"Give our friends time to escape . . .

She raised her rifle to her cheek, squeezed the trigger. Dirt and rocks kicked up in front of the lieutenant's mount, causing the creature to snort and skip back. Auna-yi quickly scurried to another location, then fired off three rounds from her pistol while Big Woodpecker, immediately catching the nature of her game, moved away from her and fired also.

The officer shouted an order, and his troops scattered heading for a ravine that led back to the lava beds. Auna-yi ran, stooping low, paused to fire another round from the rifle, and went on—while Big Woodpecker moved further away, firing random shots from his pistol as he dashed along.

Then he glanced back, saw Auna-yi stumble and fall, lie still, heard the report of a rifle and the distant sounds of men cheering.

He retraced his course, circled wide, and climbed up onto a low lava rim, and looked over the edge. Two troopers had already strapped Auna-yi onto a stretcher. With aching intensity Big Woodpecker stared at the still form of the girl. Then he saw her fingers clutching and uncurling at her side.

Alive, at least. What will they do with her? Prisoner of war? Ship her down to the Indian territory? You bastards, you take care of her, damn you. Do you hear me, Jesus Coyote? You look out for her, or I'm coming after you too. . . .

Also by Bill Hotchkiss

PEOPLE OF THE SACRED OAK

Fire Woman

✛

BILL HOTCHKISS

BANTAM BOOKS
TORONTO · NEW YORK · LONDON · SYDNEY · AUCKLAND

FIRE WOMAN
A Bantam Book / March 1987

ISBN 0-553-26452-4

Published simultaneously in the United States and Canada

Bantam Books are published by Bantam Books, Inc. Its trademark, consisting of the words "Bantam Books" and the portrayal of a rooster, is Registered in U.S. Patent and Trademark Office and in other countries. Marca Registrada. Bantam Books, Inc., 666 Fifth Avenue, New York, New York 10103.

PRINTED IN THE UNITED STATES OF AMERICA

KR   0 9 8 7 6 5 4 3 2 1

For Steve, Jenny and Anne

CONTENTS

III: When Eden Burns [1874]   315

Massacre at Table Mountain

[October 1850 to July 1851]

IT WAS THE MONTH of ripe acorns, and long ridges to the east of the big river were shrouded in a thin blue haze, for fires were burning in the mountains, close by the snow-crown of Yana Wahganupa, the high sacred place of Yana peoples. Wahgalu, as it was more commonly called, had grown up after the destruction of Tehama, or so the stories of the Old Ones claimed, and it occasionally vented steam into the sky. The mountain marked the point where the territories of the four Yana groups met, yes, and the lands of the Atsugewis and the Maidus as well, people to the north and south, respectively. When a Yana died, the spirit made its ascent to Wahgalu's summit and then stepped off into the stars, following the long white band over heaven and into World Beyond.

Smoke Woman did not know with certainty if the Atsugewis and the Maidus followed the same death trail. Different peoples did things differently, and she'd been told the Maidus, for instance, revered some small mountains rising from the floor of the long valley, far off to the south, peaks visible at times on clear days after rain fell—visible at least if one were up high, on a crest of one of the long ridges separating various rimrock canyons where the Yahis, her own people, had their semipermanent villages.

3

The snow mountain of Wahgalu rose above its lesser fellows, broken rims of Old Tehama according to the stories, and glittered in late afternoon sunlight.

Smoke Woman laughed—laughed because all things were as they should be, as much as was possible since the coming of the Whitemen, the *Saltus*—or Wawlems, as Maidu people called them. For a number of years these Whites were few, but even then they had caused much trouble. During the previous two years, however, the number of Whites had multiplied many times over. In Wintun lands, where the green river came down into the valley, these men were searching for gold and were digging holes everywhere, and the same was true in Maidu lands to the south. But here, beneath Wahgalu, apparently no gold was to be found. Wolf Tracker, Smoke Woman's father, was of the opinion that Old Coyote Man had covered the gold when Tehama blew up—or perhaps there had simply never been any of this substance along the canyons where Yana people lived.

But for the moment things were as they should be. In a swale below where Smoke Woman stood, beneath great oaks that lined the big river where it looped around Table Mountain, her father and her husband, Floating Hawk, were standing side by side. They would be speaking the Man Language, for among the Yanas men and women spoke differently, and all women pretended not to understand when their men conversed with one another. In speaking to women, men used the Woman Language. Just as the Yanas had always lived close around Wahgalu, so there had always been two different languages. Old Coyote Man had directed that things should be this way.

Now Wolf Tracker claimed the world was changing again, and to support his contention, he cited the many Whitemen who'd come into the land—men known to be violent and extremely dangerous, far worse than grizzlies. These Saltus had guns, and they killed people for no reason at all. Several years earlier a troupe of Whites, some wearing blue uniforms, had ridden up from Peter Lassen's Rancho and attacked a conclave of Yanas—a gathering, just as at present, when people from all four groups came together to harvest acorns. The Whites had murdered nearly a thousand—not only warriors but women and old people and little children as well. The leader, the Yanas learned later, was a man named

Carson, and the attack was brought on because some of Lassen's cattle had wandered back into the creek canyons, into Yana lands, and so had been slaughtered and eaten.

From that moment onward, all the Yanas perceived the Saltus as their enemies and so struck back at them in whatever ways they could, even though short bow and spear were no match for guns. Furthermore, the Whitemen rode horses. Only superior knowledge of the land and a mastery of the rugged canyons allowed the Yanas to elude their enemies after a revenge-taking for always the Whites came on horseback and carried their deadly weapons. Fires might be set behind the pursuers, and ambushes from atop bluffs were reasonably effective countermeasures, but the Saltus could kill from such a great distance. . . .

The Whites dug everywhere for yellow metal, something they valued very highly. They saw no value in woodpecker scalps or in strings of shells that came from the Karoks and Yuroks who lived near the ocean. No, the Saltus wanted only gold. It was a kind of madness with them. Gold, then, might be used to buy horses and weapons from the Whites themselves, and yet there was none of the substance to speak of in the canyons beneath Wahgalu. Besides, what warrior would be willing to spend his time digging holes in the ground, as the Wintuns along the river to the north did, working for pay from the Whitemen, Major Reading and the others? Even if the Yanas were able to find gold, the situation was all but hopeless—for very few White traders would sell guns to Indians.

Horses, though, could be stolen from the ranchos—and several had been. The Atsugewis on Pit River had already become skilled horsemen. Yes, and some owned rifles as well, but the Pit River people were unwilling to trade when all villages gathered at the salt marshes near Wichuman'na.

For all these reasons, Wolf Tracker was at first opposed to leading his village down into the valley, where the best acorn trees grew. Bands of Whitemen were everywhere now, and not just around Lassen's Rancho. Peter Lassen led wagon trains in from the east, and now there were other ranchos— more houses and many more cattle. Some of the newcomers stayed, while others moved away, a few heading northward to the branches of the big river, but most ventured southward, deep into Maidu lands where much gold was to be found, or so the stories went.

But this year the acorn harvest was scant, and so finally Wolf Tracker consented—upon learning the other Yana groups had agreed to gather where the river looped about Table Mountain and where big white oaks nearby would be heavy with shelled fruit that, when leached, was turned into flour that would sustain the people through even the worst winter. Now, with a few more days of gathering, the season's needs would be met.

Smoke Woman shouldered a heavy basket full of acorns and began to walk toward her husband and her father. She smiled, and felt like singing—felt almost like a young girl again, one newly emergent from the woman's lodge and beginning to think about taking a mate. In truth, she had not been married long to Floating Hawk—only for the passage of two seasons. Perhaps before long his seed would take hold in her belly. Then they would have a little new one of their own.

The oaks beyond where Wolf Tracker and Floating Hawk stood were filled with children who had climbed up to shake acorns loose.

NEAR SUNDOWN half a dozen Yahi boys drove three cows into the encampment at the bend of the river. The youths were singing and shouting and quite full of themselves. When Malki, woman chief of the Halhala Yanas, inquired where the cattle were found, the boys insisted the animals had, of their own volition, swum the river and presented themselves.

"They're from the new rancho, then," Floating Hawk declared. "I do not know why the cattle came across the river, but I think there may be trouble in this. The young men have listened to Coyote instead of Long-tail Lizard. These cattle are not ours to kill."

"We are many," another warrior argued. "Only one new Saltu *wawi* stands across the river, just one Whiteman's dwelling. The animals came to us, so now they are ours. Not even with a rifle will one Saltu attack us. I say we must butcher cattle and eat them."

Malki turned to Wolf Tracker, and the two leaders ex-

changed glances. It was abundantly clear to both that the
mood of the people was in favor of devouring the cattle.

Pashahi, Saikolohna, and two or three other band chieftains
stepped forward, apprised themselves of the situation, and
then turned to Malki and Wolf Tracker.

"Perhaps Kalchauna the Lizard himself told the cows to
swim the river," Pashahi grinned. "Kalchauna knew we were
hungry for meat, and so he sent these animals to us."

Wolf Tracker shrugged and turned his back, walked stiffly
to where Smoke Woman was standing. Within a moment
Floating Hawk followed.

"We will leave this place in the morning," Floating Hawk
said. "We will be gone before the Saltu realizes his cattle are
missing. The new ranch belongs to Clayton, one who came to
the valley with Peter Lassen. That is what I have been told."

"These Saltus," Wolf Tracker replied, "they always come in
groups. One man does not ride out alone. We must leave
early, then, when it's still first light. We will return to
Woxinstca or perhaps Wolopti. For now the will of the people is clear, and we must hope no bad thing happens because
of it."

"Perhaps we should leave tonight," Smoke Woman suggested. "The moon's full, and we could cover a far distance
before daylight comes again. I am afraid of the Saltu men."

Floating Hawk nodded, and put his arm about his young
wife's middle.

"We must not seem to go against the will of the others,"
Wolf Tracker said. "Tonight we feast, and tomorrow we return to our own lands. We have always been safe there. After
we've eaten, perhaps Malki will tell the story of how Kalchauna
defeated the Wintuns long ago, and how he made things so
our people would always have enough pine nuts to eat."

"Sometimes he forgets about acorns, though," Floating
Hawk said. "And he made a great mistake in allowing the
Whitemen to come into our lands."

"I think Coyote brought the Saltus here," Smoke Woman
whispered. "He's the one who likes mischief."

BIG DAN CLAYTON was well aware of the Yana encampment at
the bend of the Sacramento River, and one of his hired hands

came in late in the afternoon to report the Indians had
somehow managed to get some cows across to the east bank.

Clayton rode north to Good's place, and when he returned
the hour was nearly midnight. Hi Good was with him, and so
were Bob Anderson, Henry Curtis, and a total of about forty
men, all mounted and carrying rifles.

"We'll harvest us a few savages," Anderson laughed. "Take
us a few squaws to boot. We got law, damn it, and the law
says we can indenture as many Injuns as we need. Ain't
nothing more than wild animals, when you get right down to
it. Good workers, though, the females is. Clayton, you'll get
the hang of things after you've been here a spell. The men,
they don't train too good."

"Not interested in having an Injun housekeeper," Big Dan
shrugged. "Just want my damned cattle back. A man brings
animals across half a continent and over Lassen's damned
Death Horn to boot, he don't want them decorating no Injun
village."

"One way of putting 'er," Hi Good laughed. "If the Yahoos
has got your cows, they're already et by now. Easier than
huntin' deer, the way them boys see it."

"They hunt our cattle, and then we hunt them," Henry
Curtis said. "Thievin' bastards'll take anything that ain't by
Gawd nailed in place, and that's a fact. Gov'ment's goin' to
have to round up every divvel's son of 'em and haul 'em out
into the desert somewhere eventually. Right now, we got to
take matters into our own hands. Get ye a little squaw, Dan.
The missus don't have to know about it. Jest kinda keep her
around to diddle with when ye're of a mind."

"Want my damned cows back."

"Bones," Anderson nodded. "That's all you're going to
find, Clayton. Might as well get used to the idea."

THE RANCHERS hit the Yana encampment just before dawn,
horses pounding among sleeping forms. The Indians staggered up and then leaped for their short bows, attempting to
fight back, but to no avail.

Floating Hawk placed himself between the Whites and
Smoke Woman, but almost instantly a fifty-caliber lead slug
tore through his throat, and he fell backward into his stunned
wife's arms, blood pulsing from a ragged wound and spatter-

ing her deerskin tunic. Then he went limp as she clung to him, his weight dragging her, as well, to the ground.

The Yanas were in confused flight as shot after shot struck home. Within no more than a few minutes nearly a hundred Indians lay dead on the dry grass beneath gnarled, spreading branches of great oaks.

Small children who had not managed to flee were casually gunned down or clubbed to death, and several men who captured girls or young women proceeded to have their way with them.

Smoke Woman clung to her husband's dead body, her mind a stunned blankness, and when she finally rose to attempt to flee, it was too late.

"There's one for ye!" Henry Curtis laughed. "Show 'er what kind of tool a big Whiteman's got inside his britches!"

Dan Clayton, having killed his first Indians that morning, was feeling good about things. No matter the lost cattle—that was water under the bridge. Now, with a frightened squaw surrounded, he dismounted slowly, strode forward, and grabbed hold of Smoke Woman's long hair, backhanded her repeatedly until her head began to flop back and forth and she crumpled to the grass.

"Believe I will at that," he said, unbuckling his belt. "By God, I'm in a fair mood for it. Never thought of myself wanting to do this kind of thing, but by heavens. . . ."

As Clayton pulled down his pants and nudged the Indian woman's legs apart, Curtis and the others began to whoop and laugh.

"Sure you're up for it, Big Dan?" Bob Anderson yelled out. "Maybe you better let an expert handle that job. . . ."

"Quiet," Clayton grunted. "Can't you boys tell when a man needs to concentrate on what he's doing?"

"Put a bullet in 'er when you're finished," Anderson advised, turning his horse about and looking to see what else might be of interest. "You lads find anything young over there? Clayton here, he's put me into the mood, damned if he hasn't. . . ."

Along the eastern horizon, had anyone been looking, a delicate crimson began to form above the jagged line of peaks that culminated in the high dome of Mt. Lassen, and a sweet, soft wind began to blow, waving through tall dry grass of October and rustling among yellow-veined oak leaves.

EVEN THROUGH A HAZE of semiconsciousness, Smoke Woman realized what was happening to her. She made no movement, however, gave no hint of response as the tall Saltu thrust away at her, then grunted, and ceased. Other Whitemen whooped and laughed.

"Think you kilt her, Dan!" someone said, the strange-sounding *Yenglish* words slowly registering upon her.

Her mind, numb, came hazily clearer as she fought to understand what had been said.

Kilt. She knew that word, and sensed the meaning of the assertion. A season earlier a buckskin man had ridden into Wolopti village, an old man astride a mule. He had shown no fear, and indicated he wished to share venison he had killed. Wolf Tracker had made him welcome, and she had listened as the man and her father attempted to communicate across the barrier of different languages. The strange old Saltu had stayed a week or more, and she had grown to like him. All Whitemen, apparently, were not dangerous—only ones who raised cattle or dug for gold. . . .

Kilt.

The man who had raped her struggled to his feet, pulled up his trousers, and buckled his belt. He laughed and gestured at his companions, then turned back to where she lay, kicked her in the side. She groaned slightly but made no other sound, and the man appeared grimly satisfied with himself.

"Not yet, she ain't. Your turn, whoever wants her."

"Think you busted her neck. Hell with that—Hi Good's got a live one. Leave that bitch for the vultures."

"What do you think, Dan, was it fair grass?"

"Like humpin' a sheep, I guess. You really think her neck's broke?"

Smoke Woman did not move. She breathed as shallowly as possible, and waited for what would happen next. Then the group of Saltus turned and strode away toward where some of their companions had begun to shout once more.

A pistol shot. Another.

Smoke Woman summoned what strength remained to her, rose to her feet, fell, and rose again.

Escape.

She forced herself to run—to the river, beyond the line of oaks. She heard more shouting, but did not look back. Then she was at the low cliffbank above the river, its green water almost black in early light. She hurled herself forward, rolled down, slid onto a gravel bar beside a thicket of willow brush.

On the far side of the October-low current emerged the broad, humpbacked form of Table Mountain, steep, rocky in places, sheaves of stone like broken ribs, otherwise splatched with scrub oak and greasewood and manzanita. Cattle grazed beneath oaks, and one animal had a bell about its neck. As if hypnotized by the bell's oddly dissonant sound, Smoke Woman stood trembling for a few moments. Three vultures, one after another, began fanning their big wings in a digger pine's upper branches and vaulted out into the air, gliding for a space and then flapping to gain altitude. Off to the southwest the Bolly Mountains, in the lands of the Wintuns, rose blue-gray and solemn, their upper slopes touched with morning sunlight.

Then she heard shouts—turned quickly—saw half a dozen Saltus standing astride the low bluff she had tumbled down. One of the men was pointing a rifle at her. She saw a puff of blue smoke. Wet sand spurted up close by her feet, and then the crack of the rifle's report echoed off across the river.

She leaped into the water, wedged her moccasins against a half-submerged snag, and shot forward through coldness toward the stream's center.

Perhaps the current will carry me away from the guns, she thought.

SHE STAYED in the water for some time, struggling back to shore within sight of yet another rancho, this one situated just as the river entered into a long loop. For a while she lay confused and panting, hidden among tangled roots of a washed-out cottonwood at the stream's edge. She listened intently but could hear no further voices. Possibly the Whites had lost interest in her, or possibly they'd decided to pursue those of her people who had escaped—for without question, most had. How many dead? Smoke Woman could only guess, but she surmised the number amounted to thirty or forty, perhaps even more. And of these one was Floating Hawk, her husband. . . .

She withdrew the obsidian blade from within the folds of her deerskin tunic, stared at the carefully chipped stone, then grasped her long hair close by the scalp and cut away several handfuls. In the normal course of things, a woman would cut her hair at the death of a loved one, would weave it into a belt to signify her mourning. . . .

"Floating Hawk, go well into World Beyond," she whispered.

Trembling, almost numb with cold, she let out one long, agonized wail and then was silent again. Her husband was gone, and so long as she continued to repeat his name or to rehearse the times they had known together, so would he be prevented from making his journey to Wahgalu and then on to the place where the dead lived.

I must find my father, I must find my way to where my people are, otherwise Wolf Tracker will come back to find me, and the Saltus will kill him. We should never have come to Wamatiwi, we should have remained in the canyons where the Saltus do not come—only Lassen and the ones he leads, they bring their wagons down the long ridge, but they do not bother us.

SHE MADE her way through brush country toward the landmark summit of Tuscan Buttes, and nightfall brought her down to Salt Creek. Exhausted and hardly caring whether she lived or died, she took cover in a hollow between basalt boulders and fell into profound and dreamless sleep.

The sun was well into morning sky when she awoke, opening her eyes but remaining otherwise motionless.

Someone was close by. She knew it without knowing why she knew it. Then she became aware of a soft panting sound.

She sat up.

Across from her, beside a black stone face, a coyote sat on its haunches.

"Go away," she told the animal. "Look. I am not dead yet. Lizard Man gives me his protection. You eat only the dead, you must not bother me."

She reached quickly for her stone scraping knife, but then

she realized the song dog apparently meant her no harm. A female, yes, and heavy with unborn young.

"Have you been watching over me, then?" Smoke Woman asked. "Why are you big with pups, little sister? You will have to raise them during the time of snows."

The coyote opened its mouth, tilted its head back, and gaped at the air, displaying a fine set of shiny white teeth. The animal stood up, approached more closely, and thrust its head forward, sniffing.

"Where is your man, little wolf?" Smoke Woman asked. "My husband is gone. Have you come to tell me something? You mated with a Whiteman's dog, and now you will bear its offspring? Is that what you're telling me? The seed that was put in my belly, it will take root? I am to have a child because of what happened to me? I couldn't give Floating Hawk a child, but now. . . ?"

The coyote sniffed again, seemed to satisfy its curiosity, turned about quickly, and was gone, its long tail streaming from the hollow between slabs of fractured stone.

Smoke Woman got to her feet, braced herself against a rockface, and bit down on her tongue.

"This thing must not be," she whispered.

ON SALT CREEK she found sign that a large group had passed by. Further up the canyon she noted where the group had divided into two bands, one turning south to ascend a ridge separating the drainage of Salt Creek from that of Antelope Creek beyond. Without hesitation she followed to the south, for those would be her own people—such, at least, as remained alive after what had happened at the big bend beneath Wamatiwi, Table Mountain.

Was Wolf Tracker, indeed, among those still alive? In truth, she had no way of knowing whether her father as well as her husband might not have been among the dead.

At the ridge crest she stopped, uncertain now whether to continue or to turn back.

"Is that your voice, my husband, he-who-is-dead? Are you telling me to return to the death place, to gather dry grass and brush so that your body may be consumed in flames that will aid the release of your spirit? Is this what you now wish me to do?"

But whatever she had heard did not answer her.

"Tell me what I must do—speak to me!"

Far ahead, as though floating dreamlike above the backs of lesser mountains, rose the rounded cone of Wahgalu, its perpetual snows glinting in sunlight. Vaporous clouds were beginning to swirl about the mountain in a way that sometimes happened, often during the time of new leaves, though seldom at acorn harvest.

"Floating Hawk, I speak your name yet one more time. Do you wish the one who once shared your bed and your love to live or to die?"

Drifting to her ears from either side of the ridge crest on which she stood came the sounds of falling water—or was it nothing more than movement of wind among yellowing oak leaves and gray-green thatch of pines?

Smoke Woman scanned the horizon, searching for a sign, but no big-winged birds were in the sky—not eagle, hawk, or vulture. The land appeared just as it always had, undulating endlessly from Wahgalu's snow crown westward to the broad valley and beyond that to the jagged Bolly Peaks of the Wintuns and the even higher and more rugged forms to the northwest. But dominating all, drawing the entire world into perspective, rose the giant peak of Shasta, mountain of the Achomawis. Hidden among folds of all this vastness, she thought bitterly, were villages of the hated Saltus, white-faced and bearded and looking like owls, men who came from somewhere far to the east, men with pistols and rifles and horses and cattle.

She waited motionlessly for some sign, but there was none.

At length, with a single backward glance toward Uht'anuwi, the Tuscan Buttes, Smoke Woman turned and began her way downslope to the stream her people called Halhala, Antelope Creek.

She was within sight of the sunlight-filled running water when she first discerned her father, Wolf Tracker, walking toward her.

THE YAHI BAND, numbers now diminished to fewer than three hundred, made their way eastward into a fastness of canyon and rimrock and forest and came at length to the semiperma-

nent village of Ya'muluk'u, situated at a point where Sulphur
Creek joined with the larger flow of Deer Creek.

A great fire was built to honor those who died by the big
river, a cremation without bodies. Old Ke-tip-ku-ni, Civet
Man, insisted that this was the proper thing to do. He was
very old, and his health had failed rapidly after the escape
from the Acorn Massacre, but his position as shaman was
respected by all. And so a big fire was built. The shaman
himself stood vigil until the last trailing wisp of smoke vanished, some three days after the ceremony. Then he sat down
beside the heaped ashes and began to chant. When that
happened, everyone knew another cremation would be held
soon—and so it was, for by the evening of that day Civet Man
was dead.

Smoke Woman stayed in her father's *igunna* now, she and
he together, for the mother had died several years earlier.
Life in the village went on almost as though nothing had
happened, though Wolf Tracker sometimes spoke of striking
back at the Saltus. Acorns were harvested, but there were
not nearly enough for winter. The young men hunted deer,
and much meat was dried, curing fires burning day and night
until the time of rains began.

Wolf Tracker traveled to the east of Wahgalu and traded
for acorn flour—and returned with an elaborate story concerning a huge Whiteman who had married a Maidu woman,
she the actual leader of the Panos, a band whose sole purpose
was that of taking revenge against the Whites. Rumor of
these Panos, the Grizzly Bear People, had spread throughout
the mountains. They had weapons, and they struck quickly
and fiercely. But now they were apparently at peace and
living among the Oidoing-koyo Maidus near Wahgalu's eastern base. Lest anyone should doubt his tale, Wolf Tracker
was quick to display both a fine rifle and a single-shot pistol
the big Whiteman had given him.

"That one is our friend," Wolf Tracker grinned. "Not all
Saltus are devils. When summer comes, he and his wife, the
medicine woman Ooti, will visit us. We will exchange gifts at
that time, and the Yahis will listen to what these people tell
us. He is called Ben McCain, Bear-who-cannot-see-well. He
is not like the others."

* * *

BY THE TIME of the first snows, Smoke Woman knew without question the message the coyote bitch had given her was true, for she was with child. She would bear the offspring of the Saltu who had raped her, a man called Dan Clayton. It was a name she would not forget. She considered feigning that the child inside her body actually belonged to her dead husband, but at length she explained to Wolf Tracker, told him about the coyote that visited her that night in the hollow in the rocks.

When summer came, a child was born—brown-eyed but light-skinned, hair reddish-brown, not black.

"She must be called Wahtaurisi-yi," Wolf Tracker said, "Sits-by-the-ladder, for that is the name we give to a father-less child. In the old days such a new little one might have been put to death, but now our numbers have grown few. Many have died of diseases we have gotten from the Whites, and others have been slain in battle. No, this child must live. When she reaches the time of the woman's moon, we will find another name for her. She was begotten in hatred, not in the love of a man and a woman. But I will love her as my granddaughter. You, too, Smoke Woman, you must love this child, even though she is not the one you wanted. Sits-by-the-ladder has been granted special protection by the coyotes. Coyote Man is usually our friend, even though he urges us to do foolish things, but we have Gray Squirrel and Lizard to protect us from most of his whims. He sent that coyote bitch to visit you, and so this is his child as well as yours. Perhaps she will live to be our link with the future during the time when the world changes."

I

✚

Beneath Wahgalu

[1864–1865]

ONE
Sits-by-the-ladder
[June 1864]

WOLF TRACKER'S BAND of Yahis returned to their summer encampment along Deer Creek, to meadows hidden at the foot of high basalt rims, and the people were happy to be back to this special place they considered their stronghold—hidden far up in the big canyon, where Saltus had never bothered them. Indeed, even after all the years of their ongoing confrontations with valley cattlemen, the Yahis could still take solace in a belief that Whitemen had never discovered the village on Deer Creek. Surely, Coyote Man himself had reserved this one village site, had hidden it away in a spot so remote that ranging cattle never came and Whitemen never followed.

The Yahis worked quickly to erect their hide and brush lodges above shallow excavations that had served as summer and autumn dwellings from the time of the beginnings of things, and within a day the encampment was complete, with lodges arranged in a series of half-circles about a larger dwelling where the chief would live with his widowed daughter and her child, the girl now thirteen years old, fatherless because the man whose seed produced her was Saltu.

While the others were building, teenaged boys went hunting, some upstream into the narrow part of the canyon, others climbing to red-black rims above the village site. By late afternoon the boys returned in good spirits, for both hunts had gone well. The people would be able to feast for the next three days.

Times would be good again, at least for a while. Wildlife was plentiful, and the stream was full of trout and big, sleepy pike that lurked in deep water beside boulders. Salmon had returned to the creek three years earlier, and some villagers took this event as a good omen.

But no one spoke any longer of a presumed time when the Whites would all go away. No, it was enough now to live season to season. Survival itself was a precious gift. Lizard and Gray Squirrel smiled upon the people, and so long as Old Coyote Man could be kept happily occupied with other matters, so long would the Yahis survive, moving from village site to village site among the broken canyonlands to the west of snow-hung Wahgalu.

A fire circle was arranged, and boys and girls alike dragged in sections of deadwood while grown women prepared the slain deer, carefully skinning the animals and cutting up portions of flesh, scattering entrails at forest's edge in deference to wolf, coyote, and vulture.

SMOKE WOMAN was worried about her daughter.

The girl's life, begun in violence beside the swirling Sacramento River, seemed blighted from the beginning—and not even the protection of Wolf Tracker himself, revered leader of the people though he was, really sufficed to shield Wahtaurisi-yi from occasional waves of resentment directed at her by other children and fueled, without question, by bad feelings of some of the elders, old women in particular, those who insisted the newborn child should have been bound hand and foot and left among the rimrocks for badgers to feed upon. When Wolf Tracker made it abundantly clear no such thing would happen, the old women clucked their tongues, chose to shun Smoke Woman, and made much of blaming the very existence of Wahtaurisi-yi for every minor reverse the Yahis suffered.

The women, of course, could do nothing really obvious. But it was almost as though a conspiracy were underway—for word came to her, often from Wahtaurisi-yi herself, of occasional sneering remarks by other children and a pattern of the young ones leaving her out of whatever group activities were going on—even during early bathing sessions in the creek. Smoke Woman observed the ritual that very morning—all girl children running to the pool, entering the water, and then the others Wahtaurisi-yi's own age moving inevitably to the far side, away from her.

Lately it had been much worse—and complicated by the fact that Wahtaurisi-yi had apparently come fully to accept her outcast position within the tribe and no longer even made feeble attempts to join in.

More and more Sits-by-the-ladder chose the company of Wolf Tracker, her grandfather. The chief, if not fully aware of what was going on, sensed his favorite's need for special attention. Just as Ben McCain had taught Wolf Tracker to speak the Yenglish tongue, so now the chief was instructing his granddaughter in the language of the Saltu people, something Smoke Woman silently disapproved of. What was the point? Was it not enough that nearly everyone in the village resented the one who is half-Saltu in her blood?

Certainly, being able to speak Yenglish could do no more than to enforce the distance between Wahtaurisi-yi and the others.

Word spread among the people that Wolf Tracker was not only teaching Sits-by-the-ladder the tongue of their enemies, but he was also conversing with her in Yahi Man's Language—the chief himself violating one of the oldest and most important taboos.

Still, Wolf Tracker persisted. He was Smoke Woman's own father, yes, and though she lived in the same lodge with him, having found no new husband since the death of Floating Hawk, she had no idea where the chief's spirit wandered. When he was not teaching Wahtaurisi-yi or going on long walks with the girl, he seemed to be staring somewhere ahead, out into darkness. Sometimes he went off by himself for several days at a time; and when he returned, it was as though he had been staring into fire—only it was a different kind of fire.

A fire of passing time—a fire that would destroy the Yahi people at some point down the future. With each new season

*the group's numbers were smaller, and there were strange
diseases for which the shaman had no cures. Young men
struck out on their own, attacking the Whites and sometimes
not coming back. Two years earlier the Whites had ambushed
the Yahis close by the stinking-water springs, and many were
killed. A terrible night when the creek rose suddenly into
flood, and a little boy was washed away, sucked down into
roaring waters in an attempt to retrieve a bow his uncle made
for him. . . .*

WAHTAURISI-YI CLIMBED to the base of the canyon's high rim,
where an outcropping of black, glassy rock could be chipped
off into fragments Yahi men used for the crafting of arrow and
spear points. She would break loose some excellent pieces for
Wolf Tracker to work on, should the desire to create new
hunting points come over him. Perhaps that would happen
when he saw what fine stones she'd carried back from the
bluffs, her woven willow basket containing lumps like black
eggs ravens ought to lay but didn't.

Yet in truth, she had not really come to gather obsidian.
No, her motive had more to do with a simple wish to be
alone—high above Wolopti village, where she was not obliged
to concern herself with how others thought of her, where she
did not have to deal with the shame of being a bastard child,
an offspring of the hated Whites.

Once, when she and her mother sat together preparing
leached acorns for grinding and baking, a rare instance when
Smoke Woman chose to speak of Floating Hawk, the handsome young man who had been her husband before the
massacre near Table Mountain, she actually asked Smoke
Woman to describe the Saltu who was her father. But the
mother's eyes grew narrow, and her mouth went hard. Smoke
Woman shook her head and said nothing further for a long
while.

From this somewhat unexpected response, Sits-by-the-
ladder concluded that Smoke Woman, caught off guard,
found the experience too painful to think of, even after all the
time that had passed.

On another occasion when she and her mother were alone
together, Wahtaurisi-yi again demanded information about

her White father. What did he look like? Did Smoke Woman know who he was, know his name?

"Do not ever ask such questions again, my daughter. If I knew the man's name, I would never speak it. He is my enemy, and he is your enemy as well. If he met you now, right now as we're walking beside the stream, I think he would rape me again and you too, Wahtaurisi-yi. You have always had to bear his shame, even though you have done nothing to deserve it. I will tell you the truth. It's not something you wish to hear, but you must have thought about it—how it would be for any Yahi woman who. . . . When I realized I was with child from what happened, I hated the seed within me, the life growing in my belly. I thought about climbing to the canyon rim and leaping down— and so finding a quick way to join Floating Hawk in World Beyond. I didn't wish to bring such a little one into the world."

Wahtaurisi-yi remembered Smoke Woman had avoided eye contact as she spoke.

"But Wolf Tracker read my thoughts," Smoke Woman continued, "and he told me of one of his visions. My father's a strange man, and often his spirit wanders out into places the rest of us cannot even dream of. So he told me, yes, that the ghost people had spoken to him of the child I carried— that you, Wahtaurisi-yi, would be a woman and that it would be your fate to enter into the Saltu world during a time when our people all go off into darkness. They told him you had a special mission and that he must convince his daughter not to do anything that might harm you. I listened—I studied Wolf Tracker's face as he spoke to me. That time he used Man Language, just as he often does with you. And I believed him, even though I still hated the idea of what was going to happen. But when you began to move within me, my daughter, and when you came into the world, then I loved you dearly—and I have prayed many times to Coyote Man so he might forgive what I once felt. I. . . ."

"I understand, Mother. It couldn't have been any different than it was. I promise never again to ask questions. I love you, Mother."

Wahtaurisi-yi was silent for a little while as they continued walking, but then a bluejay shouted through the afternoon air, and the girl could contain herself no longer.

"How could I enter into the Whiteman's world?" the girl asked, actually phrasing the question in English. "I do not understand what Wolf Tracker meant when he told you that."

Smoke Woman nodded.

"Neither do I. Your grandfather believes we live in a time of the endings of things as they have always been. Each year we are fewer, and each year the Saltus advance deeper into our lands. Perhaps it's so. Perhaps one day the Yahis and the other Yanas will be only a handful . . . and then only one . . . and then we will be no more. But you're half-White in your blood, and that's why your skin and hair are a little different from everyone else's. Maybe because of that you will one day be able to live among the Saltus almost as though you were one of them. I know that's why Wolf Tracker teaches you to speak their language. He'd show you how to read from the black medicine book too, if he could."

Sometimes the girl had picked up the mysterious book, held it, opened it, stared at the strange little markings on thin paper pages.

Wahtaurisi-yi resolved to query her grandfather. If the vision concerned her, shouldn't she be allowed to know? And her real father—she'd given her word not to ask Smoke Woman again, but perhaps Wolf Tracker knew things that he would be willing to share with her.

And yet, what difference did it make? She was Yahi, not Saltu. But because of what had happened before she was born, she realized, her chances of ever having a husband and a family of her own were very poor, even though she was granddaughter to the chief himself.

Occasionally Wolf Tracker told her stories about women who didn't marry—women who became shamans or even village chiefs instead. Lizard and Gray Squirrel singled such women out when they were still merely children, and yet she herself had never experienced any such vision.

The thought of being a medicine woman or an interpreter of dreams didn't really appeal to her, though maybe it would when she grew older. For now, however, there were moments when odd sensations came over her, tingling feelings in her private woman's place, and she fantasized what it might be like to lie down with a man. A prospect of living her entire life without ever knowing—she hated that.

Well, the situation might change. After all, she might meet some young man during one of those times when all the Yana peoples gathered together at the Salt Marshes. Or maybe she'd meet a Maidu boy or an Achomawi, for those people also went to the Salt Marshes. At such times the groups talked happily and exchanged information. Young men of different tribes might not be concerned with the fact that she was half-White. The Achomawis, she knew, respected Wolf Tracker. She had sometimes listened when other chiefs asked his advice on various matters. Since he was her grandfather, it was possible she'd be able to find a husband when the time came.

That might be in another year, more likely in two. Her breasts were beginning to bud, and sometimes girls even teased her about it—when they bothered to speak to her at all. But she had not yet reached the time of her confinement to the woman's lodge. Only after that happened and her moon blood began to flow would she need to worry seriously about such matters.

FOR THE MOMENT, everything was all right. The Yahis had returned to Wolopti, and no one was thinking about Whitemen. Soon the salmon would swim up the creek, and after that would be the time of acorn harvest.

It was not actually very far from Wolopti to where several Whites lived, however. Above the deep canyon was a ranch where cattle grazed in wide meadows, but those people posed no threat and were not seen as enemies. For this reason, the Yahis left their cattle alone. Beyond the ranch, over into the next drainage, lived another Whiteman who was friends with Wolf Tracker—a huge man who wore thick glasses, one who several times had visited the Yahi village. He too had a ranch and raised cattle, but he lived among Maidu people and was married to a Maidu woman. Her name was Ooti, the leader of the Panos, a small group who at one time acquired rifles and pistols and repeatedly attacked the Whites, exacting revenge upon them. Such, at least, was what Wolf Tracker told her. This Ooti, Wahtaurisi-yi had long since decided, was someone she wanted very much to meet again.

Perhaps Wolf Tracker's vision was not as Smoke Woman said. Perhaps she, Wahtaurisi-yi, was fated to be like Ooti of the Pano Maidus. Maybe she, too, would be able to lead a revenge-taking, possibly even against that nameless man who raped her mother and fathered the child who was outcast in her own village. But if the moment ever came, would she somehow recognize the man? And if she did, would she truly be able to kill him?

Wahtaurisi-yi put such thoughts away, the idle dreamings of a child (as she knew well enough), and set about prying loose a few pieces of shiny black stone from the outcropping at the base of the high rim.

The work went quickly, and soon her willow basket was filled with so many choice stones that she knew she'd have difficulty carrying the load back to the village. Or maybe the basket itself would rupture from the weight, and then she'd have to come back with two baskets.

Sunlight glared down pleasantly, and Wahtaurisi-yi scrambled over to a small pool cupped as though between two huge rocky hands at the rimrock base. A trickling waterfall came down from above, a stream so thin that any fluttering of breeze caused the water to burst into mist as it fell. High up, close by where the small stream leaped out, a number of swallows had built their mud-and-twig nests, basketlike structures seemingly bonded to the dark stone surface.

Of all the places round about Wolopti vollage, this was her favorite. The water in the pool was almost like a mirror during late summer, when the small cascade stilled to a trickle.

She lay down, placed her lips to the surface, and drank.

Then, rising, she glanced back toward the village. No one else would climb to the black rock this day—nor would it really matter if anyone did. Even if a young man saw her naked and alone, that would not really matter—not until after she had gone to the woman's lodge.

Wahtaurisi-yi removed her cedar-bark shirt, folded it, placed it on a smooth stone surface beside the pool. For a time she stood there, studying her reflection. She was, she decided, certainly as pretty as the other young Yahi girls, even though she didn't look very much like them. She postured once or twice, studied her changed image, and overcame an impulse to grin. But girls who spent too much time admiring them-selves, according to one story, were sometimes devoured by huge salmon that waited for the idlers and leaped up out of the water at them.

There were no big fish in this pool. Nevertheless, she resisted temptation to turn half about and gaze over her shoulder so that she might admire her buttocks. Instead she stepped out into the water, waded in to her knees. This was the deepest place. She stood there, eyes closed and hands raised above her head, palms toward the sun, and basked in a delicious sensation of complete freedom—freedom from all human concerns, a sense of release even from herself and the kinds of thoughts that sometimes troubled her greatly.

In her imagination she was suddenly several years older, her body that of a beautiful woman. On the far bank stood a young man, a very handsome young man, and he called out her name. . . .

Wahtaurisi-yi's eyes came suddenly open, and for an instant she half believed such a young man was indeed standing across from her.

But it wasn't a man at all.

A coyote sat there on its haunches, pointed ears forward, an expression of puzzlement in the strange amber-colored eyes.

"I was dreaming," she said softly, directing her words to the brush wolf. "Did you come here to drink and maybe to swim? The water isn't deep enough for me—unless I simply lie down in it."

The coyote didn't move.

Wahtaurisi-yi laughed, then sat down in the water and splashed about with both arms.

The coyote backed up a step or two, lowered its nose, and began to wag its bushy tail. The animal jumped about, almost as though engaged in mouse hunting in a twilight meadow, and then pranced forward, stared directly at the girl, lowered its muzzle to lap at the water.

"Someday I'll have a medicine vision, just as the young men do," she told the coyote. "When that happens, you must come to me and be my Spirit Helper. Will you do it for me?"

The coyote finished drinking, then sidled to a rock, and lifted its leg.

"I knew you were a man coyote," the girl laughed, "even before I saw your. . . . I suppose men are all the same. All of you like to lift your legs and make water on things. I tried once, but I can't do it. I have to squat. But I'm going to have a medicine vision anyway. . . ."

Then the coyote was gone—a sharp, quick movement, almost as though he had simply dematerialized.

Wahtaurisi-yi lay back in the shallow pond, stared upward at a silver-yellow disc of sun, blinked, and then closed her eyes once more.

BROKEN WILLOW checked woven fish traps she had set upstream from the village, where the big creek's current stilled, water veeing out from occasional large rocks in its bed and glimmering clear green by morning sunlight.

Sits-by-the-ladder accompanied her friend, a young woman of perhaps twenty winters, and tended to her child as Broken Willow waded out carefully, inspecting each open-throated basket in turn, resetting those that were empty and bringing in traps into which too-curious trout had swum. Flopping fish were deposited into a large tule basket, and then Broken Willow waded back into the water and submerged her traps once again, weighting them with stones.

The child was a little boy, only three winters of age but extremely agile and difficult to control. On this day he particularly wished to follow Broken Willow into the creek, being more or less convinced he was old enough to do the work himself.

"Patience, Wood Duck," Wahtaurisi-yi cautioned, "you must stay here with me. When you're older, you'll be able to build your own fish traps and set them wherever you want to. Do what your mother tells you."

The child stared at Wahtaurisi-yi, his mouth pursed.

"Why can't I be old enough now?" he demanded.

Wahtaurisi-yi smiled, reached out to stroke his forehead.

"I can't understand you," she said. "You're speaking the Man Language, like your father. I think you copy everything he does."

Wood Duck nodded seriously, made a shrugging motion,

and then grinned, displaying two even rows of milk teeth. At that moment he caught the sound of a chirring squirrel, the long-tailed creature apparently having some sort of treetop dispute with a bluejay. The boy said nothing further, but instead went stalking off into the brush, his posture almost that of a coyote on the hunt.

Broken Willow emerged from the stream, sunlight glistening from droplets of water on the tan flesh of her bare belly and breasts.

"He's being difficult, my little Ishi, my little man? Thank you, Wahtaurisi-yi. I wouldn't have been able to bring him along if it weren't for you. He's wonderful, but he's a terrible pest. When we're alone together, Salmon Man suggests we send him to live with our cousins in Big Foot's village. My husband doesn't mean what he says, though. Already he's made Wood Duck a small bow of his own."

Sits-by-the-ladder nodded. The previous afternoon she'd watched Wood Duck shooting his short, blunt-nosed arrows at three sleeping village dogs, the spotted animals growling softly to themselves as missiles fell harmlessly about them, then getting up and walking off stiff-legged to find a better place to drowse in sunlight.

"You've caught some very fine fish today, Broken Willow," she said. "I wanted to put that last one back into the water—he's beautiful."

"When I was younger, I hated to watch fish die. But we'd starve to death if we didn't have them. Fish are fine people, and that's why we always say a small prayer for them. . . ."

"So their spirits will come back and be fish again," Wahtaurisi-yi said, finishing the young wife's sentence. "I'm getting good at weaving fish baskets—don't you think so?"

"Indeed you are. My husband agrees. Perhaps when you're older and have been in the woman's lodge, Salmon Man will wish to take you for a second wife. We're very grateful to have you help us with so many things—but maybe you should spend more time with the other girls your age."

Sits-by-the-ladder ignored this last remark, and neither did she choose to respond to the idea of being a second wife to Salmon Man. When the time came, she vowed silently, she'd have a husband of her own. In any case, Broken Willow was merely being kind.

A great blue heron swooped downcanyon, wheeled about, flared its wings, and dropped silently into shallow water across from where the girl and the young woman sat together. The big bird stood in the water, long beak pointed downward.

"He's fishing too," Wahtaurisi-yi whispered.

"If he gets any nearer to my trap, I'm going to toss a pebble at him."

"But the basket's empty. . . ."

"It's better he doesn't get any ideas, though. Is that Wood Duck—making bluejay noises in the fir tangle up above us? I saw him go running off."

Wahtaurisi-yi stared at the gray-blue fishing bird, startling slightly when the long beak thrust down into green current. A small, silver-gleaming fish wriggled for a moment and disappeared as the heron swallowed several times and then resumed his study of the stream flowing about the one thin, scaly leg the bird was standing on.

"What is it like?" Wahtaurisi-yi asked suddenly. "I mean . . . when Salmon Man makes love to you. His manhood becomes hard, and then what? Does he just push it into you? That's what all the other animals do."

Broken Willow laughed, shook her head.

"You're still young," she replied. "My husband only does that when he knows I want him to do it. The woman is usually the one who decides when it's right to make love. Making love isn't . . . at all like what we see the dogs doing. It's warm and close and wonderful, Wahtaurisi-yi. It's—well, it's like pollen flowers on black oaks during the time of new grass. We all pretend our men are in charge of things, but women know better. Sometimes Salmon Man is more of a child than his son. No woman would live in the same lodge with a man if he really meant all the threats he made. We let them think they want to do the things we want them to."

"I don't understand," Wahtaurisi-yi said. "Last week Red Otter beat his wife, Slippery Root—everyone in the village heard her crying out. I think she should tear down his lodge and go back to her father. That's what I'd do."

Broken Willow picked up the largest of the trout, admired the dead fish, then placed it back into the carrying basket.

"Perhaps she will do that, and perhaps not. Maybe she'll

decide to keep him, but she'll have to figure out a better way of making Red Otter think he's happy. Several of us spoke with her afterward. We told her she should do just what you said. I don't know."

"Men are much stronger than women," Wahtaurisi-yi mused. "That was another of Coyote Man's tricks, I guess."

"Not in their heads, they aren't. Otherwise they could never believe we don't understand everything they say to one another. It's all a kind of game. Besides, the other men disapproved of what Red Otter did. He and Wolf Tracker went off together for a long while the next day. Your grandfather's a wise leader, Wahtaurisi-yi. I don't think any of us would survive without him. He's not foolish like most men, and that's the difference. Some few men become wise as they grow older."

Broken Willow stood up, called Wood Duck to come back from whatever venture he was on.

In a moment the little boy appeared, a bleached white legbone of a deer in one pudgy fist.

"Look what I have found!" he said. "I'll take it to the big dog who's my friend. . . ."

"I'm sure he'll love it," Broken Willow said as she and Sits-by-the-ladder picked up the carrying basket between them and began to walk toward Wolopti village.

TWO

Fire Under the Mountain

[July 1864]

AN EARTHQUAKE rolled through the hills, not a single sharp jolt, but ground swelling and heaving several times, almost as though waves were passing unseen through the underlying strata of basalt and cinder. Dwellings of some of the older Maidu Indians in Oidoing-koyo village, traditional *hubos* dug into the ground and roofed over with rough planking cut at Ben McCain's little sawmill, were untouched. Two Wawlem cabins, however, the nearly uniform log structures of the hinterlands of the California outback, shifted about, with roofbeams cracking. In other cabins the windows shattered—those that had glass in them. As for the much larger and more elaborately constructed McCain ranch house, no structural damage was apparent, yet the upper three feet of a stone block chimney cracked with the first surge and fell apart with the second.

For a day or two afterward children in the rancheria village whooped with delight whenever they felt a minor aftershock and quite a few times, in fact, when they only imagined they felt something.

Benjamin McCain, the huge, bearded Whiteman who ten years earlier was designated acting though unpaid Indian agent for the reservation farm called Upper Eden, set a ladder against the roof and began to climb up and down, hauling cinder stones and buckets of mortar, resolutely intent upon repairing his chimney.

Mt. Lassen, Wahgalu as it was called by Yanas and Little Tehama by Maidus, drew bandings of lenticular clouds about its summit and hid, even though the sky was otherwise clear. Had old Kuksu shaman Hurt Eagle still been alive, he might have predicted the fire mountain was about to erupt, but that man of indeterminate age had died the previous summer, and his passing was mourned at the time of *Ustu*, a fire ceremony held at the conclusion of acorn-gathering. Few Maidus continued to observe the traditional rites of Kuksu, but memory remained even in an Indian village that had become, for all practical purposes, very much like various small White settlements hidden away in folds of the volcanic Northeastern California mountains.

Indian children and some of their parents stood about watching as Ben McCain, straddling the roof of his house, set to work replacing chunks of stone. Blue Loon laughed and pounded his thirteen-year-old son, Big Woodpecker, on the back.

"Earthquake doesn't make the house fall down," he said, "but McCain's weight may. Well, that house is strong—we all helped build it the year you were born."

Big Woodpecker, half smiling at this show of affection from his father, watched intently as Mizz McCain, a beautiful Pano woman many years Ben's junior, nimbly climbed the ladder and stood balanced on the crest. Her name was Ooti, Acorn Girl, and she was wearing a dark red dress that clung to her lithe body. She was True Bear's mother, William True Bear, Big Woodpecker's best friend, but she didn't look at all like anyone else's mother—certainly not like his own. No, she was *beautiful*, and the sight of her caused strange stirrings of something between pleasure and pain. When he grew to manhood, Big Woodpecker resolved, he would also have a wife who looked like Mizz McCain. He had heard many stories about her, stories of what happened in the old days, but such tales were hard to believe. When he asked True Bear, the only response had been a shrug and a "Guess so. Heard Mom and Dad talking about it after Hurt Eagle died,

how they blew up a mining camp down south. They were
renegades all right, and that's the truth."

TRUE BEAR and Big Woodpecker urged their ponies ahead,
away from broad meadows where whitefaced Hereford cattle
grazed, and on up a meandering stream that fed down from
Black Butte and Diamond Peak, satellite mountains to Wahgalu
itself. Ben said the creek was North Branch of the North Fork
of the Feather River, *Rio de las Plumas*, as the Spanish had
named it—but here simply a stream, running eastward and
southward, gathering tributaries and eventually making its
way to the little town of Chester and Almanor Meadows
before dropping down into a big canyon and cutting southwestward through the heart of the mountains and eventually
finding the great Valley of the Sacramento River, *Nem Seyoo*.

"You think whitefaces are really as good as Spanish cattle?"
Big Woodpecker asked his friend. "My dad don't think so."

"They put on weight quicker," True Bear shrugged. "Bring
lots better prices in Sacramento. You ought to see the Clayton herd—he's got thousands of 'em."

"Doesn't get cold out in the valley," Big Woodpecker
replied, snapping the reins along his pony's neck.

"Yeah. But Herefords are easier to work with, you know
that. Pretty soon nobody's going to be running Spanish.
That's what Dad says. . . . Why we talking about cows? To
hell with that. You scared of going up the mountain, or
what?"

Big Woodpecker scowled at his friend.

"Maidus ain't scared of no mountain. Why do you say
dumb things like that, True Bear?"

"Just wondering, that's all. There she is, up ahead. Clouds
all pulled in around her."

"Coyote Man's sleeping," Big Woodpecker laughed. "That's
what my father says."

"Ignorant Injun."

"You're Injun too, no matter what you say. Your ma's
Maidu, just like me. That's the trouble with being your
friend, True Bear. I have to listen to your damn Wawlem
ideas all the time—and read an' all that stuff. The Old Ones
say it's bad, the way Ben makes us read and do numbers and
the rest of it. The Yanas, they're still wild, and so are some

downriver Maidus. Your pa's turning us all into dark-skinned Wawlems."

True Bear was silent for a few moments.

"What's it like, do you think?"

"What are you talking about?"

"Living like that—the way the Yanas do. They keep hidden, then they attack, then they disappear back into the canyons. They don't have to go to school."

"Some of them live on ranches, I guess," Big Woodpecker mused.

"But some don't—they just hunt and move around. They hate the Whites. Last summer they killed those Lewis kids over by Chico, Big Foot and his bunch did. Dan Clayton told my pa all about it when we went down to get our new herd of Herefords. Only the girl got away. Why do the Yanas kill kids, anyway?"

Big Woodpecker pursed his lips and then spat.

"Because Clayton and his friends hunt them, just like they was animals. You know that. Besides, the Lewis girl, she pointed a finger at some Yanas, and Lewis and Clayton and Anderson tied them up and shot 'em. They'd come shoot my people too if your pa hadn't got rifles for everyone. That's true, and you know it."

True Bear nodded.

"And if Ben ever died, Clayton and the others would come to Upper Eden and take charge of everything, and my people would either have to work for him or go live with the Yanas. You too, True Bear, and your ma. Because there's no law to protect Indians. That's what Ben told us, and Ooti agreed with him. They leave us alone because your pa's a Whiteman, that's all."

"We've got guns," True Bear said. "Plenty of guns. Clayton would have to bring a whole army with him. We'd all go live with the Yanas, or maybe the Modocs. There's no way the Whites could ever catch us. Maybe it'd be better like that. . . ."

The boys rode on silently. When they reached a high crest and the meadows that lay between Black Butte and Diamond Peak, they reined in their ponies and gazed toward Wahgalu, but the mountain was still partially shrouded in swirling gray clouds.

"That's why Pa says everyone has to learn to read and

write," True Bear said. "The law will change eventually, but
the world's not going to hold still. It won't be long before
there aren't any more wild Indians. It can't be helped. . . ."

"I guess not," Big Woodpecker mumbled. "Your pa's going
to send you away to school, isn't he? I heard him talking
about it. Probably you won't ever want to come back after
that, will you?"

"We're being blue-faced and grumpy today, both of us. I
ain't going to go if I can help it. But if I have to, I'll come
back just as soon as I can. Why would anyone want to live
anywhere else? You afraid to go all the way up Wahgalu or
not?"

"Of course I'm not afraid. Was I afraid the time we ran into
that big grizzly?"

True Bear laughed.

"That was probably one of the ones my ma raised from a
cub," he said. "Didn't attack us, did it?"

"Well, it might have."

"Just stood there and watched us—like a big brown dog."

"She really raised two of them and turned them loose?" Big
Woodpecker mused.

He had often heard bits and pieces of the story, how fifteen
years earlier, when the Wawlems first found gold, and Ooti
McCain had spoken with Pano the Bear Spirit and after that
she raised two grizzly cubs and exacted her revenge upon the
miners who massacred her people—she and Ben McCain,
whom she found shot and close to death. There were rumors,
in fact, of one band of Grizzly Indians, still wild and still
attacking ranch houses and kidnapping children, just like the
Yanas. No one knew for certain, of course, not positively, and
not even True Bear had much to say on the subject. Maybe,
Big Woodpecker reflected, his friend didn't even know for
sure. But the older Oidoing-koyo Maidus all believed Ooti
and Ben McCain, Bear-who-cannot-see-well, had been the
original group's leaders. Why else would Ben McCain, the
big Whiteman with the thick glasses, prefer to live in an
Indian village, and why else would he have been so careful
over the years to see to it everyone was armed and capable of
holding his own against any possible threat from the outside?

The boys urged their ponies forward, crossed the seldom-
used wagon trail that led over Wahgalu's shoulder and on

toward Hat Creek and the town of Burney. They rode around the margin of an extensive snowfield and angled up a ridge, entering at last into cold, gray dampness of what seemed exactly like winter fog, a shroud of vapor that continued to surround the mountain's summit.

At timberline they tethered their ponies and continued on foot, ascending bare rock and then climbing steep slopes covered with scalloped snow, very irregular, melting in the heat of midsummer when no clouds hovered about the mountain. The boys had climbed silently for half an hour when grating noises began to pour up from the rocks they stood upon, sounds followed by a considerable jolt that tossed both of them off their feet and onto their backs.

"Another earthquake!" Big Woodpecker shouted.

"Jesus!" True Bear gasped. "You think maybe old Wahgalu's really a volcano—like Mount Etna in our history book? What if it's going to erupt?"

"Blue Loon says it's never done that since long, long ago. The mountain's asleep now."

"Well, what if the damned thing decides to wake up? Maybe we ought to get back down."

Big Woodpecker rose to his feet.

"I am not afraid," he said. "You go down. I will go on to the top, Whiteboy."

"Not without me, you son of a bitch! Okay, we'll both get blown up, then. Come on, I'll race you. Can't be far from here. The mountain rounds off just above. . . ."

They tried to run but soon stopped, hands on knees, bent over, and sucked for breath.

"Air's . . . thin," True Bear managed.

"Look!" Big Woodpecker pointed. "What's that?"

Just over the rise, a great column of steam had begun to vent, and in a moment the sound reached them—an intense hissing, shrieking, wailing sound, as if some huge monster, trapped beneath the rounded dome of the peak, were screaming in pain and terrible anger.

The boys turned instantly, and ran wildly downslope, leaping over boulders and scrambling madly, oblivious to anything except an urgent need to get away from whatever it was that inhabited the top of Wahgalu.

When they reached timberline, they discovered one of the

ponies had broken loose from its tether and the other's mouth
was flecked with foam as the creature struggled, wild-eyed,
against a braided rope fastened securely to a twisted juniper.

True Bear untied the rope, and the horse immediately
plunged off downslope, mired briefly in a snowbank, fought
its way free, and galloped onward.

The boys had regained some of their composure by now.
They looked sheepishly at one another and began to laugh.

"It was a big sulphur spring, just like the ones at the head
of Mill Creek," True Bear said.

But thinking: *Maybe the mountain's really getting ready to
erupt, maybe it is a volcano like Mount Etna. Maybe fire will
come down and everything will burn up—like Pompeii. . . .*

"That's what it was, I guess," Big Woodpecker agreed.
"Well, we're down now. How we going to catch our ponies,
True Bear?"

"They'll calm down. Let's go find 'em."

The two friends moved off after the vanished horses. They
walked rapidly at first—and then broke into an easy run,
careful not to act as though they believed they were being
pursued by a monster of unknown dimensions and possibly
carnivorous purposes.

ONCE DOWN from Wahgalu and over to the drainage below Black
Butte, the two boys halted, allowed their recaptured ponies
to drink from the stream and graze on sweetgrass. The animals were still somewhat skittish but otherwise amenable to
human guidance.

True Bear withdrew an oilcloth-covered bundle from one
of his saddlebags, untied rawhide laces, and sat down with his
back to a ponderosa pine. Big Woodpecker squatted next to
him, nodding.

Acorn-meal bread and slices of pickled beef.

Big Woodpecker broke off a chunk of bread, took a bite,
and chewed thoughtfully.

"We could of got killed up there," True Bear reflected.
"What if Wahgalu had split open and swallowed us?"

"You think it does that all the time?"

"Don't know. Listen. . . ."

A series of explosions, muted, rang heavily through the air,
noises lasting for a minute or more, then ceasing. After an

interval a camp-robber jay began to croak—joined within moments by several of his fellows.

"Old Coyote Man was playing," True Bear grinned.

"You believe that stuff?"

"I guess. Sometimes I do. Maybe we should've stayed up there and watched what was happening. Wonder what it was like when Tehama Mountain blew—if it ever happened at all, I mean. Dad says just listen when Crane and the other old women start telling stories—listen but don't believe 'em."

"Could of happened, though," Big Woodpecker said, taking a mouthful of beef, chewing at stringy meat.

"Well, we could have been killed. That was a real adventure, huh? I mean, I bet we're the only ones who ever saw anything like that. Maybe that was our medicine vision. What do you think?"

"Nope. My father had one when he was a young man, before he married Ma. He climbed up on Brokeoff and stayed there for two nights—nothing to eat all that time. A red-neck loon came and talked to him. It was a woman, like Ishanahura, only it didn't have a string of dried hearts around its neck, just red feathers. The rest of it was as blue as the sky."

"And that's how he got his name?"

"Uh-huh. Hurt Eagle explained the meaning to him. The loon was warning him of what would happen if he chose the wrong woman, and that's how he knew he was supposed to marry Ma. Because of what the loon said. Anyhow, nothing like that happened to us. I think you've got to fast and pray to Lizard or Gray Squirrel if you want to have a medicine vision. The prayers keep Coyote Man away. If he gives you a vision, it's bad luck, and nothing ever goes right for you after that."

True Bear swallowed, wiped his mouth, and stood up.

"Guess so. The mountain's quiet now. It's probably underneath the mountain, that's all. So some steam came shooting out. We could climb back up there and look . . . ?"

Big Woodpecker shook his head.

"That's dumb, True Bear. What if the mountain explodes? You really want to do that?"

"Naw. Maybe some other time. But I know what you and me ought to do. We been best friends for a long time, ain't that so?"

"Yep. It's true, all right."

"You remember Bully O'Bragh, that crazy old bastard who came to visit about four years ago—took the gang of us swimming down to Childe's Meadows? Well, he's the one who led my dad across from St. Louis, and he used to live with the Cheyennes out on the plains. He used to hunt buffalo with 'em. O'Bragh said when two men are close friends, they cut their wrists and press them together. Afterwards they're blood brothers. Maybe that's what we should do—even if what happened up on Wahgalu wasn't a real medicine vision. What do you think?"

Big Woodpecker laughed self-consciously.

"That's almost like two men getting married, ain't it? I remember when Old Bully told the story. You think he really done all those things he said he did?"

"My pa believes him. Bully O'Bragh saved his life a couple of times, and Ma's too. They never would have come here if it hadn't been for O'Bragh."

"How deep do we have to cut ourselves?"

"Just enough to make the blood run, that's all."

Big Woodpecker pulled out his skinning knife and ran his thumb tentatively along the whetted edge.

"You're half Pano," he mused, "and I'm Oidoing-koyo. If we do this thing, then your people and my people are joined."

"Sure, but they are anyway," True Bear shrugged. "Another few years and I'll bet no one remembers who's who any more."

"Ain't you afraid to cut yourself?" Big Woodpecker teased.

"Hell no. I cut myself all the time without meaning to."

"That's different. You go first, then."

True Bear withdrew his own knife and touched its point to the side of his wrist.

"No good if you shut your eyes," Big Woodpecker grinned.

"Who says? O'Bragh never mentioned anything about that."

"You think the Shy-anns is the only ones who have blood brothers? You've got too much White blood in you, that's the problem. Only half Indian."

"That's a dumb thing to say. All right, then, I'll do it with my eyes open."

True Bear gritted his teeth and jabbed the point of the

knife into his flesh. A trickle of blood ran down, dripped from the wrist.

Big Woodpecker started to do the same, but hesitated.

"Go ahead, Big Mouth. Cut yourself!"

Big Woodpecker jerked the knife, but the scratch only turned red. He jabbed again, this time producing a small flow of crimson.

"There. . . ."

The boys pressed their wrists together and nodded at each other.

"Now we're the same as brothers," Big Woodpecker said.

"We are brothers. Now we will always share things and each will always protect the other in case he has to."

"What about women when we get older?"

"Can't share women," True Bear said. "But what if we both fall in love with the same girl? What do we do then?"

"Let her decide."

"She probably won't want either one of us," True Bear grinned.

"What do you mean?"

"That's how come we get along so well—because 'one's about as ugly as the other.' "

"We ain't ugly, are we? You think that's so, True Bear?"

"Naw. Dad's always sayin' stuff like that, but most of the time he don't mean it."

"He sure is big, though. Lots bigger than any of the Maidu men. Twice the size of your mom."

Big Woodpecker inspected his knife closely, then replaced it in its sheath.

"Should we tell the others?" he asked.

"About being blood brothers, you mean?"

"All of it."

"Of course," True Bear laughed. "That way even the bigger boys will know if they push one of us around, they'll have to push both. Together, we could whip just about anyone. Two are always way tougher than one. Just like Patroclus and Achilles in that book Dad's been reading us in school."

"*The Iliad,*" Big Woodpecker nodded. "That book's even crazier than stories old Crane tells. And the Bible too. My dad says none of it ever happened, but he don't even know how to read."

"Probably he's right. Think we'd better get back to the rancheria? Sun's already down behind the ridge."

They stuffed the last of the food into their mouths and strode to where the ponies were grazing.

AS THEY RODE in past the McCain ranch house, True Bear's father walked out to meet them.

"Where the hell have you boys been? Well, you've got a little search on your hands tomorrow, Son. Three of our Hereford heifers either strayed off or got taken by Yanas, in which case they've probably already been slaughtered. Right after lessons tomorrow, True Bear, I want you to head down to Childe's place and see if our cows are eating his grass. Not even branded yet, but you'll recognize them. Stop in and tell Seth Childe what you're about—so he doesn't put a load of buckshot into your rear end."

"Big Woodpecker and I are blood brothers now," True Bear blurted, displaying the inch-long cut on his wrist.

Ben McCain nodded, smiled slightly, and adjusted his glasses.

"Good to hear it, good to hear it. In that case, Big Woodpecker can ride along with you—providing Blue Loon doesn't have some other work cut out for him. Blood brothers, eh? Partners in crime is what I'd call it. Now put your spotted mule into the barn and get on into the house. Ooti's got dinner just about ready for us. Suppose your *blood brother* wants to eat with us tonight? Connecticut pot roast, lads. It's only taken a dozen years or so, but Ooti's by-Gawd learned the art of civilized cooking. Well, Woodpecker Monster, what do you say?"

Big Woodpecker glanced at True Bear and grinned.

"Sure he would," William True Bear Goffe McCain replied.

THREE

In Wolf Tracker's Village

[July 1864]

THE BOYS SPOKE briefly with Seth Childe and then made a long ride about the perimeter of some big meadows, but did not find the three young Herefords among grazing Spanish cattle that composed the greater portion of Childe's herd. At length they passed back by their neighbor's ranch house, waved to Childe and his two young sons, father working with a bow scythe and children standing not far away, watching. True Bear and Big Woodpecker continued, alert for strayed cattle, to Mill Creek. Here they noted tracks in a mudbank close to streamside, tracks that led down into a forested canyon, the grassy area close by rushing water growing ever narrower as Mill Creek passed beneath Morgan Mountain and on into the fastness of long, twisting canyon that emerged far to the southwest, as they knew, into the Sacramento River Valley.

"What makes you think these are your cows, True Bear? I bet those heifers have wandered down Lost Creek. If cows is lost, don't Lost Creek seem like a good place to look? Or maybe down to Stump Ranch. You might be good at understanding what's in books, but I don't think you know how to find cows at all. What if we run into some Yanas, what then? They'll murder us, just like they did those Lewis kids."

"Probably. I guess they'll cut off our heads and roast us for dinner. Maybe they'll eat our horses too. Since when is an Oidoing-koyo afraid of a Yahi? Just yesterday you was telling me how brave you are."

"They kill kids like us, and you know it, too."

"Naw they don't. That probably wasn't Yahis at all. Besides, Wolf Tracker and his people don't like valley ranchers. They never attack us, do they?"

"No. . . ."

"Of course not. My dad and mom have visited Wolf Tracker half a dozen times. And your dad says the Oidoing-koyos and Yahis used to get together at the salt swamps every year."

"That was a long time ago—not since I was first born. Everything's changed since then. Oidoing-koyos are civilized now, and the Yahis still wander around and hunt and. . . ."

"Murder kids?" True Bear laughed.

"Damn right. That did happen, didn't it?"

"Guess so."

"Well, then?"

"Dad says the Yahis are probably over on Battle Creek. This is their time of year for root digging and deer hunting. I'll bet we find our heifers grazing in the next little meadow we come to."

"I heard what he said last night. He said them cows might of got taken by Yanas. If he wasn't talking about Wolf Tracker, then who was he talking about?"

True Bear shrugged, snapped the reins along his pony's neck, urging the animal ahead at a faster pace.

"Probably Long Tooth the Fool Killer."

"You bastard. There's no Yana chief named Long Tooth."

"No Yahis in this canyon, either. Just three stupid Herefords. Come on, *blood brother*, we got to hurry if we want to be home before dark."

"I'm not your damn blood brother if you're going to get the both of us murdered and eaten for dinner, no sir. Ben never said for us to ride down the canyon. We ought to be up by the lake. I bet that's where the cows is."

AT THE NEXT MEADOW'S lower end, just where hoofprints crossed over a damp sandbar, True Bear and Big Woodpecker drew up their ponies and dismounted. The boys stood side by side, staring down at some new impressions in the sand.

Moccasin prints.

"No Yahis, huh?"

"Probably someone from the rancheria," True Bear replied quickly, kneeling to take a closer look.

"Nobody wears moccasins anymore except the older people, and you know it too. What would any of our people be doing down here? Besides . . . those ain't Maidu moccasins. Look. I think we better get out of here."

"You're right, Woodpecker. Look at the edge of the prints—lacings are different. Whoever it is must have stole our heifers—or else found 'em and started driving them along."

Both boys' voices instinctively dropped to whispers, and True Bear stood up, and looked around. He felt chill water run on his spine—had a distinct intuition he and Big Woodpecker were being watched. He scanned the forest that came down to meadow's edge, saw nothing, and gazed up the west slope to a rim high above and the still-recognizable summit of Turner Mountain barely visible beyond.

"What's the matter?"

"Nothing," True Bear replied. "For a moment . . . this is a big canyon, ain't it, Woodpecker? I half remember it—the last time I was just . . . five. I was riding behind Mom, hanging on. We went further down than this. Met Wolf Tracker and maybe a dozen of his men, never did see the village."

They heard the mating trill of a screech owl—unusual for afternoon. And it didn't sound quite right, repeated three times in quick succession.

"Let's get the hell out of here," Big Woodpecker whispered, moving toward his pony.

True Bear turned, not contesting the idea this time. But when he glanced across the meadow—some movement caught along the periphery of vision—he realized a man had stepped out from behind a thicket of young madrones. He was barechested and wore a band of white leather around his forehead, his hair long like a woman's. The right arm was raised, fist clenching a spear.

Then other Indians emerged from cover of brush and firs,

five men in all, some armed with short bows, some with spears.

Yahis.

True Bear's pony whinnied and pawed at the sand with a forehoof.

The Indians didn't move again for what seemed to the two boys a virtual eternity. Then, as if satisfied True Bear and Big Woodpecker were indeed without weapons, the man wearing the white headband walked slowly toward them, staring first at one, then the other. Without speaking, he grasped the reins of the ponies in either hand and gestured to the boys to follow him.

The remaining Yahis approached, now their weapons held at the ready and yet not in a manner that seemed particularly threatening.

"My name's True Bear McCain"—his voice seemed to come out a squeak in spite of his intentions—"we're Maidus, friends of the Yahis."

The leader did not even look back, either ignoring or not understanding what True Bear said.

"My father's Ben McCain—he's friends with Wolf Tracker. . . ."

Again no response from the leader, but one man behind them laughed, as if enjoying a good jest, and then mumbled the words *Oidoing-koyo Saltus.* Another murmured apparent agreement.

"Are they taking us prisoner?" Big Woodpecker whispered. "What will they do to us?"

"I guess—hell, I don't know," True Bear replied. "But we mustn't act afraid. They're not taking our knives away from us—not yet, anyway. . . ."

The Yahis and their prisoners proceeded downstream into the heart of precipitous Mill Creek Gorge, into a world of long shadows and grotesquely piled boulders, great fragments of black rimrock that had in the past fractured loose from a dark lip high above. The Yahi leader moved ahead quickly and certainly, as though he were walking along a well-known trail. Yet no trail was visible—only the hoofmarks of three Hereford cattle.

As darkness filled the canyon and first evening stars began to appear above the ridge spine to the east, the Indians stopped momentarily. One man, not the leader, gave a hawk cry—or of a bluejay imitating a hawk. And then they moved on.

Beyond a sharp bend in the gorge, the land opened out into a meadow to either side of the alder-lined creek, and the two boys could see campfires, smell the odor of roasting meat.

ONCE WITHIN the village of makeshift huts, a randomly distributed collection of *Mat'adjuwa*, brush lodges used during summer months, True Bear and Big Woodpecker took note of the three Hereford cattle they'd been looking for. The animals were lying down beneath a huge liveoak, chewing cud and seemingly undismayed by their new surroundings and likely fate.

The ponies were tethered, and the two boys were pushed ahead toward the largest of several cooking fires. Men, women, and children crowded about them, in a great show of curiosity. Two or three older Yahi youths shouted what were apparently insults of one sort or another, but for the most part the Yahis acted as though they were examining specimens of peculiar-looking wildlife that had been driven into the encampment.

An old woman, grinning a toothless smile, cautiously approached the boys, finally stepped forward, and touched her fingertips to True Bear's face. Then, satisfied, she retreated.

"They going to kill us?" Big Woodpecker whispered.

"Maybe. But if they decide to wait until morning, maybe we can get away. Dad will come looking for us, you can bet on that. He'll stop by Seth Childe's place and find out which direction we went."

"It'll take half our village to do any good. . . ."

The group around them parted, and a man stepped forward, a tall man wearing a cone-shaped hat of woven tules—a man, True Bear judged, about the age of his own father, sixty or so. From his bearing and general air of authority, the boys understood him to be the chief.

Wolf Tracker? It's got to be him, but he doesn't look the way I remember him. . . .

The old Indian spoke briefly to his scouts, nodded, and

appeared satisfied with whatever they had told him. Then he
turned to True Bear and Big Woodpecker.

"*Achi djeyauna?*" he asked. And then, in English: "How
are you called?"

It took a moment for the words to register.

"I'm True Bear McCain, and this is Big Woodpecker, son
to Blue Loon of the Oidoing-koyo Maidus. Your name is Wolf
Tracker—I was with Ben McCain eight years ago. I'm his
son."

The Yahi leader, no expression whatsoever on his weathered face, stared first at True Bear and then at Big Woodpecker.

"We were looking for those cows over there," True Bear
continued, pointing toward the three animals. "My father
sent us to find them. He has always said that you were his
friend, Wolf Tracker."

"Young Saltu devils," Wolf Tracker muttered finally. Then
he spoke quickly in Yahi, turned, and walked away.

Several men placed their hands on True Bear and Big
Woodpecker, guiding the boys away from the fire, passing
through a crowd of excited villagers and across the meadow to
a young blue oak, where the boys were pressed to the ground,
their backs to the tree. A length of braided deerhide lariat
was wrapped around their waists and cinched tight, then
loosely about their throats. Their hands were bound in front
of them.

The Indians returned to their cooking fires, and the Yahis,
as if suddenly having completely lost interest in their captives, went about the business of eating an evening meal.

"Haven't killed us yet anyhow," Big Woodpecker observed.
"Guess they're going to wait for morning. You think they'll
post a guard on us?"

"Maybe. Can you get at those straps on your wrists? I think
I can use my teeth to untie them. Maybe they want us to run
away. I don't know whether Wolf Tracker recognized me or
not, but he must remember Dad's name. I was just a little
kid then."

"Didn't act very friendly, if you ask me. I don't think he
cares who you are, or me either. The Yahis have been at war
with the Americans for years now, and your dad's American.
I bet they're going to make slaves of us. They used to do that
sometimes."

"This is a dumb thing to say, but I wish they'd bring us some of whatever it is they're eating. I'm starved. If the Yahis are going to kill us, they ought to let us eat first."

"Venison stew and wild carrots and acorn bread, just like my grandmother makes. Smells the same, anyway."

"I've got the thongs loose from my wrists, Woodpecker. You think they want us to run off?"

"So they can track us down and stick spears into us—I'll bet that's what it is. Like a game. They see us gone, and then they all come running after us like a damn bunch of wolves."

"Shut up a minute. Can you get your hands free?"

"Yes. But let's wait."

"Until the Yahis post a guard on us?"

"Those old women over there—they keep looking this way. If we get loose, they'll yell, and we won't have a chance."

Across the way, the Indians were laughing.

Then a slim figure emerged from the throng of people and began to walk toward where True Bear and Big Woodpecker were bound. In the dimness of firelight, the person appeared to be a boy carrying a basket.

"I have brought you something to eat."

The words were in English, and the voice was that of a girl.

For a moment neither True Bear nor Big Woodpecker was certain as to how to respond. There was only a rich smell of steaming deer flesh and vegetables, drifting sounds of amusement from the gathering of Yahis, distant cries of a pair of horned owls talking to one another from canyon rim to canyon rim, a half-discernible echo of a solitary coyote, perhaps high on a ridge above, and the silhouetted form of a boy who had turned that instant into a girl, a girl about their own age, a wild Indian girl who spoke to them in their own language. These, and the sounds of flowing, tumbling water and a gentle wind moving insistently among oak leaves and pine needles.

"You speak English?" True Bear asked, startled.

"Have I not spoken correctly? Here is something for you to eat. Wolf Tracker says you must be hungry."

She placed the basket before them and stood by, waiting.

"How can we eat?" True Bear asked. "Our hands are bound, and the leather cord presses against our throats. We couldn't swallow even if our hands were free."

"Can you not untie yourselves? Any Yahi could do it easily enough. Wolf Tracker said you would be nearly loose by the time I brought the food to you."

"We're supposed to escape?" Big Woodpecker asked. "Then everyone tracks us down and kills us, right? Is that the game?"

"There is no game, Maidus. I have brought you something to eat, that is all. I am to stay here with you until later. Then another will take my place. Do you wish me to untie your hands for you?"

"My hands are free," True Bear admitted. "Will you take the cords away from our throats, at least?"

The girl did not answer—instead stepped behind the oak and unfastened the upper strand of woven deerhide.

"Do you think you can swallow now?"

"This food poisoned?" Big Woodpecker asked.

"You do not have to eat it if you don't wish to do so. We are all eating the same thing tonight. My mother and the other women have prepared it. If you die, then we will all die."

True Bear took a small portion of warm, mushy substance from the basket, first touched the food to the tip of his tongue, breathed in a savory odor, and then chewed, and swallowed. Big Woodpecker had his hands free within moments and proceeded to follow his friend's example.

The girl, her features half-shadowed, half-revealed by light of flickering campfires, an odor about her like that of oak leaves and something else, something indefinable. Her hair bound tightly behind her head, long, trailing down her back. And her breasts were bare in the manner Maidu women had once followed but no longer did, breasts merely suggested in a dimness of light, those of a girl who'd begun her magical transformation into womanhood—a girl who wore a skirt of woven tules laced with willow whips, a garment that clung to her waist and hips and descended nearly to her knees. Pretty girl, one who didn't look entirely Indian, whose features in some way were suggestive of True Bear's own.

She watched them intently as they ate, slowly at first, then almost ravenously. True Bear swallowed a final morsel and looked up.

"Thank you. The food was good, and we were very hungry.

I'm True Bear McCain, and this is Big Woodpecker. We're blood brothers. What's your name?"

She did not answer.

"Are we going to be killed?" Big Woodpecker demanded.

The girl smiled then.

"I do not think so. Wolf Tracker says we must take you back to your village when tomorrow comes—but I was not supposed to tell you that."

"What's your name?" True Bear persisted—thinking at the same time: *If she wasn't supposed to tell us, then why was she the one who brought us food? How many Yahis know enough English to be able to talk to us? How'd she learn? Wolf Tracker himself must have taught her. Perhaps she's his daughter, then.*

"I have no real name," the girl said, her voice hardly more than a whisper. "I was born in disgrace. They call me Wahtaurisi-yi, Sits-by-the-ladder. That is the name of a fatherless child. It does not happen often among our people. A Saltu, a Whiteman, killed the one who should have been my father and then forced my mother, Smoke Woman, to lie with him. That happened near Nem Seyoo, beneath Wamatiwi, at a time when the Whites murdered many of our people—at least, that is what I have been told. If you were Saltus, then Wolf Tracker would kill you. But you are not, you are Oidoingkoyos. Wolf Tracker told those who captured you that you were not to be harmed. You do not need to worry."

"You're half White—your father was a Whiteman?"

"I don't have a father. I just told you that. But I was raised in Wolf Tracker's igunna—I have his protection, and that is why I was not left out for coyotes to find when I was first born."

"I'm also half White," True Bear said, lowering his own voice in a gesture of confidence. "I'm the son of Benjamin McCain and Ooti, Acorn Girl."

"Wolf Tracker told us that," the girl responded. "Your mother fought many battles against the Saltus. She is a medicine woman, leader of the Panos. That was before you were born, True Bear McCain. Ooti the Pano is well known. Stories of her revenge against the Whites are often told. We too fight against the Whites, just as she did years ago. Tell me what she looks like."

"Like you, only older," Big Woodpecker said, immediately wishing he hadn't blurted out the words, wishing he'd said nothing at all.

"That cannot be true. I am only a child—I haven't yet gone to the woman's lodge. I am only Sits-by-the-ladder, and Ooti was a great warrior. Some believe she will one day lead all the different peoples against the Saltus and drive them from our lands, but I don't think anyone could do that. There are far too many Whitemen. They've changed the world. That is what Wolf Tracker says."

The girl's words registered upon True Bear's mind, but he couldn't grasp what he heard. Crane, an old woman who had been married to Hurt Eagle, the ancient one, had told him tales of his mother's adventures, but he never more than half believed them. His own mother, legend among the Yahis?

By the tone of Wahtaurisi-yi's voice, True Bear sensed the girl was speaking of a great heroine, someone like Gudrun in one of his father's books, or Helen, or Caliphia the queen of the Amazons. But Ooti McCain? He loved his mother dearly, felt more at ease around her even than around his father—but she was the one who cooked meals, cleaned the house, herded cattle with his father, made articles of clothing, and took delight in saving the lives of young birds that fell from their nests in springtime. *Lead all the different peoples against the Saltus?*

The thought was inconceivable, and True Bear's first repsonse was to deny it all, to say, "No, you must be speaking of someone else, not my mother. . . ."

At the same time, however, he realized his own safety and that of Big Woodpecker were at least partly dependent upon the notion that he, True Bear McCain, was the son of an almost mythic being who had been created out of vague rumors of battles his mother had been involved in fourteen or fifteen years earlier—that even more than the fact that Benjamin McCain and Wolf Tracker knew each other.

But Wolf Tracker knew Ooti as well—how could the chief have allowed such stories to be told? Only in the back of True Bear's mind, in some dark, intuitive, prerational region, did any of it make sense. All people need a messiah, a hero-leader who will return from the dead, from the Spirit World.

They'll create their messiah out of the least trace of a rumor, the most tenuous thread of hope.

His father's words, the musings of Ben McCain, a huge, half-blind man who had sired him and who once lived a wholly different life, teacher in a great university three thousand miles to the east, in a world True Bear could only surmise from things he read in the books his father gave him.

"But you are beautiful like her," Big Woodpecker said—again wishing profoundly he had not spoken and yet unable to prevent the words from tumbling out.

Wahtaurisi-yi said nothing—studied first the face of one of her captives, then the other.

"Maidus do not understand about truth—we all know that. Don't tell me such things. I don't wish to hear them."

True Bear was about to defend his friend's judgment but then thought better of it. Instead he demanded, "If Wolf Tracker knows I am Acorn Girl's son, then why are the Yahis keeping us tied to a tree as though we were criminals, enemies of the Yahis?"

Wahtaurisi-yi laughed softly.

"So you will not wander off into the night and fall into a hole in the rocks and kill yourselves, that's why. If such a thing happened, then Wolf Tracker would have to send some of his own people to the Maidus to be their slaves."

An odor about her, she smells like oak leaves, oak leaves and fir needles that have been rubbed together in the hand. Perhaps she does that and then rubs her hands over her body. She's only a girl, but she's more lovely than any grown woman. No matter how long I live, I'll never forget what's happened. I'll never forget the taste of food Wahtaurisi-yi gave us to eat, I will never forget how she looks standing here in shadows. I have only known her for these few minutes, and yet I feel as though I had always known her, that I would like to be with her forever. Her breasts are bare, but she doesn't even seem aware of being half-naked. I'm almost afraid to look at her. Big Woodpecker feels the same things I do—I know it. I wish she lived in our village. Big Woodpecker and I will come back here to visit her. But why do the Yahis keep us tied up like this? It doesn't make sense, not if what Wahtaurisi-yi just told us is true. Maybe she likes to tell stories, but that doesn't matter either. . . .

*   *   *

THE TWO BOYS and the Yahi girl continued to talk as night hours lengthened. Wahataurisi-yi declined to answer questions concerning the Lewis children—claiming she'd heard no more than a few bits of conversation among the men, spoken in the Man Language, and so not fully comprehensible to women. After a time, however, she admitted under terms of strictest confidence that she and all the women were well aware of what the men had to say to one another—as though this capacity for comprehension were a secret, to be kept from the men at all costs. Since True Bear and Big Woodpecker were not Yahis, Wahtaurisi-yi apparently deemed it permissible to make such a confession. In any case, she insisted, the Lewis children had been captured by Chief Big Foot's band, Yana people who lived to the north, near the Salt Marshes. But more than this she would not say, and True Bear surmised that perhaps her information regarding the slayings was no more exact than his own.

The boys recounted their adventure of the previous day—their witnessing of an erupting steam vent near the summit of Wahgalu. Wahtaurisi-yi seemed greatly impressed with their tale, though whether she in fact believed it the boys couldn't tell.

"Coyote Man lives beneath that mountain," she said. "That is where he has dug his burrow. Perhaps you saw smoke rising from his cooking fire. Perhaps he and his wife were just beginning to prepare their dinner. My people don't go up onto the mountain because we do not wish to disturb Old Man. We go there only when we die, and then Old Man helps us to step off into the stars so we can make our way to the Spirit World."

"Our people say the same thing," Big Woodpecker nodded. "But True Bear's mother comes from the south, and her people climb to the place where the Great Oak Ootimtsaa grows, and from there they go on to Upper Meadows, the Sky Place. But I think it's the same place for all of us. True Bear's father is a Wawlem, and he speaks of something called Heaven, where Jesus lives with his father. Then everyone sits around and listens to music. A funny little man in black clothing came to visit last year, and he told us many stories about the Whiteman's god. But I already knew those stories. They're all in a book called the Bible."

"I know what a Bible is," Wahtaurisi-yi laughed. "Wolf Tracker has one, a Saltu medicine book. But even he doesn't know what the marks mean. Do you speak truth? Can you read this medicine book?"

"We can both read," Big Woodpecker answered. "There are many, many books. Ben McCain makes us all go to school."

"That's so," True Bear agreed. "My father believes all the Indian people must learn how to read and use numbers, for that's the only way we can protect ourselves from the ranchers in the valley. If we don't make ourselves smarter than they are, they'll find ways of taking our lands from us."

"Reading the medicine book will make a person smarter?" Wahtaurisi-yi asked. "I don't believe that. Besides, the Saltus will still have guns and horses. Those things are more important than books. I'm only a girl and one with no father, but that is what I think."

"Wahtaurisi-yi must be the one to learn about the medicine book," a voice said from the darkness. "Then perhaps the sun will not truly die in our skies. You may return to the igunna now, Granddaughter. I wish to speak to these young rascals who came to steal our salmon flour and tanned deerskins."

The girl rose, empty basket in hand, and disappeared without speaking further. Wolf Tracker, chief of the Yahis, stepped forward and then knelt close beside the tree to which True Bear and Big Woodpecker were loosely bound. The boys said nothing, still fearful as to what might happen next.

"You are the son of Benjamin McCain, the Saltu who is called Bear-who-cannot-see-well. I remember you from when you were still very small, True Bear. Your father is a friend to me and my people, and you must greet him for me when you return home tomorrow. Now tell me why you two have come down into our canyon."

"Three of our cattle strayed," True Bear managed, "and my father sent us to search for them."

"Is this true?"

"Yes, sir," Big Woodpecker said.

Wolf Tracker laughed softly.

"We thought those three deer looked strange, very slow and stupid. So my men guided them toward our village to save their lives. Wolves and mountain lions like stupid deer. That's what my scouts were doing when they found you two. Those are Benjamin McCain's cattle?"

"Yes."

"Not Childe's?"

"No, they're ours, some of the new animals Dad bought from Dan Clayton."

"Bear-who-cannot-see-well should have killed Clayton and taken the cattle perhaps. That is what I will do if I am ever given a chance. Why do you still pretend to be tied up? My warriors did not take your knives away from you."

"We didn't want to ruin a good lariat, Wolf Tracker," True Bear returned quickly. "We believed it better to wait until you wished us to be free."

"The son of McCain and Ooti the Pano speaks well. But I think you can untie the knots. It will be easier to sleep if you're able to lie down. If you are still here in the morning, you may take your three whiteface cattle and your ponies and go back to Upper Eden. Is that not the name your father uses?"

"Wolf Tracker is kind."

"I've learned to be gentle with those who are not my enemies, True Bear McCain. Still, I would keep you both except that I don't wish your mother and father to be angry with me. You would become Yahis, and perhaps one of you would one day wish to marry Sits-by-the-ladder and so become my grandson. She's a very pretty girl, very good-natured. She will make a fine wife one day, even though she is half Saltu in her blood. Yes, that is true—but perhaps she already explained about that. True Bear, you must tell your mother we saw those two grizzlies she raised from cubs many seasons ago. Last week we found them swimming together in a pond near the summit of the mountain the Whites call Turner Peak. I am certain they were the same bears—we have seen them several times before. . . ."

Then the chief turned and was gone.

Soft wind sang through the foliage of oak and fir, and from high on the ridge above came the cry of a solitary wolf, its song echoed a moment later by the barkings and yippings of coyotes on the opposite rim of the canyon.

FOUR

A Gift of Cattle

[July 1864]

BLUEJAYS WERE SCREAMING.

True Bear turned on his side, the last fragments of dream fading slowly from his mind. For a moment he was puzzled as to his surroundings, but then he came fully awake.

Oak leaves.

Dew on the grass.

Sound of running water.

He stretched his cramped limbs and sat up.

Wahtaurisi-yi was standing a few feet away, fully clothed this time, almost in the manner of Oidoing-koyo women at Upper Eden, garbed in a fringed deerskin dress painstakingly decorated with pigments and porcupine quills in geometric design. True Bear reached over and roused Big Woodpecker, who sat upright, in the same motion fumbling for his hunting knife.

She did not speak this time—instead gestured for them to follow her.

The boys watched as men and women emerged from various brush lodges and walked in small groups, men upstream and women downstream, for the ritual of morning bathing. Others were returning from the stream, some men com-

57

pletely nude, water dripping from their thick black hair. The
women, a few bare-breasted and others wrapped in deerskin
capes, talked happily among themselves. Several old women
pointed toward True Bear, Big Woodpecker, and Sits-by-the-
ladder. They laughed and called out.

Wahtaurisi-yi ignored them, seeming not even to hear the
apparent jestings, and continued to lead toward the largest
brush lodge in the temporary village. In front of this structure a fire was burning. A woman knelt close by, one who
wore a tule skirt, a sleeveless upper garment of decorated
leather, and an inch-wide headband also of leather.

True Bear guessed this woman's age to be no greater than
that of his own mother.

Wolf Tracker emerged from behind the lodge. He carried a
basket containing perhaps a dozen fish, already cleaned and
ready for cooking, catfish and trout as well.

"Whitemen eat first thing in the morning," he grinned,
"and so I have netted a few of our little friends from the
creek. You see, I know a great deal about the habits of Saltus.
This morning we will share *breakfast* with our unwilling
guests. Otherwise Bear-who-cannot-see-well might wish to
wrestle with me in payment for having abused these boys.
He's so large that he would crush the breath from me if he
accidentally fell upon me. Besides, it would not be appropriate for two old men to engage in such a contest. Smoke
Woman will prepare the food. True Bear, do you and Big
Woodpecker wish to swim first? Or have the Maidus become
so nearly White that they no longer cleanse themselves each
morning?"

True Bear and Big Woodpecker glanced at one another,
neither certain how to respond.

"We'll bathe when we reach Upper Eden," True Bear said
after a moment's hesitation.

"That is good, that is good. Hurry, Smoke Woman. I can
tell these young men will die soon if they aren't fed."

Smoke Woman spoke in Yahi tongue, something half intel-
ligible, and True Bear, recalling Wahtaurisi-yi's explanation
of Man language and Woman language, realized that Wahtaurisi-
yi's mother was obliged to await instructions, whether in fact
she understood Wolf Tracker or not.

The chief spoke to her, and she immediately began to

insert a willow whip through the gills of the fish, a task she accomplished quickly. She then attached the switch ends to posts set in the earth on either side of the fire.

The men use Woman Language when speaking to women.

"Your ponies are ready, but you must check them to make certain my warriors haven't stolen anything. The animals are tethered close by the cattle."

Wolf Tracker gestured to Wahtaurisi-yi, and with downcast eyes she began to walk in the direction Wolf Tracker indicated. True Bear and Big Woodpecker followed.

Everything was in place, as True Bear realized it would be. He completed a perfunctory inspection, nodded, and turned to Sits-by-the-ladder.

"Is he kind to you—Wolf Tracker? Aren't you allowed to speak when he's near?"

The girl stared at her two companions and smiled.

Straight, even teeth . . . high-bridged nose . . . close-set brown eyes . . . thin face . . . full lips . . . a tiny cleft in her chin. . . .

"Grandfather is very good to me and to my mother. I wouldn't be alive if it were not for him. I would have been left for the wild animals as soon as I was born—because that is the usual thing. My name—in your language it would be *Girl-bastard*, but because I have the protection of the chief, I am in some ways honored by my people, even though they disapprove of me. It's very strange. Smoke Woman has always said I would understand much better after I reached the age of a woman. That time is coming closer now, but I still don't understand very well. My mother and Wolf Tracker explained what happened, when the Saltus killed many of us and took my mother by force—that's how I was conceived. It is said I must become a great medicine woman, like your mother, True Bear. For that reason everyone is polite to me, and yet I have no close friends among the girls my own age. Sometimes I wish to leave these people and. . . . I'm sorry—I mustn't say such things. Why do I speak to you two this way? Wolf Tracker has taught me the language of the Saltus, but he is the only one I can talk to in this tongue—until now. I don't know where he learned it. Even Smoke Woman understands only a little of what we say to one another."

"I think you speak English very good," Big Woodpecker

said. "If you could come to Oidoing-koyo, you could go to
school with us and learn how to read and. . . ."

Then he stopped, realizing he spoke of what could never
happen.

"Big Woodpecker's right," True Bear continued. "He feels
embarrassed for having spoken so quickly, but he's right. We
have only known each other a little while, but I. . . ."

Wahtaurisi-yi nodded.

"I feel that way also," she said.

Then she lowered her gaze and turned away from the boys.

"Come with me," she murmured. "Your meal will be ready
by now. Fish tastes very good when it's still hot and steaming."

"Do you know how to find your way home?" Wolf Tracker
asked, his coppery, weathered face revealing no trace of a
smile.

True Bear and Big Woodpecker glanced at one another,
wondering for a moment whether the chief spoke in jest or
seriously.

"How could we get lost?" True Bear asked. "All we have to
do is follow the creek until we reach Childe's Meadows,
where the stream branches. Big Woodpecker and I have
wandered all over. . . ."

"Remember not to ride your ponies up the side of the
canyon, then. I hope you will tell my friend Bear-who-cannot-
see-well that Wolf Tracker and his *Nozhi* have treated you
well. When my warriors took you captive, True Bear McCain,
they didn't know who you were. Perhaps they thought you
were blue-coated soldiers, I don't know. You two are only
boys now, but soon you will turn into men. When that day
comes, Wolf Tracker hopes you will be his friends. Perhaps
after a time I will come to your *Upper Eden* to visit. If so,
then I will bring Wahtaurisi-yi with me. I think perhaps she
would like to go with you even now, for when a girl reaches
her age, she forgets all the good things her grandfather has
done for her and remembers only the times when he scolded
her. Young women are very difficult to live with at times.
Remember that, both of you, when you decide to take a wife.
Find an old woman, a good fat one, for a *Mahala*. That's the
advice I give you. Skinny young ones with small breasts do

not know how to prepare food properly, and often they are afraid to be touched in the way of a man and a woman."

True Bear grinned, wasn't exactly certain why he was grinning, and glanced at Wahtaurisi-yi, who was standing to one side of and half a pace behind Smoke Woman. The girl stared resolutely at her own feet, pretending to hear nothing at all, even though Wolf Tracker was speaking in English.

The chief nodded and gestured toward the waiting ponies.

"Good-bye, Wahtaurisi-yi," Big Woodpecker blurted.

But the girl still did not respond.

The blood brothers mounted their ponies, shouted at the three whiteface heifers, and clapped their heels to the sides of their mounts. The cattle moved slowly forward, grudgingly, as if realizing they had a fifteen-mile trek ahead of them and were trying to think of some elemental reason why it was better to stay right where they were. One heifer bawled plaintively, and then all three turned their noses upcanyon and began to plod along.

After no more than a few yards of progress, at the meadow's limit, True Bear turned in his saddle and gazed back to where the grandfather, the mother, and the daughter had been standing. Wolf Tracker and Smoke Woman were walking in the opposite direction, with Sits-by-the-ladder behind them.

At that moment the girl turned for a last look at True Bear and Big Woodpecker. Young eyes met across an intervening distance, but only for an instant. Then she waved once, not exuberantly, but with restraint, as if she were not altogether certain it was the proper thing to do.

Big Woodpecker had also turned in his saddle, following True Bear's lead. He let out a wild whoop and gestured with both hands held high above his head.

They moved ahead into a dark forest, following a faintly discernible trail alongside tumbling waters of Mill Creek.

A kingfisher screamed at them and went darting upcanyon, a blur of metallic blue scratched against chill morning air.

"Jesus Kirimity!" Big Woodpecker laughed. "We've had ourselves a real adventure, True Bear. We might of got kilt, and that's true. But it was worth it, even being tied up that way. Wahtaurisi-yi's the prettiest girl I ever saw. There's no one like her in Oidoing-koyo, an' probably no place else, either."

True Bear mumbled agreement and moved his pony so as to head off a heifer that seemed to be having second thoughts about going any further.

"I think you're stuck on her, that's what," Big Woodpecker persisted. "Well, maybe one of us will marry her someday. I'll bet I'm the one, though. Ben's going to send you off to Massa-chew-sets to go to school, just like you told me. When you get back, me an' Sits-by-the-ladder will probably have three or four kids. That's what you get for being half-White, Billy McCain."

True Bear squinted, felt a sudden and intense sensation of jealousy because of his friend's good-natured banter.

"Why would she want to marry you?" he demanded. "You're as homely as a basic pile of cow flop."

"That shows all you know about things," Big Woodpecker laughed. "Girls always fall for me. An' that's true, too."

"College is a long way off. Besides, maybe I won't go at all. Maybe I'll just sneak away and go live with the Yahis."

Big Woodpecker yipped and urged his horse forward.

"And you'll end up marrying with a fat old woman, just like Wolf Tracker said," he laughed.

BELOW MORGAN MOUNTAIN, where the troughlike formation of Childe's Meadow joined the drainages of Mill Creek and Deer Creek, True Bear and Big Woodpecker saw a band of riders approaching. Even at the distance of half a mile, there was no mistaking the man leading the group—a huge individual astride a Percheron.

"Ben's come looking for us," Big Woodpecker said, laughing nervously and at the same time waving wildly. "If Wolf Tracker hadn't let us go when he did, we'd of had a genuine gun fight in that Yahi village."

"Wish we'd made it home on our own," True Bear nodded. "After all that's happened, it don't seem right for us to get herded back like a couple of kids."

The distance between the boys and Ben and his search party diminished rapidly, and the identities of the others in the group became apparent. Ooti was there, riding alongside her husband. Trailing after them were Big Woodpecker's father, Blue Loon, and half a dozen other Oidoing-koyo men.

"Where in thunderation have you lads been? When I sent you out to find some lost cows, I didn't mean for you to trail them all the way to Oroville. You all right, son?"

"Why did you not come home last night?" Ooti demanded. "Perhaps you will be a man soon, but that doesn't mean you can stay away whenever you choose. Big Woodpecker's mother was certain one of you had fallen from your pony and broken a leg. Where have you been, True Bear McCain? I suppose you have a good story made up to amuse us with."

True Bear glanced from his mother to his father and then back again.

"We got captured by Yahis," Big Woodpecker gestured helplessly. "Old Wolf Tracker had the heifers an'. . . ."

"Is that true, son?" Ben asked.

"We followed the Herefords downcanyon, and that's when Wolf Tracker's men surrounded us and took us to their village."

"Tied us up an' everything."

Ooti squinted at the boys, glanced toward Ben.

"My son imagines wild things," Blue Loon said. "I will beat him with an oak branch so he learns to speak the truth—otherwise there's no hope for him."

Ben McCain's big hand moved nervously to his thick spectacles.

"Wolf Tracker, eh? Would have guessed him to be over on Battle Creek this time of year. Well, doesn't look like the old renegade scalped you two, in any case. The Yahis had the three heifers, then? Wouldn't have known they were my animals, not if they strayed down the gulch. How's His Nibs getting along? He's had a couple of run-ins with Clayton and Breckinridge lately, from what I've heard. Maybe he figures to go into the cattle business himself."

"He says he wants to come visit you after a while," True Bear nodded. "The village is just a few miles downcanyon."

"Is it true the Yahis tied you up?" Ooti asked. "Didn't you tell them your names?"

"The men who captured us couldn't speak English. We got tied up all right, but then a beautiful girl brought us food, and after that Wolf Tracker came to talk with us. He fed us good and even caught some fish for breakfast."

"Beautiful girl, is it?" Ben grinned. "Ooti, look at the
expression on our kid's face. The young rascal's in love. From
now on we're going to have to keep him on a leash. Otherwise he'll be disappearing down the gully every other day."

Blue Loon squinted at his son and then began to laugh.

"Both of them," he said. "If I've ever seen guilty boys,
these are the ones."

"Wolf Tracker allowed you to bring our heifers back to
Upper Eden?" Ooti asked. "Are the Yahis doing well? Did it
seem to you as though they had enough to eat? There aren't
as many deer as there used to be. My husband, perhaps we
should leave the heifers for Wolf Tracker's men to find. We
have plenty of cattle in our pastures."

"Deer all over the damned place," Ben returned. "The
beasties are no doubt wandering into the Yahi village and
committing suicide. Hell, Wolf Tracker and his friends aren't
in any danger of starving. Come winter, that's another matter, perhaps. But let's don't be giving away our new breeding
stock. The lads have returned our worthless offspring to us,
so I guess we're going to have to potlatch them something or
another though. Two or three longhorns ought to do it. One
kind tastes as good as the other, as far as I can tell."

"Wolf Tracker and his people will already have moved
their village," Blue Loon said. "He knows you, Ben, and he
trusts you as much as he trusts any Wawlem, but he won't
remain where he is. His people are hunted by the Whites,
and it would be very foolish to allow the site of his village to
be known. Wolf Tracker knows you bought these new cattle
from Dan Clayton, and he knows that Whitemen exchange
conversation as well as money when they do business together. The Yahis are able to remain wild only because
they're always able to keep a few jumps ahead of their enemies. But maybe if you took some cattle down the canyon
and left them, then Wolf Tracker would find the animals and
know they'd been left as a gift."

"It's a good idea," Ooti agreed. "That is what we must do."

THUNDERHEADS FORMED over the mountains, and lenticular
clouds wrapped themselves about the summit of Wahgalu,
completely hiding the peak. Lightning snapped and thunder
roared out of darkness, with heavy raindrops drumming on

the roof of the McCain homestead. The creek that ran through Oidoing-koyo village began to rise during the storm's second day, and the Maidu people found it necessary to chop fire-wood and to light fires in their cabins and brush lodges. Smoke trailed from the newly repaired chimney of the McCain house, and for a brief interval summer seemed to have vanished.

On the third day, however, the heavy clouds drifted east-ward, and brilliant sunlight returned. The upper portion of Wahgalu gleamed brilliant white, the result of a new accu-mulation of hail and snow.

By noon the whiteness diminished, and only a few streaks remained high on the mountain.

Ben McCain and his son, on horseback, cut out three lean Spanish cattle from the herd, two young bulls and an old cow, and proceeded to drive the animals over the crest past Wilson Lake, across Childe's Meadows, thence northward to Mill Creek, and down into the canyon. Turner Mountain rose ahead of them, and True Bear found himself filled with a strange anticipatory anxiety. Would the Yahi village still be where it had been, or had the wild Indians moved on, as Blue Loon said they would?

If the village was still where it had been, would Wahtaurisi-yi be there? Would he have the opportunity to speak with her?

Big Woodpecker wanted to come along on this *potlatch* venture, but Blue Loon said no and set the boy instead to doing a math lesson Ben had assigned, a lesson Big Wood-pecker was supposed to have finished the previous day.

Driving three longhorns before them, Ben McCain and his son rode on into the depths of the precipitous canyon. King-fishers screamed at them, and ouzels darted above tumbling waters. The forest was even thicker than True Bear remem-bered, and the sensation of greenness, after summer rain, was almost painful to look at.

Ben drew back on the reins of Blue-Two, his ungainly Percheron, and pointed toward the far end of a small meadow ahead. A family of wolves was hunting mice in tall grass, so intent upon their activity they inexplicably failed to become aware of plodding cattle and humans who rode behind them.

One of the wolves was as if frozen in position, tensed like a cat. The big gray dog sprang suddenly upward, arcing down with forepaws together, nose to the ground.

Then one wolf turned its head slowly toward the intruders, stared at them—indignant to be caught engaged in so mundane an activity. Immediately three pups darted away, each in a separate direction. But the two adult animals did not move at all—completely unafraid, half in challenge to those who came to interrupt this lesson they were giving their young.

"Just stay here in the canyon," Ben laughed. "Hunt whatever you want, but stay the hell away from my cows, my lupine friends."

"They're pretty," True Bear said. "That one looked like . . . a dancer or something."

"Doesn't appear they intend to move out of our way, son. We're trespassing on their ground. As long as they leave us alone, by heaven we'll leave them alone. That's what a man's got to do—make a special pact with each species of varmint. Now if you and Big Woodpecker could just manage to get some coyotes trained, we'd have fine watchdogs to keep track of our cattle. If there's coyotes around, the old mountain lion, he'll stay clear. Three or four coyotes can worry a big cat half to death. We've been lucky the past couple of years. Just that one grizzly. . . ."

Grizzlies, True Bear knew, enjoyed the specific protection of his mother's medicine—medicine, she said, that derived from bears themselves—the two grizzlies she'd raised from cubs before he was even born.

The wolves moved grudgingly away, melting off into the forest, and Ben urged his Percheron ahead, driving the indifferently grazing cattle before him.

At length the canyon opened out into a long meadow, but at first True Bear didn't recognize the place.

Empty. The village has vanished.

Ben glanced at his son.

"This is the place, is it?"

A single elaborately woven basket had been left conspicuously placed beside the remnant of what appeared to have been a cooking fire, though the charcoal had been scattered. Indeed, after an interval of rain, one might suppose no humans had been here for a month or more.

"Yes," True Bear said. "This is where Wolf Tracker's village. . . ."

His voice trailed off.

A girl, her features half-revealed by the light of flickering campfires, an odor about her, like that of oak leaves and something else, something indefinable. Her hair bound tightly behind her head, long, trailing down her back. And her breasts were bare. . . .

FIVE

How to Solve the Injun Problem

[August 1864]

"McCAIN, I'm telling you the Goddamned truth. You want to keep your cattle safe, there's only one thing to do, and that's to join in with us. As long as those damned Yahoos has got free run of the canyon country, there ain't a one of us will ever be certain his whitefaces will be there when he goes to look for them. Wolves and catamounts are bad enough, but the Mill Creeks are subject to run off a hundred head at a time. They got coyote brains and coyote strategy, and that's worse than having to deal with Goddamned professional cow thieves. I tell you, they'll run your animals off into some damned ravine or another and then slaughter the lot of them— and not just for meat, neither. They do it out of pure malice. Your Wintuns or your Maidus are capable of being civilized

after a fashion, but not the Yahoos. The only solution to the
Injun problem's to kill every last one of 'em, and I sure as
hell ain't the first one to say so. Pardon me, Acorn Girl. Your
blood's red, but you think like a Whitewoman. Hell, you're a
cattle rancher, same as me. It's those wild ones I'm talking
about."

Dan Clayton interlocked his large, freckled hands, pressed
one against the other, made the knuckles pop.

"Wolf Tracker and his people have never caused us any
trouble at all," Ooti replied. Her voice remained calm, but as
Ben noted, the muscles about her eyes had grown taut and
the eyes themselves were narrowed.

McCain recalled vividly that night, some fourteen years
earlier, when Ooti had led her Pano warriors on a great
revenge-taking against miners at Steephollow Creek—yes,
and with old Bully O'Bragh there to urge her on. Well, he'd
played his own part in the battle as well, taken lead into his
hide for his trouble and damned near died of it. At the time
he had come to detest his fellow Whites with every fiber of
his being. In truth, he had been just as set upon exacting a
terrible revenge as his wife and the Maidus had been. What
would Clayton and the other ranchers say if they had even
the slightest inkling the beautiful Ooti McCain was, in fact,
none other than the legendary leader of the dreaded Pano
Maidus?

But years had passed, years. The world, just as old Hurt
Eagle the shaman said so often, was a trail of changes. The
Great Dreamer was visioning once more, and all was transformed. Smallpox, tuberculosis, and syphilis had decimated
the Indian populations, while starvation fairly well took care
of the remainder. Between the dredging for gold and the
hydraulic placer mining, salmon could not survive in brown,
silt-laden waters of the rivers along the west slope of the
range. Only recently had a few of the migrating fish begun to
find their way upriver again. The great influx of Americans,
their towns and booming young cities up and down the valley
and scattered throughout the hill country to the south of
Upper Eden, had long since dispersed the once overwhelm-
ingly abundant wildlife. Vast herds of tule elk had all but
disappeared from the valley of the Sacramento and San Joaquin, and deer herds in the mountains were nothing to what

they once were. The remaining animals grew ever more wary, adapting to a world characterized by rifle fire, so that men armed with the native short bows found it increasingly difficult to take game. The one road to survival lay in becoming a part of the White world—in becoming red-skinned Whitemen, as was the case with the Oidoing-koyo Maidus.

The fierce Shastas were essentially tamed by now, and even the Modocs were slowly being brought under control, despite rebellious declarations of such young leaders as Kintpuash, Captain Jack.

Of all the Indian groups, only the southernmost branch of the Yanas, Wolf Tracker's people and a handful of other bands, clung fiercely to their ancient ways, putting their full energies into a hopeless resistance to the Whites. They remained in their all but trackless canyon mazes and struck back at cattle ranchers when opportunity presented itself.

"One answer," McCain said, "is to keep your cows out of the canyon bottoms. There's hardly enough forage to make the thing profitable in any case. You really figure Wolf Tracker and Big-Foot Jack and the others would be any threat to the cattle then?"

"It's a matter of principle, damn it. You're an educated man, McCain. A college teacher back East, from what I hear. Sure as hell you can understand about *principle*, even if all your hired hands are Injuns. No offense, Acorn Girl, but you can see what I'm getting at. California's a state, a full-fledged member of the Union, and now that the Confederacy's just about whipped, we figure to grow into the most important state of all. One day there'll be a Western Washington D.C., you mark my words. Hell, maybe we'll even end up running the whole shooting match from out here. We're fair to being the richest land in the world, between gold, cattle, and orcharding. So it's by God not right that a man can't run his cows on public domain without a bunch of half-human Injuns cutting off beefsteaks whenever they're of a mind to. You and me, Ben, we can look ahead—we can see the potential of what's here. Bears, wolves, cats, and Injuns—wild ones, that is. They've got to be wiped out. I've spent a dozen years, more than that, trying to civilize this land, and yet for all of it, the Mill Creeks are still out there, running bare-ass naked and sticking arrows into cows whenever they want."

"Mr. Clayton," McCain said, glancing at Ooti and sensing his young wife was on the verge of an explosion. For a moment he saw her face daubed with war paint, smelled powder smoke, and could discern those fierce and all-too-familiar points of light in her eyes. He imagined her rising from her chair, pulling out a knife, and calmly proceeding to scalp Dan Clayton without the valley rancher even being aware of what was happening. "Don't you think you're overreacting just a bit? My guess is that your ranching operations would go a great deal more smoothly if you'd just forget about the canyons. It's not as though you don't already have enough land to pasture your animals. Now that's so, isn't it?"

Big Dan Clayton shifted in his chair. In the first place, he felt distinctly ill at ease around Ben McCain, to say nothing of the man's disconcertingly attractive squaw. At six foot three, Clayton simply wasn't used to feeling small around anyone, and Ben McCain, gray-haired and maybe half-blind though he was, made him feel, physically, as though he were a mere kid—a child talking to an adult.

"Overreacting, am I? Listen here, McCain. I'm not calling you an Injun-lover, though there be some that do. Let me rehearse one or two things. Could be you don't always get all the news up here by the butte."

"No point in turning red in the face, Dan. Go ahead, have your say—but I think I've heard it before."

Ooti rose and walked stiffly from the room.

Goddamn it now, Ooti, don't go fetch that skinning knife of yours. . . .

"Problem is, the boys in Sacramento have changed the law. Used to be we could just capture Diggers an' civilize them, whether they wanted it or not. Some of them make damned good hands, just like your Maidus. I admit it."

Ben squinted, used his index finger to push his glasses back into place.

"I've told you before, Clayton, they're not my hands. We live together, that's all. The land's in my name, but we run a cooperative venture. I'm agent here in name only. I'm not on government pay, and I wouldn't take the money if the Washington people offered it."

Clayton smiled, glanced at the door through which Ooti had exited, and winked.

"You've got a way with Injuns, McCain, I'll give you that much. Strange damned method, but she works for you, and that's all that matters. Don't make no difference, though. The Yahoos has got to be driven out of the hills, and you know it as well as I do."

"The Battle Creek Yanas are still at Nome Lacklee, on the reservation, aren't they? I'd suppose that might have satisfied you fellows."

"Yep, those as haven't found their way back yet. It was a start, I guess. But you know about how Good and Breckinridge and the boys and me all went with Bob Anderson five years ago—we was going to solve the problem for once and for all. What happened? The bastards led us a merry chase clear over to Hat Creek country, where we lost 'em. Must have split their force, and half of them doubled back to Anderson's ranch, stole his horses, and set his barn afire."

"So you ended up murdering some peaceful Maidus outside of Chico—it was you, I believe? The Yanas outsmarted you, but you took revenge on some tame Indians."

"Good's idea, not mine. But there was Yahoos in amongst them, and that's the gospel. Then, three years later, the Mill Creeks burned Anderson's barn again and stole half his horses."

"They don't bother me," McCain said.

"Kidnapped your boy, didn't they? Tied him up and was ready to burn him when you arrived—that's the story I heard."

"Inaccurate in all significant details, Mr. Clayton. The truth is, Wolf Tracker and I are friends."

"Maybe ten years ago you was. Had dinner with the old thief lately? One of these days he'll have you for dinner, Ben. Look what happened last year—just you think about that and tell me those savages should be allowed to wander about wherever they're of a mind to. They stole Solomon Gore's horses and then killed the Lewis boy and took off with the other kid and the little girl. God only knows what they done to her."

"Yes, Thankful Lewis—isn't that the name? The Indians never touched her from what she said."

"At least the government come in and removed a few of the bastards over to Round Valley with the Covelos. Cap'n Starr managed to eliminate two, three hundred of them on

the way over, and that's the best thing he's done. I half think
the government's told him to pretend he's looking for the
Yahoos, going through the motions is all. And what about
what happened just this month? Over to Millville, I mean.
The Allen and Dirsch women, both of 'em murdered while
they was on the way to Ball's Ferry."

"In fact," McCain said, "we don't really know who killed
the women, now do we? But you and Good and Anderson
and your men went flying off half-cocked, as usual. How
many Yanas did you kill at Oak Run? A hundred or so?"

Big Dan Clayton grinned, shifted about in his chair.

"Nope," he said. "Three hundred and seven. At least that's
how many bodies we found when the shooting was all over. A
few more hunts like that one, and the problem will be solved
permanent. If the government can't or won't protect our
cattle, we've got to join forces and handle matters on our
own. For Christ's sake, McCain, pitch in with us. You've put
guns into the hands of your Maidus, not that I approve of it,
but apparently they'll do what you tell them. So you've got a
couple hundred men here at the upper end of Mill Creek
Canyon. If me and the boys move upstream, and you and
your tame Injuns ride downcanyon, we can trap the bastards
in between, and that'll be the end of our problem. Turkey
vultures and coyotes can take care of the mess."

Benjamin McCain stood up, purposely towering over his
guest.

"No," McCain said, "I don't think so. You're twisted up
inside, Clayton. It's like a sickness that's taken hold of you, a
fever that's going to kill you before it's run its course. Possibly you ought to consider getting some religion. I've known
about your Indian hunts all along, but I never realized until
now just how utterly satanic you've become. There was a
time in my life when I allowed hatred to rule me, but I've
had time since to regret it—at least some of it. There's a
better way, damn it. If a man hates as long as you have, he
becomes the very evil he imagines he's trying to eliminate. I
can't justify what happened to the Allen and Dirsch women
or to the Lewis kids either, of course. The men reponsible,
be they Indian or White, need to be punished—tried in a
court of law, that is, and then hung if they're indeed guilty.
But Jesus Christ, Dan, you don't exterminate an entire peo-

ple because of what a handful of outlaws did! Good God, I see what it comes to now. You've gotten to like killing for its own sake."

Clayton's lips went thin, and his face contorted with a rage he no longer saw any need to contain. He spat upon the table and stood up slowly, took a step or two backward toward the fireplace, and let his right hand settle toward his revolver.

"You're a coward, McCain. You make me sick to my stomach. . . ."

"Bad idea," Ben said, his voice not rising at all. "You're our guest here, Clayton. Get hold of your temper. It seems I'm unalterably opposed to what you have in mind, even if there's nothing I can do to stop you and Good and Anderson and the rest of the madmen. Tell you what. Pull that gun, and I'm going to break your back for you. Even if you manage to get three or four slugs into me, that's not going to save you. I'm pretty good at holding my lead, as the saying goes. We've broken bread together, Dan, and we've done business. Maybe we will again. But right now I'd like you to be on your way. Let's call this a little flare of tempers and be done with it."

"You're no longer welcome in my house," Acorn Girl said from across the room.

The pistol she held was pointed directly at the valley rancher.

Clayton glanced in her direction, considered spitting again, and then decided against it.

"Aw shit," he said. "I should never have drunk that whiskey with dinner. Acorn Girl, ma'am, I'm harmless. Just sort of lost my head there for a moment is all. Put the gun down, gal. The damned thing might go off accidental."

"Not accidental," Ooti said.

TRUE BEAR was not directly privy to the discussion concerning the proper solution to the *Injun problem*, but the following day, with Ben and Acorn Girl still rehearsing details of their disagreement with Dan Clayton, the boy was able to assemble in his own mind a fairly accurate account of what had transpired. It was completely clear to him that the valley ranchers, Clayton and Good and Anderson and their friends, would almost certainly make a concerted effort to find Wolf Tracker and the other remaining bands of Yahis—for the

specific purpose, not of forcing them to relocate to the re-
serves at Nome Lacklee or Round Valley, but of massacring
them. A terrible empty feeling ran through him, for in his
active child's imagination he could see Wahtaurisi-yi's mutilated body lying beside Mill Creek, her flesh being torn at by
vultures and coyotes. This vision was too terrible, too horrible for him to bear, and, without expressing his feelings in
the matter, he resolved to renew his demands that his father
allow him to carry a pistol during his times of tending cattle
and the more or less aimless wandering of the woods that he
was so obsessed with. He thought of various arguments he'd
advanced on previous occasions when he'd attempted to
secure a revolver for himself, thought about Ben's dismissal
of such things as the need to protect himself against everything from rattlesnakes to grizzlies, and realized that a whole
new strategy would have to be employed.

At evening meal he said simply, "Dad, I'd like that old
Colt Navy revolver you never use any more."

Ben glanced at Acorn Girl, adjusted the thick spectacles
onto the bridge of his nose, and replied, "Now why would a
kid like you be needing a pistol? Isn't it enough that I let you
use a gun when we're out riding together? Left to your own
devices, you'd probably shoot your foot off."

True Bear sat tall and stared his father in the eye.

"Because I'm a man now, and a man ought to carry a gun.
Them as don't look after themselves has early funerals. That's
what your friend Bully O'Bragh says—you've told me so
hundreds of times."

Ben shrugged, and turned to his wife.

"Among the Maidus," she nodded, "a boy his age would be
allowed to go off hunting on his own. His manhood is not
very far away now."

"Big Woodpecker doesn't have a pistol—so you figure you'll
score a coup on him if you've got one, is that it, son?"

"No, that's not it. But it's right for me to have my own
pistol now. I'm already a better shot than any other . . . boy
. . . in Oidoing-koyo, and I'm a better shot than most of the
men as well. You know that's true, Dad."

Benjamin McCain laughed, tugged at his beard.

"Ooti, the lad's got a point. Billy True Bear, you wouldn't
be thinking about wanting to impress that little Yahi gal who's

been running through your imagination, now would you? Best you forget about her."

True Bear stared at a half-eaten portion of venison on his plate, and shrugged.

"I'm a man now," he insisted.

"He look any taller than he did this morning?" Ben asked Acorn Girl.

"Perhaps so," Ooti replied. "Besides, manhood does not depend upon height. It's what is inside that matters."

Ben growled, wiped at his mouth, and rose from the table, striding quickly from the room. True Bear glanced helplessly at his mother, felt for a moment like a foolish child, forced a stoic expression onto his face and resolutely cut off another bite of deermeat.

In a moment Ben returned. He was carrying the old Colt thirty-six, now encased in a brand-new holster, an embossed *T.B.M.* burned on leather.

"Been meaning to give this to you, son," the elder McCain grinned. "I figure it's about time. Just don't you be holding up any stagecoaches, though. You hear me? And the first time you shoot off your foot, I'm taking the gun back and keeping it until you're thirty years old."

TRUE BEAR rode alone, past Seth Childe's place and on to where Mill Creek Canyon dropped away southward beneath Morgan Mountain. Blue Loon insisted that Big Woodpecker help with the shoeing of some horses, but True Bear was, in fact, secretly pleased his blood brother had not been able to come along.

With luck he'd be able to discover the whereabouts of Wolf Tracker's village and so be able to see Wahtaurisi-yi again.

An image of the girl lying dead beside a stream still haunted him, but now he began to modify the vision. She was not dead. Wounded, yes, but not seriously. A bullet had passed through the flesh of her leg. Big Dan Clayton was standing over her, laughing, speaking obscenities: and at that point True Bear McCain rode into the meadow. Numerous men with rifles looked up, the gunfire ceasing. True Bear did not speak. He dismounted and stood facing Clayton. The rancher laughed at him, asked him if he wanted the little squaw.

"Yes," he answered in a voice that was deep and con-

trolled, "but first I want you, Clayton. If I win, the others are
to ride back to the valley—and the Yahis are to be allowed to
have the canyons to themselves. You hear what I'm saying?
Go for your gun when you're ready."

Beyond this initial scenario, there were several possible
resolutions to the confrontation. In one, the Navy Colt cleared
leather like magic—before Clayton's hand even moved. Clayton knew he was beaten and muttered something like, *You're
a better man than I am, McCain*. Thereafter the rancher
turned away, his men following, and he vanished down the
canyon. In another version two bursts of pistol fire occurred
simultaneously, lead grazing True Bear's shoulder. But Dan
Clayton lay sprawled in the grass. With his final words the
rancher admitted he was wrong about the Indians. In yet
another version Clayton was mortally wounded, but so was
True Bear, who died with Wahtaurisi-yi kneeling beside him
in such a way that the flowing blood from her wound was
mingled with his own.

The trek downcanyon, past Turner Mountain and on to
meadows beneath Mill Creek Rim had by now become familiar terrain, but for all that, the twelve- to fifteen-mile ride did
not go any more quickly.

August sun burned from an utterly cloudless sky, and the
temperature had no doubt risen above a hundred degrees by
the time True Bear reached the site of the former Yahi
encampment. The cattle Ben had left were nowhere to be
found along the length of still-empty meadows. True Bear
dismounted and looked about for sign, but found nothing
fresh.

The basket is gone. That's why the longhorns aren't here. . . .

For nearly an hour True Bear attempted to track the cattle,
hoping to discover which direction they'd gone—or rather,
been driven. There were many hoofmarks, but none seemed
to lead anywhere in particular. Then, just as he was about to
give up his search, he noted a discontinuity among mixed oak
leaves and pine needles of the duff on the north side of the
canyon, indicating that cattle had apparently been herded up
a precipitous slope toward the rim high above. He turned
immediately, ran to his pony, and vaulted into the saddle.

A few hundred yards beyond, True Bear was forced to
dismount and lead his horse. The trail he followed was clear

now—hooves of cattle having dislodged rocks as the beasts were driven first one way and then the other, zigzagging up the canyonside, finally between two escarpments of vertical black lava and into a narrow ravine that was now dry but which had carried a considerable flow of water just a few days earlier, during the downpour.

Within an hour he reached the rim, but there, in thick mixed forest that covered a rolling crest, True Bear lost the trail he was following.

He scanned the country around him for some sign—smoke, perhaps, any evidence of human presence.

Nothing. Vanished as if into thin air. Wolf Tracker, you old sonofabitch. Didn't you know I'd want to come visit? Where the hell are you?

To the northeast rose a saddle-backed dome of what True Bear was certain must be Turner Mountain, and beyond that, as if floating in the atmosphere and distant perhaps another fifteen miles, brooded the high dome of Wahgalu itself, its rounded peak marked with a single band of white.

True Bear McCain unsheathed his Colt and fired two shots, listened as sound reverberated across the wilderness around him.

Then he turned his pony and began to ride toward a pine-covered swale to the east of Turner Mountain. From that point, as he noted on his ride downcanyon, he'd be able to make his way back to Mill Creek perhaps four or five miles below Childe's Meadows.

A bluejay screamed at him as he rode along, following him, warning all other denizens of the forest: *It's True Bear McCain, defender of the Yahis, and the young fool's armed and dangerous!*

Vultures circled above, five of the big birds. True Bear thought about taking a shot at one and then decided against it. He had a distinct impression the forest he rode through was utterly at peace—that he himself provided a single discordant note.

SIX

The Yahis Return

[September 1864]

EQUINOCTIAL RAINS CAME, several days of light but steady
precipitation. Then skies cleared, and temperature rose once
again. Sparse stands of black oak around Upper Eden flamed
thin gold, and creek maples shouted rich amber. Brown drifts
of pine needles lay about on the ground, newly fallen from
ponderosas and sugars. Only blue willow and wild lilac remained apparently unchanged in this time of changing seasons.

Ben and Ooti sat their ponies and surveyed the upper
pastures.

"Indian summer!" Ben McCain laughed. "That's what we
call it in my other world. Ooti, little girl, maybe I'll have an
opportunity to take you back to New England before old
Grim Reaper comes whacking away at me. I tell you, the
trees turn blood red right about the time of first frost, maybe
a bit before that. It's the one season of the year when I miss
Connecticut—for a minute or two, in any case."

"You wish to go see the one who used to be your wife?"
Acorn Girl asked.

"What the hell was her name? What was my name in the
States? God, no. That life has vanished so far behind me it
doesn't even seem real. Nope, this child doesn't regret a

thing. If I'd wanted to be with that lady, whatever her name was, I'd never have come looking for gold."

"Etta," Acorn Girl nodded, "that was her name."

"God rest her soul—she's no doubt married to a senator or some other swindler these days. If she's still alive, Ooti, she's an old woman by now."

"Was she beautiful, Bear-who-cannot-see-well?"

"Homely as four mud fences—cross-eyed and bald to boot."

"How could she find another husband, then? I think you'd rather be with her than with me. Maybe I'll ride off toward Wahgalu and die of starvation. That way you will be free to return to Connecticut and find your *Etta* again."

"One thing about Maidu women," Ben mused, "it's certain they aren't jealous."

"Your friend O'Bragh told me there were two women."

"The Irish Vulture was lying, of course. I wonder how that thief's getting on. He's as old as the hills, but it's my distinct impression he never had even the slightest intention of dying. *Meat don't spile in the mountains*. That's his philosophy, the full breadth and extent of it. Truth to say, I wouldn't be surprised if Bully showed up here one of these days. The man's a wandering fool."

"It would be good," Ooti said. She gazed toward the gleaming white crown of Wahgalu, clucked her tongue twice, and turned her pony toward the ranch house—thumping her heels against the horse's sides and urging the animal into a gallop.

"Wait for me!" Ben yelled, turning Blue-Two the Percheron about and giving pursuit. "Wait for your husband, you little hellcat!"

SUPPLY WAGONS CAME up from Oroville, following the route of the old Lassen Trail, the final few miles of the *Death Horn*, as it had been called, and Oidoing-koyo men assembled immediately to begin the task of unloading and storing merchandise and foodstuffs that Ben McCain had purchased with money from the sale of cattle.

Among other things, a bundle of newspapers from Sacramento arrived, and once the work was finished and the details of business attended to, Ben McCain settled down in the large oaken rocker before the fireplace and began to inhale reams of newsprint.

The following day he lectured to his pupils, True Bear, Big Woodpecker, and other Maidu youngsters whom he'd selected as his special charges.

Yellow Grass, he noted, had apparently decided to sit beside Big Woodpecker. Perhaps a new boyfriend-girlfriend relationship was underway. The girl was a month or two older than Blue Loon's son and would, in the tradition of her people, soon be going through the *Yupu-kato*, the girls' adolescence ceremony. Thereafter she'd be adjudged a woman. At that time, Ben reflected, she would no doubt lose interest in Big Woodpecker or any of the other boys, since they would be essentially beneath her dignity. For the moment, however, young love was allowed to flower.

But getting the two of them to pay attention to their lessons, in the present moment, was a difficult matter.

"I've marked all the newspaper passages that I want you to read," Ben said, adopting a formal tone of voice that he once used with his students at Yale College. "For the time being, though, I want you to pay close attention. We've talked many times before about the Civil War that's going on in the eastern part of the United States. This new information suggests that many expectations of the North have been or are about to be realized. The Confederates continue to fight bravely. General Grant's Army of the Potomac has taken position opposite Lee's army, some twenty miles south of Richmond, and the U.S.S. *Kearsarge* has sunk the *Alabama*, a Confederate raider that's captured some sixty-five Union merchant ships. But the South under General Johnston has defeated Sherman in a battle at Kenesaw Mountain in Georgia, and casualties were apparently very high. . . ."

Ben continued with his lecture for an hour or more, and even True Bear, devoted student that he was, began to lose interest—having concluded the sequence of the interminable succession of battles might better be dealt with by means of the simple expedient of reading through the stack of news sheets.

The tide of the war, True Bear surmised, had clearly swung in favor of the North, and President Lincoln would probably be reelected to a second term. The Democrats had

nominated General George B. McClellan, with Pendleton as
a running mate. Casualties mounted into the tens of thousands on both sides, numbers of humans that True Bear could
hardly conceive of, and it was evident the public was becoming bone-weary of both destruction and death. Even the issue
of Negro slavery seemed to have been all but forgotten as
America continued to eat at its own intestines like some huge
gray and inchoate wounded shark. Ben's sympathies, reasonably enough, were clearly with the North, and on a purely
abstract level, True Bear agreed totally. The bravery and
determination of Southern forces, however, compelled his
imagination. Well, possibly Lincoln wouldn't win the election
after all—so much depended upon outcomes of battles still to
be fought.

True Bear's thoughts turned to the plight of the Yahi
Indians—their continuing skirmishes with valley ranchers.
In some ways, scale infinitely smaller, the Yahis were like the
confederates. They fought a desperate and losing battle for
their homeland.

And then his mind drifted, inevitably, to the image of a girl
named Wahtaurisi-yi.

He stood in front of her, protecting her with his own body.
A gang of ranchers, Dan Clayton among them, approached
from downslope, climbing toward the entry to a basalt cave
in which he and she had taken refuge. He raised his Navy
Colt and leveled the weapon at the chest of the cattleman. . . .

WILLIAM TRUE BEAR GOFFE MCCAIN mounted his pony and
rode out into pale gray light of early morning. This was a day
with no chores, no studies, no responsibilities whatsoever. It
was a day for adventure—for wandering the forest. He'd
asked Big Woodpecker to accompany him, but his blood
brother seemed to have other matters on his mind these
days, and those other matters were apparently all spelled
Yellow Grass. The two were virtually inseparable, and True
Bear, in spite of himself, was feeling what amounted to pangs
of rejection. His close friend had virtually deserted him in
favor of this round-faced slip of a girl, daughter to Tied Wing
and his own mother's close friend, Small Ears.

True Bear directed his horse upward, toward a saddle
beyond which lay Wilson Lake. When he reached the small

body of water, he stopped and scanned the marshy area on the far shore for the pair of great blue herons that were usually close by, often standing stilt-legged in shallows, their long-beaked heads poised above the water. He recalled a time, months earlier, when a third heron had appeared, and a territorial mock-battle had ensued.

The huge birds had performed a strange dance, posturing, puffing, hissing, and stabbing their beaks into the air—all at a distance of perhaps fifteen yards or more. Two male birds— and whether the issue at hand was favor of the female or a matter of primary fishing rights, True Bear could only surmise. In either case, the battle was conducted at a safe distance, and he felt privileged to be able to observe it. He had expected the strange performance to progess into actual combat, with long beaks clashing in the manner of sword fighters, but instead, at length, the newcomer seemingly decided his rival had made the better show and so had flapped away, skimming the lake's surface and disappearing down the ravine toward Childe's Meadows.

At first True Bear did not see the birds, but then he caught sight of two ungainly forms perched side by side in a young pine, perhaps a hundred feet back from water's edge.

"Time to be up and about your business!" he shouted to them. "Early birds catch all the fish—don't you know that?"

The creatures ignored him, moving only sufficiently to touch beaks, as if in some silent language comprehensible to blue herons alone.

A raven croaked from a nearby fir copse, then took wing and came gliding by for a closer look at this human astride a horse. The big black bird swooped past, dipped its wings, and flapped on across the still water from whose surface threads of white mist were rising.

True Bear had not specifically decided upon venturing once again down into the recesses of Mill Creek Canyon—at least not consciously. But now he realized the canyon was, of course, precisely where he would go. He clucked his tongue to his pony and tried to determine whether he was sorry or glad that Big Woodpecker had chosen not to accompany him on this mission.

The women of Oidoing-koyo had made a foray to an oak-covered bench beneath Morgan Mountain a few days earlier, taking a buckboard with them and returning with nearly a full load of acorns. Yellow Grass was expected to assist in the shelling and leaching of kernels, naturally, and so Big Woodpecker decided to spend his day with her, doing woman's work.

Once, True Bear knew, the time of acorn harvest had been the most important of all seasons for Maidu people, but now, even though Ben procured quantities of rough-ground flour from the mill at Chico, the Indian women continued to observe at least the forms of older customs. So long as they remained in this fashion true to the ways of the Old Ones, they believed, *Ka-awk*, the hard times, would not come to them. Whatever the belief, one thing was indeed certain. Steaming acorn mush, *Oosaw*, was very good on cold mornings—the grainy gelatinous cakes fried in a skillet and then doused with butter and molasses. Such had been the breakfast his mother prepared that very morning.

Soon would come the Ustu ceremony, the Maidu time of ritualized mourning for all the dead of all past years, as well as for those who had died in the previous twelve-month period—except that this year no one at all had passed away in Oidoing-koyo village. Nonetheless, the high poles would be erected, just as they were every year, and baskets full of acorn bread and dried meat and various sorts of trinkets and baubles would be hung from the poles, and then fires would be ignited from below. The result was almost that of tall, spindly, flaming Christmas trees—a spectacle in some ways similar to ceremonies performed by ancient Druids, or so True Bear had read in one of his father's books.

True Bear rode onward, and after another mile was looking down into the still-shadowy trench of Childe's Meadows. The grassy area was splashed irregularly with white, the first real frost of the year, though at Upper Eden only lower branches of a few scrub junipers were touched by the cold. And behind him, spread across the eastern sky beyond a fir-cloaked rim, torrents of luminous red-orange burned, a glorious sunrise. Long bands of thin cloud streaked the sky, but the day would soon become pleasantly warm.

He urged his pony forward. Perhaps in this time of acorn-gathering the Yahis would have returned to their Mill Creek encampment.

*   *   *

WHEN HE HEARD the trill of a screech owl, he knew he'd been detected. The Yahis did not confront him, however, and he continued his ride downcanyon. Only when the cry was repeated back and forth from rim to rim did it occur to him that the Indians into whose territory he had come might not be Wolf Tracker's band at all. Perhaps Big Foot Jack's people had traveled south and made encampment this season of ripe acorns.

Then half a dozen bronze forms, men armed with bow and spear, appeared mysteriously from either side, not threatening and not approaching too closely. They fell in behind him, effectively blocking his only possible avenue of retreat, and followed along as he continued his ride southwestward.

The forest opened before him at length, and he found the meadows inhabited. Temporary brush lodges had been erected, and close beside the creek, next to the very tree to which he and Big Woodpecker had been bound two months earlier, a throng of women, most bare-breasted and wearing tule skirts, were busily engaged in shelling and grinding and leaching acorn kernels. Across the way some men were in the process of skinning an elk, while others prepared a charcoal pit. Two older men sat beneath a liveoak, flaking arrow points, while several children stood closely about, watching.

Faces turned to observe him, but True Bear continued to ride, slowly now, toward one brush lodge conspicuously larger than the others. He dismounted, tethered his pony, and walked to the shelter's entryway. He sat down, crossed his legs, and waited—for such, he remembered old Hurt Eagle saying, was the proper way to gain entry into the home of another.

Activity within the village continued unabated, and even the men who had followed him downcanyon disappeared, perhaps having returned to take up their positions as guardians. For some minutes no one paid him the least attention, an interval that seemed far longer than indeed it was.

Then the one whom he had for so long wished to see turned back a deerhide entry flap and stood silently before him.

"Wahtaurisi-yi!" he exclaimed, rising to his feet.

She did not answer but gestured for him to come in.

Had he violated propriety by speaking out immediately? He grinned, shrugged his shoulders, and held out his hands in a gesture of placation, then passed through the entryway.

"Has the son of Bear-who-cannot-see-well brought another gift of cattle, or does he come to this village for some different purpose?"

"I didn't bring cattle, Wolf Tracker. I came to visit."

"Smoke Woman," the chief said in English, "our young friend has returned so that you will fix him another breakfast of fish. At least, I cannot imagine why else he would have come."

Smoke Woman glanced at her father and then at her daughter, as if uncertain whether it was proper to answer.

English. Do the rules of Man Language and Woman Language apply?

"Why have you come to visit my lodge, True Bear McCain?" Wolf Tracker asked, gesturing for the boy to sit down. "Do you have a message from your father, or are you simply out hunting?"

For a moment True Bear's mind was an utter blank.

"Perhaps you didn't expect to find us here," Wolf Tracker suggested, raising one eyebrow. "Yet I don't think this is the first time you have returned. We have found sign of your passing. I think maybe you have come to see my granddaughter. Is this so? You are very young to be searching for a wife. I will tell you how it's done. When you are older, you must come to visit often, and each time you must bring me a present of some sort. I tell you this because you are not one of us and therefore are ignorant of our ways. Have I guessed rightly?"

True Bear could feel himself blushing, thankful for halfdark of the inside of the brush igunna.

"I didn't know Wolf Tracker's people would be here, but I hoped it might be so. I've come simply to visit those who were kind to me."

Wolf Tracker, True Bear realized, was on the verge of actually smiling.

The chief made a slight nod of his head, and Smoke Woman and Sits-by-the-ladder disappeared from the lodge. Wolf Tracker sat down opposite True Bear and reached into a leather bag for a stubby, hand-carved stone pipe. Without speaking further, he filled the bowl with tobacco from a metal cannister similar to several Ben kept on the mantel above the fireplace at home, then ignited a twig by thrusting it into the faintly glowing coals of a small firepit between them, and lit his pipe.

"You've ridden into my village as a man would, True Bear, so now you must smoke with me. This is good tobacco, but I don't like it so well as that which grows wild. Well, the world has changed much during my lifetime, so now I have acquired this bad habit from the Saltus. One of my warriors found the can inside an abandoned wagon beside the old emigrant trail that leads down into the valley. He gave it to me. We didn't even have to kill any of our enemies to get it. Does your father allow you to smoke?"

True Bear hesitated before replying but at length shook his head.

"If Ben asks you, then, you must tell him I insisted you smoke with me. A boy must always answer truthfully when his father asks him a question."

Wolf Tracker puffed four times on the pipe, made a hand gesture almost like that of the missionary who'd visited Upper Eden the previous year, and then passed the implement to True Bear.

"Draw the smoke into your mouth but don't swallow it or breathe it in," the old chief said. "Otherwise you may make yourself sick in your stomach. Sip at the smoke, as though it were soup that's still too hot to drink."

True Bear did as he was told, nodded, and then returned the pipe to Wolf Tracker.

The chief puffed several more times, made a low grunting sound, and nodded.

"Dan Clayton stopped at Oidoing-koyo. I know Ben has bought cattle from him, but was there any other reason? Is this something you can tell me, True Bear?"

How does he know? How could he possibly know . . . ?

True Bear shrugged.

"I wasn't present in the room when my mother and father talked with Clayton, but I could hear their voices anyway. Clayton is your enemy, Wolf Tracker. He's planning to attack your people."

The chief's face remained impassive, weathered features strangely highlighted in the dimness of the lodge.

"Clayton's an old enemy. He is always planning to attack us, though usually we manage to evade him. He and his friends will kill all of us at last, though. Many Yanas died on the stream Saltus call Oak Run this past summer. Soon we will be nothing more than a memory in the mind of One Who Dreams. After that the world will go on changing, always changing. It's the way of things. Even the Saltus will vanish one day, that is what I think."

The old Yahi smoked in silence for a time, staring at some point just beyond the embers of the fire. Then he straightened up, tapped ashes from his pipe, and spoke again.

"But we will continue to live for a little while yet—perhaps even long enough for me to have a great-grandson. That would be good. Or perhaps my people will have to change their ways, as the Maidus have done. Perhaps we should come to live near Oidoing-koyo, but Yahis and Maidus have never truly been friends. Ah, we do not wish to live like Saltus anyway. What would we do if we were forced to leave these canyons? No, I don't think our men and women are suited to living in this new world of yours, True Bear. It is sad, but one must not complain when the sun begins to rise differently."

ONCE BACK OUTSIDE the lodge, True Bear stood in late September sunlight, uncertain what to do next. He felt awkward, ill at ease, half-wishing he hadn't chosen this day to ride down the deep canyon.

Then Wahtaurisi-yi came to him, hesitating before raising her eyes to his.

"It is you I came to see," he said.

"I'm glad, True Bear. I have thought of you and your friend Big Woodpecker many times. It was fun—talking as we did. Smoke Woman has told me I must climb up to the rim to gather some arrow stone. There's a big black ledge of it there. She said I should ask you if you wish to accompany me."

"Yes, I'd like that. We can ride together on my pony."

She smiled, then looked away from him.

"It would be wonderful, but I don't think a horse can climb the canyonside. Too steep. No, we must walk. You will not have to carry the basket when I fill it with pieces of black glass, but I would enjoy your company."

They climbed together, the girl in a fringed leather skirt and halter, the boy in red flannel shirt and denim saddle trousers, the former home-sewn, the latter purchased in Oroville. He wore boots, and she moved on nimbly ahead, barefooted but oblivious to sharp fragments of cinder that lay loosely along the faint path they followed.

A small stream cascaded from a high black rim above them, gusts of wind turning the water to spray as it splashed down the rock face to a small pool at the base. To one side of the pool projected a ledge of obsidian, fractured in places.

Wahtaurisi-yi utilized a wedge-shaped stick to lever one portion loose, and a number of large chips clattered to the ground.

"This is very fine stone for arrowheads," she said. "Many of our men prefer it to the other kind. They say it flakes more easily, but I don't know whether that is true. Only men are taught how to make tips for spears and arrows. Often they work for a long time on a point and then ruin it and have to start over."

"They should have guns," True Bear said.

"You have a gun now. I don't like the looks of it. Isn't it dangerous?"

"No. I'm very good shot, much better shot than most of the men in my village. You want me to show you how it works?"

Kneeling side by side, the two stared at each other for a long moment. Then Wahtaurisi-yi reached out and placed the tips of her fingers to True Bear's forehead.

"Wolf Tracker shouldn't have said what he did—asking if you came to find a wife. I couldn't look at you after that. I. . . ."

The girl faltered into silence, delicate lids sliding down to half-cover her bright, brown eyes as she turned her gaze upon the shards of stone near the fringe of her skirt. Then she withdrew her hand, stood up, and walked quickly to the edge of the little pool. She sat and dipped her fingers into rippling water.

True Bear rose, perplexed, and then followed her.

"I've thought of you almost every day," he said. "I've even dreamed about you. . . ."

"That is strange. The other girls in my village still tease me about the night I brought food to you and stood guard over you and your friend. They say it's because I am half-White in my blood—that is why. . . ."

True Bear flushed again, furious with himself for having done so. He picked up a pebble and hurled it far downslope, looked about for another.

"You can throw a stone better than any boy in my village," Wahtaurisi-yi laughed. "I have never seen anyone who could throw so far."

"Is that true? I've always liked throwing rocks. Watch this one."

He threw so hard his elbow ached afterward, but the nearly oval-shaped piece of basalt sailed out in a long arc, catching the wind at just the right angle, and finally striking the crown of a fir growing far down the steep slope to one side of the narrow ravine through which the small stream of water made its way to Mill Creek at canyon's bottom.

"That was wonderful! I've never seen anything like it!"

True Bear rubbed his elbow, grinned.

"Just looks like a long way," he said. "It's easy if you're throwing downhill like this."

"I wish you could teach me how, True Bear. Girls cannot throw very well."

"That's because you don't practice. Big Woodpecker and I have contests all the time. I usually win, but not always. The secret's in finding the right-shaped stone. . . ."

Wahtaurisi-yi got on her knees, leaned forward, and scooped water with both hands. She drank.

True Bear, confused, resisted an inexplicable urge to put his arms about her from behind.

"The water's good. Very cold. It comes from a spring just above the rim."

"Do you suppose we might?" the boy blurted out. "When we're grown up, I mean?"

"I don't understand what you're saying, True Bear."

"Get married to each other. I. . . ."

Once again he felt blood flaming in his cheeks, and he turned away quickly, pretended to be searching for another stone to throw.

SEVEN

Boarding School

[October 1864]

Ustu, the burning time, the cry time, the Hill of Dead People carefully prepared, just as it had been every year that True Bear McCain could remember. . . .

The men of Oidoing-koyo village erected an open enclosure perhaps a hundred feet across, a brush fence that followed the line of a circular form scratched into soft ground, with one entrance leading to the west, one to the east.

Ooti McCain presided, acting ceremonial director, even though she was not of Oidoing-koyo, in deference to her universally acknowledged power as a shaman of the Kuksu religion, her *Sila* extremely potent, her medicine deriving from none other than Pano, spirit chief of all grizzly bears. Whether any of this was more than time-honored superstition, True Bear did not know. But what difference did it make? When his mother wore her ceremonial robes, she seemed almost a totally different person—no longer the one who cooked his meals and sewed his shirts. At such a time as the Ustu, Ooti became beautiful in a way that was very strange. Her son almost supposed she could walk through great boulders or even disappear completely and reemerge from nothingness in a place that might well be miles distant. Perhaps

90

she indeed went off to visit with the two grizzlies everyone
said she'd raised during the time before he, True Bear, was
born. She seemed like a being from a dream. That's what one
side of his mind said. The other side said simply, "Mom's all
dressed up again."

On the first night no mourners came to the enclosure—
since no one had died that year. True Bear stood beside Ben,
outside the sacred circle, as Ooti moved about, chanting
words she had learned from old Hurt Eagle and from her own
father as well—*Grandpa Kuksu Man*, as True Bear knew
from hearing various stories about the exploits of his deceased
grandparent, one who had been killed shortly after the discovery of gold near Kolo-ma, on the American River.

Ooti proceeded to the village gravesites, sprinkling a special variety of acorn meal over the ground, waving a pitch
pine torch about in circular motions as she moved. At length
she finished her ritual and walked back through the sacred
circle, from east to west, her motion indicating a passage
from the Spirit World into the everyday realm of the living.

"Back from the dead, are you?" Benjamin McCain chuckled, his face illumined by a torch his wife held, smears of
yellow light jumping from the thick lenses of the glasses he
always wore.

"Odoing-koyo has been fortunate this year," Ooti answered.
"All the time since we came to Upper Eden we've been at
peace, so no men have died in battle—only very young and
very old have gone on to the High Meadows, and sometimes
a woman in trying to give birth. Whiteman's medicines have
made some things better—my husband—and I would be
satisfied if only I didn't remember how it was before all the
miners and the ranchers came to these lands. My people
were ignorant of much in those days, and now we are learning to be just like Whites. How long do you think the people
in Oidoing-koyo will continue to respect the Ustu and the
times of holy dancing? A few more years, and then. . . ."

"We all have to change eventually," Ben McCain replied.
"Everything turns inside out in the long run. The United
States of America? The lads back East are bleeding one
another dry, and most of them are satisfied they know what it
is they're fighting about, but they don't. No, it's just change,
that's all. I believe it. There are hundreds of new worlds

ahead, and it won't end until the bunch of us, White and Red
and Black, get so clever we ruin the whole stew. That's what
I think, at least. But for now, Acorn Girl, my little termagant,
let's get on back down to the house. It'll be a big day
tomorrow, putting the poles in place so the people can hang
them with baskets and burn up half their earthly fortunes.
Just watching—it's hard on a parsimonious old New Englander like me. But True Bear here, he likes fires. Isn't that
right, son?"

True Bear shrugged, didn't reply. He was still toying with
the string of words his father had just uttered—yes, and what
his mother said as well. He thought of his friends the Yahis,
in his boy's mind *beautifully free and wild*, people who didn't
have to *do anything*. Maybe that wasn't true after all. In fact,
he thought, they had to fight in order to survive at all—yes,
and fight against great odds. *Soon we will be nothing more
than a memory in the mind of One Who Dreams.* Wolf
Tracker's words. Were they true? Was that simply an inevitable part of the change his own father spoke of?

True Bear tried to imagine what the world would be like
when he himself reached his father's age, but no vision would
come. How could things ever be different than they were at
the present moment? Yet he knew, knew down deep, that his
father was right—and Ooti was right—and probably Wolf
Tracker was also right. For such reasons Ben McCain expended so much of his time in the apparently thankless job of
teaching the children of Oidoing-koyo to read and write and
cipher. He was helping them, with the only means he knew,
to find their way into that mysterious time ahead, a world in
which the term *wild Indian* would refer to conditions long
since past.

THE VILLAGE was busy the next day, older adults moving
about as though in a trance, tending to those matters necessary for the night's burning. Many younger men, however,
looked askance at the activity and shook their heads.

True Bear fancied himself as being aware of the cross-
purposes of the people among who he lived, as if for the first
time.

Big Woodpecker: He didn't believe in any of this "foolish-
ness," and yet he was there on the hill, with Yellow Grass's

father (who did believe), helping to raise one of the basket-bedecked burning poles.

Half of True Bear wanted to believe, and he wondered if it were his Maidu half. Or maybe it was just like Christmas—he wished the thing to be so, and thus is had been until after his fourth birthday—St. Nicholas or the Frost Giant or some other mythic being had actually managed to slip down the chimney to leave presents that were reverently opened the following morning.

In any case, he walked forward into the sacred circle and fell in line beside Big Woodpecker.

"You won't want to do this next year, because Yellow Grass will have gone to the woman's lodge by then," he whispered. "After that she'll be a woman, and she won't want to have anything to do with you. I bet she ends up marrying John Goat's Beard, who's always visiting Tied Wing and Small Ears."

Big Woodpecker grunted as he pushed against the pole.

"We'll see, we'll see. I'll borrow your pistol and shoot old Goat's Beard in the back if I have to. Besides, Blue Loon gave me four heifers. What do you think about that, True Bear? In a few years, I'll have a whole herd of my own. I'll be able to buy whitefaces from your dad."

True Bear chuckled and shook his head. His friend's evident intensity surprised him.

"I was teasing, that's all. Hey, what's going on down below?"

The skinned fir slipped into its appointed hole, tilting to one side. A few of the men glanced toward the small cluster of people who had formed to one side of the McCain ranch house. Then they shrugged and went about the business of pushing rocks and earth into the hole, levering the skinned fir into vertical position as they did so.

True Bear shaded his eyes with one hand and stared down the hill.

"Hey—that's old Wolf Tracker, isn't it? Who's with him?"

Big Woodpecker squinted.

"I'll be damned. I think it's Sits-by-the-ladder—he's brought her to Oidoing-koyo!"

And then the two boys were engaged in a footrace to see who would reach the bottom of the slope first.

* * *

"BEAR-WHO-CANNOT-SEE-WELL," Wolf Tracker said, "I have come to visit, as I told your son I would. We have known each other for a long while, many seasons, without really knowing each other well. But your son and I are friends, I think, and I believe that one can learn much about another man by observing the one who follows after him, just as one can tell much about the son by observing ways of the father. You are Saltu, but you are not like the others, and that's why you live here among the Maidu people and are the mate of Ooti, the one who took full revenge upon the Whiteman who massacred her village, depriving her of a family. You fought alongside her, Ben McCain. The man who calls himself O'Bragh told me all this long ago and assured me of its truth. Now I come to you to ask a great favor."

McCain's hand went nervously to his spectacles as he nodded and then glanced about at the throng of Maidus who'd gathered.

"Wolf Tracker is welcome in this village," Ben said. "Come into the house—we will eat first and then speak of the matter. Is this your granddaughter? From the expression on True Bear's face, I suspect that it is. Come in, come in, both of you. Blue Loon, everyone, let's get on with preparations for the Ustu burning. Tonight we'll have an honored guest amongst us."

Ben gestured toward the open door of his home, and Wolf Tracker followed him inside, Sits-by-the-ladder half a pace behind, the girl's face without expression and her eyes lowered.

Big Woodpecker turned to True Bear, who nodded, and the two friends quickly entered the house in the wake of the others.

Ooti was standing in the middle of the front room. She was dressed in ceremonial robes of her people, a full deerskin garment of white leather, a cloak over one shoulder, her *Huku* cape, made for her by old Hurt Eagle a dozen years earlier.

"We're honored by this visit," she said solemnly. "Wolf Tracker of the Yahis, I am pleased that you have entered my *K-um*. It's a strange time for all of us. We speak to one another in English, and the lodge is a Wawlem house. Have you come to watch our burning ceremony? I forget myself and speak to you in the new way. Please do not be offended.

Come, sit down next to the fireplace and make yourself comfortable."

"It's a pleasure to meet Acorn Girl once more and to be in her lodge," Wolf Tracker nodded.

Ben cleared his throat.

"Would the chief of the Yahis like a cup of coffee? We've got some on the stove."

Wolf Tracker's lips went tight, and then he grinned—grinned almost like a child.

"I would enjoy that very much," he said.

Ben poured the mugs, handed one to his guest, one to his wife, and then sat down on the hearth.

"Even when he's sitting down, your husband is taller than I am," the Yahi said to Ooti and then sipped tentatively at his steaming coffee.

"Hello, Wahtaurisi-yi," Ooti smiled. "That's who you are, isn't it?"

The girl glanced up momentarily and then lowered her eyes once more.

"The cat stole her tongue," Wolf Tracker said, glancing from Ooti to Ben to determine whether he had used the expression properly.

Ben nodded his appreciation of the use of English idiom and gestured to True Bear to fetch a chair for Sits-by-the-ladder, for the girl was shifting her weight nervously from one foot to the other.

"I have come to ask a favor, even though I have no right to make such a request," Wolf Tracker said. "My granddaughter knows English, though perhaps not very well. I am the only teacher she's had, and I am in need of a teacher myself. Still, I have done my best."

"The chief speaks very well," Ooti nodded.

"Wahtaurisi-yi has been as my own, even though she has no father. That's what her name signifies. I will speak the truth. In her blood she is half-Saltu, though she is Yahi in all other ways. I believe she was given to my people for a special reason. Perhaps in some ways she will be to my people as Ooti has been to hers, I do not know. Bear-who-cannot-see-well, you have taught the Oidoing-koyos much of the Whiteman's medicine. You have even shown them how to speak from your books, and now they understand the marks on the pages. That is a very great gift. Once you read from a book and then gave it to me. I remember the things you read, but I cannot read them myself. For that reason I cannot teach Wahtaurisi-yi. Now I wish to give you my granddaughter. I wish you to teach her how to read what is in books, and in exchange she will be your slave. That is the favor I came to ask."

McCain glanced at Ooti, cleared his throat, but Wolf Tracker continued without pausing.

"I do not know what Rabbit, Gray Squirrel, and Lizard may have planned for my people, but I fear the men called Anderson and Good and Clayton will attempt to drive us from our lands. For many seasons now we have managed to elude them, and often we've been able to strike back, as is proper. But each year there are fewer of us, and each year the lands we are able to wander about in grow smaller. There are new ranches in the hills, and I believe our time grows short. Many Yanas were slain at Oak Run, and soon we will not be able to defend ourselves. That is what I believe. Will you accept my granddaughter and at the same time teach her your ways? Of all the Saltus I have met, Ben McCain, you're the only one that I have reason to trust."

Ben's mouth fell open. Whatever he was about to say vanished before the words were spoken.

"My husband does not understand, not completely," Ooti said. "He doesn't believe anyone should be slave to another."

"Perhaps I have used the wrong expression, Acorn Girl."

"We welcome Wahtaurisi-yi into our home," Ooti said. "I too am still a student, though I've learned to read and write. I will act as though I were this girl's mother, and I'll help her to learn."

"Does Bear-who-cannot-see-well say the same thing?"

"Yes," Ben stammered. "I didn't mean to be impolite. Wolf Tracker, I will teach her the *medicine*—we'll all help to teach her. If this is what you wish, then she's welcome for as long as she chooses to stay here. But when she wants to leave, no one will prevent her. I give you my word."

Wolf Tracker turned to his granddaughter, nodded.

"I am hungry," he said. "Sits-by-the-ladder and I have walked a long distance this day. We will eat with you. But you must allow the girl to work when she is not being a student. She will not be happy here otherwise."

USTU FIRES BURNED throughout the night, and the entire Maidu village attended, people observing in reverence whether they continued to believe in the efficacy of the ceremony or not. A few older women, remembering times past, began to wail after Ooti had performed a ritual chanting appropriate to this most crucial time of the year. In all, however, the tone was one of restraint, though even a few skeptics entered into the spirit of observance as evening wore on and flaming poles sent trails of red-orange sparks up into a star-flung October sky.

Wolf Tracker stayed with the McCains until the fires diminished, tall poles like skeletons against night, marked only by guttering coals and trailing smoke. Wahtaurisi-yi stood close beside her grandfather, and next to the girl were True Bear, Big Woodpecker, and Small Ears' daughter, Yellow Grass. Other Maidu youngsters approached in groups of two or three, studied this newcomer for a time, whispered among themselves, and then vanished.

Well past midnight Ben left Ooti to continue with her task of presiding over the Burning and walked downhill toward the ranch house, Wolf Tracker beside him, and True Bear and Wahtaurisi-yi following at a distance of a few steps.

Ben strode across the porch, opened the front door, and gestured with a coal oil lantern he was carrying.

Only True Bear and Sits-by-the-ladder were still there.

From off across the meadow a screech owl trilled and then was silent.

"IT'S STRANGE HERE, but I like it. In many ways I am happier than I ever was in my grandfather's village. Many things are different—the times when we eat and the manner in which our meals are taken, living inside the big log house, different kinds of clothing that Ooti makes for me and is showing me how to make for myself, everyone talking in English and men and women all speaking the same, not moving about from one place to another. Everyone is very kind to me here, and there's much laughing. Often I feel embarrassed about that, but I try to join in and act the same as everyone else in

Oidoing-koyo. The greatest difference, though, is that no one ever seems to be afraid of anything. The men are not constantly on lookout, for they all have rifles and pistols. Sometimes other Whitemen come to visit with Ben McCain, and I can see that they're all a little uneasy around him. It's because he is so large, I think, and also because he knows so much. He seems to know about everything, and the other Whitemen listen to him and nod. It's funny the way they always seem to end up agreeing with whatever he tells them.

"In the afternoons we often sit in the front room of the McCain house and listen to Ben talk about books and things that are happening in other places in the world, and it's almost as though I knew who these strange people were. A man named Fremont was trying to become the chief of all the Saltus, to replace a man named Lincoln. But now Ben says Fremont has become Lincoln's friend. Lincoln has another friend named Grant who's a great warrior and who fights battles against other Saltus who don't like Lincoln. I do not understand any of this very well, but Ben says there's no danger to us. Even though the ones who are fighting have huge guns and many men, they will never come here.

"I can read things in books now, though I am not very good at it. True Bear and Big Woodpecker help to teach me. And I also know how to write. Ink pens are hard to work with, and I always forget to dip the point into the ink in time. But I can make all the letters and put them into words. Ben has more than one copy of several of his books, but I don't understand how the pages can be exactly alike in them. I've looked closely, and I cannot find any differences. The letters and words are all exactly the same.

"Ooti says I am very intelligent, but maybe she's being polite. True Bear and the others know much more than I do, and I'm not sure if I can ever learn so many things. True Bear says I will—it's only that the others have been going to school for years, ever since they were small children. Some Oidoing-koyo adults are just now learning how to read and write, like me, but I learn faster than they do. I can tell that easily enough. So perhaps what Ooti says is at last partly true.

"During the mornings True Bear takes me to some wide meadows where cattle graze, and I've gotten quite good at riding a horse, even though I didn't think I would ever be able to do that. I believed only men could ride horses, but Ooti is better at it than any of them except maybe True Bear and Big Woodpecker, who compete with one another at doing tricks. Ben's horse is larger than any of the others, but that's because he's so big. His feet would touch the ground if he tried to ride the pony he gave me.

"At first I thought of Smoke Woman and Wolf Tracker and the others in my village all the time, and I wondered if I should run away from Oidoing-koyo and return to my own people. But Wolf Tracker told me not to do that, and so I have obeyed. Now, though, I'm very happy here. At times I even feel disloyal, for I don't really wish to return. No, I would like to stay here. There's still so much to learn. Ben says he will take me and True Bear with him when he goes down to the big Saltu village of Chico, and that's exciting, even though I am afraid of being around so many Whitemen. I fear they will realize I am from Wolf Tracker's village and try to murder me.

"I told True Bear of my feelings, and he laughed at me. But that's because the Saltus do not hate him.

"Sometimes I try to think of what it will be like when I become a woman. I would like to be True Bear's wife some day. It is strange. I knew how I felt about him from that first time when the men took him captive and brought him into our village. When I dream, I sometimes see myself grown up, and True Bear's grown up also. In my dreams, he's nearly as big as his father, and I feel very small beside him. He seems like a different person then, even though I know it is still True Bear. We've become very close friends, but does that mean we will always be friends? He says Ben wishes for him to go away in a few years, back to where Lincoln and Grant are, to go to a big school where he'll be able to read all their books. After that happens, he won't be interested in me anymore. I think that's how it will be. I am still a child because I haven't yet gone to the woman lodge, but I know that I love True Bear in the way of a man and a woman. It's almost time for me to be a woman though. My mother said that it would happen very soon. Already I feel things, I feel different. I dream that True Bear and I lie down together out in the forest somewhere, and all the birds are singing. I know what's supposed to happen next, but I always wake up. Maybe tonight I'll have the dream and not wake up. Then I'll know, not as it will be someday, but. . . . It makes me sad to think that when I am a woman and have a husband, it will not be True Bear. But I won't ever forget him. Did not Wolf Tracker tell me he believed True Bear McCain and I would one day share the lodge of a husband and a wife? Grandfather was teasing me, but I hoped then that it would be so, and I still do.

"Yesterday True Bear and I walked up to see if the blue herons were at the lake, and he put his hands on my shoulders and kissed me on the mouth. After that he acted as if he were ashamed of himself, but I wanted him to do it again. I wished to tell him so, but I could not speak."

EIGHT

The Rites of Spring

[November 1864–April 1865]

RAINS CAME, long days of grayness as one storm after another swept in from the west, spawned of steel-gray Pacific waters and working their way down the continent's length before turning inland, across Bolly Peaks and Sacramento Valley, moisture-laden air lifting one more over the southern extremity of the Cascade Range. During sunny intervals between periods of intense downpour, Wahgalu's high crown gleamed unbelievably white against faultless blue sky, while eagles and hawks, unable to hunt during the rains, glided air, their amber eyes keen for any least motion of gopher or ground squirrel or rabbit below.

Yellow of oak and maple vanished as autumn leaves drifted down to soggy duff below. Grizzlies and black bears prowled canyon bottoms in search of salmon and edible vegetation, grunting and roaring at one another, tearing apart rotten logs in order to get at woodgrubs and big black carpenter ants. Territorial squabbles ensued over rights to bee trees and favored fishing spots.

Herds of blacktail and mule deer moved gradually toward lower pastures, and wolves, whether solitary or in pairs, followed after, their canine eyes on the halt and the lame, sometimes driven from prey they had taken by either mountain lions or the seemingly insatiable bears, while coyotes, ravens, and vultures kept track of all that was happening, intent upon leavings.

The men of Oidoing-koyo village hunted as well, their rifles securing a plentiful supply of venison, whose flesh this time of year was dried over beds of coals and stored away against the intervals of winter snows.

Christmas came, and Ben McCain strode in from the woods with a young red fir over his shoulder. He secured a section of planking to the base of the tree and placed it in the front room corner, to the far right of the fireplace.

At first Wahtaurisi-yi was astonished, then fascinated as the McCains proceeded to adorn this tree with brightly-colored candle holders and painted oak galls, as well as a few gleaming baubles of colored glass. A delicately wrought angel with starched linen wings was placed at the fir's tip.

Wrapped packages appeared mysteriously beneath the branches, individual names inscribed upon them. Only then did the girl fully understand that a potlatch was to occur—a time of gift-giving, but to what end? All presents were handed out at once, as she was told, but no obligation lay upon anyone after that.

During intervals between study sessions, Wahtaurisi-yi retired to a small room that Ben and Ooti had furnished for her and spent her time frantically decorating a fine bleached section of deerskin that Big Woodpecker had given her in exchange for her assistance in butchering a buck he had shot. She had worked pigment and porcupine quills into a design of English letters: THANK YOU.

On the day of the potlatch, Ben read from the Bible, another copy of the same medicine book that Wolf Tracker had, and then the presents were unwrapped.

Clothes.

The girl took these to her room and, in silent wonder, ran her fingers over the garments—denim trousers, a red woolen sweater, underwear such as Yellow Grass and the other Maidu girls possessed, a blue gingham dress with puffy lace sleeves, a pair of pliable leather boots with brass hooks, a second pair of shoes—so many other things! She had, she realized, received far more presents than anyone else in the family, and her own present, embarrassingly little and without utility of any sort, was well received by all and made much of.

Though she worked eagerly at any task given her, her own contribution to the McCain household, she understood too well, was pitifully meager. They praised her not only for whatever help she was able to render but for the progress in her *school* also, even though the latter was in fact a gift she was being given.

Benjamin McCain was indeed an unusual Saltu, and the matter could not be explained simply by his choice to marry a Maidu woman. His generosity, Wahtaurisi-yi quickly realized, extended to all the people of Oidoing-koyo. Yet, why was it this huge man, who could barely see at all without his thick spectacles, preferred Indian people to his own kind? Perhaps he had been made an outcast in that place far away, Connecticut, where he lived at one time. Wahtaurisi-yi resolved to ask True Bear—but was not Connecticut the place where Ben intended to send True Bear to *college* when he was older? None of it made sense, and sometimes Wahtaurisi-yi actually doubted whether such a place existed, even though it was clearly indicated on a map in that big leather-bound book called *Atlas*.

At last the girl, hands trembling slightly, put on both delicate underthings and blue gingham dress, stood before a small mirror Ooti had hung on the wall in her room, and turned this way and that, admiring herself and yet hardly recognizing the image.

Still wearing her dress, she ventured out to the front room, where Ben was reading a new stack of newspapers that had arrived from Chico two days earlier and where True Bear was engrossed in working grease from a blue-and-white metal cannister into the leather of a new pair of boots.

Ben glanced up from his reading.

"Ooti!" he thundered. "Come take a look at this, will you! We've been visited by a goddess, by heaven!"

Wahtaurisi-yi resisted a sudden impulse to flee from the room in embarrassment, took a deep breath, and turned to observe True Bear's response.

Puzzlement in his eyes, almost a look of sadness.

But he nodded.

"You're . . . beautiful," he stammered. "You're. . . ."

Ooti came into the room, smiled, her eyes gleaming.

"Sits-by-the-ladder will be a woman soon," she said softly. "It's almost time for her to receive a new name. I will speak with Crane. She is old and wise and will know exactly how this thing is to be handled."

Then Ooti laughed and shook her head.

"In the old days," she continued, "our son would have to lose his playmate for a time. Ben, is that how things happen among the *Yengees* as well?"

"It all depends," Ben chuckled. "It all depends upon 'how the stick's floating,' as Bully O'Bragh would say. Well, no two ways about it, we've got a proper young lady on our hands now."

SHORTLY AFTER the first of the year, heavy snows began to fall, and with passage of the first cold storm, the forest about Upper Eden took on a wholly different aspect—broad meadows blanketed with a foot or so of whiteness and conifers mantled, boughs springing back and loosing their burdens in rattling showers of frozen wetness by midday of the interval of sunlight following a night of intense cold that came on when skies cleared.

Blue woodsmoke hung over Oidoing-koyo village, hearthfires inside log cabins and k-um lodges as well. Cattle moved about disconsolately, their hooves breaking crusted snow, trickles of steam rising from their mouths and noses as they snuffled for bits of dry grass. At Ben's direction, Blue Loon

and the other men and the boys hauled out wagonloads of hay
from the big barn, forking the good-smelling forage into piles
in several locations.

Then more snow fell, sometimes snow mixed with rain or
hail, and during one interval of extreme cold, four cattle were
found dead in the morning. The animals were butchered,
their meat distributed among the people of the village and
the hides stretched and tanned.

For a period of nearly two weeks, Wahgalu was not visible
at all as low running clouds blotted the sky, a time of "dry
storms," as Ben called them, without more than occasional
heavy mistlike rain that did little to melt snow from the
pastures.

Then warm rains, and the creek rose to flood stage, over-
topping its usual banks as a torrent of red-brown water surged
away eastward toward Almanor Meadows and the little town
of Chester, its scattering of log cabins and general store and
trading post.

Springtime, *Yo-meni*, the season of flowers, *Laila* moon, the
month of new grass.

WAHTAURISI-YI NOTED traces of blood on her underthings and
knew the proper time had arrived.

She found Ooti in the big barn, intent upon gathering eggs
the red chickens had taken to laying in hidden places where
the remains of hay lay bunched in corners of the building.

"I must return to my own people now, even though I don't
wish to go," the girl said. "It's time for me to enter the
woman lodge."

Ooti turned, stared at the young Yahi girl, and nodded,
reached out, touched at her hair, and smiled.

"It's not necessary, One-who-is-like-a-daughter. Crane and
I and the other women will furnish a woman lodge at the
other side of the village. It will soon be time for Yellow Grass
to go there as well."

"No," Wahtaurisi-yi replied. "I must return to my own
people for a time. I will come back here later. Smoke Woman,
my mother, she spoke with Wolf Tracker before I left my
village. After a time he agreed, and so they are expecting me
to return to Wolopti, the encampment in Mill Creek Canyon.
My people will be there very soon, if they haven't arrived

already—it is a good place to be when the time of new grass
comes. If the people are not there yet, then I'll do what
needs to be done. My mother explained everything to me. A
tightly woven basket of acorn meal has been left cached in a
hollow tree and sealed in with stones. I'll have enough food
even if the people have not returned yet."

"Smoke Woman is wise," Ooti replied. "But what if the
pack rats have found a way to get into the basket? Pack rats
are very clever little people, and they are also hungry during
the time of the snows. Is it truly necessary for you to leave
us, Wahtaurisi-yi?"

The girl nodded, took note of a guilty-looking chicken as
the bird emerged from a mound of straw close by the horse
stalls.

"It's good to honor the old ways, Little One," Ooti continued. "And for your people, the old ways are not old at all. I
understand. This is what must happen then. You are to take
the pony Ben gave you, and you must fill the saddlebags with
food, just in case the rat people were more clever than usual.
True Bear will ride down the canyon with you, and perhaps
Big Woodpecker will wish to go also. If your people have not
yet arrived at the village, then True Bear will stay close by
until they come, and Big Woodpecker will come back to
Oidoing-koyo to tell us. If that's the case, then Small Ears
and I will ride down in order to be near, as is proper. We'll
be your attendants until the Yahis come back."

THE RIDE downcanyon was a solemn outing, not at all like
other times during the preceding few months—with True
Bear and Wahtaurisi-yi urging their ponies ahead, sometimes
during periods of light snowfall, horses frisking and occasionally undertaking maliciously to rub their humans off against
oak boles or low-hanging branches, at other times through
warm spring sunlight, the horses' hooves making sucking
sounds in muddy earth and crushing newly-emergent grasses.
No lighthearted races this time, and indeed not much talking
at all.

True Bear and Big Woodpecker rode behind the Yahi girl,
the boys mumbling to one another that Wolf Tracker's people
would probably not be at the long meadows at all and that

after a day or two in this *woman lodge*, Wahtaurisi-yi would see the folly of what she was doing and return to Oidoing-koyo.

But the Yahis were there.

Wahtaurisi-yi embraced Smoke Woman, the two of them speaking in subdued tones as Wolf Tracker gestured to the boys to enter his lodge, insisting they smoke the pipe with him.

"My granddaughter isn't happy," he intoned. "I think that now she will not wish to remain with her own people but will want to go back to Oidoing-koyo. Well, that's as I suspected all along. Does she know how to read and write now? Tell me if she has learned the White medicine."

"Yes, yes, she has learned very quickly. Already she can read better than some of the grown-ups in our class," Big Woodpecker grinned.

"Is this so, True Bear McCain?"

"It is so. Sits-by-the-ladder has been very much a part of our family, and we're all sad that she had to return so soon. I. . . ."

Wolf Tracker passed the pipe and nodded.

"Do the two of you continue to enjoy one another's company, then?"

Big Woodpecker laughed.

"True Bear is already saving up things to bring you for a bride price," he said. "Even Ben teases him about it."

Wolf Tracker studied True Bear's embarrassed expression and nodded.

"No one knows what future times will hold. No one knows the mind of the Great Dreamer of things. But listen to what I say now: friendship endures, even though those who are friends are apart for long periods, even though one should die and the other not know it has happened. We keep those we love alive within our memories, and sometimes they come to us in our dreams and help us. Many seasons may pass between meetings, but if the friendship is real, why that hardly matters. When we meet once more, it is as though we had never been apart. True Bear, you must not pay any attention to Big Woodpecker's jestings. Friends are that way, and it is all in good nature. But I will tell you this: when the time comes, if you and Sits-by-the-ladder should wish to be man and woman together, and if Ben and Acorn Girl agree, then I will not refuse whatever presents you may be able to bring me. Yet what am I talking about? Many seasons must pass first. In the meanwhile, I will bring Sits-by-the-ladder back to Oidoing-koyo myself when this little matter of the lodge is finished. She'll be a woman then, but I won't encourage any suitors for a time. I think my granddaughter still has much to learn. No one can understand all about the Saltus in so short a time. Tell me, True Bear, has she been a good worker for Ben and Ooti?"

"She would work all the time if my mother did not tell her to stop. She even knows how to use a sewing machine my father bought for my mother last year. She can use it almost as well as Ooti herself."

Wolf Tracker puffed once again on the pipe and then handed it to Big Woodpecker, along with a caution not to breathe the smoke but only to taste it.

"A machine that will sew clothing?" he asked. "It must be a wonderful machine, then. I would like to see if sometime— perhaps Ooti will show it to me when I bring Sits-by-the-ladder back to Oidoing-koyo village."

When True Bear and Big Woodpecker exited from Wolf Tracker's lodge, Wahtaurisi-yi was nowhere to be seen—and neither was Smoke Woman.

The boys mounted their ponies, waited about uneasily for a few moments, waving to groups of Yahi men and women, dallying, not yet wishing to leave the encampment in the meadows.

Then they moved off, upcanyon, and entered the forest.

Wahtaurisi-yi stood beside the path, her arms folded across her developing breasts. She didn't look up—her actions like those of an earlier time.

True Bear gestured to Big Woodpecker, and the latter rode on ahead, passing the Yahi girl. He grinned, winked, and cautioned her against staying away from school too long.

True Bear dismounted and approached Wahtaurisi-yi. She raised her eyes to meet his, and for a long moment neither said anything at all.

"I . . . I'm going to miss you very much. Will you really come back to Upper Eden? I feel a knot inside my stomach, as though we were saying good-bye. When you weren't there after we smoked the pipe with your grandfather, I thought. . . ."

"I came here so that we might speak together and not have all the people in the village trying to hear what we were saying, True Bear. Yes, my mother says I am to return as soon as . . . if your mother and father are still willing to have me in their home."

"Of course they are—you know that."

"Yes, I know. And that's what I wish also. At first I was lonely for my own people, but now I am even more lonely for . . . all of you. But when I come back after one moon, probably Yellow Grass will be your girlfriend and not Big Woodpecker's. I like her very much, but she is always looking at you and laughing at things you say. Maybe she wants to be your girlfriend."

"You're just being silly, Wahtaurisi-yi. I'm not interested in her."

"She's much prettier than I am. And I think you like her, too. Well, I wish to go back anyway. I want that so much it makes me feel disloyal to my own mother and to my grandfather."

"If you don't come back, then I'm going to come here to live."

"You would soon grow tired of moving about all the time, True Bear. Besides, you will one day be sent to *Connecticut* to go to college. Then you'll meet some girl with yellow hair and blue eyes, *like the ones in the book-pictures.* You'll forget all about Wahtaurisi-yi then."

"Don't . . . say such things. I'm getting all confused. It's like you're trying to say good-bye or something. You just said Wolf Tracker wants you to return to Upper Eden."

"If it's possible, yes. That is what my mother has told me."

"Then don't say dumb things, Wahtaurisi-yi. Look. I'm going to ride back down here next weekend."

"No, you mustn't do that. I wouldn't be able to see you anyway because. . . . Do you understand, True Bear? We must wait to see what will happen, but I am certain Wolf Tracker will let me. . . ."

True Bear stepped closer and clumsily put his arms about the Yahi girl, trying to do it just the way his own father embraced his mother.

Wahtaurisi-yi did not return his embrace, but neither did she resist.

He nearly pulled away, thinking he had once again over-stepped his bounds, thinking that he must apologize immediately. But then he resolved to plunge on ahead, and so he pressed his lips to hers.

For a moment neither of them moved, stood there almost as though frozen in place. Then Wahtaurisi-yi closed her eyes and clung to him, her lips slightly parted and working against his. She put her arms about him, and the two of them held desperately to one another, neither wishing to be the first to relax the embrace—and both of them thinking to themselves that this was happening only because they were saying good-bye for a month—a month, certainly not longer.

NINE

The Vultures Circle

[April 1865]

THE CONFEDERACY, Ben told his students was reduced to a desperate holding action, beyond hope of victory. Peace commissioners for the South had met with President Lincoln, who had insisted on an unconditional restoration of the Union, while Southerners grimly demanded that any peace agreement would have to be concluded between two fully independent nations.

Sherman had captured the capital city of South Carolina, Columbia, and Charleston fell almost immediately there-

after. On the verge of total defeat, the Confederates even
authorized the use of slaves as soldiers, and Schofield took
Wilmington, North Carolina, without meeting any resistance.

Ben McCain even read his charges the concluding portion
of Lincoln's second inaugural address:

> With malice toward none; with charity for all; with
> firmness in the right, as God gives us to see the right, let
> us strive on to finish the work we are in; to bind up the
> nation's wounds; to care for him who shall have borne
> the battle, and for his widow, and his orphan—to do all
> which may achieve and cherish a just, and a lasting
> peace, among ourselves, and with all nations.

"The whole thing may be over by now," Ben said, stroking
his beard and adjusting his spectacles. "The last of these
papers from Sacramento is dated the first of April, and even
that news is no doubt two weeks in arrears, Pacific Telegraph
Company or no Pacific Telegraph Company. Well, scholars, I
suppose there's little cure for it. Here at Upper Eden, we
must learn to be patient concerning word from the outside."

THE LAST WEEK in April, Blue Loon and Goat's Beard rode in
from a trip to Chester, driving their horses. The two Maidus
reined up before the McCain house, did not bother to
tether their mounts, and pounded on the front door.

"You gents look as though you've come face to face with
the great *Kakini Busda* itself," Ben said. "Has the world
ended while I was tending cattle?"

"A hundred Wawlems are riding toward Oidoing-koyo,"
Goat's Beard blurted, absently removing his felt hat and then
putting it back on again. "They're heavily armed, and they've
got blood on their hands. I think they're coming to attack us."

"Is this so?" Ben asked, turning to Blue Loon. "Ooti! Come
on out here!"

Acorn Girl appeared almost immediately, True Bear with
her.

"I think they've been hunting for the Yahis," Blue Loon
said. "I do not trust this many Whitemen with guns. Shall we
alert the men in the village, Ben? Clayton's the leader—I

recognized him even from a distance. You know what they did at Oak Run. . . ."

"Goat's Beard," Ooti said, stepping forward, "alert everyone. Tell the men to arm themselves. Get the others inside—women and children. Did you come by way of Childe's Meadows or Stump Ranch?"

"Childe's Meadows," Blue Loon nodded. "The Wawlems were riding up toward Wilson Lake—we took a shortcut over the rim. We saw them from the crest."

"Tell the men to come here, then," Ooti said. "We'll confront them as they come down from the low pass."

"Hold on, now," Ben cautioned. "Nobody starts shooting. Get the men up here, as Ooti says, but nobody—nobody—is even to think about firing off a shot unless we give the word. Only damned fools would make an attack on Oidoing-koyo, and whatever else he may be, Dan Clayton's no fool. Let's find out what this thing's all about. You gents didn't catch wind of news in Chester, did you?"

Blue Loon shook his head, and Ooti gestured toward Goat's Beard to go—to sound the alert.

True Bear studied the expressions on the adult faces, turned, and went to his room to get his Colt pistol. When he came back, Ben and Ooti had both strapped on their weapons, and Blue Loon was leading Ben's Percheron and Acorn Girl's roan toward the house.

"Son," Ben said, "you stay inside the house. We're not going to fight our own Civil War right here in Upper Eden, but you stay inside anyway. Latch the door. I suspect we're blowing this whole thing out of proportion."

True Bear started to protest, but Acorn Girl shook her head.

The boy glanced from one parent to the other, and shrugged.

BENJAMIN MCCAIN, Acorn Girl, and Blue Loon rode slowly away from the ranch house, up a trail past the Ustu site and on toward Wilson Lake. Just short of the summit, they confronted Clayton, Anderson, Good, and their men. Everyone was indeed armed, and Clayton's band seemed to be composed partly of cowhands and partly of drifters who'd volunteered to ride along for the excitement, whatever the nature of that excitement was.

"Hold up, Dan!" McCain shouted. "You're welcome here,
but what's the army for?"

Clayton, Good, and Anderson rode forward, all three grinning and apparently in high spirits.

"News from the outside!" Clayton laughed, "but not all of
it's good. First off, the damned war's over. Lee's done surrendered to Grant at a place called Appomattox in Virginia."

"It was bound to happen—just a matter of time," Ben
nodded.

"Bad news too," Clayton continued, "or maybe not so bad,
depending on your politics. We got us a new president.
Andrew Johnson's the one. Some Reb or another has killed
Abe Lincoln. Sure as hell it's official. That log-splitting
sonofabitch has gone under, and that's the truth. Deader than
your basic doornail. The bastard caused the war in the first
place, but now it's over, and he's over into the bargain."

Ben, intent upon the expressions on the faces of the three
ranchers, sensing something that, in fact, had nothing to do
with the war or, for that matter, the stunning surprise of a
president's death, was not aware that True Bear, disobeying
what his father told him, was riding up the trail. Ooti noticed, however, and waved for the boy to return to the house.

At first pretending not to understand her gesture and finally shaking his head, True Bear continued to ride toward
them, drawing up his pony a few paces behind his mother's
animal.

"Are you gentlemen certain about all this?" Ben asked.
"The President's . . . dead?"

"Got shot while he was watching a play—that's the word,"
Hi Good answered. "The news was telegraphed to Sacramento, and some of the boys here rode up to tell us."

"Damned rights," Bob Anderson agreed. "So we got together and had a little celebration."

"What are all the guns for?"

"Well," Clayton grinned, "since the lads back East have
managed to get their problems settled, we decided to do
likewise."

"Killed all but half a dozen or so, as I figure it," Hi Good
laughed. "We was just on our way over to Chester to do a bit
more celebrating."

Ben glanced at Blue Loon and Ooti, and became aware for the first time of the presence of his son.

"True Bear, damn it . . . ," he began.

"What are you talking about?" Ooti demanded.

"Why, the damned Yahoos, Miz McCain," Clayton grinned. "Me and the boys left bodies strewn all over Mill Crick Canyon—a meal for vultures and coyotes."

"So I guess that problem's took care of, at least until the monkeys that got away have had time to breed 'em up another tribe," Bob Anderson said. "Ben, you won't be having to share your whitefaces with 'em anymore, not unless dead men eat beef, at least."

"A massacre . . . ?"

"Call it what you like, McCain," Clayton said. "The military couldn't get the savages on over to Covelo or wherever, so we saved our bluecoats a bit of work. As I see it, the canyons are more or less safe for running cattle after today."

"Now you wish to slaughter the Oidoing-koyos as well?" Ooti demanded. "All our men are armed and ready. It will not be easy for you to murder us, as you say you have the Yahis. Turn around and ride away in peace, Dan Clayton. You're not welcome at Upper Eden. I'll kill you myself the next time I see you."

A moment's silence followed Ooti's outburst, and then Bob Anderson began to laugh.

"Hell," he said, "we ain't got nothing against *civilized Injuns*, have we boys? Make damned good workers an' good bed partners, as long as they don't go forgettin' they're just Injuns."

At that moment True Bear kicked his pony forward, letting out a wild scream of rage as he did so. Pistol in hand, he rode directly toward Clayton.

Ben saw what was happening and turned Blue-Two quickly about, lunged for his son, and dragged him from his saddle.

The pistol went off, the shot missing Clayton, and weapons suddenly appeared in the hands of the ranchers' men.

Ben hurled True Bear to the ground, shouting as he did so.

"Turn around and ride away from here," Ooti said during an interval of deadly, stunned silence. "If you men attempt to come into Oidoing-koyo, my warriors will kill all of you."

A whistling sound, like the cry of a marmot.

"What in hell's the matter with you, McCain?" Clayton
demanded. "You've done forgot you're White, is that it? If
there's going to be permanent bad blood between us, just
remember that it runs both ways. It'll be a cold day in hell
before I sell you any more cows, and I guess that goes for the
rest of us, as well. As for your half-breed brat here, the day'll
come when I put a round of lead into his hide. Mebbe the
truth is them rumors about you being a renegade a few years
back was right. Mebbe your Maidu woman here really was
the leader of them that attacked the mining camp down
south. I met Dan Fischer up in Redding two, three weeks
ago, and he told me they was a Whiteman with the Injuns
that time, one who was riding a plow horse, just like the
beast you're sitting on. Almost makes sense, don't it? We get
us any evidence, Big Ben, and we'll bring the U.S. Army up
here if we have to and string up the lot of you. You've been
holed up with these savages so long, you're no better than
one of 'em, by Gawd."

"Fischer's a drunk," Ben shrugged. "He's poisoned his
brain with whiskey. I don't know what stories he's telling
now, but face-to-face with me, that's a different matter."

"The man didn't accuse you, McCain, but I started putting
two and two together. . . ."

Again the shriek of a marmot.

True Bear, stunned from the fall, found his Colt revolver
and stood up, the weapon once more pointed directly at Dan
Clayton. His hand was trembling.

"Get out of here, all of you!" he shouted.

"Tell the whelp to put his toy away," Anderson growled,
"or the boys'll stick plugs in him."

Ooti was off her horse in a moment and standing between
True Bear and the ranchers. She took the pistol from her son
and then turned once more to face Dan Clayton. She smiled.

"Shall I tell the Oidoing-koyo men to open fire, or would
you and your friends like to turn your horses about and
leave?" she asked.

The Maidus, on foot, had come up through the forest,
spreading out to all sides of the band of armed cattlemen,
staying back and away, behind cover, but well within rifle
range.

The valley ranchers glanced about, realized the vulnerable position they were in.

"This ain't over, McCain. For once you've bit off more than you can chew, that's what I'm thinking," Good said, gesturing to the men to turn their horses.

Clayton began to laugh.

"Bunch of your friends lying around a few miles down Mill Crick, but they seem to have lost most of their hair. McCain, mebbe you and your Injun pals ought to go down there an' have a burying party. Lots of good baskets they ain't got use for anymore. . . ."

GOAT'S BEARD volunteered to follow the Whites at a distance, tracking them to Childe's Meadows, where they stopped for a few minutes to confer with Seth Childe and his wife before continuing their ride toward Chester, some fifteen miles eastward. When it was clear that Clayton, Anderson, Good, and the others had no intention of doubling back toward Oidoingkoyo, Goat's Beard returned up Lost Creek and on to Upper Eden.

Ooti warned the Maidus to keep their weapons at hand and then sent Goat's Beard on down North Fork, but with explicit instructions not to enter the town of Chester. At first indication the ranchers and their men were heading toward Oidoingkoyo, he was to return, post haste, with warning.

"We must ride to the Wolf Tracker's village," she told her husband. "Whatever has happened, we must find out if Wahtaurisi-yi is still alive. Perhaps she's among those who were able to escape. Wolf Tracker is a wise leader. It's possible he managed to lead a number of people away from the slaughter-place. Clayton had whiskey on his breath. I think all those men were still half drunk. If the Yahis had had rifles and pistols, none of this could have happened."

Ben nodded, glanced momentarily at his True Bear's stunned and blank expression.

"I have to go," the boy said.

"All right, son. It's a dirty piece of business that we've got ahead of us, though. I don't think you're going to want to see. . . ."

"True Bear is still young," Ooti half-whispered, "but now

it's time for him to become a man. Later there must be a revenge-taking."

"Guess he's turned a man already," Ben said. "True Bear, you lunkhead, a fourteen-year-old can't go fighting the whole damned world. Why didn't you stay in the house? I ought to tan your rock-headed hide."

"No," Ooti replied. "He is a man now. You've just said so."

TRUE BEAR accompanied his father and mother and half a dozen Maidu men into Mill Creek Canyon, to the site of the village where he had so recently left Sits-by-the-ladder to enter into her time in the woman lodge.

An odor of death was indeed in the air as they approached the long meadows, and they discovered that what Dan Clayton said was true.

Yahi men, women, and children—all dead, their mutilated bodies lying heaped about, bullet-riddled and scalped. The brush lodges had been torched, and wisps of smoke continued to rise. The entire area was pockmarked with splatches of black where grass fires had burned, sometimes missing the bodies of the dead, sometimes scorching flesh. A woman lay in the center of one blackened area, her dead infant still clutched to her bare breasts and her tule skirt nearly burned away, her flesh charred.

True Bear felt nausea rising in him. He gritted his teeth and looked away.

Ben and Ooti surveyed the scene, walking from one corpse to another:

"We've looked upon this kind of thing before," Ben said. "When I go blind eventually, perhaps it will be a blessing. How can human beings perform this sort of butchery upon others of their own kind? The satanic impulse turned loose— and all over . . . what? Marginal pasture lands, utterly unneeded. So that isn't it at all. A terrible hatred of *others*, of people whose way of life is sufficiently different so that they are not regarded as human at all. A war of extermination. *Thou shalt not kill* was never supposed, from the very beginning, to apply to Philistines. Ah, Ooti, I'm sick inside. The older I get, the less able I am to deal with things like this. War, organized frenzies of slaughter, a perpetual way with the human creature."

"I would not feel so bad, my husband, if we had found all those Whitemen lying about this way. Yet I'd still know the horror of it. Fifteen winters ago you and I killed many men, though we had deep reason. No, it was my reason. Johnson and Lindley and the others, they butchered my family, my village, my firstborn children. Now we must help these people on into the Spirit World."

Ben and the Maidus carried bodies to a central location and laid them out, side by side. When this grim task was completed, they began to gather dry grass and brush, sections of rotten downfall logs, whatever would burn. Dry fuel was heaped around and over the dead, and Ben poured out a flask of coal oil he'd remembered to bring along in grim anticipation of the necessary pyre. Despite these elaborate preparations, the fire burned slowly at first, and the men were obliged to bring in yet more fuel. Then flames caught hold, growing to yellow-white intensity and sending up a long plume of smoke into the clear blue of late afternoon.

Neither Wolf Tracker nor Wahtaurisi-yi was among the dead, and a faint, desperate hope rose in True Bear. Was it possible that she and her mother and her grandfather had actually been able to escape? Clayton and the others said a few managed to get away. As if sleepwalking, True Bear continued his search, not wishing to find what he dreaded most but unwilling to allow the bodies to lie off in the forest unattended. True Bear tried to think of others who were not among the dead. Salmon Man and Broken Willow, Wahtaurisi-yi's friends, they were not there. Broken Willow's young son, Wood Duck, U-Tut-Ne. . . .

At length True Bear, having convinced himself that Wahtaurisi-yi was nowhere about, returned to where the big fire was burning fiercely at the center of what was once a Yahi encampment.

In a world of death, was it possible that Sits-by-the-ladder still lived? Was she safe? Or wounded and dying, alone, too numbed even to be frightened, hiding somewhere and waiting for oblivion? He shouted her name many times as he searched the surrounding bluffs, the place where obsidian was gathered beside a small pool under a black rim, hidden glades here and there along the canyon wall, everywhere he could think of. . . .

Not far from the funeral pyre, just at the edge of the
meadows and half-hidden among tufts of tall grass, three
coyotes sat on their haunches and observed the proceedings.
True Bear caught sight of the song dogs, and a shudder went
through him. Brush wolves were scavengers, and they would
certainly come in to gorge themselves on whatever roast flesh
remained after the big fire died down. It was simply the way
of things. For this moment, however, the animals merely sat
there, observing human activity as they no doubt had on
many occasions when the Yahis were preparing an evening
meal or perhaps simply going about the business of their
lives. Later the coyotes would snuffle about the remains,
chew at charred flesh, and carry away whatever bones might
still provide edible marrow. The eyes of the three coyotes
were almost hypnotic, unblinking and terribly wise.

"Son," Ben said, "you didn't find anything, I gather? I'm
thinking maybe old Wolf Tracker and a few others must have
gotten away, including little Wahtaurisi-yi. It could very well
be the case that our friends weren't even here when Clayton
and his butchers came riding in. What I can't figure is why
the Yahis didn't have scouts posted downcanyon. When you
and Big Woodpecker brought the girl back to the village, was
there any sign of sickness among these people? That's about
the only thing I can think of to account for it. Wolf Tracker's
been keeping a few steps ahead of Clayton and Anderson and
Good for years, and a sudden lapse just doesn't make sense."

Ooti shook her head but didn't speak. A strangeness had
come into her eyes, and her son was immediately aware of it.
He sensed both terrible anger and resolve. Would she attempt an attack against the ranchers? Did more horror lie
ahead?

"Possibly," Ben went on, "Wolf Tracker and his family will
show up at our place. He knows he's always been welcome. . . . Hell, maybe I'm just clutching at straws, I don't
know. But Wahtaurisi-yi's not here, and that means there's
still some reason for hope."

The deep canyon of Mill Creek had already filled with
shadow when the riders began their return trek to Upper
Eden, though high rims to either side remained in bright
sunlight.

Earlier three of four vultures floated across the blue sky,

but now a great band of the dark birds gathered, redtail
hawks and golden eagles among them, in all perhaps as many
as fifty of the winged forms in a wide spiral, drifting with
currents of springtime air.

TEN

Vanishing Trail
[April 1865]

OOTI STOOD on the front steps of the McCain ranch house and
looked out over the assembled villagers, her eyes fixing first
one face, then another. Finally she began to speak. "Listen to
my words, people of Oidoing-koyo. You all know what's happened, and it must be entirely clear to you that Clayton,
Good, Anderson, and the other Sacramento Valley ranchers
are our enemies. Perhaps they leave us alone for the time
being, but a day will come when they decide they wish to
possess our lands to make summer pasture for their cattle.
We're Indians, and in the eyes of White law, we have no
rights—none at all. These Wawlems pay lip service to their
little Jesus god, and he tells them they must not kill—it's a
sin to commit murder. The Whiteman's wisdom is in his
Bible, and if Wawlems practiced what's contained in the
Medicine Book, then it would be possible for our people to
live in peace with them. But no, that's not the way of things.
The Book prevents them from murdering all of us, just as

they've murdered the Yahis, yet that is all. I think it's not
long before they decide Ben's claim to these lands is invalid,
and when that occurs, the Whites will try to herd us to Nome
Lacklee or Covelo, just as they've done to other of our
people. Do you wish to live there, out of sight of Wahgalu?"

"No one wishes to do that," Goat's Beard replied, "but
what reason have we to believe such a thing would ever
happen? It's different with us. We have followed the Whiteman's way, just as Ben McCain told us we must. Most of us
live in houses, like the Wawlems themselves. We raise cattle
and cut timber and saw the trees into boards. We sell what
we produce—to the Whites in Chester and to the Valley
ranchers as well. Wolf Tracker and his Yahis persisted in
living in the old way, wandering about, hunting, and fishing.
Sometimes they stole cattle from Clayton and the others. Is it
not true? So now the Whites have attacked Wolf Tracker's
village and killed most of the people there. We've seen a
terrible sight, Acorn Girl, but we have to realize the time of
old ways is past. I do not believe the Whites will bother us,
not here in Oidoing-koyo."

"Ben McCain is protected by Whiteman's law," Blue Loon
added. "Everything's in his name, and he's been designated
our agent. The Sacramento men did that, the ones who run
the government. Then how can the Whites take away our
lands without violating their own law? Wolf Tracker and the
Yahis chose one way, we chose another. Now the Yahis have
been destroyed. Their choice was wrong."

"The Whites have committed murder," Ooti persisted.
"The massacre was murder. Yet we all know Wawlem law
will do nothing about what has happened. The ranchers don't
care about law—they do what they wish, they take what they
wish to take. And they'll take our lands as well as soon as they
can find a way of doing it. Maybe Dan Clayton will claim
we've also stolen his cattle. If the ranchers have friends in
Sacramento, then the government will send blue-coated soldiers to force us to move onto a reservation—they'll say the
Upper Eden rancheria is causing trouble, and they'll force us
to leave. Not us. No, I'll be able to stay here because I am
Ben's wife, and for that reason I'm protected by the law. You
are the ones who will have to go to Nome Lacklee. Then
there will be no more Oidoing-koyo Maidus. You'll be reser-

vation Indians, those who survive the march. I don't need to tell you what happened to the others who were sent there."

"What is it that you wish us to do, Ooti?" Goose Leader asked. "I'm old now, but once I rode with your Panos—yes, after my own village was destroyed. You led us then on a great revenge-taking, but Hurt Eagle was still alive, and his Kuksu medicine was strong. He gave you counsel and strength. That was fifteen winters ago, and I have grown weak. Nevertheless, I'll ride with you if that's what the people of Oidoing-koyo decide. Bear-who-cannot-see-well has grown old also. I want to hear his words."

McCain glanced at his wife, her eyes fierce, just as they had been years earlier—when she had found him at the bottom of a canyon, left for dead. There were times, he reflected, when it was very difficult to oppose the intense moral sense that governed Ooti, however impractical her perceived mode of action might be.

He rose from his chair, stood beside Ooti, his sheer physical bulk dwarfing her.

"A terrible crime has been committed," he said, "and several of us have seen its aftermath with our own eyes. What we've witnessed will play in our dreams for a long while to come. Acorn Girl wishes to take revenge upon the ranchers, and deep in my heart, that's what I want to do also. We know enough about Clayton and his wretched companions to know they're no friends of ours. Indeed, they are our enemies—beyond question. But if we attack them, however much they deserve it, then the United States Army will send troops here. Ooti and I will both be arrested, and the people of Oidoing-koyo will be forced onto a reservation. Those who've been identified as leaders will also be arrested. I'll have a trial before I'm hanged. You Maidus won't—you'll be executed by military order. Those are the simple, unpleasant facts of the matter, my friends. Nothing will be gained—Wolf Tracker's people cannot be brought back to life. The cost of revenge will be very great, and we'll all lose everything we've worked for here at Oidoing-koyo. Perhaps my wife will despise me now and see me as a weak-willed old man, but this is how I see it. Still, I am like Goose Leader. I'm willing to go on a revenge-taking if that is what the people decide."

McCain gestured apologetically to his wife and then sat down.

"My husband speaks the truth," Ooti said. "I don't doubt his wisdom, for he has lived among the Whites and knows their ways very well. But have we now grown so much in love with our barns and cattle and houses that we're unwilling to fight for what we know to be proper? If the ranchers suppose we're weak, we will lose our barns and cattle anyway. Could we not go east, into the desert? Are there truly so many Wawlems now that we cannot find someplace where they won't be able to bother us? I say it's worth more to be free and untamed than it is to be governed by a law that does not protect us."

"Acorn Girl is brave," Blue Loon replied, "but she counsels us to go to war in behalf of people who are already dead—people who chose to live the way they did. I say we can gain nothing but revenge, and we'll lose everything, just as Ben McCain says. I vote to protect ourselves and to fight back only when we've been attacked. That makes sense. Wolf Tracker's war was his own, and now the Kodos are dead."

Three or four others spoke then, each in turn echoing the counsel of Blue Loon. As Ooti listened and observed the faces before her, she realized a consensus had been reached. The people would remain armed and alert, even though Sacramento law forbade their having firearms at all. Yes, they would indeed defend themselves if the ranchers and their men attacked. But when soldiers finally came and ordered the Maidus to leave their lands—what then?

The people would have to obey. They would no longer have any choice in the matter.

Ooti sat down beside Ben, reached out, and took his hand.

The old ways were gone. They had vanished with the Yahis—had vanished even before that. The change that Hurt Eagle had predicted was complete now.

The sun had vanished from out of Maidu skies, and what appeared to be a sun was different, pale. Ooti knew as well as anyone else what the intelligent thing was. She, too, wished to live to see her son grow to manhood. True Bear was the new generation—perhaps he could find a way to live among Whites and yet retain a sense of honor. Perhaps there were even advantages to living in this new world where everything would eventually become civilized. But what was absolutely clear: her own world, now merely memories of a time when it was unusual even to see a Wawlem, a time of gathering acorns and hunting and fishing and moving from one village site to another—all had vanished, vanished forever.

"I'LL BET there was a trail," Big Woodpecker said. "Everyone leaves a trail. You were probably so sick to your stomach from seeing all the dead people that you just didn't find it. Wolf Tracker can probably cover his sign even better than old Goose Leader, but not while he was trying to get away from the ranchers. I think I could find it."

True Bear tossed a pebble across the stream, squinted as the projectile missed by a foot or more a thin-boled aspen he'd been aiming at. He stooped, found a likely-looking stone, and threw again, this time striking his intended target.

"Let's ride down there, then," he said. "You won't like what you see. . . ."

Charred bodies, a heap of blackened bones, many of them scattered around by now, the work of badgers and coyotes and wolves. The powerful jaws of wolves, well able to crack open a human leg bone to get at the marrow. . . .

"You think it's right to do that?" Big Woodpecker asked. "I mean, it'll be like wandering around in the Ustu place, only no one's buried."

"If she's alive, I have to find her. She's. . . ."

"I know, True Bear. All right. I think Mom and Dad will let me go tomorrow. It's too late today—be way after dark when we got back. You know they went somewhere—Wolf Tracker wasn't there, or Smoke Woman, or Sits-by-the-ladder. Wherever she is, she's got a new name now. She went back to her village to be in the woman lodge, and so. . . ."

"Doesn't make any difference what her name is. She hasn't changed any. That's strange, isn't it—how girls start *bleeding* whey they start growing up. I don't want to talk about that. Can we start first thing in the morning—or have you got chores to do first?"

"Will your dad let you go? You sure of it?"

True Bear nodded.

"I'll take my Colt revolver," he said. "We'll be safe enough, even if we run into some of those damned ranchers."

"Oh, hell. They won't be anywhere near. If you were them, would you go back? I wonder how many Yahis managed to escape? It's strange that Wolf Tracker ever let the Wawlems get close to his village. Maybe the Yahis were having a celebration or something."

A BIG BLACK BEAR was sleeping perhaps fifty yards from the charred heap of human remains, and a raven was perched on the creature's back, oblivious to human presence, drowsily engaged in preening its wing feathers. True Bear and Big Woodpecker watched spellbound from the meadow's perimeter, neither boy saying anything and neither even bothering to point.

A large chunk of meat lay nearby, the half-eaten remains of a human leg.

Then the raven became aware of them, ceased grooming, drooped wings to either side, and turned its head sideways—holding that posture for a minute or more. Late morning sunlight glittered from a single visible eye, a small, white-hot, silver point of brilliance.

Wings began to fan, not hurriedly or out of fright, but slowly, lazily, at length lifting the creature upward so that for an instant the raven appeared to be walking on sheer nothingness. Then the bird vaulted upward, circled twice, and alighted in the upper branches of an oak.

The black bear awakened, snorted, sniffed, rose heavily, paused to scratch behind a cuplike ear, and stood up, head moving first one way, then the other. The monster growled, coughed, dropped back to all fours, and slowly ambled away downstream, past the dark human remains of Wolf Tracker's village.

True Bear and Big Woodpecker rode forward once the blackie was gone, reined in their ponies well short of the burned heap of bones and portions of unconsumed flesh. A soft downcanyon breeze ceased momentarily, and the boys became aware of an odor—an odor that neither would ever forget. *Death—death smell—burned flesh—rancid and penetrating*.

Big Woodpecker turned away, seemed on the verge of

vomiting, but True Bear steeled himself. His previous visit to the massacre site had allowed him to prepare for the spectacle.

A skull, no longer attached to its skeleton, tilted crazily to one side and seemed to grin at them. Bits of burned flesh still clung to one cheekbone and the chin.

"*Ulisi*," True Bear whispered, using a Yahi term Wahtaurisi-yi often resorted to during her time at Upper Eden, "I don't understand."

He shook his head.

"Why hasn't Wolf Tracker returned—to do something? No one's been here since. . . ."

"*Kakini-Busda*," Big Woodpecker muttered, "the spirits of dead people. They're all around us. It's difficult for them to leave. Wolf Tracker and the others, whoever is still alive, they will not return to this place for a long while. You remember that story Crane told us—about a village where so many died of Spanish sickness? No one went back there for ten winters. Let's go, True Bear. I don't feel good—this smell. Show me where the black glass is. Maybe Wahtaurisi-yi and the others were able to hide there while. . . ."

THE BOYS LED their ponies to Mill Creek Canyon's rim and continued northward for perhaps a mile, coming to a shallow brook that coiled along through a narrow ravine with standing basalt boulders to either side. There was a path now, a deer trail, and they followed that upward—no sign of human passage, but they continued their search.

Then True Bear saw something lying plainly atop a shelf of stone. He dismounted quickly, picked up the object, a bracelet of woven swamp grass.

"This is like the one Wahtaurisi-yi made the day we all walked toward Stump Ranch. Maybe it's hers!"

Big Woodpecker examined the bracelet, and nodded.

"I think we've found the right trail, True Bear. Let's keep going."

Half a mile further along they detected a small area between two big liveoaks, a place where moss had been disturbed. They searched carefully and had nearly come to the conclusion that it was nothing more than where some deer had bedded down.

"Look at this," Big Woodpecker said, pointing. "It's blood—

dried blood. I'll bet the Yahis were here all right. Someone was wounded."

True Bear felt his stomach knot up, and he had to force himself to breathe. In his mind's eye Wahtaurisi-yi had not only escaped, but she was unharmed. His will insisted that it be so. But now his will broke as he stared at the bloodstain, and he began to sob—dry, painful wrenchings of his entire body.

Big Woodpecker put his hand on his friend's shoulder, uncertain how to console him but feeling the need to do something.

"Let's keep looking," he whispered. "This could have been . . . anything. Anyone. Wolf Tracker's leading them toward Turner Mountain, perhaps on to Oidoing-koyo. They might even be there by the time we get back home."

True Bear rubbed his wrist across first one eye and then the other. He walked slowly toward his pony.

EVIDENTLY NO REAL attempt at all had been made to cover the trail they followed—either because Wolf Tracker was confident the ranchers wouldn't be able to follow in any case or perhaps simply because the need to flee was so compelling it overrode all other considerations.

True Bear and Big Woodpecker, now clearly perceiving a basic line of flight, moved ahead rapidly, ascending one shoulder of Turner Mountain and then dropping into a mile-wide valley along Nanny Creek and from there upcanyon to the small stream's head at a large shallow pond high on a ridgeback, within view of the big white dome of Wahgalu, Lassen Peak, visible between Brokeoff Mountain and Black Butte.

But the Yahis' trail didn't veer eastward here, as True Bear and Big Woodpecker had anticipated. Such a route would have led them across Mill Creek's upper canyon, that stream rising high on the mountain in a region of boiling sulphur springs, then over a rim beneath Black Butte and so on down the fledgling North Branch of Feather River to safety at Upper Eden.

"Perhaps Wolf Tracker has some old people with him," Big Woodpecker suggested. "Descending the canyon and climbing the other side would be too difficult for them—or perhaps they're carrying the one who's wounded. I bet they went to the boiling springs—maybe they're camped there, waiting."

True Bear nodded.

"Wolf Tracker would send out a scout—or he'd go himself— through the pass behind Black Butte and down to North Branch from there, the same way we go when we want to climb up onto Wahgalu. . . ."

"Probably they've already reached Oidoing-koyo, just like I said. Should we cut across, then, and get on home as quick as we can? I'll bet Wolf Tracker and Wahtaurisi-yi and the others were walking along North Branch when we rode out this morning—we've come all this way, and they'll be waiting there when we get back!"

True Bear shook his head.

"You cut across if you want, Big Woodpecker. I'm going to keep following the trail. Maybe the Yahis are afraid to leave the sulphur springs. Maybe that water's good for healing, just as Crane says it is. How could Wolf Tracker know whether he'd be safe, even at Oidoing-koyo? He wouldn't take any damned chances unless he knew for sure."

"I'm going too, then. Ain't riding home alone. I guess we've got time to make it before dark."

"Before it's too dark, at least," True Bear replied.

THE SUN DROPPED beneath the high red-gray rim of Mt. Diller, a jagged crest north of Brokeoff, by the time the boys reached the place where boiling water and sulphur gasses wheezed and bubbled from a nearly barren mountainside, air strangely both pleasant and unpleasant at once.

The Yahi trail remained visible here and there—moccasin prints, trampled vegetation, an occasional stone displaced, a cutback where someone apparently slipped—as though those who had passed this way did so at night, half-feeling, half-seeing where they were going. True Bear and Big Woodpecker, in fact, began to congratulate themselves on their skill as trackers, for they continued to have no difficulty in detecting sign.

"You think the Yahis might be at the high lakes?" True Bear asked.

"I don't know. Going to be dark soon. You think we've got time to get up there to see?"

"Not if we keep talking. Let's go, Pecker-Wood. I think we're close to them now."

Not heading toward Upper Eden. No, Wolf Tracker's on his way to the high pass below the volcano itself, then on north, toward Magee Peak and Hat Creek. Dad says there's no one out there except a few cattle drovers. Maybe Wolf Tracker's taking his people far away into a wild place that I've never even heard about. . . .

Somewhere above them, on a rocky scree above the uppermost trickle of water that drained away southward to form Mill Creek, all signs of passing vanished.

The boys continued to the lakes nestled beneath the snow-splashed dome of Wahgalu, but they found no one and nothing. A single white-throated loon cried out, danced across a few feet of still water, and then fanned itself aloft, darting off into shadows cast by great boulders and wind-bent firs. The lake's surface grew still once more.

It became clear now that Wolf Tracker knew precisely what he was doing—yet as to what that was, True Bear and Big Woodpecker had only the most vague of surmises.

ELEVEN

With Bully
[May 1865]

MORE NEWS, Ben reported, had arrived from the world beyond Upper Eden.

A funeral train bearing Lincoln's body had made its way from Washington D.C. to Springfield, Illinois. Huge crowds gathered along the way to view the remains of the slain leader. A second Confederate army had surrendered, and John Wilkes Booth, Lincoln's presumed assassin, had been surrounded by Federal troops near Bowling Green, Virginia, and killed. A conspiracy trial was set. More Confederate troops surrendered to General Canby, and a week later Jefferson Davis himself was taken prisoner—to be tried as one of the conspirators in a presumed plot to kill Lincoln. West of the Mississippi, Confederate forces under General Kirby continued to offer resistance, and President Johnson had designated General Sheridan to move against them and to force their surrender.

"For all practical purposes," Benjamin McCain told his students, "the great American Civil War is over. Slavery's now a thing of the past—except, of course, here in California, where Indian people like yourselves are without rights and may still be indentured. But the time will come, soon, I trust, when sheer logic will enforce the conclusion upon those in Washington that all human beings have been endowed by their Creator with precisely the same rights. We're all human beings—that is our common bond. In the meanwhile, those of us here at Oidoing-koyo will do well to keep our pistols and rifles loaded. So long as we're able to defend what is ours, I firmly believe that we will remain free. What, after all, is a reservation but an impoundment of one's enemies? It's a place designed to contain prisoners of war, and we must remember that our own war of liberation is not yet concluded. Were the Modocs under Captain Jack actually given any choice? No, they've been forced to live among their ancient enemies, the Klamaths. It will be interesting to see how that works out. Well, I predict difficulties. If the Modocs attempt to leave the reservation, they'll discover they're indeed to be treated as enemies of the Federal Government. We must have patience, though how much patience I do not know."

GRASS IN THE HIGH MEADOWS was beginning to turn brown in places during the last week in May, though perpetual springs bubbling from under seams of basalt would keep the McCain pastures verdant in most areas until a time of first autumn rains. Cattle browsed here and there, some younger animals frisking about. A pair of yearling whiteface bulls dug at sod and grunted warnings to one another, made all the gestures preparatory to charging, and then went back to biting off mouthfuls of forage.

One calf, straying from its mother, suddenly broke into a stiff-legged run. Catching sight of a pair of swallowtail butterflies, the animal stopped, stared, and then began to stalk the small winged-beings.

True Bear and Big Woodpecker thumped their heels to their ponies' sides and raced toward an aspen grove at the meadow's edge, neglected to make any particular note of who'd won, dismounted, and walked back in among dancing green aspens.

Big Woodpecker withdrew his hunting knife and proceeded to engrave YELLOW GRASS upon the soft bark of a tree.

"I'll bet you've done that twenty times so far," True Bear laughed. "How come she doesn't put your name anywhere?"

"My name's too long, that's why. It won't fit."

"What about BW? That's easy enough."

"I don't know. In the books, it's always the boy who carves initials—not the girl. Yellow Grass wrote my name on the blackboard the other day, didn't she? That ought to count for something."

BIG WOODPECKER EATS BUGS.

True Bear remembered, laughed. Ben McCain had walked from the room for a moment, and Yellow Grass, giggling, flounced to the board, stuck out her tongue at Big Woodpecker, and quickly wrote out the short sentence—causing great amusement among the other children and even the three adults present. When Ben returned, he had immediately noted the inscription, adjusted his spectacles, and without any question as to the matter of authorship, complimented Yellow Grass on her handwriting.

"That's true. Maybe you ought to carve YELLOW GRASS SUCKS TOADS. Put it on a tree where she's certain to find it."

"Not funny," Big Woodpecker scowled. "Where do you think they are?"

True Bear's expression turned serious.

"Wolf Tracker and the Yahis? Dad says a guy from Burney found a deserted camp on top of Hat Creek Rim—and it wasn't Atsugewi, either. None of those people are wild anymore. You know that. Either they're working for ranchers, or they went over to Hoopa Valley."

"Could have been some Modocs, though."

"Captain Jack and his people are all up near Klamath Lake—just like Dad said. No, it was a Yahi camp."

"I hope so," Big Woodpecker nodded, staring off toward Wahgalu. Long streamers of white cloud were trailed from the mountain's summit, so that for all appearances, the volcano seemed to be jetting steam.

True Bear broke off an aspen twig and chewed once or twice at the end of it.

"You suppose they'll ever come back here?" he asked.

Big Woodpecker shrugged, saw a troubled look in his friend's eyes.

"Probably. Yes, in autumn, when Tem-tsampauto moon makes the acorns ready. The Yahis will come back to gather acorns. Ain't no oaks around Hat Creek—that's what Blue

Loon says. Pop and Tied Wing went over there two summers ago. I wanted to go along, but Ben said I had to stay home and do schoolwork. . . ."

"You think she's all right?"

"Sure. Why wouldn't she be? There's no reason why Clayton and Anderson and those men would go over to Hat Creek. They're happy enough now the Yahis aren't in the canyons anymore. Probably aren't even interested. Not enough Yahis left to make a difference."

"It was only a month ago . . . ," True Bear mused, his voice trailing off. "Now everything's changed. Goddamn it, why do things have to be this way? Dad keeps talking about how it'll be *Back East*, when I get sent there to go to college. That's three years from now, and yet he talks like it's next week. Grown-ups don't have any sense of time, you know it? They're always talking about things that happened ten years ago or five years from now. All the same, I almost wish it was next week. Everything seems so empty around here. I. . . ."

"Don't get moody, True Bear. We were having a good time until you started thinking about Wahtaurisi-yi again. What happened—it can't be helped. You've gotta keep your mind on what's real. Let's target practice with your pistol, what do you say? Some friend you are. Hell, you hardly ever let me use your gun. If I had a real blood brother, he'd let me—he'd even loan it once in a while."

"I'll tell you a secret," True Bear said, withdrawing his Navy Colt from its holster and checking the cylinder. "I'm going to kill Dan Clayton when I grow up. I mean it. I'm going to make him beg for mercy, and then I'm going to shoot him five times—just to watch him bleed for a while. Then I'll use the sixth bullet right between his rotten eyes. I'm going to do it, I swear on the Bible."

Big Woodpecker took the offered pistol, sighted in on a nearby cow, grinned, and then fired at an outcrop of stone.

"You'll end up getting hung. That's what happens to murderers."

"No I won't. I'm going to track him back into one of the canyons and then wait until he's all alone. That's when I'll do it."

"Okay, then," Big Woodpecker replied, firing off another

shot. "I'll help you bury him—as long as there's no way we can get caught."

"Bury him, hell. I'm going to scalp him and leave his body for vultures. That's how the Indians in the Rocky Mountains do it."

Big Woodpecker glanced at his friend.

"Some Wawlem or another'll find the body, and he'll know you did it. Maybe we ought to cut Clayton up and scatter the pieces around. Just kind of drop them every mile or so."

True Bear shrugged.

"Let's climb to the ridge," he suggested. "The cows are starting to get nervous. I guess Herefords don't like gunfire very much."

As THE BOYS prepared to ride back to the village, a strange apparition confronted them: a man mounted on a mule, a second mule trailing behind. The stranger was wearing worn, grease-stained leathers and a beaver cap. He had a green-colored pouch slung from one shoulder, and his eyes were like twin points of dark light staring out from beneath bushy black eyebrows, the rest of his face covered with a thick, stringy white beard—so that his lips were hardly evident at all. A buffalo rifle rested across the pommel of his saddle.

For a long moment no words were exchanged. The boys stood, puzzled, and True Bear's right hand dropped slowly toward his pistol.

"Goin' to shoot the Irish Vulture, are ye, lad? Wagh! That won't do no good, not a whit. This child's been plugged lots o' times, an' he's still hyar to brag on 'er. Ye be William True Bear McCain, if I ain't mistaken?"

"Bully? Bully O'Bragh, is that you?" True Bear yipped, momentarily annoyed with himself for allowing his voice the childlike octave. "It is you! Does Dad know you're here?"

" 'Course not, 'course not. Ye're the one this coon's come lookin' for. Figgered it were time to teach ye a thing or two. Injun chiefs, they've all got to have medicine visions, an' I'll bet ye ain't had yours as yet. Who's yore compadre, if it ain't out o' the way to ask?"

Big Woodpecker glanced at True Bear, then nodded, spoke his own name.

"I remember you," he said. "You're Ben McCain's friend. You came to visit four years ago. . . ."

"Shore enough," O'Bragh grinned. "Guessed that's who ye was. We all went swimmin' down to the hole on Mill Crick, that's what. So ye two leetle thieves is still friends, eh? Wal, one's about as ugly as t'other, so I guess it's all right. True Bear, ye had a vision or not? I've done rode a powerful long way thinkin' I had a job to do before I packed 'er in. A man gets to be a hundert an' twenty-nine y'ars old, an' crossin' half a continent turns troublesome."

The boys laughed.

"Dad says you're only forty-five," True Bear replied. "You're actually his younger brother."

"Big coon never could tell the Gawd-awful truth," O'Bragh grinned. "But lyin' about a man's age, wal. . . . Guess I'll have to whomp him good for sullyin' me repu-tation. Must be gettin' close to lunchtime, ain't it? For civilized folk, anyhow. This child's got a powerful hunger—so let's go see what leetle Ooti's got fixed up. After that we'll talk about your future, young Mr. McCain. By damn, ye're startin' to get shoulders on ye. Skinny as ye used to be, I wondered if it'd ever happen."

Bully O'Bragh.

This was the wraithlike mountain man of utterly indetermi-nate age with whom Ben McCain (then Benjamin Goffe, recently resigned Professor of Literature at Yale College) had fallen in with one night at the El Sombrero tavern in St. Louis. Ben was then readying himself to head up country, the lure of California goldfields bright in his imagination. Ben had left behind him a secure and prestigious career, a faith-less wife many years his junior, Etta, who'd married him apparently because no better catch was immediately available to her—yes, and family ties that went back to his distant relative, the regicide, swordsman, and aventurer, William Goffe, a New Englander out of necessity after the Restoration and eventually husband to an Indian wife.

His meeting with O'Bragh, McCain recalled, had been very much like a segment from some perplexing dream—as though Bully had emerged as a stereotype of a repressed portion of his own nature. In any case, O'Bragh was apparently waiting for him, like a kind of destiny, and knew about him as well, his name, where he'd come from, even tantalizing hints of knowledge of the marital situation that, among other things, McCain had journeyed west to escape. Ben's first response to the irrepressible Bully O'Bragh was that of comparison to the "graybeard loon," the strangely compelling figure of an old sailor in opium addict Coleridge's insanely grotesque poem. O'Bragh had accosted McCain in much the same way the mariner grabbed hold of the wedding guest, and, indeed, immediately began telling some outrageous tale of presumed vast import and profound moral significance. But in St. Louis the telling was cut short by a bar room brawl in which Ben knocked several men unconscious and lost his glasses, without which he was blind as the proverbial bat.

O'Bragh, naturally, found the specs. And the two men, a most unlikely pair at the time, walked into a St. Louis night and spoke briefly of their plans.

Ben took a steamboat up the Missouri to Independence, gathered together an outfit, and ultimately set out, *solus*, for the Far West. Not too far up the road to Eldorado, Bully was waiting, waiting like the being out of myth that McCain still believed him to be—or at least pretended that he did.

On to California!

A very late start, and in the midst of freezing weather along the Humboldt River, O'Bragh had taken time out to court an old Te-moa widow, whose man had been slain by an earlier band of emigrants.

The trail had taken them at last to the settlement of American Valley (Quincy, as it was now called) on the Feather River, and from there McCain had proceeded alone to Sutter's Fort in Sacramento City, then to Grass Valley in the goldfields, and ultimately to a dark ravine where Ooti had found him, slowly bleeding to death from gunshot wounds, and saved his life.

McCain, drawn into the Maidu cause, had turned renegade, and managed to purchase pistols, rifles, horses, dynamite. And that was when O'Bragh had again mysteriously appeared, ready to assist Ooti in taking her revenge and finally leading her band of Pano outlaws northward, to Upper Eden, a place Bully himself had found congenial, having lived for a season with the Oidoing-koyos. Furthermore,

O'Bragh was the first Whiteman to make peaceful contact with Wolf Tracker's Yahis.

"Where's Rabbit-chaser," Ben McCain asked now. "You haven't deserted your wife, have you?"

"Wagh! How can ye be thinkin' such a thing, Sonny? Don't ye have no faith in me after all this hyar time? Rabbit-chaser, she's livin' with the Cheyennes, Leg-in-the-water an' that bunch. Up in the mountains since the massacre at Sand Crick. That news get out to ye? Chivington come in at dawn, an' his soldiers cut down men, women, an' toadstools. Jimmy Beckwith was with 'im, can ye believe it? Wal, the colonel, he had a gun pointed at ol' Medicine Calf's back, but Beckwith testified against the big preacher at a inquest they held. Anyhow, it were after that when this nigger an' Rabbit-chaser tied in with Leg-in-the-water. Been an outlaw all my life, by Gawd, an' I figgered I might be able to help out one way or t'other."

"You didn't answer my question," Ben persisted.

"What question were that?"

"Why'd you leave her behind?"

"Got 'er into a family way, ye mud-suckin' idjit. Kid was born last winter. Cain't jest go haulin' a leetle one across the mountains an' deserts, now, can ye? I told her I was figgerin' to come visit ye. She's a good woman an' knows I'll be back. Got to have someone as will bury me, but I guessed I had to help yore boy first. Needs someone to assist with the medicine vision, ain't it gospel, Ooti? That way with yore people too, or so I been told."

"It was good of you to come, Irish Vulture," Acorn Girl said. "But I don't know if Ben believes. . . ."

"Shore he does. Ain't that right, Sonny? Mebbe ye are goin' to send the lad to college, an' all that, but it don't make no difference. True Bear's half Injun, a leetle more, an' certain things has got to be done."

Ben McCain nodded. Whatever he might have felt about the matter, he knew from experience there was little sense in trying to argue with Bully O'Bragh, who was profoundly worse than Acorn Girl in that regard.

The man's finally beginning to show his age, Ben thought. *He's thinner, and the hair's gone completely white. He looks more like a ghost than before, and that's saying something.*

Back in '49 he claimed he'd been dead for several years—got impatient with the way things were going, and so dug his way back to the surface. Only this time I think it's real. Well, no one, not even Bully O'Bragh, can live forever. He's had a good life, from all accounts, and now there's this one last thing he thinks he has to do for me—no, for my son. A little superstition, what can it hurt? Only maybe it isn't superstition at all. I guess I've learned that much from my young wife, at least. Yes, yes. When I die, and it's not too far off either, I'd much prefer to step off the top of a volcano and hike on over to Upper Meadows. Never was much of a harp-player. . . .

"What do you think about all this, William True Bear, my boy? Bully says you ought to dream for a while—make a little premature visit into the Spirit World."

"Ye Gawddamned hulking skeptic!" O'Bragh hissed. "Ye wouldn't believe in mule piss unless it were poured onto yore topknot."

"If the fool would persist in his folly," Ben grinned, thinking of the obscure poet Blake, "he would become wise. Who am I, then, to stand in the way of wisdom?"

"Damned rights. True Bear, what do ye say? Ye up for it?"

True Bear studied the old mountain man's face, smiled, and nodded his head.

"I'm ready for a Kuksu vision," he said. "My mother's told me about it. You will be my spirit-assistant, then?"

"See what I told ye, Goffe—I mean, McCain? The lad's got more common sense in one finger than ye've got in that three-hundred-pound body, an' he weren't never no college teacher, nuther."

BEN McCAIN, Bully O'Bragh, and True Bear rode to the high lakes beneath the peak of Wahgalu, dismounted, built a campfire, and brewed a pot of coffee.

"Not suppose to have nothin' to eat, Billy True Bear," the old mountain man said. "Plenty o' time to fill yore meatbag later. Drink the coffee, though. She's good for what ails ye, an' that's life itself. A Gawddamned disease, is what. But we all got it, for a while at least, an' after that we ain't got it no more. Me an' Benny hyar, we're gettin' along. We've took about all the coups we're goin' to take. But ye—ye've got the whole infernal thing ahead of ye, an' that's why the mountain up yonder is callin'. Heard it in the wind from clear out to Platte headwaters, an' that's a fact. What ye got to do: Go up clean to the top an' find a sheltered spot among some rocks. This buffler robe I'm givin' ye, it'll keep the hurricanes off an' the ice out o' yore bones. After that ye jest wait. Then one o' the Animal People'll come palaver with ye. When it's time to come back down, ye'll know it. . . ."

"That's what I call 'concise instruction,'" Ben laughed. "Anyway, Son, we'll be here. Bully'll have a pot of medicine stew waiting for you in case the mountain's made you hungry."

True Bear was no longer certain exactly how he felt about the thing that was supposedly going to happen, but he nodded his head and forced himself to appear serious-minded.

He took a swallow or two of O'Bragh's peculiar-tasting coffee, stood up, and put on the *Huku* cape Ooti had made for him, a garment of white deerskin decorated with various strange figures and designs, including the stylized head of a grizzly, its mouth open in a way that seemed vaguely threatening. No one else, his mother told him, was to be allowed even to touch the cape. In old times, she said, to handle a *Huku* garment meant death to anyone but its owner. In most ways the garment resembled the one she herself wore at the Ustu ceremony, and True Bear realized his mother had been working on it, secretly, for some time—apparently in anticipation of this ritual that was now to be enacted.

Well, he'd climb the mountain. He'd done that before. This time, if a steam-jet began to hiss, he wouldn't run away. He'd stay the night, at least, and then come back down. He doubted whether any Animal People would come to him, except maybe in a nightmare, but putting on the *Huku* cape, in some inexplicable way, made the whole thing seem more likely.

"Leave yore pistol hyar, lad," O'Bragh said. "Won't be needin' it. Jest get in the way o' matters is all."

Ben pounded his son on the back a bit more vigorously than usual.

O'Bragh pulled at his whiskers and touched the tip of his tongue to his upper lip.

True Bear picked up the folded buffalo blanket Bully gave

him, turned determinedly, and then and began his solitary ascent of Wahgalu.

A marmot whistled and scuttled into its burrow. A bluejay screamed, pretending to be a hawk.

Beyond those things, the mountain air smelled slightly different than True Bear remembered it.

TWELVE

A Vision of Flame
[May 1865]

HUNGER WOKE HIM, hunger and a sensation of thin gray mist suffused with light. True Bear sat up, pushed the buffalo robe away from his arms and chest, and looked out into windblown streamers of fog dancing across Wahgalu's stony crest. The illusion was that of actually being inside an inchoate aurora, such as the one his father had called him outside the house two winters past to see. But this—was it indeed an illusion, a figment? Was he actually awake at all?

True Bear breathed deeply, got to his knees, and then stood up.

Was steam issuing from the mountain, or were bands of cloud merely passing over the high summit?

He tried to remember if he'd dreamed at all—but nothing, nothing coherent.

Strands of vapor, gyrating, endlessly shifting, the wind

*producing strange, low, moaning noises, almost sounds of
many people dying, wounded and bleeding, groaning and
wailing. Wild movement, and yet a dizzying sensation of utter
stillness. New light, as if thrown from some source far distant—
faint violent tones gaining, gaining, then flooding to intense
crimson and orange.*

"This is not actually happening, I'm still asleep. Is it
possible?"

*Flames, a wall of fire. Spellbound, he walked toward it—
could hear his own voice being called from somewhere beyond
a surging curtain of crazily twisting redness. No sensation of
heat at all, and he strode into the fire. . . .*

*Then he was standing on a ridge above Upper Eden, in the
center of the Ustu grounds. Someone was close by—who was
it? He could feel the presence, tangible but invisible. He
turned, frantic now, gazed first in one direction, then in
another.*

"Ulisi, True Bear, I do not understand. How did I get to
this place? The Saltus came at us after dark, and then they
began to shoot. There was nowhere to hide, but Wolf Tracker
called to me, and I ran toward his voice. Several others came
also, and we slipped down into the waters of the big creek,
stayed close to boulders, let current carry us downstream.
After that we climbed to the rim and hid. . . ."

"Wahtaurisi-yi? You're alive? I searched for you, Big Woodpecker and I both looked. We found your trail but then lost it
high on the mountain. There was blood. . . ."

"I am here. Can't you see me? True Bear, I've chosen you
to be my man, just as you have chosen me to be your woman.
We must be patient now. Winters must pass over our heads,
and then. . . . I am not Wahtaurisi-yi any longer, my name's
been changed. Dearest one, how shall I speak to you?

"I can stay with you now only a moment longer. Bad things
have happened. I have lain with a Whiteman, but that was
against my will. There will be others, many others before we
meet again. Will you still want me then? The fate which
carries me is stronger than I am. . . ."

"You're not making sense. Come closer. Look—down there!
Fire's burning all around my parents' house—all about
Oidoing-koyo! It consumes the house—where are my par-
ents? They're not inside?"

"I must leave you, True Bear McCain, I have no power to remain . . . remember me . . . we will meet again . . . after that I can see nothing . . . True Bear. . . ."

Flames closed in about him, lifted him from the Ustu grounds and flung him through the air, high up, high among stars and on into absolute blackness. Next he felt stones beneath his bare feet.

"You wished to dream," the grizzly said. "Do you like what you saw? It's dangerous to wander into the Spirit World unless you've prepared yourself first. Well, I'll stay with you for a moment. I miss Ooti, your mother. She raised me and my brother after our own mother died. Tell her you spoke with Bear-who-comes-before. That's the name she gave me. No, I am not dead at all. You've seen me in the forest—don't you remember? Your own name came to you because Ooti wished to remember me and my brother. He's well also. You must tell her that. He's down by the sulphur springs, chewing apart a rotten log to get at woodgrubs. I was there too, but I heard you cry out, and so I came to find you. Strange lights burned on the mountain, and at first I was afraid. Usually we bears are not afraid of anything, so long as we can understand it."

"Are you the Animal Person Bully O'Bragh said would appear to me?"

"For this moment I'm allowed to speak with the voice of Pano. He's off somewhere with Coyote Man, so I came to you. . . ."

The huge bear, fire glittering from eyes and mouth, rose on his hind legs and waved his great arms about. He took a step or two, then turned, dropped to all fours, and began to shamble away.

"Wait! Before you leave you must tell me—did Wahtaurisi-yi speak the truth? Will we see each other again?"

"That's not her name anymore," the grizzly replied. "I cannot speak what you ask unless you use her correct name. Tell Ooti we're happy, even though we miss her. . . ."

CONFUSED, True Bear McCain found his way back to the sheltered place between slabs of lava rock where he'd slept. Everything was gray now, and the top of Wahgalu itself seemed suspended in mists, a floating island caught somewhere between heaven and earth. He shivered, suddenly aware he was cold, and drew the buffalo robe up about his shoulders, over the Huku cape.

Full sunrise couldn't be far away, he concluded, and so he waited patiently, needing time in any case for the fragments of what he had seen in his waking dream to fade and in the process to fall into place, to make sense.

Bully had suggested an animal guide, and so the grizzly appeared—one of the creatures his mother raised before he was born, naturally. And Wahtaurisi-yi appeared simply because that's what he wanted to happen. He wished desperately to see her again, and so his mind tricked him into believing she was there. It was certainly not the first time he'd dreamed about her during the month since he and Big Woodpecker followed Wolf Tracker's trail from the massacre site to the slopes of the snow-crowned volcano. In earlier dreams, however, he and the girl were always involved in doing something or going somewhere, just as though nothing had ever happened in Mill Creek Canyon.

This time, though, it was different—and in truth he had not actually *seen* her at all. Felt her, yes, and heard her voice, but. . . .

She said her name was changed?

Of course. He knew that. After the woman lodge, Smoke Woman or Wolf Tracker or one of the old medicine women would have given her a new name to take with her into her adult life. In his vision Wahtaurisi-yi did not, he remembered, tell him what that name was.

But there was more.

Why did she tell him she'd slept with a Whiteman? Or that there'd be others, "many" others before she would see him again? A great deal of time would pass. Perhaps he would not even wish to be with her when they finally did meet once more.

Possibly he was just tormenting himself.

Why would she be with a Whiteman? And the other— impossible to think of. She'd never do such a thing—perhaps only after he and she were married, perhaps they would do it once in awhile, but he'd always be careful to apologize afterward. Maybe they'd do it only to have children. Grown-ups spent a great deal of time joking about sex, mostly the men, but sometimes the women as well. It was a mystery he could not as yet quite fathom—except that with Wahtaurisi-yi there would be nothing dirty about it, not like the crude adult jokes at all. Perhaps it would even be wonderful. In the darkness they would touch one another, and there would be nothing wrong with it. . . .

He roused himself, shook his head. He'd allowed his mind to wander into the maunderings that often came to him. In the time before the massacre (how distant that time seemed now, how precious and how utterly vanished), he indulged in fantasies about Wahtaurisi-yi—how he'd find her half-drowned beside some raging stream, lying there, shivering uncontrollably. He'd lift her and carry her (himself grown big and powerful, like Ben) to a cave mouth, and there he'd build a fire and remove her clothing as she slept, dry her off. He'd cover her with a blanket, and when she awoke and found herself naked beneath the covering, she'd know what had happened. Or they were be at Wolf Tracker's village. The two of them would go downstream and swim together, and neither would wear anything. . . .

Foolish visions.

Then a thought came—like a powerful fist striking him in the midsection. Was it possible she had not escaped at all? Could one of the Whites who murdered her people have carried her off—to have her for a servant girl? Clayton and the others . . . that day at Upper Eden . . . they didn't have her with them. No, but maybe another man took her from the village, back toward the Valley?

True Bear's mind went blank as he continued to stare eastward. The mists were vanishing now, dropping away, dispersing in wind. Then a sensation of silver-white, a crescent. The familiar horizon came visible—Mt. Harkness, Mt. Hoffman, Red Cinder Cone. Sun appeared to burn its way up out of black rock.

He rose, folded the buffalo robe, and walked away southward along the high rim, then downslope, catching sight of the lake far below where Bully O'Bragh and Ben McCain were waiting. He could see a wisp of smoke from their campfire.

He began to run easily, leaping at times, jumping onto a

snowbank and sliding for a hundred yards, then running
again, running toward the first wind-twisted grove of hemlocks.

HE DRANK a cupful of steaming coffee and felt momentarily
dizzy. Bully, true to his word, had brewed up a pot of stew—
venison from the taste of it—and ladled a hefty portion onto a
tin plate. True Bear closed his eyes, took a mouthful, decided
the concoction, whatever it was, wouldn't poison him, and
swallowed. Then he decided the taste was in fact quite pleasant, however unusual, and he ate greedily.

"The lad takes to mountain cookin'," Bully grinned. "At
least someone in yore family knows what's good an' what
ain't."

"No accounting for tastes," Ben laughed. "Well, William
True Bear, did the Spirit Communicators come to you?"

True Bear nodded between mouthfuls of stew.

"O' course they done did, ye idjit. Don't think I rambled
out hyar a thousand miles for no goose chase, do ye? A coon
gets to my age, he cain't be wasting time, no sir. What kind
o' varmint was it, True Bear?"

"A grizzly," the boy managed. "One of those two that Mom
raised. . . ."

"O' course it were. Makes sense, by Gawd. A proper link
between one world an' t'other, ye might say. Wagh! She
sounds powerful."

"The cubs," Ben mused. "Well, they're around here somewhere. Any messages from beyond? Tell us about it, Son."

Bully poured True Bear another cup of coffee.

"Not exactly," the boy answered. "I saw Wahtaurisi-yi—no,
I didn't actually see her. But she was there. I saw fire
surround our house, and then everything went up in flame. It
was like I was thrown up among the stars, and I landed back
on the top of the mountain."

Ben nodded once more.

"Ezekiel," he said. "The one who views the world from
above. We'll take a look at that passage when we get back to
the house."

"Ye seen the little gal, though?" Bully asked. "Benny hyar,
he told me the whole story. Wal, she's alive then, that much
is certain. No two ways about 'er. Ye got a spell to go, True
Bear, but by the flat feet o' Jesus, a man needs an Injun wife.

Ain't no other kind is worth a damn. Ye're half-Injun, an' so's she, from what this child understands. Makes a interesting match. Lots o' things got to happen first, I figger, but one way or t'other, ye'll find each other. Two born thieves, they always manage to meet up. Jest like me an' Benny hyar. Old Man Coyote, he takes care o' such stuff."

"I'm waiting for Mr. O'Bragh to explicate the vision of flames," Ben smiled. "Was it a dream of purification? In literature, fire often has that implied meaning—the impact of metaphor itself. An old order of being is consumed, and out of its ashes a new realm emerges, phoenixlike."

O'Bragh snorted.

"Wagh! There's gibberish for ye. Lad, don't never pay no attention to pro-fessors. They'll mud up the water every time. Wal, it's peculiar, outright peculiar. . . ."

WHEN BEN, Bully, and True Bear returned to the ranch house at upper Eden, Seth Childe was there, obviously agitated, talking to Ooti and old Crane, Hurt Eagle's widow.

"Seth," Ben said, extending a huge paw toward the much smaller man, "what seems to be the problem? Have some of your cattle found their way up over the hill to my pastures?"

Childe shook McCain's hand, his fist seeming to vanish within Ben's grip.

"Seems I got a barn full of Injuns," the neighbor said. "Yahis I guess—some that Anderson and Clayton didn't manage to butcher. My wife went out to collect eggs, and there they was, and I don't mean eggs. It was Injuns, a bunch of them. Said they wanted to talk to me. Martha, she come running for the house, and it must have took me five minutes to get her calmed down so's I could understand what she was saying. Anyhow, I grabbed my pistol and went out there. The chief, he spoke English all right, just like Martha said. Wolf Tracker—you know the man, Ben?"

True Bear stood by silently, studied Seth Childe's face.

"Of course," McCain replied. "I'm surprised he didn't come here. . . ."

"Cautious, I guess," Childe said. "Anyhow, he promised not to steal nothing if I'd come fetch you. A pitiful damned looking bunch, like they'd been run through hell, and I guess

they have been. So he give me his word, and I give him
mine. Said I'd bring you on down to palaver with him."

"How many Indians?" Ben asked, glancing at his son. "A
girl about True Bear's age maybe?"

"Can't rightly say. I glimpsed a few of 'em, back in the
barn, half-hid. One squaw had a little boy, maybe four, five
years old. At least one buck and another female. Didn't go in.
Wolf Tracker and I did our talking on the outside, but I could
see faces through the open door. . . ."

THE McCAINS and Bully accompanied Childe back to his
ranch, to the barn where Wolf Tracker and the Yahis had
indeed remained.

The old chief saw them ride in and stepped outside the
rough-hewn structure, stood with arms folded across his chest.

"Greetings, Ben McCain," he said. "Hello, Ooti, hello
True Bear. And Irish Vulture—it's been a long while since
we've met. I lead only a very small tribe now. Rabbit, Gray
Squirrel, and Lizard have deserted us, and now even our
camp dogs have run away to hunt on their own."

"Heard what happened to ye," O'Bragh nodded, for once
not bubbling over with verbiage. "The stick don't float so
good. . . ."

"Greetings, Wolf Tracker," Ben said, stepping forward and
embracing the Yahi chief in traditional manner, complete
with several slaps on each shoulder. "Mr. Childe said you
wished to speak to me. You must bring your people to Upper
Eden now—live among us, damn it. It's safe there, for all of
us, because we keep ourselves armed. There's room for
everyone."

The embrace concluded, Wolf Tracker stepped back—and
almost smiled in spite of himself.

"You have not grown any smaller, Bear-who-cannot-see-
well. When you hug me, I feel like a young child, even
though I am older than you. Acorn Girl, how do you deal
with this man? He's as large as my entire lodge, except that I
do not have one just now."

"The offer is made sincerely, Wolf Tracker," Ooti said.
"The ranchers came to Upper Eden after. . . . We ran them
off, and then we went down to your village, several of the
men from Oidoing-koyo went. We built a funeral pyre for the

dead. My heart grieves for you and for those who have gone to the Spirit World. Now we wish you and your people to come to Upper Eden. . . ."

Wolf Tracker folded his arms once more and shook his head.

"No," he replied. "Your offer is generous, and no doubt we should accept. We could live there and be safe. We could help with whatever work needs to be done and in that way not be a burden to you, Acorn Girl and Benjamin. But such a life is not the way of the Yahis. We made our choice many winters ago, and it was the right choice for us. I have already spoken with those inside—they've told me what to say, for I knew you would make this offer. You've invited us before, and you took my granddaughter into your home and taught her to read and to write. I'm grateful, and yet there is no way for me to repay you. But my people and I wish to return to our canyons. We went north of Wahgalu, but we had no luck. It was not the right place for us."

"Is Wahtaurisi-yi inside?" True Bear burst out, unable any longer to wait patiently for the formalities to be done with.

"True Bear," Wolf Tracker said, "I had hoped you would be my grandson one day, but that is not to be. I'll tell you what happened because you have a right to know. You loved my granddaughter very much, and I could see that. It was easy to see, and that's why we stopped here instead of going on down into Deer Creek Canyon, for that's what we must do now. I hoped you would come with your father so I might speak to you directly, as men should. Robert Anderson and some of his men are in Chester right now. I think they're riding north to find us. That's why we are going in the other direction. But this is what happened. You brought my granddaughter back to the village, and after that she went into the woman lodge. When the right time passed, she became *Auna-yi*, Fire Woman. That had just happened when the Saltus attacked us. We couldn't defend ourselves—it was night. The Whites must have surprised our sentries and killed them. But we escaped—Salmon Man and his wife, Broken Willow—and their young son U-tut-ne, Wood Duck— and Smoke Woman and Fire Woman also. We crossed over Wahgalu and made a small camp near Hat Creek, the stream that flows north from the mountain. Once we were there,

Fire Woman began to set nets in the stream, and each morning she went to tend them, just the way I taught her. I should never have given her that lesson, for she was captured by some men who were moving cattle. I found tracks later and followed, but it was no use. They had ridden away northward, and they took her with them. Probably she's dead, but I do not know. It is likely that they killed her after a time. . . ."

Pain, pain like a whiplash across his face. The vision—now that much of it made sense, but did any hope remain?

True Bear turned away. He fought back tears. He didn't want Wolf Tracker or Ben or Bully to see him sobbing like a small child.

"We cannot help these things," Wolf Tracker continued. "Our time is past, and now only darkness remains. We will live for a little while, I think, but there is no hope. Well, perhaps Wood Duck will be able to grow up. Maybe there will be time for him to become *Ishi*, a man, but where will we find a young woman for him to marry? If we can do that, then for a while we will prevent the sun from setting. No, our way is the way of Death. Ben McCain, we cannot become like Saltus—as the Oidoing-koyo people have. We must search to the west of Wahgalu to see if any of our cousins are still alive. That's our final hope."

O'Bragh walked over to where True Bear was standing, eyes closed and mouth open, struggling for breath. Bully put his arm around the boy's shoulder, patted softly.

"She's alive, lad," the mountain man whispered. "Wolf Tracker, he don't know it, but it's so. I'm tellin' ye, she's alive. Ye saw her in yore vision—jest keep thinkin' on it. Knew they was a reason for this old cahuna to come moseyin' out hyar. Ye're a man now, damn it, so by-Gawd ye got to act like one. Time ain't run out yet, ye'll see. . . ."

True Bear opened his eyes, stared into Bully's face. And something he saw there made him *will* that what the old man had just said might actually be true.

WOLF TRACKER and his remaining Yahis walked away south, through Childe's Meadows toward the head of Deer Creek Canyon, and Bully and the McCains went on back to Upper Eden. They rode in gloom, and not even O'Bragh's continual chatter and tale-telling were sufficient to break the sense of great loss.

That night, after Ben and Ooti retired, Bully O'Bragh slipped out of the house, went to the barn to fetch his mules, and rode away eastward.

True Bear *felt* him go.

II

✠

Land of Burnt Rocks

[May 1865–December 1873]

THIRTEEN
The Voices of Owls
[May 1865]

SOMETHING WAS WRONG with midmorning stillness—Auna-yi felt wrongness before she thought about it. She was kneeling beside the clear water of Hat Creek, checking wicker traps she'd set in the stream before sunup to catch trout. The gurgling and gentle splashing of the big creek, a dreamy quality of light filtering down through water to a brown-pebbled bottom, lulled her, and her mind drifted—first to the terrible time, those shattering minutes when Dan Clayton and the other Saltus rushed in without warning, out of darkness, thunder of rifle and pistol fire, people screaming and falling everywhere, men and women and little children, almost everyone she'd ever known, and the world turned upside down in the space of a few breaths. Clayton's murder-obsessed face—a mask of hatred and repugnance that would be etched forever upon her consciousness.

Now there were very few of her people left, she and Smoke Woman and Wolf Tracker and the others, a handful only of the villagers escaping, living from day to day, moving all the time, not knowing where they would be or how they'd live when winter came. She flinched from pain of those memories, and thought of another time, a happier time,

remembered kneeling beside the pool at the foot of the
waterfall where she gathered obsidian, when she and True
Bear McCain embraced before the world came apart.

*Will I see you again, True Bear? We thought a month, only
a month. . . . Wolf Tracker says the end has come for us, for
my people, yet I want to see you again. I would be your wife
when the proper time came. . . .*"

Then she felt it, something beyond a murmur of running
water, some indefinable change that made the skin at the
back of her neck cold. She rose, looked around her, saw
nothing, and yet knew there was a difference, some quality of
light or sound changed, an extra measure of silence, perhaps,
an extra clarity in air above this meadow where the creek ran.

A bluejay shrieked, its warning taken up by others, and
Auna-yi became aware of a new sound, a low rumble seeming
to come up from the rocks themselves. Cattle came into sight
around a bend up the canyon, half a dozen animals moving at
a quick walk, all heading with apparent purpose in one direction, not rambling aimlessly as the big red beasts normally
did.

Someone's driving them. Saltus. . . .

She stepped back away from the water and broke into a
run, heading for cover of some trees upslope, but before she
reached them she heard a shrill *Wahoo!* and, looking over
her shoulder, saw a horseman, a flank rider, turning off from
the herd, perhaps thirty cattle altogether, to give chase. She
ran frantically, tears coming to her eyes, her breath painful in
her chest, but the rider overtook her easily, and when she
looked back again, he was pounding down upon her. She
caught a glimpse of a lean, sun-bronzed face, eyes a startling
pale blue, teeth bared white as the horseman laughed, twirl-
ing a loop of rope over his head.

Auna-yi stumbled and fell heavily, breath going out of her,
tried to push herself up to hands and knees, fell forward
again, and only then realized the loop of rope was around
her, holding her arms to her sides, the cowboy pulling the
line taut, backing his pony and laughing loudly.

"Hey, McLaughlin!" he yelled out, "Come see what I've
caught us down here. Little wild heifer, sure as hell. Right
purty one, too."

"Please," she said, her gaze fixed on the stranger's face, the milky eyes. "Please. . . ."

"You speak English?" he asked. "By God. Hey McLaughlin, she talks English."

"How about that!" called a second rider, apparently McLaughlin, cantering up.

This one was older, thicker through the waist and shoulders, but his face narrow, shrewd-eyed, his hair reddish and thin, going gray at the sides. Beyond him Auna-yi could see two others, these staying with the small herd of cattle but staring curiously in her direction, grinning broadly.

"Please," she said, thinking quickly and addressing the newcomer. "Perhaps you can help me. I come from Oidoing-koyo, but I'm lost. Do you know where that is, Benjamin McCain's ranch?"

McLaughlin stared at her, his eyes traveling over her body, lingering at her bare breasts, continuing down over her short bark skirt.

"Naw, you ain't one of McCain's tame Diggers, not dressed like that, you ain't. I figger you for one of the Yahoos, probably one of them that escaped Clayton's little action a couple of months back. Where's the rest of your folks, gal? How'd you learn to talk like a human, anyhow?"

"I . . . told you. I'm alone. I don't live at the McCains' village, you're right, but I know them. If you could take me there, perhaps Benjamin McCain would pay you for helping me."

"Crazy Ben's ranch, you say? Hell, I got no time to be traipsing clear over there," the man replied, his eyes still on her body. "We got cows to take down to Shasta City. Why don't you just tell us where your people are, I'll ride you back to 'em."

"I'm alone. All my people died when the Saltus. . . ."

"Sure you are. Well, we ain't got time to hunt for 'em, neither. Tell you what. You just come along with us to Shasta, and after we get rid of this herd, we'll haul you back to Ben's place right enough. Over close to Chester, ain't it?"

He's lying, of course. The way his eyes look at me—the way a cougar looks at a wounded deer. The other one too. . . .

She felt a cold shiver of fear, repressed it.

"Thank you, Mr. McLaughlin, but I can find my own way,

I suppose. If this man will untie me, I won't bother you any-more."

"Think you better stick with us, Missy," said the pale-eyed one, still grinning broadly. "No telling what might happen to a' purty young thing like you all on her own. We've heard tales of wild Injuns running loose. Damn—you've got some nice little tits there. Young."

"Jake's right," McLaughlin nodded. "Why don't you just slip a few turns of rope around her hands? She can ride with me."

Jake glanced at the man who was apparently his boss, touched the brim of his hat, and dismounted, keeping the rope taut as he approached the girl, then catching her in his arms, one hand traveling over her body, touching her breasts, running up under her skirt to her buttocks, sliding between her legs. She gasped, cried out, kicked at the man. He chuckled again, pressed his mouth roughly against hers, and wrestled her to the ground.

McLaughlin's whip cracked in the air above them, and Jake released her, looking startled.

"None of that, you trail-riding scum," McLaughlin snapped, climbing down from his mount and standing above the two, hand on the butt of his pistol. "I won't have this girl harmed. She's just a pup."

"Want her all for yourself, eh, Weasel?" Jack sneered. "Have it your way, then. You're the boss. Hell, I was just checking her for weapons. Never can tell where one of these wild squaws might be hidin' a hogsticker."

"It's Mr. McLaughlin to you," the other said. "You get on back to those cows, you jackass. It's my business what I do with this young lady."

Jake rose slowly, staring hard at the older man, his hand going to his hat brim again in mock salute, and mounted, tossing the coil of rope down to McLaughlin before he saun-tered back to the other riders, the two men sitting their horses a short distance away and watching, the herd of cattle stopped now and pulling at mouthfuls of grass, unconcerned with this small human drama.

"Just doing this for your own protection, Missy," McLaughlin grunted as he wrapped several loops of rope around her wrists and tied it tightly, cutting the cord with a short length still attached as a lead. "You don't quite trust me, and you're likely to run off and get yourself in trouble again. See, most men you come across, they're going to be like Jake there. A pretty young girl traveling alone and half-naked, well, it's just asking for trouble. You want to survive, you'd best start covering yourself. You stay with me, I'll get you through safe and sound. Here, now you grab onto the saddle horn—that knob there—and stick your foot into the stirrup. I'll give you a boost on up."

The red-haired Saltu half-lifted Auna-yi onto the back of his big bay and swung up behind her, holding the reins in front of her, his body touching her back, his breath unpleasantly warm and damp against her ear.

"You boys move 'em out!" he bellowed to the three grinning cowhands. "I ain't paying you to set around staring like a pack of Goddamned monkeys. Let's get these animals on the trail. We still got a good three days ahead of us."

THEY RODE on through the afternoon, pausing once in a small valley where they rested the animals and ate a cold lunch— an area of green amidst a sage-dotted volcanic jumble of land through which they drove their herd.

They continued then, crossing out of Hat Creek's drainage and camping for the night at the edge of a lava flow, ten miles short of the village of Burney—this by design on McLaughlin's part, since he felt it wise to keep his hands well away from saloons until his thirty head had been safely delivered in Shasta City.

When they halted, the sun was an orange-red blob balanced on the rim of mountains to the west, in a cloudless sky, shadows stretched long from dark clumps of pine and fir that dotted the plain.

Auna-yi almost fell from the saddle when McLaughlin assisted her down. She'd become a good rider while at McCain's ranch, but she had never become accustomed to travel on horseback, and after a long day riding ahead of McLaughlin, she felt as if all her bones were broken, the joints of her hips displaced permanently. Jake and the two other hands set about scrounging deadwood for a fire while McLaughlin secured Auna-yi to a tree, a leash of rope tied about her neck.

*   *   *

WHILE THE EVENING meal was cooking, the men squatted around their fire, drinking coffee, McLaughlin leaving Auna-yi to join them. They were several yards distant from her, and their backs were turned toward her, apparently feeling that in this way they'd effectively screened off their conversation from her, for although they initially spoke in murmurs that were indeed inaudible to her, the tone of their voices rose as they continued. There was obvious discontent among the men, and at length she had no difficulty following every word of the dispute.

"Shit-fire, McLaughlin," Jake said loudly, then glanced around at Auna-yi and lowered his voice, but not enough. "Injun gals ain't worth nothin' in Shasta. Hell, a man can go out in the hills and round up twenty Wintuns anytime he gets the urge."

Auna-yi focused intently on the words, sorting them out as the foreman replied in a softer tone.

"Keep your damned voice down. This one speaks English real good, and in case you jackals haven't noticed, she's a looker. Ain't many like that, no matter what. Probably hasn't even been stuck yet."

"I noticed," said another, a sandy-haired individual with a sullen mouth, one who looked to be no more than two or three years older than Auna-yi herself. "I damned well noticed you droolin' down her neck all day. Tomorrow, how about you chase cows, an' I take the little squaw with me?"

"You forget who's workin' for who, Jonesy? I already said it, but I'll say it again. I don't want the damned girl touched. She'll fetch us a good price in Shasta, but not if she looks like she's been had by a trail gang. You boys are gonna get a nice bonus out of this, believe me."

"I'd rather take my bonus now," Jake said. "Maybe it's better to put a bullet in her—after we've all had a turn. You're asking for trouble, McLaughlin. Ain't you heard they outlawed slavery?"

"Shit, not for Injuns, they didn't. But I'm not *slavin'* anybody. Just takin' a fee as her agent, so to speak. You be a little bit patient, an' you boys will get enough extra out of this to hire two or three ladies at the best fancy house in Shasta."

"Likely, McLaughlin. I trust you about as far as I can

throw a yearling bull. Like you say, you're the boss, but we'll
be watching real careful, Weasel."

"Goddamn it, Jonesy, you fuzz-faced bastard, you know my
name. It's *Westley*, not *Weasel*. You watch it, or you'll end
up yelping back home with a load of birdshot in your tail, so
help me. . . ."

As she listened, Auna-yi worked silently at the knots binding her wrists. *Slavery.* She tried to remember what Ben
McCain had said on the subject—something to do with that
great war among the Saltus, a war that was supposed to make
it *illegal*—another fuzzy term—for people to own other people. But this Saltu, McLaughlin, clearly intended to sell her
to some Whiteman in the place called Shasta City.

*They hate us in the Saltu villages. Smoke Woman and Wolf
Tracker, they must have found the tracks by now—must
think I'm dead. I should have listened to them, shouldn't have
gone off by myself. My mother, I'm sorry. . . .*

McLaughlin came over with a plateful of food, beans boiled
with chunks of fat bacon. He untied her hands and then sat
beside her as she ate. She kept her head down and her eyes
averted as she silently spooned up her food. She was ravenously hungry but found it difficult to swallow, partly because
of the pressure of the noose against her throat, but more
because the food seemed to stick against a knot inside—this
knot compounded of grief and fear and anger.

"You sure are a quiet little critter," McLaughlin said after a
time.

Auna-yi glanced at him, her eyes hard, then dropped her
gaze back down to the plate in her lap. The red-haired
rancher looked over at the men near the fire, then reached
out a thick, heavily calloused finger and stroked it down her
cheek. The girl jerked her head back and shot him a look of
pure hatred.

"No cause to be that way, Gal," he said. "I'm the one who
saved your little tail-end from these cowpokes, remember?"

Auna-yi continued to stare at him in warning, then scooped
up another spoonful of beans, chewed, gagged, swallowed.

"Bet you heard what we was saying over there. That's it,
ain't it? You really figure I'm going to sell you in Shasta?
Hell, that's just what I was sayin' to keep those horny damned
coyotes off of you. Once we get to town where there's firewa-

ter and fancy women, those three are gonna forget all about
you, the way I figure it. Then I'll take you on back to
McCain's place, if that's where you want to go. But maybe by
then you'll want to stay with me. I'll take real good care of
you. What's your name, anyhow? Look, I ain't got a wife, you
don't need to worry about that. I'll treat you just like a White
lady—pretty clothes, anything you want. You look like you're
part-White anyway, as a matter of fact. Halfbreed, eh? You
sure are a pretty little thing, you know that. Just call me
Wes. We'll get along real good."

He stroked at her hair, the back of his hand brushing
across her breast as it moved down the black braid. She
stared into his eyes, small and murky blue, the lashes sparse,
pinkish. His expression, she thought, was both avaricious and
falsely self-effacing, half-hopeful, half-greedy and cruel, dog-
like. She spat, started to laugh as his face froze in surprise
and then twisted to quick fury, the drop of saliva sliding
down one cheek.

He wiped his face, then backhanded her, his arm lashing
out with astounding speed and force. Auna-yi fell to one side,
the noose bringing her up short and choking her so that for
an agonizing moment she couldn't breathe as she struggled to
right herself.

"Thought you didn't want her bashed up?"

Jake stood over them, thumbs hooked in belt loops, his
face noncommittal. Jonesy was beside him, and just behind
stood the third hand, dark haired and with a dirty-looking
growth of whiskers ringing a red mouth.

"Now that you gone an' ruined her marketability, we might
as well. . . ."

McLaughlin was on his feet, Colt Paterson in hand.

"You bastards back off," he snapped, then turned on the
girl in fury. "See what you've done, you dumb bitch? Back off
now, Goddamn it, Jake!"

The men retreated, laughing among themselves, and
McLaughlin knelt beside Auna-yi again.

"All right, you damned little wildcat," he said. "Have it
your way. Afraid I'm going to have to tie you up tighter for
the night."

Auna-yi sat quietly, her heart still pounding with fright.
For a few moments, as the men ringed her, their eyes shin-

ing, she thought she was to be torn to pieces, raped and beaten and left bleeding where she lay. She saw now that McLaughlin, however much she distrusted him, was the only thing standing between herself and the savagery of the other men.

"I'm sorry," she whispered as he snugged the rope around her wrists again, this time behind her back, then ran a cord from wrists to noose, this still fastened to the pine tree behind her.

McLaughlin grunted, and tossed a blanket over her.

"Try to get some sleep," he said. "Got a long haul ahead of us. Come on, now, what the hell's your name? You got one or not?"

She stared at him, uncertain whether to answer.

"Auna-yi," she whispered. "It means 'Fire Woman.' "

Westley McLaughlin nodded.

"Fits your damned disposition," he said. "I like the Injun name better. Anna. Well, you act decent, we'll get along just fine."

THE CAMP QUIETED, the three hands pitching their bedrolls near the fire, McLaughlin lying down close to Auna-yi, his blankets between her and the cowboys, pistol at hand. Auna-yi lay uneasily, ropes biting her flesh, and after a few minutes her arms began to ache intolerably from the strain of her position. She shifted, trying unsuccessfully to get more comfortable. Cold seeped into her bones from the hard ground, and a breeze stirred the needles in the tree above her. Beyond that, stars glittered in blue-black sky, while somewhere off across the flats coyotes sang, thin notes like bands of quivering light out in the darkness.

She dozed despite her discomfort, but awoke with McLaughlin breathing into her ear, one calloused palm rubbing at her breasts. She gave a gasp and struggled to sit up.

"Easy, now, Anna. Why don't you try bein' nice to me for a change?" he whispered. "I don't want to hurt you, Gal, just want to have a little fun. You might even figure out you like it."

Must not cry out. The others. . . .

"Wait, McLaughlin," she whispered, trying to make her voice sound seductive. "Maybe you're right, Wes. . . . But how can I make love with you when I'm all tied up this way? Unfasten my hands, at least. You'll like what I can do with my hands."

The man hesitated, then kissed her, forcing his tongue into her mouth. She relaxed, tried to mimic the movements of his mouth with her own, made her breath come in short gasps the way Yahi women did. Once she had crouched outside Broken Willow's brush lodge, listened as she and Salmon Man. . . .

"You promise to be good? No tricks now, damn it. I really like you, Anna."

"No tricks, I promise. Perhaps I like you too, Wes McLaughlin. . . ."

"What the hell? Not much you can do, anyway."

He fumbled at the knots for a moment, then with a gesture of impatience he drew a knife and slashed the rope. His eyes glittered with starlight as he pulled her to him once more, cupping her buttocks and pressing his belly against her. She chafed at her wrists, then slid one hand down to his groin, squeezed softly. Broken Willow had told her about that. He sucked in a breath, tried to push her legs apart.

"No. My neck," she whispered against his ear. "I'm choking. . . ."

He drew back a little, stared at her, his face a white blur, and then he sliced through the lead rope, tossing his knife carefully away to the far side of the blankets. Auna-yi watched, then moved her hand to his crotch again, working at the buttons.

"Now," she whispered. "Wes, I want you to lie with me now."

She saw the flash of his teeth as he grinned, then knelt above her, holding her shoulders pinned as he pushed one leg between hers, shifted his weight to move her other leg. She pulled her knee up hard, felt the give of soft flesh, and then she was up as he crouched forward, heaving for breath.

She found the knife on his blanket, slashed at him as he came toward her again, and then she was running blindly, no idea of direction, darker clumps of sagebrush against barely visible earth, branches scraping painfully at her legs, dark presence of lava rock close by. She stumbled, caught herself, and ran again, struggling over uneven ground. She heard a question mumbled into the night, one of the hands half-waking at the commotion, heard McLaughlin's reply—*God damned coyotes after our grub.*

She kept running, pulse throbbing in her ears, breath coming hard in ragged, half-sobbed inhalations.

Then she was down, sprawled on her face, knife flying out of her hand and clattering against stone. The man was on top of her, panting against her neck, arms clutched around her waist. She wanted to cry out but couldn't, couldn't seem to find air.

"Damned little hellion," he hissed. "You don't want to do it the easy way, eh? All right, then. I'll get you tamed down. Be still, now. You want the other three as well?"

He pulled her hips up, rough, sandy soil grating against her skin. One hand fumbled at her breasts for a moment, pinching the nipples, moved down, probed her private parts, and then he was thrusting at her, dry and hard.

Pain, tearing something inside. It hurts. My first time. . . . This is not the way it should be. . . . True Bear, forgive me, this isn't what I wanted. . . .

Her face was wet—tears or blood, she didn't know. Her head was turned to one side and she could see the horizon, black and jagged against swarms of stars. Pain continued as he pounded against her, but growing less, growing distant. He grunted as he moved, like a man doing hard physical labor, and she had a momentary mad impulse to laugh. She saw the quick arc of a falling star.

That means someone has died, a soul is moving to the other world. Who is it? Who has died? My mother, this is how I was conceived. You told me that story. It comes full circle, then. . . .

IT WAS OVER.

The man gave a final groan and collapsed momentarily against her, withdrawing, turning her over now and kissing her on the mouth, stroking her breasts and laughing softly.

"Still feel like fighting, Anna? By God, Missy, you're all right, even if you are a ball-cutter. Be tempted to keep you myself, but I don't think I can afford the wear and tear. Little more of this taming and gentling and you'll make somebody a right decent little lady's maid, you will, yet. Hell, I'll even throw in a few more lessons for free."

Auna-yi sat up wearily and let him tie the rope around her wrists again. She watched as if from a great distance as he went on laughing and gloating. Nothing seemed to be of any great importance.

Tears, she thought, *it is only tears on my face, not blood. I'm not hurt very much, no, hardly hurt at all.*

Crickets sang in the sage, while far off in the vast and star-encrusted darkness a horned owl called a question, and after a few moments another answered.

Beautiful. The night is very beautiful with the voices of owls. I listen to them talking. I almost understand what they're saying. What are they saying?

FOURTEEN
Sold to Hank Bitler
[June 1865]

SHE RODE *a horse the color of flame, the mane hissing and giving off sparks where it touched her fingers. True Bear galloped beside her, and on the other side Ooti, seated on a charging grizzly, dark hair streaming out behind her, a lance in one hand, a pistol in the other. Before them was a city of the Saltus, lodges like great stone monoliths towering to the sky—and thousands of White men pouring out, all armed and firing at the three riders, but she was not afraid.*

"I am Auna-yi," she shouted, her voice issuing from her throat in a roar, "my name is Fire Woman, and I am here to burn your village."

A man reached for her, grinning, and she recognized his pale eyes. She stretched out her hand, and flames leaped from her fingers. She laughed as the man fell, blazing like a star. More came at them until they were surrounded by a sea of white faces—some she recognized from the burning of her village, others she did not know. Ooti fired her pistol and one fell, his head dissolving into smoke. Together she and Ooti and True Bear fought the Saltus, who kept coming in waves and falling, burning, smoke rising in dense black clouds until everything was obscured.

Suddenly she realized she was alone, utterly alone, Ooti gone, True Bear gone. She couldn't see anything, and then McLaughlin walked toward her, unbuttoning his trousers and grinning. His manhood was a knife, the blade glittering against surrounding darkness.

"You don't want to have it the easy way, eh? All right, then."

She stretched her hand toward him, saw flame leap out. He hissed like fat melting into a cookfire, still smiling as his face twisted, blackened.

"Better be careful where you point that, Missy," he said, and then the clouds parted, and she saw that behind him was her village, the people all on fire, women and little children running frantically about and screaming, screaming. Yes, and with them Benjamin McCain and Ooti and True Bear. True Bear's mouth opened, he was trying to tell her something, his eyes pleading, even accusing.

"No!" she sobbed. "I didn't do this terrible thing. I didn't mean. . . . True Bear, I can't hear what you're saying. Please. . . ."

She reached out to embrace him, but when she touched him, he also burst into flame, his hair blazing around his head, fire dripping from his mouth as he struggled to speak words she couldn't hear.

*   *   *

AUNA-YI SAT UP, heart pounding heavily and face slick with
tears. It was quiet and dark, and for a moment she couldn't
remember where she was. No, not completely dark, not
completely quiet. Across from her a little square of dim light
and a distant noise of voices, laughter, occasional cries from
cattle and horses, rumbling of wagons.

Shasta City, she remembered, *the Saltu village. And
I'm locked in this room—McLaughlin paid the big, yellow-
haired Saltu woman money to make sure I couldn't get away.*

She rose from a narrow iron cot, the contraption screeching
as she released her weight from it. She moved to the window, looked down three stories to a street below, still busy
even now, well after dark. Gaslights burned on posts in front
of the buildings, and shone onto the dusty street, a knot of
men in boots and hats, laughing loudly as they passed from
one saloon to another, a tinkle of spurs barely audible to the
girl. Horses stood patiently, heads down, tied to porch rails
and hitching posts, and a small, single-seated buggy drove
past, the man holding the reins dressed in black and wearing
a tall hat.

There was still no way out, Auna-yi realized wearily for
perhaps the tenth time since McLaughlin left her there many
hours before, when the sun was still some distance above the
horizon, just after they'd ridden into town. He sent Jake and
Jonesy and the other hand ahead to the stockyard with the
cattle, and then he brought her to this tall Saltu dwelling. He
spoke to a woman who sat at a desk in a big room with red
walls and mirrors, a woman with a pink face and hair the
color and texture of grass in midsummer. She was as tall as he
and a good bit heavier, as Auna-yi noted when she rose. This
woman, whom McLaughlin called Maude, took her to another room, one with a big, scoop-shaped tub, and watched
the girl as she bathed, McLaughlin explaining to her that
he'd be just outside the door in case "the little savage gets a
fool notion to bolt."

"You're a pretty one, Honey, even though you ain't got
much meat on you," Maude said as Auna-yi undressed, removing the faded blue flannel shirt and canvas britches
McLaughlin had given her. "You could make good money
staying right here and working for me, but it's up to you. I

don't believe in keepin' gals here if they don't want to be.
Bad for business in the long run."

With a shudder of pleasure, Auna-yi settled into the warm
water. It felt wonderful after long days of having her bones
pounded by McLaughlin's horse, her body growing gritty
with dust and unpleasantly sticky with her own perspiration
and that of McLaughlin and his horse as well. The big blonde
woman seemed kind, her bright red mouth smiling, little
lines of laughter at the corners of her eyes. Auna-yi thought
perhaps she might, indeed, wish to stay in this place, although she didn't understand why the woman had suggested
it.

"What would I do? Do you need a servant, someone to
clean and cook? I can do those things."

Maude threw her head back and laughed.

"Not exactly, Angel-face. You're a young one, ain't you?"

"You mean that the women lie down with men who pay
them money?" she asked when Maude had explained further.
"I have heard of such a thing, but I wasn't sure it was true."

"Law of supply and demand, Sweetie. Women are still
scarce in these parts. So what do you say?"

Auna-yi shook her head, remembering with a shiver
McLaughlin's thick body on top of her, the smell of him, the
pain.

"Have it your way," the woman said cheerfully. "If you
change your mind, I'll probably still be right here. But I'll
warn you—Big Wes has it in mind to make some money out
of you—tradin' you to some damned cowboy, and chances are
you'll end up doing it for nothing and not liking it any better.
You take care of yourself now, you hear? And remember, the
offer's still open."

Maude gave her a Whitewoman's dress, a pretty yellow
cotton with ruffles around the high, scooped neck, and after
that McLaughlin took her to the room.

"By God, it's tempting," he grinned. "Real tempting. We
probably won't get another chance to play, pretty Anna. Aw,
hell, I just got you all cleaned up, and there's business to tend
to. Maybe another time, then. Could be I'll see you again. . . ."

He kissed her on the mouth, ran his hand up under her
long skirt, grunted, and left, the key rattling in the door as he
locked her into the small room.

*   *   *

SHE CONTINUED now to stare into the street. Even if she
could manage somehow to climb down three stories to the
earth, she'd still be in the White town, surrounded by strangers who seemed to enjoy killing her people, and even then
she wasn't sure she could find her way back to the place where
the cattlemen had stolen her away from Wolf Tracker's little
band. She thought again of Maude's offer, but rejected it with
a quick shake of her head.

"I must be patient," she thought. "I must wait. I'll find a
way back to my people, to Smoke Woman and Wolf Tracker."

*Perhaps even to you, True Bear McCain, although you
may not want me now that the Saltu McLaughlin has had
me. . . .*

She leaned her forehead against the glass, swallowing hard
to fight off tears. A wagon rattled along the street, a big,
square buckboard drawn by a pair of mules and loaded with
crates and sacks. Auna-yi recognized Westley McLaughlin
sitting up on the seat beside the driver.

The rig stopped in front of the building. The two men
climbed down from the buckboard and disappeared beneath
an overhang. Auna-yi drew a quick breath, turned away from
her window, and stood tensely facing the door, awaiting the
rattle of a key in the lock.

*So that's the man Weasel McLaughlin has sold me to,
she thought. What is he like? Taller than Wes, dark clothes.
What else? Nothing. He walks oddly, a limp? Perhaps an old
injury? If he tries to touch me, I'll kill him. Maybe I'll kill
him anyway.*

My name is Fire Woman, I am here to burn your village. . . .

McLaughlin was red-faced and chuckling when he entered,
a candle in one hand, using the other to slap the stranger's
shoulder heartily as he stood aside to let him pass. A strong
odor of whiskey entered with the men.

"There she is, by God. Told you she was a beauty, now
didn't I? Didn't I tell you that? Anna, honey, this here's my
good pal Frank—uh—Butler. You're gonna get along fine,
jus' fine, ain't she Frank?"

McLaughlin winked and grinned as he stepped toward a
small table next to the cot to put the candle down. He

stumbled against furniture and sat noisily on the creaking
bed, laughing as if he'd done something remarkably clever.

"It's Bitler, Ma'am, Hank Bitler. Well, I'm pleased to meet
you, Miss Anna," the stranger said, ignoring McLaughlin's
antics and fumbling with his hands, beginning to hold one out
as if in greeting and then moving it instead to the brim of his
battered black felt hat, which he first tipped to the girl and
then removed entirely.

"Din't I tell you she's a looker, eh, din't I now?" Mc-
Laughlin insisted.

"That's what you said, all right, but to be truthful, I didn't
believe you until now. I don't know that Eleanor's going to
take all that well to Miss Anna here. She's a fine woman, my
Eleanor, but a trifle insecure."

"Hell with Eleanor, eh Frank? Woman does what her man
tells her, way I see it. Eleanor'll get over it. I bet *you* like
little Anna jus' fine, eh?"

Bitler shook his head and made a sucking sound through
his teeth.

"You ain't got anybody—well—a little more on the ordinary side, do you Wes? This one's not much more than a
kid—and a halfbreed from the looks of her."

"What you think I am, a Goddamn slaver? Hell, no. Just
found this little gal over by Hat Crick, no family or nothin',
and I thought, this little gal needs a place to stay, prob'ly
somebody down here could use a maid or somethin'. Jus'
tryin' to help out all parties. Look, Frank, you don' want her,
I'll go talk to somebody else. Quite a few men around that
ain't gonna object none to the way she looks, by Gawd!"

"I'm not objecting. Hell, probably Eleanor would like a
pretty young face to brighten things up. You say she speaks
good English?"

"Real good. Say somethin' for Frank, here, Anna."

Auna-yi didn't respond. She continued to stand with her
back against the wall, next to the window, as far away from
the two men as it was possible to get while she assessed the
stranger. He was indeed taller than Wes McLaughlin, but
also considerably thinner. The face was long-jawed, with
deep vertical grooves around the mouth, and burned red-
brown by sun, except for a narrow band of white visible
below the hairline when he removed his hat. His clothes

were nondescript—baggy, dark brown coat to below the knees, battered black hat, heavy, low-heeled boots rather than the high-heeled, narrow-toed kind McLaughlin and his men wore. For some reason Auna-yi found this reassuring, and she thought the man's face looked kind, although he didn't smile, his expression friendly but cautious, his eyes steady, intelligent.

"Well, I gotta tell you the truth—she's a little bit on the moody side at times," McLaughlin went on when Auna-yi continued to watch without speaking. "But I guarantee you she talks English just fine. And she's real healthy, still a virgin, I reckon, although I gotta admit I was tempted, ha ha." McLaughlin nudged the other man with his elbow. "Look, Frank, you want to try her out, get acquainted so to speak, why I got this room for the whole night. You're welcome to use it. Anna, why don't you slip out of that dress, let the man see what he's gettin'?"

Auna-yi stared steadily at Hank Bitler.

If you touch me I will kill you. . . .

"No," Bitler said with sudden decision. "The young lady will do just fine. Miss Anna, my business in town is finished, and I'll be heading back to Goose Lake right away. Are you all set to go?"

"My name is not Anna," she said.

"Well. I'm sorry, then. What is your name?"

"Auna-yi. It means 'Fire Woman.' "

"All right. You need to pack some things? I can wait."

The girl still didn't move, continued to study him.

"Look, miss, if you don't want to go with me, I won't force you. I fought on the side of the Confederacy for a time, but I'm no slave-trader."

"I have nothing to pack, Hank Bitler. I'll go with you," Auna-yi said and stepped to the door.

"WELL, ma'am, you're not the sort to talk a man's ear off, I'll say that for you."

Auna-yi glanced sideways at Hank Bitler on the high seat of the buckboard next to her. He was looking straight ahead over the rumps of his long-eared mules, tending to his driving as they came down a long grade from Hatchet Mountain Pass, but the corner of his wide, rather mournful-looking mouth was twitched up in a halfhearted grin, and when he turned his head briefly and winked at her, she couldn't resist returning the smile.

"Look, you want to crawl in the back and sleep some more, it's all right with me. I know I kept us both up pretty late last night, travelin' until 'most dawn. I guess I just don't take to towns much. Soon as I'm in one, I start gettin' itchy to 'shake the dust,' if you know what I mean."

"No, I don't know, exactly. I'm not sleepy, though."

"Well, that's good, that's good. I'm not really in a mood to keep myself company. Biblical expression, I believe. Shake the dust from your feet, something of the sort."

"Biblical. From the Bible? The Saltus' Medicine Book?" Auna-yi nodded. 'I've read some of that, though I can't read very well yet."

"For a fact? Well, you're a young lady of surprising accomplishment. Did you get hooked up with some missionaries, or what?"

"No. Benjamin McCain taught it to me."

"Ben McCain. I've heard of him. Great big man, rides a plow horse. Some folks call him Crazy Ben. Lots of stories about him, and a few hard feelings, I'd guess. He really keep a whole Indian village on his place?"

"Yes. His wife is Maidu. She is. . . ."

Auna-yi broke off abruptly.

Ooti, Acorn Woman, warrior woman of the Pano Maidus, riding against the Saltus, her hair streaming behind her like a banner, two grizzly bears shambling along beside her.

Hank Bitler cast a quick glance at the girl, studying her for a moment as if he'd read her mind.

"Yeah. I've heard some stories about the two of them would as make your hair stand on end. I don't put much credence in gossip, though. Folks are prone to envy and wild speculation, especially about them whose habits are a little different from the ordinary."

Auna-yi bit at her lips and studied the landscape around her. They had rounded the shoulder of a mountain, and she could see Burney Plain below, dotted with sagebrush and stands of pine, the same valley across which she had passed with McLaughlin and his men two days previously. Above the plain a big bird drifted, vulture or perhaps eagle, playing on currents of air and roughly at a level with them, although too distant for her to see the bird's color against blue sky.

She thought, *I nearly told this Saltu stranger about Ooti. How could I have done such a thing? This man seems to have some magic that makes me want to talk to him. Careful, be careful.*

"That's fine, though," Bitler said when he determined she was not going to reply to his last remarks, "excellent, about you having an acquaintance with the Good Book. Eleanor— Mrs. Bitler—she's pretty strong on religion. Good bit stronger than me, truth to tell. Well, I figure she can pester old St. Pete into lettin' me through the Pearly Gates if anybody can. That is, if she's feelin' kindly disposed toward me when the time comes. Never know in advance with Eleanor. You a Christian, Miss Oona-ee? I get your name right that time?"

Auna-yi detected a flicker of mirth at the corner of Bitler's mouth again. She followed very little of what he was saying, but she smiled in response to his smile.

"Not exactly."

"Not exactly what? You mean about the name, or about bein' a Christian?"

"Both. I meant about the name, but I'm not a Christian, either. I don't really know what that means, except most White people say they are, I suppose, and it has something to do with the Medicine Book and a god who lets men torture him to death. Even McLaughlin said he was Christian. Benjamin McCain tried to explain it to me. . . ."

Bitler laughed abruptly.

"Not sure I know much more of what it's about myself. Don't let on to Eleanor, though. She's a mite touchy on the subject. Was you one of McCain's Injuns, or what?"

Auna-yi did not answer. Instead she studied Bitler's face, saw lines of weariness beneath the flicker of humor when he spoke of *Eleanor. He doesn't really like his wife,* she thought, *or perhaps he's afraid of her. Yes, I've seen that among my own people.*

She remembered Painted Duck, who was plump and pretty but had a very sharp tongue, and her husband, Smoking Rock, who usually said very little for fear of offending his wife, except for a few times when he felt he'd endured more than his pride could bear, and then he'd beat her ferociously.

Dead, both dead. Now she wondered if this man Bitler
sometimes beat his Eleanor.

Bitler glanced at her with a trace of uneasiness, chuckled.

"You got a way of looking right through a person, Miss
Ona-eye."

"I'm sorry. I know it's rude to stare."

"That's all right. I'd give a heap to know what you were
thinking, though."

Now Auna-yi shifted about uncomfortably on her seat.

"I wasn't thinking of anything, really. I'm afraid your wife
may not like me."

"Don't you worry about that, ma'am. She'll like you once
she gets to know you—be like havin' a daughter, sort of. I
figure I can grease the goose for you a little. We've been
married for twenty years, now, and I've learned a few things
to get along."

Auna-yi nodded, but she wasn't entirely convinced by Bitler's
assertion. She'd seen that weary, resigned look come back
into the lines on his forehead.

THE TRIP to Bitler's ranch in a valley at the foot of the Warner
Range on the eastern shore of Goose Lake took three days.
They followed Pit River after winding through the Adin Hills
to the northeast of Big Valley, and Hank Bitler kept up an
intermittent flow of conversation as they traveled, this interspersed with songs and occasional bits of rhyme. There were
also long periods of comfortable silence in which both rancher
and Yahi girl soaked in the vast, ringing silence of the wide,
dry land they were crossing—until Auna-yi at times felt as if
either she, herself, had shrunk to a point and ceased to exist,
or perhaps her being had expanded until she was as vast and
diffuse as the blue and mirage-haunted distance.

During the journey's course, Auna-yi had learned a good
deal about the man whose home she was apparently to share
now for an indeterminate time. She had also learned to trust
as well as to like Hank Bitler. Although he was invariably
courtly, she was certain he was attracted to her—even though
he made no attempt in all the time they were alone together
either to seduce her or to take her by force—a fact which
caused her some puzzlement as well as relief.

"You're about as much White as you are Indian, aren't you

Ona?" he asked as they sat beside their cooking fire for a few minutes before retiring, Hank Bitler smoking a long, curved pipe, and Auna-yi sipping at a cup of dark, heavily sweetened coffee, a beverage she'd developed a taste for at McCain's place.

She glanced across at him, her eyes points of yellow firelight.

"My mother was raped by a Saltu rancher at a time when the Whites killed many of our people," she said. "I cannot help what is in my blood."

Bitler coughed, poked a twig at the ashes in his pipe bowl.

"Didn't mean to stick my nose in," he said. "I'm sorry."

Auna-yi nodded, sipped silently at her coffee.

"There's plenty of things about my own kind I'll never figure out," Bitler said, staring off into darkness beyond the circle of firelight. "One reason I came out here, to get away from the insanity. Had a place back in Missouri before the war. Raised horses, real fine horses. When things started heating up, folks around there were about fifty-fifty. It got bitter, nasty, to the point where fellows who'd been friends one day were ready to lynch each other the next. I wasn't even sure which side I came down on. All I wanted to do was raise my animals. Abolitionists burned me out the first time, set fire to my barn and shot a half-dozen of my best stock. After we rebuilt, I decided I was a reb, and I went off to fight Yankees. They burned us out again while I was gone. Then the damned Confederates requisitioned all my stock—that's military talk for *stole*—and set fire to my fields so there wouldn't be anything for the other side to requisition. That's when I decided it wasn't my war anyhow. I just walked away after a battle—figured they'd never miss me among all the dead. I walked home and packed up Eleanor and Tod—that's my boy—and headed west. I thought I could get away from the craziness by heading out to where the people were a little less thick. Turns out you can't really get away from nothing, I guess."

The pipe had gone out, and Bitler sucked at it several times before lighting a stick in the fire and applying the glowing end to the bowl. The lines around his mouth were elongated, sad, and Auna-yi had a momentary impulse to reach out to the man and stroke his face, cradle his head against her. Instead she spoke softly, apologetically.

"Benjamin McCain tried to teach me about the war between the Eastern Whites, but I didn't pay much attention.
I'm afraid I don't understand it very well. . . ."

"Not much to understand, I reckon. Logic doesn't have a
lot to do with most human action. You learn to live with that.
I'm sorry for Eleanor, though. I don't think she ever quite
forgave me for making her leave Missouri, bad as things was.
Well, you know—kin and friends and all. She had notions of
being a gentlewoman. War or no war, she blames me for
taking her away from civilization. My boy too, I'm afraid.
He's more hers than mine. Well, in a way they're right. It
was my fault. . . ."

THE WEATHER held fair, sky faultless blue, for the first part of
the trip, but late in the afternoon of the third day a thunder-
storm overtook them—great piles of cumulus forming above
the eastern mountain and moving over them with astonishing
speed, air suddenly growing dark and then flowering with a
great stalk of lightning, a crash of thunder following almost
instantly, and torrents of rain mixed with stinging hailstones
descended.

Hank Bitler pulled his wagon into the slight shelter of a
stand of creek alders. The two humans crouched beneath the
wagon for a time, but when the weather showed no signs of
letting up, he rigged a shelter from a canvas tarp, tying one
end of it to the rim of the buckboard and pegging the other to
the ground.

Auna-yi insisted they must have a fire, and, against Bitler's
objections, darted out and upslope from the river, quickly
gathering dead wood and sage despite the downpour. Bitler
came after her, calling her crazy, but when she couldn't be
persuaded to come back into the shelter until she had loaded
her arms with damp combustibles, he joined her.

"It's not going to burn anyway, you capricious female critter," he said, following her back into the doubtful shelter of a
rain-soaked tarp.

"Why do you think my name is Fire Woman?" she said,
grinning into his eyes as she piled twigs together at the
opening of their makeshift tent. She was out of breath, her
face slick and shining with wetness, her hair and clothing
plastered against her.

"Got 'big medicine,' do ye? Well, I don't think it's going to be potent enough for this," he laughed. "We'll try some Whiteman's magic."

Bitler pulled out a powder horn from under his coat and sprinkled a quantity over the damp sage, then struck flint and steel. The powder hissed into quick, sputtering flame, and a few twigs caught. Auna-yi crouched and blew repeatedly, nursing the small blaze, adding twigs, intent on her job.

Bitler sat back on his heels and watched her, still smiling, until she looked up. Their eyes met, and Auna-yi saw his expression change as they continued to look steadily at one another, the lines around his mouth softening, his face suddenly appearing youthful, eager. He touched softly at one of her cheeks, then drew her into an embrace, and kissed her, his lips touching first at her mouth, then her eyelids, her throat. Auna-yi didn't resist as his hands traveled down her sides, over the curve of her hips.

But Bitler drew away then, holding her shoulders and giving her a kiss on the forehead.

"I'm sorry," he murmured. "It won't happen again, I promise. You looked so. . . ."

"Why are you sorry?" she asked, puzzled. "I wondered why you didn't try to make love to me, like McLaughlin did. I thought you wanted to."

He drew her tightly against him in another embrace, then released her with a little push.

"Young enough to be my own daughter, that's part of it. No. You tend to your fire, Fire Woman," he smiled. "Don't tempt me beyond my feeble capacity."

Auna-yi knelt and blew on the embers of the little blaze, nursed it back to life, added larger pieces of wood, filled a coffee pot with water and set it to boil once the fire was crackling healthily.

Neither of the two spoke for some time.

"There is one to whom I promised my heart," the girl said at length. "Yet when you touched me—I wanted you to go on holding me. But if we had lain down together in the way of man and woman, I would have felt that I had torn my own heart in pieces, for I love this other one. Is that how it is for you also, Hank Bitler?"

"Not exactly," he said, staring into the flames. "But close

enough, I guess. More like, where I was raised, if you make a promise, you keep it. I'm a married man, and there doesn't seem to be any help for it."

Auna-yi studied his face for several moments, then dropped her eyes and nodded, still troubled in her own mind.

They went to sleep with rain drumming on the canvas above them, although the storm diminished somewhat after nightfall. Auna-yi dreamed that True Bear embraced her as Hank Bitler had done.

But when they lay down together, and she had closed her eyes, she realized that what she clasped in her arms was icy cold, repugnant. She opened her eyes, saw the corpse of a dead Whiteman lying between them, the flesh of the face half eaten away by scavengers, eyes blank and ragged holes in their sockets. She knew, somehow, that the dead Saltu was her own father, his identity still unknown to her, although what was left of his face resembled Westley McLaughlin's. She cried out to True Bear, but he was walking way, weeping, his chest torn open and bleeding, the heart visible and beating but in two separate halves.

She awoke with a sob of horror and guilt, and felt tears on her face. She could hear Hank Bitler breathing regularly in sleep, realized then that the rain had stopped, the night utterly still.

It crossed her mind that she might simply get up and walk away. She'd go south, and soon she would come within view of Wahgalu Mountain. . . .

FIFTEEN

A Right Decent Little Lady's Maid
[May–July 1865]

HANK BITLER DROVE his wagon along the main street of the White settlement of Alturas and on northward, continuing to follow Pit River, the road winding over formations of reddish rock dotted with sagebrush and junipers.

The sun was just past midpoint when they came to the southern tip of a wide, shallow sheet of water Bitler identified as Goose Lake. Light glittered on the surface, and as they drew near in the creaking, rumbling wagon, a flock of big birds appeared as if by magic, geese rising up out of brilliant water, wings beating wildly and cries issuing from long, outstretched throats.

Auna-yi caught her breath as the long, laboring wings passed nearly directly overhead, shadows crossing her face, and then, picking up altitude and speed, the creatures executed a half-circle against the sun and disappeared up the lake northward.

Beautiful. The world is so beautiful. We're the only ones who don't quite fit, never seem to be happy.

Yet in spite of her troubled feelings, memory of the previous night's dream kept returning to her, and she couldn't help responding to her surroundings with a little surge of pleasure, a physical sensation of joy that had nothing to do with reason.

Bitler abruptly broke into a loud chorus of "Sweet Betsy From Pike," grinned at her apologetically, and continued with his song.

They continued along the eastern shore, passing a few scattered ranch houses and hugging the foot of the mountains, and at some indeterminate point Bitler stopped his buckboard and pointed in a sweeping gesture to the north and east.

"My land starts here," he said, "four sections in all. Another half hour and we'll be at the house."

Auna-yi looked around her, but could see nothing to mark any boundary.

"How do you know this is where your land begins?"

"Does a bear know his den?"

"It's a very large den," she said, thinking: *Crazy in the way of all Whites, even Ben McCain, thinking they own the land when they only live on top of it, just like anyone else.*

They began to see cattle in twos and threes, and small aimless herds, shortly before Bitler turned onto a pair of wagon tracks leading up a draw away from the lake and into the mountains, passing soon through a post-and-wire gate across the road, several strands hooked to rough, hand-hewn split cedar rails and fastened with a loop at the top to the fenceline. Then they crossed over a low rise, and below were the ranch buildings, a sizeable frame house, a not-quite-finished barn, and several log outbuildings set in a beautiful green valley sloping up to a steep canyon with mountains rising behind, pine ridges on two sides, and a stream flowing through the center. In a large fenced pasture below the house, twenty or more horses and a pair of gawky colts grazed, all of them slender, long-legged creatures that looked as if they belonged to another, more elegant world than this.

"I still keep my hand in with a little breeding," Bitler said, mouth barely smiling but eyes glowing. "Cattle are the mainstay in this country, though. What do you think of it?"

"McCain's place is nicer," she said, her face straight.

Bitler turned to her, his expression one of disbelief and disappointment, and Auna-yi couldn't keep from smiling. He understood, then, and laughed, the two of them laughing together like conspirators, each sending the other off into fresh fits of mirth.

Bitler was roaring "Sweet Betsy From Pike" again when they rolled down the hill to the house.

A WOMAN EMERGED, and stood with hands folded beneath an apron and face set as she watched them approach.

Bitler broke off his song immediately, and glanced at Auna-yi, nodding.

"That's her," he said, his voice becoming apprehensive. "Just remember what I told you, now. You'll get along fine."

For most of the morning Hank had coached her on how to behave with Eleanor, had described the woman in a dozen different and conflicting ways—so that Auna-yi had mentally prepared herself for anything from a thin, pale-complexioned invalid to a great, brawny harridan wielding a butcher knife. What she was not ready for was a pretty woman of perhaps forty years, medium height, female curves tending toward plumpness, brown hair not showing a trace of gray and skin of a healthy ruddiness. Further, Eleanor Bitler was clothed in an attractive blue cotton dress, and her hair was pulled into a thick chignon at the back of her neck, both frock and coiffure impeccable.

She was smiling as she walked to the wagon and held her face up to be kissed even before Hank had climbed down. She continued to smile, corners of lips curved up in greeting as she turned her gaze on Auna-yi, and the girl, jumping down from her own side of the high seat, began to think Bitler had spoken very ill indeed of his wife, when she noticed the woman's eyes, hard as blue marbles and unwavering.

"Well, Henry Thomas, always full of surprises, aren't you? What have you brought us here? Hello, dear, what's your name?"

Something about Eleanor's voice, like the trill of a sage thrush but with the warning hiss of a rattlesnake hidden in undertone, paralyzed Auna-yi's own tongue.

Saltu warrior woman—she's like Ooti, perhaps, only now I am the enemy. . . .

"This here's Oona-yee, darlin'. That means Fire Woman, or so she tells me. A Yahi—one of them Mill Creeks from down south. I sort of bought her from a rancher who'd hauled her in to Shasta City. Guess I figured you could use some help. . . ."

"I see. Well, that will hardly do here, will it? We'll find you a better name, dear."

Still the honeyed smile, but a sting underneath.

"Uhh. . . . Oona's going to help you out around the house. She's got no folks. I thought maybe a little fee-male companionship might cheer you up. Says she can sew, cook, that sort of thing. And she knows English. Even knows how to read. Maybe she can read to you when you got one of your sick headaches."

"How lovely of you to think of me, Henry."

Eyes like ice down under mountain snow, where it never melts.

"Fanny's a good enough name, don't you think? Remember, Henry, that was the name of my mama's little Nigger girl back home."

"My name is Auna-yi."

"Not any more, child. If you're going to stay here, you must learn some manners. You address me as ma'am, always, Fanny, and Mr. Bitler as sir."

The voice suddenly lost its superficial music, and was all hornet buzz now. The woman turned as a pair of young men walked up behind her. One, coming from the house, had brown hair and the same hard blue eyes as Mrs. Bitler. The other, approaching from the direction of an outbuilding, was black-haired and brown-eyed, his broad-cheekboned face expressionless and obviously Indian, although he wore the same costume of blue jeans and flannel shirt as the White youth, and his hair was cut short.

The young Whiteman studied her openly, his red mouth twisted into a loose, unpleasant grin, his eyes traveling up and down the length of her body.

"Tod, this is Fanny," Eleanor Bitler said. "She's our new serving girl. Fanny, this is our son, Master Tod. Remember yourself, Tod dear. Lust is as much a sin as fornication, and she's not our kind, as you can see. The Lord knows what manner of diseases she might be harboring."

Auna-yi's face went hot, and she checked an impulse to spring at the woman, whose fixed smile did not change in the process of uttering those last words.

Tod Bitler nodded, touched his tongue to the center of his upper lip.

Hank's face flushed.

"Eleanor. . . ."

"Hush, Henry. It's easy enough to see your motives in bringing this girl here. Now I must make the best of it. Doesn't she have anything less provocative to wear? I'd just as soon not have my son corrupted too."

"Christ! Oona, I'll take ye back to Shasta City soon as I can if you want to go," Bitler said. "Guess I should have known better."

"Matthew," Mrs. Bitler spoke calmly, as if her husband had said nothing, but now addressing the Indian youth, "take the new servant's things out to the barn—if she has any. You can fix up a space for her in the loft or somewhere."

"No, Goddamn it," Bitler exploded. "I'm not gonna have her treated like some animal. This is my house too, by Christ, and I say she stays in the spare bedroom."

"Henry, I'll not listen to this. I'll not have you taking the Lord's name in vain. Isn't adultery bad enough—without adding blasphemy?"

"I should do it, Eleanor, by God I should. I've kept my marriage vows for twenty years, like a poor damned fool, and I'm beginning to wonder why. . . ."

"Oh!" Eleanor gasped, putting a hand to her well-padded bosom and swaying a little. "Tod, darling, help me to the house. Your father upsets me so, sometimes. My heart. . . . Well, it's the cross our sweet Jesus gave me to bear, and I won't complain."

"The barn will be fine, Hank," Auna-yi said, shuddering at the thought of staying in the same lodge with Mrs. Bitler and her son.

"Mr. Bitler, *sir*," Eleanor corrected, her voice now faint as she leaned against Tod. "Really, Henry. Matthew?"

"Yes, ma'am," the Indian hand said, expressionless still as he watched the White woman. "Come with me. . . ."

Without looking at Auna-yi, Matthew climbed up onto the wagon seat to take the rig to the barn. Auna-yi glanced at Hank, who wouldn't meet her eyes, then climbed onto the buckboard.

"Dinner in a half hour," Eleanor Bitler said. "You may

serve, Fanny. Put on a more suitable dress, something in a
dark color if you have it."

"This one is all I own," Auna-yi replied.

"Really. Well, I'll send old Mamie out with one of my
throwaways for you. And, Fanny,"—she smiled again, paused—
"it's 'This one is all I own, *ma'am.*' "

AUNA-YI STIRRED the sheets boiling in a big washtub, moving
the heavy wooden paddle in a continuous swirling motion,
lifting and turning soggy, steaming linen. She worked in an
area of hard-packed, bare earth behind the house, and sun
reflected mercilessly from the ground, steam rising from the
water adding to the heat until perspiration ran down her face,
dampened her hair, and left spreading dark patches on the
ill-fitting, coarse brown smock Mrs. Bitler had decided on as
her habitual uniform.

In a few minutes it would be time to move the smoking
laundry from the boiling tub to a washtub, where she'd have
to rub the clothing with harsh yellow soap and scrub the
material up and down a corrugated washboard.

She stood up for a moment, stretched, and put her hands
to the small of her back, which ached now continually, even
after she had lain down to sleep on the straw pallet in a
curtained-off corner of a hayloft that served as her room. Her
hands were red, cracked, and swollen from harsh laundry
soap and water, palms blistered and beginning to form cal-
luses from milking and from wielding rake and hoe in the
vegetable garden, broom and mop and scrub brush in the
house.

STILL, Auna-yi preferred the hard physical labor of ordinary
days to Sundays, when Mrs. Bitler gave them a half-day's rest
and spent the afternoon teaching *Fanny* and Matthew about
Christianity, her sermons being short on "love," which she
mentioned from time to time as a primary attribute of the
Jesus God, and long on lovingly detailed descriptions of the
fate that awaited sinners.

If Auna-yi answered a question wrong, often a ruler came
down across her knuckles. She noticed that Eleanor did not
try this method of discipline with Matthew. In any case, the

physical punishment was as nothing to those vivid descriptions of torture and the terrible, hateful Saltu God.

On Sunday nights Auna-yi invariably had nightmares of that *Loving God* burning the skins off those He had damned, flies crawling on open wounds, wild beasts devouring the unelect—whose blood, at the Time of the End, ran up to the withers of horses. All the while this Saltu God hung grotesquely on his cross and laughed to see the torments of His enemies. In some vague way he resembled Big Dan Clayton.

But perhaps worst thing of all was Tod's presence at these Sunday school sessions, his eyes always on her, glittering while he listened to account of the gruesome tortures, winking at her if she flinched—as though he were imagining her naked and writhing under the hooves of horses, the scourges of demons.

Matthew, on the other hand, merely listened impassively and openly satirized Eleanor's sermons when he and Auna-yi chanced to be alone. She and the hired hand had become friends during the month since she came to the Bitler place. She learned that he was of the Modoc tribe, a few of his people still living in the volcanic country to the south, though most, along with Chief Kintpuash (Captain Jack to the Whites), were on Klamath Reservation, seventy miles northwest of Goose Lake. Kintpuash, Matthew insisted, would not remain on a reservation much longer—not with the Klamaths, his ancient enemies.

The Modoc youth's real name was Red Turtle, he told her, and when the time came, he intended to rejoin his people. Together with his aunt First Rabbit, the old serving woman Eleanor Bitler called Mamie, Red Turtle shared sleeping quarters in the barn, along with Auna-yi.

What was a *real* name?

She herself was Fire Woman, and yet she responded readily enough to Fanny. This apparently minor issue disturbed her, perhaps, more than anything else. Fanny—Fanny Bitler. It was just the way Ben McCain had described Black People who were *owned* before the Civil War, the ones Lincoln-who-was-dead had given their freedom.

HANK WAS STILL kind to her, when he was there, and when Eleanor wasn't watching to make both of them pay for the attention, but he didn't spend much time around the home place, seeming to prefer riding the boundaries of his land, checking his stock, almost anything to keep him away from the house and, Auna-yi surmised, his wife. Thus First Rabbit and Red Turtle came to serve as the girl's only true companionship. The old woman had a gentle nature and didn't seem to object to doing Eleanor's bidding, but she was growing feeble, her joints swollen and painful much of the time and the strength gone out of her hands—so that she wasn't able to perform much work.

For her part, Mrs. Bitler treated Mamie with more genuine kindness than she displayed toward anyone else, with the possible exception of her son, who could do no wrong in his mother's eyes. Eleanor didn't even require that the old woman attend Sunday services.

"I tell her I'm a Christian long time ago," First Rabbit grinned one evening as the three of them sat in their little partitioned-off room near the horse stalls, her toothless gums showing pink between the lips. "I say, 'Oh, sure, I love Jesus whole lot,' an' she not bother me no more. Why not you try that, Fanny?"

"Mrs. Bitler will hate me no matter what I do," Auna-yi said. "How can anyone love such a god as the one she talks about? I couldn't even pretend."

"I wouldn't give her the satisfaction," Red Turtle laughed. "But she's hard on Auna-yi for a whole different reason, Aunt, and you know it. She figures Fanny's after her husband, or maybe it's the other way around."

The Modoc woman grinned.

"Yes, I guess Miss Eleanor don't worry 'bout Mamie that way. Long time ago, though, she have plenty to worry 'bout. One time, all the men were after First Rabbit. Lot of winters ago. Now I got no teeth, no pretty black hair."

The old woman sighed, picked up a piece of linen she was embroidering with bright-colored thread, a gift from Eleanor.

"Why do you stay here?" Auna-yi asked Red Turtle. "You know where your people are. You could go back to Kintpuash. That's what I'd do if I knew where Wolf Tracker and Smoke Woman were. Well, maybe I could find them, but it's so far away. . . ."

Red Turtle shrugged, his eyes going hard and unhappy, as they often did.

"No future in it, probably, though maybe I will," he said. "The time for my people, your people too, is finished. You either learn to live in the Whiteman's world or you die in the Redman's, sooner or later. Hank Bitler's all right, and I can stay out of his woman's way most of the time. I'm making pretty good money, I put it away. I got nothing to spend money on. When I have enough, I'll head out. Maybe I could buy a ranch of my own somewhere. Bring my folks to live with me if they want, but I don't think they'll leave the reservation—not unless Kintpuash does. You're the one I can't figure. Why do you put up with that she-devil? You're a halfbreed. Hell, the way you look, you could go to Shasta City or someplace, pass for White, snag some banker or shopkeeper or cattle rancher, and live easy the rest of your days. You're young, just a kid. Maybe when you're a little older. We've got to learn from the White People if we want to survive."

"I could never do that," Auna-yi said, uneasy with the import of Red Turtle's words in some way she couldn't define.

"Why not? I would, believe me, if I were a pretty woman."

"No, you wouldn't."

Red Turtle only laughed again, a harsh, unhappy laugh.

"You believe I should deny my mother, Wolf Tracker, my own people, and pretend to be like my blood father that I do not even know? The Saltus killed my people, and the man who was my father forced my mother to lie with him and then left her for dead. You wouldn't do what you tell me to do, Red Turtle."

"Maybe not. The Whites killed many of my people, too, but that was a long time ago. Kintpuash was there, but he was just a boy himself. Still, he's always talked of revenge. A man named Ben Wright tricked my people and then his men slaughtered them, but he may not even be alive now, I don't know. That was fifteen years ago I think. But if I ever meet Ben Wright, I'll probably kill him."

Red Turtle rose, stretched.

"I'm turning in. Sleep well, Fanny."

"Auna-yi."

"Fanny. You'd better get used to it. It's a different world now."

AUNA-YI TURNED away from the laundry boiler. The fire had died out underneath, and now it was time to drag the big washtub over and carry cold water from the well to temper hot water she'd pour in from the boiler. As she straightened up, she saw Tod lounging against the corner of the back porch, his lips parted over gleaming teeth as he watched her. She glanced at him, and walked wide around him as she went into the dim, partially enclosed area to get the tub.

Tod Bitler moved up behind her as she leaned down toward the implement, put his arms around her, pressed his groin against her buttocks, and cupped his hands on her breasts.

"You ain't been very friendly to me, Fanny," he said in his whining voice.

"Let go of me. If I tell your father what you've done. . . ."

"He'll send you back to where you come from, halfbreed. Maybe my ma will have you horsewhipped first. Ma don't like you, Fanny, but I sure do, yes sir. So why don't you just be nice to me?"

Auna-yi twisted, kicked back at his shins.

"Gonna fight me?" he said. "That'll be fun."

Suddenly she found herself flat on her back, Tod on his knees above her, his hands at her throat, thumbs pressing painfully against the cartilage.

"Or you might just disappear, by God! Fanny must of run off, lookin' for her people, I guess. Ah, I'd like to. . . ."

Tod's thumbs pressed harder, and Auna-yi couldn't breathe, stared up at the face above hers, the red lips twisted in a grin that was half a snarl.

"I seen you watchin' Matthew. Don't tell me you ain't got an eye for the Injun. You're a fancy little piece all around. I know you put out for my dad. Sometimes I think about that."

Auna-yi clawed at the hands on her throat, little red lines like the branches of trees beginning to appear against the growing darkness of her vision.

"Yeah," Tod went on, the tone of his voice almost gentle, dreamy, "and sometimes I think about how you'd look naked and tied up, with ropes making dents in this soft, soft skin, how you'd scream and writhe around when I brought the whip down, how you'd beg me, beg me. 'Please, Tod, oh please. . . .' "

She could barely see his face now for the swirls of color against darkness, his voice growing dim.

I'm dying. He's killing me.

The thought held no fear, only a distant sort of surprise.

Suddenly the pressure was gone, and she sucked in a desperate breath, another, great sobbing gulps of air. Vision gradually returned. Tod's face hung above her, laughing.

"You gonna say it now?" he demanded.

"I don't understand."

He grabbed her about the throat once more, and the pressure against her windpipe returned. Tod Bitler spoke in a mocking falsetto again.

"Please, Tod, oh please," he said, giggling incongruously.

"Your mother . . . will hear us, Tod," Auna-yi managed. "If you . . . let me go, I won't tell anyone. . . ."

"Mother's in her room with a headache," he smiled. "She has the shutters closed and the drapes drawn because she just can't bear light when her head's hurting. Father's off checking his moo-cows, and your heap-big Injun friend is with him. That only leaves the old woman, and she's upstairs putting cold cloths on mother's poor brow. Just who do you figure Ma's gonna believe, a breed squaw or her own son? Say it!"

He punctuated the last two words with another painful jab into her throat.

Auna-yi clenched her teeth, stared at her attacker with pure and perfect hate.

"I'll kill you someday," she hissed.

"That's wonderful," he chuckled, "oh, that's rich. You'll kill me. Say it!"

She pulled her knees up quickly and thrust with both feet into the pit of his stomach, twisted wildly to one side. But before she could rise, he'd caught her by the hair and yanked her back to the floor, banging her head against the boards several times—until the world spun crazily around her and blackness threatened to close in again. She tried to move, but found her limbs wouldn't work.

"God, I'd love to tie you up," he said, panting now with his exertions. "Well, maybe another time, Beautiful."

Dimly she realized he was pulling her smock up—for a moment he was occupied, his weight off her.

She twisted about, kicking hard, and this time catching him directly between his legs.

Tod stumbled backward, cursing and groaning, his face contorted with pain.

Catlike, Auna-yi was on her feet. She bolted past the bent-over Tod Bitler, escaped into an open area beyond the laundry, and sprinted for the barn. The haystack! Once behind that, she burrowed in under the good-smelling dry grass, and tunneled forward, wriggling until she was well under the big pile.

Darkness, a different kind of night. Darkness and momentary safety. Almost like oblivion, the matted hay heavy and rich-smelling all about her. . . .

Somewhere far back in her consciousness, a lost little girl was laughing and crying at the same time—at the absurdity and horror the world seemed entirely composed of. Auna-yi felt she was not very much interested in who the little girl might be, but she resolved she would never again allow Tod Bitler to maul her that way. She would kill him if necessary. Red Turtle had a knife. . . . Auna-yi let blackness swirl in around her, engulf her.

Grass seeds were in her mouth and nose.

LIEUTENANT COLONEL GIDEON WHITNEY RODE into the Bitler ranch a few days following the unsuccessful rape attempt, took note of a lovely young Indian girl carrying two buckets of slop across to a hog pen, and nodded greetings as she passed. He tethered his mount, sauntered to the front door of the ranch house, and knocked.

Mamie answered, and called for Hank.

"Henry Bitler!" Whitney said, shaking hands with the rancher. "I've got a requisition for half a dozen good saddle ponies—top government dollar for them. How's it going, Henry?"

"Fair, Gid, fair to middling. Yep—the varmints are ready for you. Matthew's done a fine job with them. Horses for the brass, eh? Well, these won't disappoint. Heard you'd gone

over to rescue some damn fools that got lost out in the Black
Rock somewhere. How'd that turn out?"

"Four Conestogas," the lieutenant colonel replied—"cats,
kids, dogs, and cows. We made it over Fandango Pass this
morning, and the folks are camped for the evening to the side
of the trail, down on Goose Lake. Why in God's name anyone
would haul housecats across country, I don't know, but the
emigrants have got five of them. Anyhow, we repaired their
wagons, and everybody's pleased to be in California at last.
They bought Valley land, sight unseen, over by Elk Creek.
Hope it works out for them. Good folks."

"Maybe the government ought to put up a rock wall out in
Utah Territory. About as many people in California already as
the land'll hold."

"Hank, you having any trouble with Indians running off
with your stock? The ranchers in Surprise Valley are complaining again, but the commandant at Fort Bidwell says it
isn't any of his. I looked over the herd those Paiutes have got
going, and everything appears okay to me. But it crossed my
mind that maybe some straggling Modocs have been moving
their operations over in this direction."

"Nary a problem," Hank replied. "Matthew, he's my Modoc
insurance, you might say. A good worker, too. Wish my own
kid had half that lad's gumption. Picked up a Yahi girl too—in
Shasta City—that's her out by the hog pen."

"I noticed," Whitney said. "A little beauty, I'd say. Doesn't
look exactly Injun—she a halfbreed?"

"Apparently so, but didn't want to give me the details. A
whiz at English—can even read and write."

"Wonder how that happened? Yahi, you say—one of the
Mill Creeks? Not many of those left these days. Ranchers to
the south have been hunting them pretty heavily—they've
had soldiers along once or twice. She tell you how she learned
English?"

"Benjamin McCain taught her, or so she says. Now there's
a fella I'd like to meet sometime—just out of curiosity. Been
hearing about him ever since I come out West."

"The McCain south of Lassen Peak? Yes, I've heard the
stories too. Supposed to have a pack of trained wolves or
something of the sort. McCain's Acting Agent to a bunch of
Maidus near Chester. Married to one of them. I've never met

the man either, but I know what you're saying. Some peculiar tales. . . . You figure he's her father? Could be he does a
bit of wandering in the woods on the side. In his sixties now,
from what I hear, but maybe he's got a wild one off in the
bush somewhere."

Bitler turned, shouted at Auna-yi.

"Like you to meet her, Colonel," he said. "Ain't much
more than a kid, but damned if she's not the sweetest little
thing you'll ever run into."

As the girl walked toward them, Gideon Whitney whistled
appreciatively through his teeth.

"How's Eleanor respond to having the young beauty
around?" he asked.

"Might say I've got a problem or two. My boy Tod's been
making a fool of himself over her, and Ellie don't like that
much, either."

SIXTEEN

The Burning Barn

[February 1866]

AUNA-YI RAISED the splitting maul and then brought it down
with all her force against a cedar round, where the blade
buried itself with a loud *chunk*, wedged in so tightly she was
forced to put one foot upon the sawn surface to lever her ax
free. She studied the grain for a few seconds, then brought

the thick blade down again. A few promising cracks opened
up, but the section of log still did not split. She wrenched the
implement loose a second time and lifted it over her head
again, but this time the staff was pulled out of her hands.

Red Turtle grinned at her, then raised the maul and brought
it down, blade slicing through the wood with a sharp
crack, and the round fell apart in two uneven pieces.

"You're much stronger than I am," she said, brushing back
a strand of hair that was plastered to her forehead with
perspiration, despite the cold. She tried to conceal the an-
noyance she felt toward Red Turtle for taking over the task
she'd set herself.

"Not a matter of strength. It's in knowing where to hit it.
You've got to take the grain into account."

"I had it cracked before you started," she insisted. "That's
why it was easy for you. Don't laugh at me, Matthew Red
Turtle."

"Whatever you say. This doesn't need to be split now,
anyhow. I told you that."

"Damn it, I want to do *something*. I couldn't help you with
the saw—I only kept getting it stuck."

"Why don't you go see if you can dig out the food? It's time
for a break, and I'm starved."

Auna-yi nodded, helped him toss several additional chunks
of firewood into the wagon, and then retrieved a tin lard pail
Mamie First Rabbit had filled with sandwiches for them
before they set off that morning. As Red Turtle leaned against
the wagon and bit into a biscuit sliced and filled with roast
beef, Auna-yi added a few sticks to the little fire she'd kept
going through the morning and set a half-full coffeepot closer
to the flames to reheat. Then she sat down on a wide round of
wood, took up a sandwich for herself, and ate hungrily.

The sky was pure and vivid blue, sun high above the tops
of pines and cedars, giving at least an illusion of warmth
although much of the ground was covered with icy snow,
more in shaded areas. A little flock of tiny, black-headed
birds gathered nearby, hopping and scratching busily at patches
of bare ground beneath the underbrush, cocking their heads
from time to time to eye the humans.

"They're waiting for us to move so they can come peck up

the crumbs," Auna-yi laughed, breaking off a piece of biscuit and tossing it in the direction of the hopeful chickadees.

Red Turtle smiled, pulled another block of wood next to Auna-yi's, and sat down also.

"I'm glad I came with you, Matthew," she said. "You'd probably rather have one of the men, though. I'm no good with a saw. . . ."

"Are you fishing for a compliment? All right, then. You're prettier than Hank and a sight better company than Tod, and he's no help at all, anyway. He just whines about the work and lets me do it all."

Auna-yi shivered a little. She raised one hand involuntarily to her throat at the mention of Tod Bitler. Red Turtle looked at her sharply.

"He did do that to you last summer, didn't he? You've never admitted it, but I knew all along you never got those marks on your neck from falling down."

Auna-yi shook her head, didn't reply. She'd told no one of Tod's attack. Mamie had discovered her lying half conscious back in their room and brought her around, nursing her for several days before the girl recovered sufficiently from the blows to her head to be able to resume work. She'd insisted to everyone that she'd slipped and fallen, hitting her head on the washtub. The two Modocs were openly skeptical, and Eleanor, while officially accepting the story, made a point for some time thereafter of keeping her son away from the "immoral influence of that girl," as she termed it in conversation with her husband, conversation that she made no particular effort to conceal from Auna-yi or the other two *servants*. Hank Bitler, when he returned, had questioned her closely, but she stuck to her story, and the man at last shook his head, assured her she needn't protect anyone from him, and gave up the effort.

She almost supposed she could tell Hank, but Auna-yi remembered Tod's words: ". . . who do you figger Ma's gonna believe, a breed squaw or her own son?"

She knew the answer without question in Eleanor's case, and it would be hard even for Hank to take her part against his own flesh and blood—or so she thought. So she kept silence, not knowing where she could go if she were sent away. She placated Eleanor as best she could, working hard

at the almost overwhelming burden of jobs the woman loaded
her with, sidestepping any situation that might place her
alone with Tod, and treading carefully to avoid any appearance of favor with the father. It was a nerve-wracking way to
live, and at times she told herself she'd simply take one of
Bitler's horses and ride south, but she knew that was an
empty fantasy. She had no idea where her own people might
be by this time; McCain's ranch was many days to the south,
and she had no confidence she'd be able to find even that.

Tod didn't attack her again, in any case, partly because of
her own efforts to avoid him and partly, she guessed, because
she'd been able to strike back, to hurt him. He took sufficient
pleasure in merely frightening her now, winking at her sometimes in the presence of his mother or father, smiling and
rubbing at his throat or making obscene gestures when the
others' backs were turned. Occasionally he'd step out of
hiding someplace as she passed and grasp at her breasts or
buttocks, leer at her when she drew back gasping—these and
many other small methods of reinforcing her terror.

One day as she worked alone in the kitchen, she became
aware of Tod's presence outside the doorway. Cold sweat
came over her face, and she reached into the silverware drawer
and took out a paring knife, the sharp one. She placed the
weapon in her smock's side pocket.

But when it came time for her to leave the kitchen, Tod
was gone. Auna-yi felt gratitude toward unknown forces, but
she kept the knife. In all likelihood, no one but Mamie would
ever notice.

In the autumn, though, Tod had gone away, Eleanor insisting
against Hank's objections that the boy needed to be educated
at a college that had been established in the city of Oakland,
near San Francisco. Auna-yi's life became almost pleasant
after that. Meeting Eleanor's outrageous demands, catering
to her uncertain temper, and listening to fire-and-brimstone
sermons seemed a small burden compared to Tod's reign of
terror.

But then he was back. He returned a few days before
Christmas, waiting until after the holidays to announce to his
parents that he wouldn't be returning south to the college—
since he'd been expelled for "irregular conduct."

He quickly resumed his campaign against Auna-yi. Whenever he was within her sight, she could feel his eyes crawling over her like icy hands, and he had lately become more daring in the winks and gestures he made to her, less cautious of discovery—to the point where Eleanor was beginning to renew her efforts to have the girl sent away, on the grounds that she was a bad influence.

AUNA-YI SIGHED unconsciously as she threw another crumb of bread to the birds. She was very grateful for the opportunity to be away from the concerns of the ranch for a time. Such opportunities did not come often. The trip after firewood had, in fact, occasioned another of many bitter arguments between Hank Bitler and his wife. It was Eleanor who insisted that Fanny accompany Matthew into the mountains to cut firewood this morning. Hank objected, saying the job was *man's work* and asserting Tod should go instead. Eleanor countered that it was for servants to perform such tasks, not the master's own son. Hank insisted he'd go himself, until Auna-yi sided with Eleanor, saying that she wished to go.

Bitler had merely stared at her, then turned and strode from the house, riding past in a few moments, headed out again, not bothering to inform his wife or anyone else of his destination.

Auna-yi stood up from her seat, and stretched her stiff muscles. The air was so cold it burned her lungs, but it was also wonderfully free. The little birds scattered at her rising, fluttering into nearby trees and bushes, and she caught movement among the pines—a single thin coyote hanging back in shadows and shying away a few steps as she moved, advancing cautiously again, amber eyes fixed on her when she reached into the tin pail and drew out a whole sandwich, held it toward him, and then tossed it in his direction.

The brush wolf darted forward, took the food, and then withdrew, vanishing among the trees.

"Yes," she said, "it feels good to be here, to be away. Brother Coyote is skinny, but he's free, Red Turtle. We should be like that."

Red Turtle shrugged, rose, and stretched also.

"Me, I like to eat. Was that the last sandwich you gave the mangy animal?"

She smiled and then handed him the pail.

"I don't think you believe what you say. I think you'll go back to your own people eventually."

"Maybe"

He moved to the fire, poured himself a cup of coffee, stood warming his hands.

"Somebody's going to kill him someday," he said.

"The coyote?"

"Tod Bitler. It may be me that does it."

"Don't say that, Red Turtle. The Saltus would hang you if you did such a thing, and then I wouldn't have any friends here. Besides, I told you he didn't hurt me."

"Let's just say I don't like him, then. Let's just say I hate the bastard's guts."

TOD WAS WAITING for them partway up the road from the back corral when they returned early in the afternoon with a buckboard stacked high with firewood.

"Thought I was going to be obliged to come after you two," he said. "Have a real good time cutting wood, did you Matt?"

He slapped the Indian youth on the shoulder and winked menacingly at Auna-yi. Red Turtle's face froze, and his hand dropped automatically to the hilt of the skinning knife he carried on his belt.

Tod was oblivious.

"Listen, Matthew old fellow, I've got to ride up to Pine Creek. One of the Clark boys just came in to tell me Pa's at their place, drunk as a bear in a rotten windfall, and I should come get him. That's where Pa goes when he wants to get sotted. Meantime, you better haul a load of fodder up to that bunch of steers below Sugar Hill. Clouds coming in from the west, and we're likely to be snowed in come morning. I was just about to do it myself when the Clark kid came in. Wagon's loaded, ready to go. Fanny, you can get this wood unloaded by yourself, can't you?"

Auna-yi nodded, puzzled by Tod's sudden energy and concern with the affairs of the ranch. He was the last person she'd have expected to take an interest in getting hay to stranded cattle.

"Right," Tod said. "Get to that, Matthew. Not many hours before dark. I'm on my way."

Auna-yi and Red Turtle watched as he reined his horse about, then stopped and called over his shoulder to the girl.

"Don't tell my ma about Dad, Fanny. She's in bed with a fainting spell, and we don't need to upset her any more. Get a move on, now."

The two brought the wagon to the woodshed, and Red Turtle unhitched the team and transferred the animals to a hay wagon that stood loaded in front of the barn, just as Tod had said it would be.

"There's something about this I don't trust," Red Turtle muttered, looking back in the direction young Bitler had taken.

"Don't be silly," Auna-yi called out, climbing up into the back of the wagon and beginning to toss chunks of cedar to the ground. "What can Tod do if he's at Pine Creek? He wouldn't have lied. He knows his father will find out if he did."

"Don't know. Just know I don't trust a bear when he starts acting like a drayhorse, that's all."

Auna-yi smiled, stifling her own misgivings.

"If I didn't know better, I'd say you're acting as if you cared about me. You'd better go. Tod's right about the cattle in the meadows by Sugar Hill."

"I know it. But he's wrong about the snow. These clouds don't amount to anything. Maybe I'll just stay. Worst that can happen is I'll get fired. I don't care about that."

"I order you to go, Red Turtle," Auna-yi said, jumping down from the wagon and standing in front of him, hands on hips.

"Don't take my orders from squaws," he growled.

"I know how to handle myself. Quit being foolish. I'm not your woman—you don't need to protect me."

"Guess not," he said. "Auna-yi. . . ."

"What is it?"

"Nothing. Be careful."

He gave her a quick, clumsy kiss on the forehead and then climbed onto the hay wagon seat and drove out of the corral and down toward the main road. Auna-yi watched until he was out of sight past the first bend, her eyes narrowed in puzzlement.

He almost asked me to be his woman—I'm sure of it. What

*would I have said? I never thought of him that way. He's
my friend. . . .*

She finished unloading the wood and then walked to the
house, still turning this new development over in her mind.

THE DAYS were still winter-short, and light was already beginning to fade when she finished her housekeeping chores and
went out to the barn to milk the single dairy cow the Bitlers
kept. As she stepped to the stall with her pail, a slight sound
caught her attention, something different from the small,
expected noises of animals breathing, chewing, moving about
in their stalls in the dimness of the barn, and she turned,
peered into the shadows behind her.

Nothing. Foolish girl, starting at ghosts.

She turned back, picked up the stool, and stepped in
beside the cow.

*A sudden, violent explosion of light, and then darkness,
impression of falling, falling a very long way.*

When she drifted back up into consciousness, she found
herself in an empty enclosure, straw prickling at her back.

*Half naked, smock pulled up around her shoulders, spread-
eagled, ropes tied around wrists and ankles and fastened to
the rails of the siding. A light growing, moving, yellowish
rays sending shadows sliding along wood, a harness hung
from hooks on the wall above.*

Tod slipped into the rear of the stall, holding a lantern,
light glinting in his eyes and from his bared teeth, breath
hissing through his nostrils as he lowered the lantern and
stared at her body.

Auna-yi watched him without speaking and felt as if paralyzed, as if she couldn't move, couldn't speak. He looked into
her wide eyes, smiled, nodded, pinched hard at one of her
breasts, twisting the nipple painfully so that she cried out.

"Ah," he said. 'That's what I like to hear. I'm glad you're
awake now. I was afraid I might have hit you too hard. You'll
be screaming, soon, pretty Fanny, but no one will hear. I was
just checking the doors so we won't be disturbed. The old
squaw's busy with dinner, but you can never be sure."

"Please let me go, Tod," she said, trying to sound reasonable, calm, but her voice emerging from a dry throat in a

croak. "I can't hide this from your father. I helped you before, I never told anyone, but this time. . . ."

"This time I have other plans," he laughed.

"What plans, Tod?"

Keep him talking. Perhaps Red Turtle will come back, or Hank. Please come back, Red Turtle, please. If I can manage to get one hand free. . . .

"Many plans, many plans," he said, smiling mysteriously. "I'm tired of this hole. Nothing ever happens here. I've apparently developed a taste for city life. Would you like me to show you what I did to a prostitute in Oakland? They didn't catch me that time. A little fire hid things nicely."

Mad, utterly mad. The fire—straw and dry wood, a dropped lantern after he has. . . .

"Tell me what you did. I want to hear about it."

Voice cracking again. Red Turtle, help me. True Bear. . . .

"You bitch, you whore, you filthy, fucking slut. Look what you've made me do—with your tits always wobbling around, your ass waggling under your dress, always there, always there."

He went on mouthing obscenities, the images becoming more violent, crueler as he continued, apparently working himself into a frenzy. He began hitting her as he shouted, punching her with closed fists in breast and belly, in rhythm with his ravings.

Then he stopped, his face changing, twisting into an obscene smile, and he pulled a knife from its sheath on his belt, leaned above her, and breathed into her face, the blade gleaming at her cheek.

She screamed, a high, piercing wail of terror, and he sat back on his heels and laughed.

"I'm not going to kill you—not yet, anyway. I'm just going to put my mark on you. Where would you like my initials to be? Here on your left tit? Maybe on your pretty forehead? Where do you think?"

As he spoke, he pressed the point of the knife against different places on her skin, pressed until a drop of blood appeared and then moved the blade elsewhere.

Auna-yi was now screaming uncontrollably, pulling against the ropes with all her strength, sobbing.

"Shut up, bitch," Tod hissed suddenly, dropping the knife and pressing a hand over her mouth, his head turned, listening.

Someone was pounding at the big front door of the barn, the noise becoming louder, insistent hammering, and a muffled voice.

"What the hell's going on in there? Open up, Goddamn it!"

Hank Bitler's voice. Auna-yi bit down on the hand covering her mouth, screamed *Help me!* as Tod jerked away momentarily.

"Slut!" he snarled, and slapped her hard, her head bouncing back against packed earth.

The pounding at the main door continued, and Tod rose, picked up his knife, looked around wildly, and ran toward the side entry, dropping his lantern outside the stall as he fled.

The glass chimney shattered, and flames licked up, growing instantly in the straw. Auna-yi watched, frozen for a moment as fire leaped, crackling, objects suddenly emerging from darkness into clarity. She pulled frantically against her bonds, her voice rising to an incoherent shriek.

The pounding at the main door ceased, and through her own cries Auna-yi heard a loud thumping sound from the rear of the barn, the hayloft. Noise of a struggle, scuffling and grunts, and then Red Turtle appeared at the stall where she lay bound, a knife in his hand, its blade smeared with blood and spatter marks on the front of his coat. He stared at Auna-yi for an instant and then dropped to his knees, severed the ropes at wrists and ankles, and lifted her to her feet.

Flames had climbed a support post, had spread over a wide area of one wall, but Auna-yi was still staring at the blood smears on Red Turtle's clothing.

"Tod?" she managed, fighting for breath.

"Had an accident. Come on, we've got to get the hell out of here!"

Red Turtle shrugged out of his coat, wrapped it around her, and pulled her toward the side entrance.

Flames danced about them as mounds of hay turned into an inferno. The milk cow thrashed about in her stall, seeking escape.

An inert form in dark clothes, sprawled in a wide red stain, fire beginning to nibble at one boot.

Red Turtle dragged her past and out the side door, where

he thrust her into the arms of Hank Bitler, just now coming around from the front of the building.

"Take care of her, Hank," he ordered, as if he were the boss and the other man the employee. "Got to get the animals out."

He turned and plunged back into the burning building.

"What in God's name. . . ?"

Auna-yi looked up at Bitler, and shook her head. She couldn't speak.

"Tod?" he asked slowly.

She nodded, blinked, rubbed at her eyes.

"He's still in there? My God. . . ."

Bitler released her abruptly and ran yelling into the barn.

Auna-yi stared stupidly after him, and then she thrust her arms into the sleeves of Red Turtle's coat and followed.

The interior was thick with smoke, flames licking through the haze. Auna-yi thought of Eleanor Bitler's visions of hell. Horses screamed, hooves pounding against stall gates, and the milk cow bellowed in fright. Auna-yi saw Hank Bitler crouched over the body of his son, pushed past him, and released the fenzied cow from her stall. Shying from flames, the animal stumbled toward safety.

Ahead, through the smoke, Auna-yi saw Red Turtle, hands raised to the bridles of two lunging horses, struggling to reach the main door. She followed, grabbed hold of the cow's lead rope so that she seemed to be dragging the confused animal along by main strength. She unbarred the stalls of the other horses as she passed, struggling through an eternity of hissing flame, billows of smoke. Then a draft of air, and the fire leaped up brighter as Red Turtle succeeded in heaving open the wide main double door.

Auna-yi pulled the milk cow through into wonderfully sweet, cold air, turned and saw that the horses were plunging about inside aimlessly, shying back from flames.

Red Turtle brushed past her, and then two more terrified animals found their way out. Red Turtle was inside, silhouetted against the orange glow, dragging at horses, flapping his hat, and shouting to drive them in the direction of escape.

Auna-yi dashed back into the inferno and tried to grab at the halter of a writhing, plunging animal, felt herself lifted into the air and then dragged along as the creature fled, somehow finding the door and taking her through as well.

"Stay out, damn you!" Red Turtle shouted at her when she turned to enter again, this time mechanically, without thought. "How many horses clear?"

"I don't know," she screamed, trying hard to count the leaping forms in memory. "Maybe six."

"I think that's all. I hope so," he said, his voice softening as he took her into his arms, held her against him while she wept, the sobs uncontrollable now.

Hank Bitler stumbled out of the inferno, carrying his son in his arms as if the young man were a child, the father's eyes blank, uncomprehending.

"I don't understand," he said in the voice of a man trying hard to remain rational in the face of utter chaos. "Fanny, for God's sake, tell me what happened. Tod's dead, I don't understand. . . ."

"I killed him, Hank," Red Turtle said.

Bitler nodded, but it was not apparent from his expression whether he actually heard or comprehended the other's words. He let Tod's body slide slowly from his arms onto the ground, knelt, and brushed at the singed, straw-colored hair.

In death the younger Bitler did not look dangerous at all. Auna-yi made this observation with an odd side-consciousness that seemed to be taking in and marking any number of irrelevancies. The dead face appeared relaxed, innocent even, like that of a child sleeping.

Hank rose, faced Red Turtle, and with the slow deliberation of a sleepwalker he drew a pistol from its holster, held it in both hands, and aimed at the other's middle. The Modoc watched him, but made no move to defend himself.

Auna-yi seemed to wake out of a trance. She sprang at Bitler, grasped the barrel of the gun, and pushed it down.

"No!" she cried out. "Red Turtle saved my life, Hank. Your son tied me up . . . beat me . . . was going to rape me. He said he . . . was going to kill me and then burn down the barn. . . ."

"Tod wouldn't do a thing like that," Bitler said, all but begging for assent as he turned on Auna-yi his strange eyes that seemed not to see anything. "He was a little lazy, a little bit of a hell-raiser. . . . Sometimes I was disappointed with

him, but Jesus Christ, he was no murderer. We can't tell
Ellie about this. . . . Goddamn world's come apart. Matthew,
you killed my son, and I'm going to kill you. . . ."

"Go ahead, Hank, it's better than hanging," Red Turtle
shrugged, his voice subdued. "But what Fanny says—it's
true. You heard the screams. You can see her dress was all
torn away. I found her, just like she says. Tod had her tied
up, spread-eagled in one of the damned stalls. He set the fire
when I jumped down from the hayloft. He tried to kill me,
too. It ain't your fault, Hank. Tod went crazy. There was
something wrong in his head. I knew that a long time ago, I
guess. Just didn't know how wrong."

Hank Bitler dropped to his knees, put his hands over his
face, and seemed to shrivel into himself and grow small.
Auna-yi touched gently at his hair but then withdrew her
hand and looked helplessly at Red Turtle.

A rending shriek slashed through the firelit darkness. Auna-yi
and Red Turtle turned, saw Eleanor Bitler dashing toward
them, her white nightdress whipping around her legs, un-
bound hair streaming. She shoved Auna-yi out of her way
with such force that the girl stumbled and fell, the mother
dropping to the ground beside her dead son. She screamed
again, a mindless, piercing, animal sound. Mamie First Rabbit limped hurriedly into view behind Eleanor Bitler, stood
silently at the edge of the conflagration's pulsating light.

Hank attempted to put his arms around his wife, but she
was not to be consoled, lashing out at him with one arm.

"Our boy's gone, Ellie. He never was quite right, and we
didn't want to see it. Tied Fanny up, was going to rape
her. . . ."

"You fool!" Eleanor screamed, pushing him away from her
a second time, rising. "I don't want to hear lies—what happened? Did you do this?"

"He tried to rape Fanny and kill Matthew," Bitler began.
"It's nobody's. . . ."

Eleanor flung herself at Auna-yi, knocked her to the ground
again with the weight of her body, and tried to strangle her.
Red Turtle and Hank pulled the crazed woman off, Hank
restraining his wife with both arms wrapped around her,
pinning her hands to her sides as she struggled to get free
and leap at the girl again.

Auna-yi rose to one knee, fumbled inside the remains of her smock, and found what she was searching for. Black anger came over her, defiance, a sudden desire to strike back at whoever and whatever had for so long been persecuting her.

She stood up and then crouched, waiting, paring knife in hand.

"That bitch, that bitch, she killed our son!" Eleanor shouted. "Let me go, Hank. Dear Jesus, how can you protect her, this whore of a squaw! She seduced our Tod, she killed him! Do you want her for yourself, is that it? Let go of me, you bastard! Let me kill her. She murdered Toddie, don't you understand that? You always hated him. . . . See, she's got a knife!"

"Come at me again, Ellie Bitler," Auna-yi hissed, "and I'll cut your heart out. . . ."

"Get back out of sight," Red Turtle murmured to Auna-yi, motioning toward the shadows of a juniper grove. Then he turned to Bitler: "I'll help you get Miss Eleanor to the house, Hank."

"Like hell," the woman raged, suddenly pulling her husband's pistol from his belt, waving the weapon about wildly. Red Turtle grabbed for the gun, but the bereaved mother fired twice, one shot singing harmlessly into darkness but the second striking Auna-yi in the arm. For a moment the girl wasn't even certain she'd been hit. There was only a sensation of dull impact, and then she looked down, saw a dark stain spreading on the sleeve of Red Turtle's coat. She placed her good hand over the bloodied, torn cloth, and stared at Eleanor Bitler as if to ask a question, feeling more puzzled than anything else. Nothing, she realized, nothing at all that had happened this night made any sense.

In her good hand she still clenched the paring knife—and that didn't make any sense either.

Then fire spread out from the wound, and she slumped to both knees.

Mamie knelt beside the stricken girl and put an arm about her waist.

"You hold still," she ordered, and Auna-yi complied automatically. The old woman eased Matthew Red Turtle's coat down over the shoulders, her own body shielding the girl's

nakedness as she wiped blood from torn flesh, probed at the
wound, grunting.

"Not too bad. I get something for it," she said. "You cover
yourself so the men can't see you."

Mamie rose, breathed deeply, and waddled away toward
the house, glaring at Eleanor as she went.

Mrs. Bitler laughed in hysterical triumph, shrieked repeatedly: "I shot her, I shot the halfbreed whore!" Then suddenly the woman went dead white and collapsed to the
ground beside her son.

THREE FIGURES bundled in heavy coats against bitter cold
stood by the corral gate in dim blue light of false dawn. Two
horses stood nearby, saddled and ready for travel. A rooster
crowed from the chicken yard, the sound breaking off in a
sleepy squawk.

"Matthew," Hank Bitler said, his voice sounding infinitely
old, his face lined with exhaustion and still smudged with
soot, "I guess I got to thank you, no matter what's happened.
The barn's gone, but if it hadn't been for you the stock would
be gone too. And for helpin' me bury—him. I know you only
done what you had to do, but it's a hard thing for a man to
swallow—to look his son's killer in the face an'. . . . You got
to understand. I'd ask you to stay on, lad, but. . . . I should
never of brought Fanny here to the ranch, much as I've come
to love her—an' you too, Matthew, damn it. You're a good
man, and I wish it was you that was my kid. . . ."

Bitler broke off, glanced toward the house, quiet now, no
lamplight showing in the windows. Eleanor had been asleep
for hours, sedated with tincture of opiated syrup.

"It's time I went back to my own people, I guess," Red
Turtle replied. "I'd like to see how they're getting on up
there with the damned Klamats. You've been good to me,
Hank. I'm sorry for. . . ."

He broke off as Bitler shook his head, stared at the ground,
then pressed his lips together, hard, regained some sem-
blance of composure.

Hank turned to Auna-yi, stared at her wordlessly for a
moment, took her head between his hands, and drew her
against him, embraced her.

"I sure as hell didn't do you any favor bringin' you here,

Fanny. Hope you'll find better on the reservation, with Matthew's folks. The bay mare's yours to keep, and I want you to take this old iron of mine. It ain't much good, but you might need it. Wish I could do somethin' more. All that's happened—it's like a nightmare, only we ain't going to wake up. There's some Fate tryin' to kick my guts out—things just keep burning, no matter where I am. I'd move on too, but there's not much farther west a man can go. Maybe I'll hire some help, get the barn rebuilt. If a man keeps busy, it keeps madness away from his door. . . ."

Bitler thrust a pistol into Auna-yi's hand, helped her up onto the slender, white-stockinged bay. Red Turtle swung onto his stocky buckskin, drew the animal around to the gate, and held out his hand to Bitler. The older man hestiated a moment, then took it and grasped firmly, his eyes becoming momentarily moist. He slapped gently at the rump of Auna-yi's mare, and the horse took a quick step forward, Auna-yi wincing at a sudden stab of pain the movement caused in her wounded arm. Then she held out her good hand to Bitler also, and he took it in both of his own, clung briefly, then released it.

"Nothin' more to say, I guess," Hank whispered at last. "Good luck to you . . . to both of you. Matthew, you take care of her, you hear me?"

Red Turtle nodded, looked as if he wanted to speak, then nodded again, and the two rode away into gaining light. At the top of a rise above Bitler's ranch, the Modoc drew his buckskin to a halt, and Auna-yi reined in beside him. They turned back, Matthew Red Turtle raising one hand to wave.

The sky against the eastward mountains glowed with coming day, a vast expanse of yellow and thin redness, but the valley below was still indistinct, dark with leftover night. Hank Bitler's figure was already small with distance, distinguishable as human but not as any particular human, a stooped form dark in its bundle of clothing. He didn't respond to the rider's salute, for his back was already turned to them as he moved from the charred rubble that had been his barn toward the dark form of a house wrapped in shadows beneath a great brassy flare of sky.

SEVENTEEN

Gunfight on Lost River

[September–December 1872]

AUNA-YI LAY with her back against a boulder, half-dozing in warm sun, hearing but not listening to the laughing chatter of other young women, shrieks of small children as they played in shallow water of the river pool assigned, by custom, as the women's bathing place. Light made red patterns through her closed eyelids, pleasant heat on her bare legs, for she had pulled her dress of cheap cotton calico to her thighs to let the sun touch at her skin. Her hair, still damp from a brief dive into the slow-moving, warm river water, was beginning to dry, and she thought about sitting up to comb it out, decided for the moment against moving. It was pleasant simply to lie in sunlight and let her mind drift.

The five years she'd spent in Lost River and Tule Lake country with Red Turtle and the Modoc people under the leadership of Kintpuash had been a time marked by trouble, but still a good time in many ways. The primary problem was that of White settlers in the region, many of whom resented and feared the Modoc presence in what was, in fact, the tribe's ancestral homeland. There had been sporadic raids, a few killings on both sides over the course of the years. And it was true that the young men, when they went hunting for

deer, were not always averse to settling for a cow if one
presented itself, many reasoning that the Whites owed them
something for the use of their lands.

Not all ranchers were enemies of Captain Jack and his
people. Some long-term residents in particular were on friendly
terms with the chief himself, occasionally bringing a cow or a
steer as gifts. One White named Jack Riddle was even married to the chief's cousin. Red Turtle and a few other young
men had worked occasionally on nearby ranches at haying or
roundup time, and many of Captain Jack's band wore White
clothing and called themselves by names Whites had given
them.

But still, they had enough enemies among the settlers, and
these were continually clamoring for government troops to
intervene and force the Modocs onto the reservation at Fort
Klamath, a result which had actually occurred twice, once
during the years when Matthew Red Turtle had worked for
Hank Bitler. Kintpuash, however, had led his people back to
their own land shortly before Red Turtle and Auna-yi joined
them.

The second time had been in the autumn of 1869, and
Auna-yi would never forget the dreadful winter that ensued.
The much larger Klamath contingent, on reservation lands
they considered their own, had bullied the Modocs and cheated
them, forcing the southern tribe to pay for lumber they cut
for their sawmill and keeping for themselves almost all the
food and goods supplied by the Indian Bureau, allowing none
to Captain Jack's people. That season the Modocs were close
to starvation; a number of old ones and a few babies died
before spring came. Then Kintpuash led his band off the
reservation and back to Lost River.

But now the Saltus were trying once again to force the
Modocs to accept reservation life. All through the summer
there had been visits by agents from the Indian Bureau,
usually accompanied by at least a few bluecoat troops, trying
to convince Captain Jack and the other leading men to move
their people onto Fort Klamath lands, requests escalating
into demands accompanied by open threats of military force if
the people did not make up their minds soon to go voluntarily.

Thus far Kintpuash had kept the Whites busy negotiating
his counterproposals, primary among these being a request

that the Modocs be given a reservation somewhere on their
own lands rather than with the resentful Klamaths. It was, in
fact, this very issue which had drawn Captain Jack, accompanied by Matthew Red Turtle and several other prominent
men, to Fort Klamath. Meacham, the Indian agent there,
promised an answer, one way or the other, at this time.

But even with the trouble, skirmishes and times of famine
as the increasing number of ranchers and their herds drove
the deer and other game away from the country where wild
ungulates had previously grazed in abundance, Auna-yi, now
known mostly as Fanny, was happy in her life with Matthew
Red Turtle. The two had begun as friends on Bitler's ranch, a
friendship born almost out of desperation, and they remained
friends, the feeling developing gradually into a deep love.

They were married within a few months after coming to
live among his people, although it had been several months
after that before she lay with him in the manner of husband
and wife. Her experience with Tod Bitler and Weasel
McLaughlin before him had left scars on her innermost being,
wounds long in healing.

Matthew was understanding, at first merely waiting for her
to come to him, later teasing and joking with her, always
holding her close in his arms each night as they slept, until at
last she consented. She bathed carefully in the river one
evening, rubbed her skin with scented oils, and slipped naked between the blankets to await him, a fire glowing in the
pit of the small brush lodge they shared.

He was very gentle that first time, almost as if afraid she
would break, and it was up to her to guide him, to touch at
his skin with her lips, to straddle him and move with the
ancient, urgent rhythms of love. After the first night they'd
taken great joy in their bodies, exploring, fondling, finding
new ways to achieve pleasure, sometimes in the quiet dark of
their lodge, at others in the open day, off from the village on
a hunting venture and hidden in a secret ravine, or among a
stand of pinyons or a grove of aspens.

For a time they were both nearly obsessed to the point
where Auna-yi's craving to be with Red Turtle frightened
her.

The frantic urgency grew calmer with time, mellowed, and
now when she thought of her husband, it was with a warm

glow of love, of long friendship, of struggle and pleasure
shared over the years. He still talked at times about going
back to live as the Whites did, of working on a ranch full-time
and putting away more money for a place of their own, a plan
that Auna-yi was less than wholly enthusiastic about, most of
her ventures into the White world having been disastrous.

But Matthew had not acted upon the notion beyond his
temporary jobs in the area, and Fanny came to believe the
threat was not very real. The one great disappointment,
which they also shared, was that they had no children—and
after five years together, it seemed unlikely that little ones
would ever come.

AUNA-YI SIGHED, rolled her head to one side on the stone she
rested against. The surface was too hard for her to be comfortable any longer. She sat up, opened her eyes. Matthew
Red Turtle's younger sister, Little Goose, sat beside her,
peering into her face, bright-eyed and grinning so that the
dimple in one cheek showed.

"If you weren't married to my brother," she said, "I would
think you were dreaming of lovers. You were smiling in your
sleep, Fanny."

"I wasn't sleeping," Auna-yi laughed. "Who told you that
you could spy on me, Little Goose?"

"No one. What were you thinking about, then, if you
weren't sleeping?"

"You're too curious for your age. Married women sometimes think of things that young girls don't know about."

"I know about everything," the fifteen-year-old insisted.
"I've been to the woman lodge, and my mother and aunts
have told me how it is between a man and a woman. Is that
what you were thinking about?"

Auna-yi tugged at the girl's braid, smiled. Little Goose was
a very pretty as well as a bright and impertinent creature,
and she numbered at least a half-dozen suitors among her
conquests.

"Soon, now," Fanny said, "you'll have to settle on a husband. You're driving the young men to distraction. They're
all afraid to leave the village for fear one of their rivals will
gain an advantage with you, and none of them is bringing in

game for the people. How will you feel this winter when we all starve because you're such a flirt?"

"I'm having too much fun to quit right now," Little Goose giggled. "It's so easy to play with the boys, to make them crazy. I think they must be crazy to begin with, and not very intelligent. Girls would never make such fools of themselves. Besides, all the ones who want me are children. I intend to marry a man."

"Do you have someone in mind? I think you want Chief Kintpuash himself."

"Don't be silly. He has a wife. Still, he's very handsome, don't you think? I bet I could make him fall in love with me. He'd forget all about his first wife. . . ."

Auna-yi laughed aloud. "I'm a married woman," she said, "and we don't notice whether other men are handsome. Your brother's the only handsome man I know about in this village."

"Married women don't always tell the truth, I think. The grown men notice you all the time, Auna-yi, even Captain Jack. When you're close by, they won't even look at anyone else. I wish I were as beautiful as you are. It's only the silly boys who want me."

Red Turtle's mother came over to join her daughter and daughter-in-law, caught a bit of what Little Goose had been saying, and laughed.

"Silly boys want silly girls," she said, smiling affectionately at her daughter. "This one is driving her father and me as well to craziness. When I was your age, Little Goose, I was already carrying your brother in my belly, and you're still playing games. I want to live to see my grandchildren."

The woman went by the name of Polly because, as she once explained to Auna-yi, she had never cared for the name given to her—which was Born-by-the-stinking-water. Polly was a handsome woman with sleek, jet-black hair, resembling her daughter in the quick, bright eyes and round, laughing face, even to the dimple that appeared sporadically in her left cheek, but she was considerably stockier, grown wide through the hips and heavy of breast.

"It's good to have grandchildren," the mother continued, nodding.

Auna-yi winced at the reminder of her own and Matthew's childlessness, although she knew the old woman had not intended the remark to hurt her. Polly noted a momentary shadow of regret pass across her daughter-in-law's face, reached over, and patted her hand gently.

"You'll give me grandchildren one day, I am sure of it. Don't worry. I've known many cases where a husband and wife did not have little ones for, oh, ten years, even, and then, after they gave up, poof. Along came two or three, even five or six, right in a row. My own mother was like that. She didn't have me until she was married to my father for six years. You're a good wife to my son, I know that, Fanny. You shouldn't listen to me. I say foolish things without thinking about them, just as Little Goose does."

Auna-yi shook her head.

"You're like my own mother to me, Polly. You could never offend me."

The three sat in silence for a time, the older woman working at some sewing she'd brought along with her.

"I wonder when they're coming back," Polly said, turning from her work to look over her shoulder in the direction of the village—as though she might be able to see through the stony, sage-dotted rise that hid this stretch of riverbank from the encampment. "I thought we would know by now. . . ."

"Councils with the Saltu chiefs occasionally take a very long time," Auna-yi replied. "They're not willing to allow us anything, and the men go on talking, hoping to reason with them, but they can never see anyone's reason except their own. Yet perhaps this time it will be different, I don't know. Chief Kintpuash speaks well, and the others with him are good men—not hotheads, but not fools who'll give away everything, either."

Except Hooker Jim, who might do anything, and maybe Scarfaced Charley, who's too quick to anger. Something about Hooker Jim I don't trust.

Auna-yi didn't speak her thought, however. She kept her doubts to herself.

"The Whitemen can't make us leave again. This is our land. Kintpuash only told them they could use it," Little Goose said, her eyes flashing. "We'll fight them if they try to make us go back to the Klamats again. That's what all the young men are saying. I will fight too."

"It's easy to say such things when you're young, Little

Goose, and haven't seen what it's like to have a battle," Polly cautioned. "I was there when Ben Wright and his men sat down to eat with us and then suddenly began shooting. It was not just warriors who died that time, but old people and little children and women too. Men like Wright are worse than crazy wolves—they don't care who they kill. Whites are not like we are. But if Kintpuash chooses the way of war now, it could be there will be none of us left when it's all over."

"That's how it was with my people," Auna-yi said, her face seeming to grow many years older as she spoke. "We never wished for war with the Saltus but only to live in peace on our own lands. The ranchers couldn't bear to let us live at all, and now there are only a very few of my people left, perhaps none. The bluecoat captain, Gideon Whitney, he told me when he came here once that he had heard the last of my people were dead, but I keep hoping Smoke Woman and Wolf Tracker are still alive somewhere. . . ."

Polly patted Auna-yi's hand and then gathered up the sewing things.

"I guess we'll know what will happen when Red Turtle and Kintpuash and the others come back," the older woman said. "Women always need more patience than Old Man ever gave any human beings. My husband will be wanting something to eat soon, so I'd better go back to my lodge. Fanny, you make sure my Little Goose doesn't disappear into the trees with some young man."

Auna-yi smiled, but her eyes were serious.

Please, Old One, Lizard, Gray Squirrel, let the men be sane. Don't let the world come apart again, not like before. . . .

IT WAS SUNSET of that same evening when the men returned from council. Auna-yi was sitting in front of Red Turtle's parents' lodge, talking quietly with Polly while the husband, Left Hand Tom, sat and smoked a pipe of tobacco, pretending not to listen to the women's conversation. When word came from the scouts that riders were approaching, Auna-yi, like nearly everyone else, ran up the trail to greet them.

Hooker Jim, Scarfaced Charley, and two other men were talking loudly in angry tones, their voices sounding at the same time so that what they said was unintelligible. Kintpuash

and Red Turtle rode a little apart and said nothing, their
expressions sober, the chief looking crushed.

Auna-yi stepped to her husband's horse, reached to take its
bridle as she walked along beside it. She looked up into
Matthew's face, and he dropped a hand to caress her hair.

"The news is not good, then, my husband?" she asked.

"The talking has come to nothing," he replied, shaking his
head. "I will tell you about it later. We have decisions we
must make. But first those of us who went to meet the agent
will have to discuss matters with the other men of the village.
Yes, we all have decisions to make, and none of them will
lead to anything good."

THE MODOC MEN gathered near the big sweat lodge, but they
didn't go inside to talk, and so the women quietly moved
near the perimeter of the circle to listen.

In short, as Kintpuash explained, the White authorities
refused to grant the tribe any concessions at all. Hope for a
reservation somewhere on Lost River was unequivocally dead,
and the Indian Bureau had ordered the people to move
immediately to Fort Klamath.

"They'll send bluecoats to move us," he said, his voice
tired. "I told them our people need time to prepare for this
journey, but I don't know how long they'll leave us alone.
Perhaps they will wait until spring, but it may be that they
will not. Three winters ago our people were starving in the
lands of our enemies. Yet if we stay here, in our own lands,
the bluecoat chiefs say we'll have to fight them. There are
many more bluecoat soldiers than Modoc warriors, and it
could be that we will all die under their guns this winter. I'm
thinking of the women and the children, for we've learned
that the White warriors don't mind killing these helpless ones
any more than they mind killing brave men. Now we must
think what to do. I will listen to you, my people."

"Bluecoats have no balls," Scarfaced Charley shouted. "One
Modoc warrior could kill twenty of them. I'm ready to fight
all of Jackson's men."

A number of younger men called out, echoing Charley's
sentiments. An older warrior called Black Lake waited for the
hubbub to die down, and then he spoke sharply.

"It is easy to say such things, harder to perform them. Do

we wish to see our women and children die because Scarface likes to boast? I don't wish to go back to Klamath country, but I want my sons and my daughters to grow up to be men and women. If we stay here and wait for the bluecoats to come, our little ones may not live to see another spring."

"What Black Lake speaks is true," Left Hand Tom said. "The Whites are numberless. We've seen how they keep coming into our country, and there seems to be no end to them. We can fight, but only if we move to the burnt rock lands to the south, to the place where they say fire came out of the earth in the long-ago days and melted the stone so that it's full of holes. The Whites would not be able to fight against us there if they sent a thousand men, because they don't know the land as we do."

Kintpuash nodded.

"We can fight them from the lava beds, that's true. If we hide out in the caves, they will not be able to take us. But our people cannot eat black rocks. If we move south to that country now, we will starve to death before spring, and it may be that the soldiers won't come against us during the cold time anyway. No one likes to fight when there's ice on the paths and fog and freezing rain in the air all the time."

"Can you promise us they won't attack before spring, Captain Jack?" Hooker Jim snarled. "You cannot. I say that it's time to drive the White settlers away from our lands, all of them. If we kill some of these men and burn their houses, the rest will leave. After that the bluecoats will have no one to protect."

"Those are the words of a fool, Hooker Jim," Matthew Red Turtle exclaimed. "You would give the soldiers the excuse they need to come wipe out this village entirely. Don't think they won't take revenge. I know the Whites better than most of you. I've lived among them. . . ."

"Yes, and maybe you want to take care of your friends," Jim sneered. "Who knows, maybe they've offered you money to speak for them. Perhaps your half-White woman sleeps with them for money, Matthew Red Turtle."

Matthew rose abruptly, reached for his knife. Hooker Jim jumped to his feet and stood before Red Turtle, grinning as his own blade glinted in firelight.

Kintpuash's voice cracked like a whip, and the chief pushed his own body between the two antagonists.

"Now you're both trying to destroy our people," he said. "How are we to stand against our enemies if we kill each other? There will be no fighting here."

The moment of crisis passed, and both Red Turtle and Hooker Jim withdrew and sat down again, although they continued to watch each other with a fierce hostility.

Auna-yi let out her breath in a long sigh, only then realizing she hadn't breathed during the short-lived confrontation.

The talk continued late into the night, the council eventually deciding the Modocs should stay where they were for the time being but to be ready to leave for the lava beds at any moment, gathering and preserving as much food as possible in the interim. Red Turtle didn't speak again after the incident with Hooker Jim but only sat listening, apparently sunk deep in gloomy thought.

"It's come," he said when he and Auna-yi were alone in their lodge later. "This is the end of my people. They will fight since there's really no other choice, but eventually the Whites will win because there are always more of them and fewer of us. And then what's left of us will be shipped off to some reservation far enough away from here so that the ranchers can feel safe, and my people will no longer exist. They will all die of hunger or diseases. It's what has happened to every tribe along the way as the Whites have pushed across the continent from the East Coast. Oh, there are a few left, a few more battles for the bluecoats among the Kiowa and the Sioux, the Apaches in the southwest, but it's not hard to see where it will end. When the Whites have finally gotten rid of all the Indian people, then they will go to work on the animals until there's nothing left but cattle and horses and Whitemen's dogs. They've already started on that, too. . . ."

Auna-yi listened to the tone of his voice—hard, bitter notes of pain. She wondered vaguely where he'd learned all these things about what had happened so many miles distant; supposed he'd probably found out from books in the White people's houses where he'd lived at one time or another. Perhaps even Hank Bitler had told him.

She didn't know what to say to comfort him—or herself.

And so she silently wrapped her arms around his middle and then leaned her face against his chest.

"No time for self-pity," he said abruptly. "It's time to get the hell away from here, time to live in the White world. I knew all along. . . . But for now, I have to stay here, Fanny. These are my people, and I have to fight alongside them even though I know the outcome already. But it's time for you to go away. I'll take you to Jack Samson's place over on the eastern side of Tule Lake. I've worked for him a number of times. He's a good man, and you'll be safe there. Maybe I can talk my mother and Little Goose into going with you. . . ."

"No," Auna-yi said.

"What do you mean? There's no reason you should get killed. . . ."

"Your people have become my people, Red Turtle. I don't have anybody else. I will not go live with the Whites while you're fighting for your home. I'll stay here like the other women, I'll get everything ready so we can go south to the lava beds when the time comes. I'm your wife. If you wish me to leave so that you can share your lodge with another woman, this is not the way to do it."

"Auna-yi. . . ."

"Hush, now. The decision has been made. We don't need to think about it anymore. Come lie down with me, husband. Perhaps tonight we will make a son for you."

AUTUMN PASSED, and the time of cold came. Geese departed from the lakes, rising and circling. They flew in great chuckling wedges toward warmer lands to the south. Every morning ice on standing pools of water grew a little thicker but melted off a little later in the day. Clouds settled in and seemed never to depart, sometimes spitting rain and sleet, sometimes dropping down to the sage-dotted hills and rock outcroppings and staying there, obscuring vision and sending chill through blankets and clothing, through flesh itself—until one felt an ache in the very bone.

The leaf-falling moon passed, and then the moon when snow first came, yet still the bluecoats did not arrive. Many people's spirits began to rise despite the misery of icy weather and never enough food, for they reasoned that if the soldiers hadn't attacked them by now, it was unlikely they would come at all during the winter months.

It was a bitterly cold day, a day of freezing rain, and with evening came fog like fingers of ice. Auna-yi kept a fire burning in the lodge all night now, spending a good part of each day just going farther and farther away from the village to find wood. But even with the fire it was very cold outside the pile of blankets beneath which she and Red Turtle slept, and when the smokehole was just beginning to grow visible with dawn, dull dark gray against blackness around, she rose to feed the red embers in the firepit, shivering as she placed sticks in among the coals.

Barking camp dogs alerted her and everyone else in the village to the presence of intruders. Matthew Red Turtle rose, hastily pulled on pants and coat, picked up his rifle, and headed for the entryway.

Now voices shouted outside, the tones harsh although the words were unintelligible. Auna-yi shrugged into her own blanket-coat, followed her husband out, and stood just behind him, watching apprehensively and concealing beneath her wraps the old pistol Hank Bitler had given her several years earlier.

Soldiers from Fort Klamath had surrounded the village before daybreak. That much was apparent at a glance, the bluecoats standing about the lodges, their bayoneted rifles at ready. Auna-yi couldn't tell how many there were, guessed perhaps forty.

Scarfaced Charley stood outside his own lodge, face grim, a pistol tucked in his belt and a rusty flintlock leveled at the apparent leader of the enemy force. The old scar marking his cheek showed dead white against leathery skin.

"No one asked you to come here!" he shouted. "We're sleeping in this village. You go back to Fort Klamath with your men."

The bluecoat leader didn't flinch, stood with his own rifle steady, his back stiff.

"Put the gun down," the officer commanded, "and fetch me Captain Jack. I'm Major James Jackson. My orders are to talk to the chief."

Scarfaced Charley continued to stare at Jackson without moving, gun still pointing at the major's midsection. Then he glanced aside, lowered the barrel as Kintpuash stepped forward and spoke.

"I'm Kintpuash," he said. "What business do you have with me to come here to our camp in the dark and scare my people?"

"You know why I'm here. I have orders from the Great Father in Washington to take your people to the reservation at Fort Klamath."

"I will go, then, and I will take all my people, but I do not place any confidence in what you Whitemen say. Come up to me like men when you want to talk, but don't sneak into our village in the dark when everybody's sleeping."

"I'm not here to make any trouble," Major Jackson said. "I want you to bring your men together here in front of my soldiers."

"You see my men," Kintpuash said, gesturing around him. "They are here. They don't hide from you."

"This all of them? You're sure about that?"

Red Turtle turned to whisper to Auna-yi.

"This is it," he murmured. "Slip away to the dugouts. The other women will be doing the same. It's time for you to leave. I'll see you in a little while."

Auna-yi shook her head and continued watching, listening to the conversation between the White major and Kintpuash.

"Damn it, Fanny," Red Turtle whispered, "you stubborn bitch . . . there's danger . . . I want you out of here!"

"You over there," a soldier called out, thrusting his rifle in their direction. "No conspiring. Listen to the major."

Jackson gestured toward a clump of sage outside the circle of men.

"Lay your gun here," he said to Kintpuash.

"Why do you ask me to do that? I've never fought White people yet, and I don't want to now."

"I promise no one will hurt you if you lay down your weapon. You're the chief, and your men will follow your lead. Now do as I say, and we'll have no trouble."

Kintpuash glanced around at the circle of bluecoats, their rifles trained on his men. With stooped shoulders, he walked slowly to the sagebrush and laid down his gun.

"Now, the rest of you," Jackson called out to the other Modocs, "one at a time."

No one moved until Kintpuash signaled for the others to do as he had, and slowly they moved forward, each stacking his rifle on top of the others. Scarfaced Charley came forward last, put his flintlock on the pile, and then stepped away.

"Pistol too," the major snapped.

"You got my gun," Scarface said easily, his eyes glinting like bits of obsidian.

"Disarm him, Lieutenant Boutelle," Jackson shouted, and another man in officer's uniform stepped forward.

"Give me that pistol quick, damn you," Boutelle snapped, reaching toward Charley's belt.

The Modoc stepped back, laughed.

"I'm not a dog to be shouted at," he said.

Boutelle went red in the face. He drew his revolver.

"You sonofabitch," the junior officer snarled. "I'll teach you to talk back to me. Now give me that damned gun."

"You're the dog, I think," Charley said. "I will keep my gun."

The lieutenant raised his weapon until it was pointing at Charley's belly, and at the same instant Charley drew his own pistol.

Gunfire shattered the icy air, two reports coming almost together, and Boutelle staggered back, clutching at his arm. Scarface twisted around to the stack of weapons, grabbed his rifle, and then all the Modoc men shoved forward and reached for their own relinquished arms.

After that the world exploded.

"Fire, damn it, fire," Major Jackson screamed, and a spattering of dull booms from military rifles followed. The Modocs ducked for cover among the lodges, and discharged their own weapons, Auna-yi firing off several rounds from the pistol she'd kept concealed until now.

Cries of men, thunder of round after round being fired, a loud scream. Bodies falling, some bluecoats, some Modocs. Where is Red Turtle?

It was over in a very short time, the soldiers withdrawing, men dragging downed comrades away from the village, bugle sounding retreat. A profound silence ensued, a silence that felt unnatural, almost painful to the ears after a brief eternity of noise. Moans somewhere, someone wounded.

Auna-yi stepped from behind cover. She saw one sprawled

form that she felt was particularly significant among several
who lay on churned-up snow and earth in the center of the
village, but it took a very long time for her to recognize the
features above a gaping hole torn in the throat another long
time before the wail emerged from her own.

*Red Turtle . . . not you, not you, Red Turtle . . . you
cannot leave me also. . . .*

EIGHTEEN
Journey to Wahgalu
[December 1872]

THEY TRAVELED southward into an increasingly jagged and
wild land of stony rims and flats, some clothed with sagebrush and greasewood, stands of pine, other areas merely
expanses of tumbled black lava flow where nothing grew at
all. The day continued cold and gray, fog drifting in and
obscuring everything at a distance of more than a few yards,
then abruptly lifting to disclose another stretch of desolate,
mournful landscape beneath a low, lead-colored sky.

The bay mare picked her way carefully through broken,
treacherous ground, and the buckskin followed along on a
lead, loaded lightly with provisions. Auna-yi moved in a haze
of unreality that she couldn't shake, a sense that soon she'd
awaken from this despairing gray dream, and the world would
be back to normal, Red Turtle would shake her shoulder and
laugh at her for crying in her sleep.

Why do I keep going? she wondered. *Why keep on blindly sitting on this horse that plods south with these people who are no longer mine? There's nothing for me here without Red Turtle. There's nothing for me anywhere, no one, no thing that belongs to me. . . .*

By afternoon they caught up to the other women, and Little Goose rode beside her. The teenaged girl was unnaturally silent, her normally bright, laughing face drawn with grief. Auna-yi's own feelings of grief and purposelessness coalesced to rage, to a need for action, to be doing something in the effort against those who senselessly murdered all native people whom they deemed inconveniently located for one reason or another. It was really this expedient, nothing more, that had caused the destruction of her own people, the Yahis, and of others in other places. The same story was told wearily in a hundred versions, different names, different parts of the continent, just as Red Turtle had said.

And when they're finished with the Indians, they'll start on the wild animals. They wish to kill every coyote, every cougar, every bear, every ground squirrel and snake, venomous or otherwise, every animal and every human that's not them or a servant to them. Some are different—Hank Bitler and this man McCain, from what you've told me—but there are far too many of the other kind. They will prevail—can't help but prevail, and when there's no wild, free place left, no animal who doesn't serve them, they'll look around and wonder where it's all gone. But they will never look into their own hearts, their fear.

The pain was still with her, but it had been transformed, it had a clear objective now.

Accordingly, when they stopped to camp for the night in a fortresslike formation of lava flows, Auna-yi approached Kintpuash, stood with her eyes modestly turned down but her bearing of tense, straight-backed determination not to be denied recognition for long.

"You wish to speak to me, Fire Woman of the Yahis?" the chief said, his voice sounding ancient with weariness and grief but nonetheless gentle.

"I wish to help in the fight against the bluecoats," she said. "I know that I'm only a woman, but I'm one who has lost her reason for wanting to cling to life. Red Turtle was my husband, and we had no children."

"I know, and I am sad. Red Turtle was a strong man, very brave. He understood the Whites, and we'll all miss his counsel. What is it that you would do?"

"We don't have enough guns or ammunition to hold out against the bluecoats very long. That's what my husband believed."

"It's true. We place ourselves in the hands of the Ancient One and hope for the best."

"I think I can get guns and ammunition for the men—enough to make a difference. I have friends, White friends who helped me when I was young, taught me to read and write. I think these people will help us now."

"Why do you believe these White people will not simply turn you over to the bluecoats and make you lead them back here?"

"Because I know them. I know their hearts, Kintpuash. How do you determine which friends you trust? Even if they cannot help us, they will never turn against me, I know that."

"I think it's been a long time since you've seen these people," the leader said. "It's not anyone who lives close by Lost River or Tule Lake, is it?"

"No. They live far to the south near the fire mountain of Wahgalu. It would take perhaps ten, perhaps fifteen days to go there and return."

The chief nodded, studying her face.

"I never wanted a war with the White people, and yet it has come to us. Many winters ago when the Achomowis and Atsugewis fought against Whitney and the bluecoats, however, the Modocs helped them. Blackbeard, the Shasta chief, had a Whiteman who lived among his people, and this Whiteman was able to buy guns for them. If we could find someone like that now, it would be a very good thing. The American you speak of—is it McCain who's married to Ooti of the Panos? I've heard the stories, though I do not know whether they're true, but Red Turtle told me you had once lived with these people in a Maidu village. If you believe McCain and Acorn Girl will help us now, then I would be glad to have you go to them. I'll ask some of my young men to go with you in the morning. Sleep well tonight. It's a long journey."

Auna-yi bowed her head in acknowledgement and withdrew to Left Hand Tom's fire back under an overhang of lava rock, where she busied herself helping Little Goose and Polly to prepare an evening meal, the work going on without the cheerful chatter that usually accompanied it. Black Lake, who was Left Hand's cousin and closest friend, came and sat beside the grieving father, the two old warriors smoking together for a time without speaking.

Suddenly a great clamor arose at the edge of the rim which protected the camp area—a volley of shots being fired off and voices whooping and shouting from thick blackness beyond. The warriors sprang to their feet, grabbing for weapons, while women and children ducked for cover among bushes and rock formations as the intruders rode down into camp.

It was Hooker Jim, leading a half-dozen warriors, a number of women and children trailing along silently. The men's eyes were bright with ferocious triumph as they waved rifles in the air, and Auna-yi immediately sensed trouble.

Kintpuash walked forward to greet the group and stood quietly as Hooker Jim dismounted.

"What is this? What have you done, Hooker Jim?" the chief asked.

"Whitemen's guns," the other laughed, tossing a rifle and a pair of pistols onto the earth.

"Where did you get them?"

"From dead Whitemen, of course. Some ranchers rode into our camp across the river from yours this morning and started shooting at us. We ran away because there were not very many of us, but still they killed Boston Charley's woman, who was fleeing with her little baby in her arms. And they killed Fish-eating Jim's mother and wounded Curly-headed Doctor. So we've been on a revenge-taking. There are twelve ranchers dead on the east side of Tule Lake, though they were alive just this morning. We didn't kill their women, though, because we are warriors, not White dogs."

"You killed the men who attacked you?"

"Whitemen are Whitemen. Who knows which is which?

The ones we killed were not expecting us to visit them, I know that."

"I think you're a fool, Hooker Jim," Kintpuash said warily. "Many of those Whitemen you speak of were our friends and spoke for us to the bluecoat leaders. Now the soldiers will come after us even here. They will not stop until we're all dead. You've brought death to your own people."

Hooker Jim stared at the chief for a long moment, then spat on the ground next to the other's feet. The warriors with Jim laughed, and the group turned away—while the chief stood as if made of stone, not acknowledging the insult, hardly seeming aware of it or of anything else, his eyes turned inward on some terrible foreknowledge, the end, inevitable now, darkness for all his people.

AS NEW ARRIVALS settled into camp, Black Lake spoke quietly to Left Hand Tom.

"This is a bad business. Hooker Jim has brought much trouble to our camp."

Left Hand stared into the fire, his eyes dull and vacant with his own grief.

"I've lost a son," he said. "That's trouble enough for me. I cannot find it in my heart to mourn for twelve dead Whitemen."

"We will mourn for many more of our own children before this is over. It's as Kintpuash has said—Hooker Jim brings us our own death. We will never go back to our lands, Left Hand Tom, and I want to see my sons and daughters grow to be men and women. Tomorrow I'll head east and cross the mountains to Fort Bidwell. My father-in-law lives there among the Paiutes. He'll be glad to see his grandchildren. Come with us, and perhaps you will not have to grieve for your daughter as well as your son."

"I no longer know what is the right thing to do," Left Hand said. "I am an old man without power."

"I know what I want to do," Little Goose said with a flash of intense anger. "I want to stay and kill bluecoats."

"Hush, daughter," Polly hissed. "You know better than to speak out that way in front of the men."

"Don't you wish to see this little one with a husband and children of her own rather than bleeding her life into the earth?" Black Lake asked, ignoring the girl's outburst. "Come

with me, my friend. If we wish, we can return and fight after
we've taken our women and children away to the safe place.
Fort Bidwell is not a bad place, because there are no Klamats.
The Indian agent even provides grain, cattle, and blankets.
Our women and children will be safe across the mountains."

Left Hand Tom stared at Polly and Little Goose for a long
time, his face appearing not merely old but dead. At last he
made a gesture of assent to his friend.

AUNA-YI SLEPT little that night, her dreams fragmentary and
haunting.

*Red Turtle embraced her, and then she saw that his throat
was torn out, the wound become a mocking mouth that
whispered obscene words of death and horror. Next it was
she who lay on the ground, dead, but she could see wolves
gathering, could feel them tearing the flesh away from her
until she was nothing but bones, and when she rose at last to
run away, her legs kept falling off, and she had to stop and
put them back on. The whole world was fire, then, and she
was much younger. She stood on top of Wahgalu with True
Bear McCain, who was was telling her something, something
very important, except she couldn't understand a word he
said. And then it was Red Turtle beside her—she was over-
joyed to see him, remembering only that she hadn't expected
to see him again. These and many more images, images of
Whitemen, their mouths ferocious and dripping blood, skulls
grinning behind them, images of wave after wave of brown-
skinned people, all stumbling and falling, flesh melting from
their bones. True Bear again, but this time he was showing
her something, pointing to his face. She looked closely and
saw that it was divided into two distinct halves, one painted
white, the other red, and she realized her own face was
painted the same way. "We must learn to live in the Whiteman's
world or die in the Redman's," he said, and she knew these to
be Red Turtle's words, spoken in the barn at Bitler's ranch,
but then fire was eating at walls around them.*

She woke exhausted at first light, rose nevertheless, and
set about making preparations for her journey. She swallowed
a cold meal of dried venison and a leftover cake of *wokas*
flour, not because she was hungry but because she didn't
wish to become weak and unable to accomplish her objective.

Left Hand Tom and his family were busy with preparations for their own departure to the east, but Little Goose slipped up beside Auna-yi and grabbed her hand, pressing it earnestly.

"Take me with you, Fanny," she said. "I don't want to go live among the Paiutes. I want to stay here and fight. My father will not chase me if I go with you to get guns from your White friends. He'll take my mother over the mountains, but you and I will come back and help our men kill the enemy."

"I couldn't do that to your father, Little Goose," Auna-yi said. "He's right. You should grow up to have a husband and little ones of your own. How do you think Left Hand and Polly would feel if you were killed also? Then they would have no children, no grandchildren ever. You must think of them. I have no one left to mourn for me, but it's different with you. The one we loved who-is-dead did not wish to fight the Saltus. He wanted to live as they did—because he knew the old ways were dying. If there is to be anything left of your people, your blood, then it must be because young ones like you learn to live in a different kind of world, and have children, and raise them—so they may live also. Then the old ways may be kept alive in memory, at least. That's the only hope remaining for your people, Little Goose. My grandfather, Wolf Tracker of the Yahis, gave me this vision when I was a girl. I didn't understand then, but I see now that he was right. Yet I don't even know whether he's alive or dead—and my mother—and the few others who escaped when Whitemen destroyed our village."

"What you say doesn't make any sense," the girl replied, her eyes filling with tears.

"Yes, it does. It's a bitter thing, but there's no other way. One path is ending, but you're young enough to find a different trail to follow. I'm sorry, my sister, but I will not take you with me."

FIRE WOMAN SET OFF with half a dozen young warriors as escort, Kintpuash having deemed that such a number might be necessary inasmuch as no one knew how many bluecoat patrols were at this moment searching for the Modoc encampment.

The sky was again the color of lead but the overcast higher, not threatening snow or sleet, the air somewhat warmer.

They encountered no White troops as they rode, skirting east around the base of the big, blown-out crater of Medicine Peak and continuing south through relatively level country.

Toward afternoon the overcast broke up, and the small band traveled for a time in dazzling sunlight, the pure white cone of Shasta gleaming off to the west, visible when they topped a rise and could see above intervening ridges. Auna-yi's escorts trotted their horses along soberly enough, talking little, presumably out of respect for her recent bereavement. But with the sudden advent of sunlight, the six young men, hardly more than overgrown boys really, the oldest perhaps seventeen, could no longer contain their high spirits and took to racing each other along stretches of level ground, whooping and laughing, playing tricks on one another.

Auna-yi caught herself smiling at their antics, and felt sudden and terrible guilt that she'd forgotten, even for a moment, the pain of Red Turtle's death. For a time thereafter, she rode on in a state of confusion.

My husband, forgive me. Are we really such shallow creatures, our feelings so transient that a thing such as a few hours of sun shining upon my face, the clowning of boys, could make me smile when so short a time ago. . . ?

Her life at Lost River, she realized now, already seemed a part of the distant past, a dream she had lived in another lifetime.

Perhaps this is how we are made, so that we can bear to go on living. But it doesn't matter very much to me whether I live or not. Too many things, too many lifetimes gone, torn apart in a matter of minutes, eruptions of violence that shattered whole worlds.

Watching the boys at play now, she felt old—ancient at twenty-one years of age—like a person who had lived too long, seen too much.

They rode on, and the light grew yellow, shadows long. The young men tired and dropped back to the jogging pace of normal travel.

They camped almost due east of Shasta, the sun appearing for a moment behind the white giant's shoulder as the group crested a rise, dropping behind the mountain again as they descended.

There was no sign of troopers—and no other human beings

at all, since the Modocs took great care to stay above valleys where ranches or settlements might exist.

That night Auna-yi, physically as well as emotionally exhausted, slept without any dreams that she could recall and felt refreshed when she roused the boys at first light to continue the trek southward.

Dawn, and a thin, high overcast—but this burned off before noon, and the sky was once more spectacularly blue, the lava-strewn plain they crossed splotched with patches of dazzling, icy snow in the sunlight, while Shasta, she noticed, had mantled itself in a covering of cloud, perfectly conical mist sworls that mimicked the mountain's shape and concealed it utterly.

But far to the south, the squared-off snow peak of Wahgalu shone through pure and icy air. She recognized the sacred mountain's form and experienced a surge of excitement, as though new life were pouring into her very being.

How long had it been?

Not even that mattered any more.

Wahgalu. Destination. God mountain of my people, place from where the spirits step off into the stars, place where all the Yahis have gone now, and I am the last one who will take that path. Or are these only stories, tales of a life beyond this one, things the old ones tell children, tell each other to comfort themselves? It's good to come back to these lands—it feels right, and yet it's very sad as well. I don't understand anything, anything at all. . . .

THEY PASSED beyond Pit River and crossed the White wagon road leading over Hatchet Mountain. Below was the settlement of Burney and east of that the basin through which Hat Creek flowed—yes, where Weasel McLaughlin and his men had captured her in the aftermath of the Mill Creek massacre.

The sacred mountain of the Yana peoples was closer now, much closer. As distance lessened, and the Modoc band proceeded toward the big volcano, Auna-yi came into country she knew from her girlhood—landforms, vegetation, even the color and odor of earth itself was imprinted at some deep level of her consciousness, so that each new vista seemed to fit into a predestined place that her mind accepted as *just right*—and her confusion grew. More and more the last five,

no, six years came to resemble a dream, one that now bore
no relation to the eternal and present reality of the country
that had spawned her. Some part of her felt at ease in a way
she'd never felt in the lands of the Modocs, even though
these people had become her adopted tribe, even though she
had married and loved Red Turtle and was his wife.

Now she was returning like a guest, like a thief, and yet
she felt herself to be at home. No amount of reasoning could
make her feel otherwise.

As they moved ever closer to the McCain ranch, she found
her thoughts turning to True Bear, wondering if she'd find
him there, what he looked like now, whether he'd recognize
her or she him. Perhaps he'd married, had children of his
own. That was possible.

She recalled her dream that first night in the lava beds, a
vision of standing on top of Wahgalu with True Bear, and
how he had tried to tell her something she couldn't understand. Irrationally, she still expected to find him as she had
seen him last, a thin boy of fourteen, scarcely taller than
herself. She remembered the night Wolf Tracker had sent
her to him with food—after the Yahi scouts captured him and
Big Woodpecker—how frightened he was, and how determined not to show fear. She remembered the day by the pool
beneath the obsidian bluff, remembered a last sweet, desperate embrace of children who anticipated separation but never
imagined it would last for years.

*We thought we would marry one another, nothing would
ever change. Children don't believe in change, and Old Coyote Man always surprises them. True Bear is married and
happy by now—has forgotten all about me. But it was a
sweet time, a time when we didn't believe in tomorrow—at
least didn't believe it would be any different from today,
didn't believe in the end of worlds, even though older people
tried to tell us. Wolf Tracker and Smoke Woman, my mother.
I cannot remember clearly what they looked like except when
I'm dreaming, cannot remember what True Bear really looked
like.*

In a moment of panic, then, she tried to call up Red
Turtle's face and found that she couldn't. She could recall
individual features, the curl of lip, slightly slanted eyes, wide

cheekbones, but she couldn't put them together to form a coherent whole.

Must we lose everything, then? Only a few days, and my husband's face is gone from my mind. Coyote, you're not kind. . . . For you, we're no more than gray squirrels or jackrabbits or trout in the streams.

She observed that, contrary to what she felt, the Modocs grew increasingly uneasy as they left lands familiar to them and entered into unknown territory, drawing together like young animals, growing quieter, no outbursts of spontaneous play now. As they rode, they peered warily about—as if an enemy were likely hidden behind every boulder, within every ravine. She took to joking with them a little, trying to tease them out of their discomfort, and found her own spirits growing lighter as a result.

THEY PASSED the eastward face of Wahgalu, riding through high forests in a land of volcanic debris and steaming sulphur vents, and approached the McCain ranch below Black Butte and Red Mountain, where she instructed the Modoc youths to stay behind and allow her to go on alone, not wishing the band of approaching warriors to be mistakenly shot as an enemy invasion before the Oidoing-koyos realized the true nature of the party.

Auna-yi rode up over the bench that separated Upper Eden from the rest of the world. The ranch complex, she realized from this vantage point, actually constituted a little town of its own—sawmill, flour mill, blacksmith shop, cabins, and brush lodges scattered among the trees—with trails everywhere worn down to bare earth among drifts of dirty snow, corrals and barns near the big house where the McCains lived, numerous chicken houses, sheds, bunkhouses for unmarried workers and temporary help. She could see a number of human figures bundled in heavy clothing and moving along paths, men and women pursuing whatever occupations they were about.

Beyond pasture lands where whitefaced cattle knotted together in groups, the great bulk of the mountain rose up, its peak partially hidden by pine ridges, huge except by comparison to the much greater mountain of Shasta.

Something about the scene, the warmth and busyness of

human activity in its small sphere beneath the vastness of mountain and sky, moved her deeply in a way she couldn't explain even to herself.

She halted her bay mare on the rim against the sky so that the inhabitants of the valley could see her and know she was not approaching in stealth before proceeding down a last stretch of trail. Oidoing-koyo was obscured now by heavily forested folds of land, and as she came around a bend in the trail, a young man approached on foot—a stocky, dark-browed individual who carried a rifle in his hands and looked wary, even hostile, until he saw the rider was a woman. Then he stopped dead still, staring at her open-mouthed while the rifle barrel dropped groundward.

Something familiar about him, but. . . .

"Wahtaurisi-yi?" he breathed. "It is you, isn't it? We all supposed you were dead. Don't you remember me?"

It came to her then. The figure was changed, of course, not much taller than when they were children, but grown thick through the shoulders, the jaw defined, hardened with maturity. He was a powerful young man now rather than a boy, but the features not really altered all that much, and there was a glint of humor, eagerness in the eyes.

"Big Woodpecker. You've grown up since we saw each other last. I guess I've changed as well."

He grinned broadly when she spoke his name, almost dragged her off the horse so that he could wrap his arms around her and squeeze her in a hug that stopped her breathing entirely while it lasted.

"You have the strength of a bear!" she laughed. "I think you've broken my ribs. You've grown up, and now you don't know your own power."

He looked embarrassed, and began stammering apologies until he managed to assure himself that the beautiful woman he'd just mauled was not truly angry, at which point he insisted she climb back upon her pony while he took the reins to lead her to the ranch house.

"Wait until Big Ben and Ooti see you! They'll shit a brick— excuse me. Where have you been all these years? Will you be able to stay for Christmas? No, don't tell me anything. Ooti will want to fix a special dinner, and then we'll talk, get caught up. So many things have changed since we saw you last . . ."

Auna-yi listened to Big Woodpecker's happy chatter as he walked and found herself unable to ask the question she wanted most to ask.

He has not mentioned True Bear at all. Could it be that he's also. . . .

No, that was unthinkable.

NINETEEN
Blood Among the Burnt Rocks
[December 1872–January 1873]

THE BIG KITCHEN of the McCain ranch was warm, almost too hot, from a great cookstove that dominated one corner, spicy-fragrant with odors of baking, a rich smell of roasting beef as well. Ooti knelt, her figure still slim and lithe, checked inside the oven, and stirred at a pan boiling on top of the stove. She spoke a few words in Maidu to a short, heavyset woman who hovered there, then poured coffee from the pot on top of the warming oven, and sat down at a long table where Auna-yi and the six Modoc warriors, the young men still rather dazed, were all eating slices of warm bread smeared with butter and jam.

Ben and Big Woodpecker also sat at the table, and next to the Maidu youth was Yellow Grass, looking both propri-etary and slightly suspicious of Auna-yi.

"Arms and ammunition, eh?" Ben was saying. "Well, after all these years, I must be getting a reputation as a gunrunner. Not what I anticipated for my old age, but. . . ."

"Of course we'll help," Ooti interrupted, patting Ben's hand. "Perhaps we'll go north with you—fight Wawlems again. What do you think of that, Bear-who-cannot-see-well? Shall we go on the warpath one more time?"

"Bear-who-cannot-see-well is now Stone Blind Bear, but my wife still thirsts for blood. I fear she may have it before all this is over. Clayton and some of the others would be delighted to see us run out of here, and our *Injun shantytown* to boot. But that's our concern, Miss Auna-yi, and we won't burden you with the details. I'm sorry True Bear isn't here to see you. I know it'll mean a great deal to him to hear that you're alive and well. I shall send off a letter immediately to let him know. We had all thought. . . ."

"Where is True Bear? You haven't told me. I was almost afraid to ask. . . ."

"Poor little one, you've lost a great many people," Ooti said. "But True Bear is well, although I'm not sure that he's very happy. Ben sent him away to the place called Harvard, near the ocean at the other end of the world, a place where Wawlems go to learn useless things."

"The elements of civilization, such worthless disciplines as literature, history, art, music, higher mathematics. . . ."

"Yes, that sort of useless things," Ooti laughed. "Then he can come home and recite *The Iliad* to the cows and tell the coyotes about the fall of the Roman Empire. See? I know about such matters."

"You know that you're as proud of True Bear as I am. It's an adventure to explore the mind, whether one finds utilitarian application for the knowledge or not. It could be argued, in fact, that using knowledge defeats the purpose of pure scholarship."

"Is that why True Bear went away, then?" Auna-yi asked. "I've heard that there's a learning place closer, Hank Bitler sent his son there, to Oakland. And there's another in Reno, only three days' ride from here, at the edge of the desert."

"To tell the truth," Ben said, "we had other reasons. I don't think our son would have chosen to go away at all. He had some trouble with a couple of Clayton's men. . . ."

"True Bear killed them," Ooti said, "which is exactly what he should have done," a fierce gleam appearing in her black eyes as she spoke.

"Uh . . . yes. Well, there's no official proof that he killed the men, but it seemed a good idea to get him away for a time. He may not come back at all, I don't know. He has two years yet to go until graduation, and after that he may find he's developed a taste for the East Coast. New England isn't such a bad place, all things considered. True Bear may find a teaching position, take up the law, something of the sort, and settle down permanently."

"He'll come back," Ooti asserted with absolute confidence. "But it's good, I guess, to learn all those things. We were talking about guns and ammunition for Auna-yi's adopted Modoc friends. News of what happened on Lost River has already reached us."

"Yes, yes. I'll do what I can for your friends, of course. Will you be able to stay through Christmas? I'll have to make a trip down to Chico, maybe up to Shasta City—or over to Susanville. It's not a good idea to buy too many guns in one place these days. I've heard something of the trouble between the Modocs and the Tule Lake settlers. And now you say Captain Jack's been driven into the lava beds? It may be that I won't be doing you or them any favor by providing weapons that merely prolong the inevitable. Wouldn't it make more sense for Captain Jack simply to surrender? From what you've said, it's this Hooker Jim fellow the bluecoats'll be after."

"The chief cannot give up his own people to be hanged, no matter what they did. They've asked his protection. Besides, the Indian Bureau will simply send the Modocs back to Klamath Reservation, and we can't live there. Kintpuash begged the Commission to give his people a reservation near their own country, but the Great Chief, as they put it, will not allow that. We have no choice."

"Typical Washington procedure," Ben said. "Send the Modocs to live with the enemies they've fought for centuries and expect everything to be fine because *they're all Injuns, after all*. You will stay for Christmas? I should be able to make my buying forays and be back by then easily enough.

It's so good to have you here with us, Wahtaurisi-yi. I'm
sorry, I've forgotten your grown-up name again."

"Auna-yi. But you may call me Fanny, if you like. That's
what most of the Modocs call me. Christmas? I had almost
forgotten about the big feast of the Saltus. But I'm afraid we
can't wait very long. It could be that the bluecoats have
already attacked our people. I hoped you might have something here you could spare. Anything will help."

Big Woodpecker had listened to the conversation intently
although in silence, but now he spoke out in a tone of final
and unshakeable decision.

"I'll go north with you, Auna-yi. If True Bear were here,
we would both go."

Yellow Grass looked stricken but didn't say anything. Ooti
nodded approval.

"You're right, Big Woodpecker, that's what True Bear would
do. It's what I would do if I could. I'm proud of you. You are
my second son."

"I wish I were as confident as Ooti about this whole venture, Woodpecker. Auna-yi, Fanny, you've got a home with
us if you want it—and your companions as well. I'll do what I
can to help your friends. I can probably round up a dozen
rifles and pistols here on the ranch and in Oidoing-koyo, and
we always keep a good stock of ammunition. I'll throw in a
couple of pack mules to carry it all as well. But I wish I could
convince you to stay on with us. If Big Woodpecker's our
second son, you have been our daughter since the first time
you came here. Now that you've returned from the dead, we
hate to lose you again."

Auna-yi's eyes filled with tears, and she couldn't speak for a
moment. Then she rose and proceeded to embrace the big
man in thick spectacles.

"I'd like that very much, but this is something I have to do.
Bluecoats killed my husband. They had no reason to do that.
He wanted to be friends with the Whites, just as Kintpuash
did once. Matthew Red Turtle dreamed of having his own
ranch, a place like this, where he could bring his mother and
father and little sister. He was a good husband to me for five
years. I owe his spirit something."

Ben nodded, and Auna-yi turned then to translate the
English conversation for her six Modoc warriors, who had sat

patiently through the whole exchange, eating bread and jam and looking vaguely ill at ease in the Whiteman's lodge.

ACTUALLY, Auna-yi had hoped to depart the following day, or at most the one after that, as soon as desperately needed supplies could be gotten together and the horses rested and fed sufficiently to make a return trip, but a blinding snowstorm caused delay, a fury of whiteness accompanied by driving wind that brought visibility down to nothing and made travel dangerous in the extreme.

Auna-yi fretted, and felt the need to move—although she enjoyed Ben and Ooti's company very much. In some ways, she thought, it was as if she had never left Upper Eden. Ben seemed to be of the opinion that school was back in—at least he insisted that she listen while he read newspaper accounts of what was going on in the White world to the east.

President Grant, the *Great White Father* of Indian Bureau patois, had been elected for a second term, and a woman named Susan B. Anthony was arrested for attempting to vote, trying to emphasize her belief, as Ben explained, that women should be allowed this exclusively male privilege.

"Universal suffrage has been an ideal of right-minded thinkers for a long time. It's an experiment that's never been tried," Ben explained. "But I expect we'll see it in this country someday. I wonder how a universal vote will work? Can the masses actually be trusted to know what's in their own interest? Will women vote their own convictions or those of their fathers and husbands? Well, that's the nature of the debate. But it'll come. In theory, at least, Negroes now have the franchise. Someday even Indians will be allowed the privileges of citizenship in this land that was theirs to start with. Do you sense the irony in that?"

"I don't even understand what this vote, this 'suffrage' means. I don't like the sound of the word. Women have suffered enough, and Indian people too, I think."

"It isn't like that," Ben chuckled, obviously delighted to be explaining something to someone. "Everyone in the country puts a slip of paper with a name marked on it into a box—the names being those of the people one wants to hold public office—various degrees of chieftainship, so to say—and the name that's marked on the most slips of paper is the name of

the new leader. That's roughly how it works. We talked about
it when you were still a child, Fanny, though you've probably
forgotten. I keep wanting to call you Wahtaurisi-yi—sorry.
But back to the subject at hand. In a way, voting is like
having the right to speak in council."

"How many White people are there in this country?"

"Maybe forty million. Hard to say—census isn't very accurate, especially in the West. . . ."

"So every person gets one forty-millionth of a say about
who should be the leader? And that's only if you trust those
people who count the pieces of paper, and if your piece of
paper doesn't get lost, or if the counter doesn't become
sleepy and lose track. It doesn't seem like very much to fight
for."

"That's what I've claimed," Acorn Girl smiled, "but Bear-
who-cannot-see-well is very interested in this voting business. Whitemen are crazy in many different ways."

"Thank God our son's at Harvard," Ben laughed. "If he
comes back, perhaps there will be one person I can speak
reasonably with."

FOR HIS PART, Big Woodpecker was teaching the young Modocs
to play draw poker. In the course of three days he'd won a
hundred and fifty nonexistent horses from a youth called
George's Son but had lost more than that to his brother
Heron, so matters were more or less even, all involved taking
the game good-naturedly and with a great deal of laughter
when the two parties couldn't understand each other, which
was most of the time.

While the snowstorm continued, those within the house
were happy enough—a peaceful interval when Auna-yi was
almost able to forget for scattered moments the essentially
tragic nature of her mission. Part of her wished she could truly
forget, could stay in this warm, safe place with people who
cared about her.

But on the third day of the storm, when winds died down
and snow stopped falling in midafternoon, clouds breaking
just before sunset, she insisted, despite all Ben and Ooti's
urgings for her to remain longer, that she and her party must
leave the following day.

*   *   *

THEY HAD INTENDED to depart at first light, Ooti rising well before dawn to prepare them a huge breakfast, but by the time they reluctantly left the warmth of the kitchen and made final preparations, oversaw the loading of pack mules, and exchanged last farewells with the McCains, the sun was well up in the sky.

"I still think you should stay another day or two," Ben said, the big, shambling form of the man made more bulky and bearlike by a heavy sheepskin coat he wore—and in contrast to Ooti's small, slender figure standing beside him. "You'll have easier going if you wait until the paths have been trampled down a bit."

"What my husband means to say is that we'd like for you to stay with us, but we know that you won't do that. Be careful, Little One, and when you've done what you need to do, come back and let us know that you're safe."

Auna-yi smiled at Ooti's name for her—Little One—inasmuch as she was now a good two inches taller than Acorn Girl. She embraced the Pano woman, then turned to hug Ben. The big man patted her back, then coughed, removed his spectacles and wiped them with a handkerchief, turned, and shook hands with Big Woodpecker.

"You too, you young lunkhead," he said, "come back to us in one piece. And take care of the Warrior Woman for us—if she'll let you. No, whether she'll let you or not. She's too much like another fierce young thing I once knew. . . ."

Yellow Grass was weeping openly, her pretty face forlorn as she wrapped her arms around Woodpecker's neck, kissing him for perhaps the twentieth time. He grinned and whispered something in the girl's ear, causing her to smile wanly, and then swung up onto his horse.

Ben gallantly assisted Auna-yi onto the bay, and she nodded to the six Modoc warriors, who were mounted, their horses stamping and blowing jets of steam throughout the protracted leavetaking. The young men whooped, momentarily galloped their ponies in a circle, and then the entire party moved away and out into heavy drifts of snow beyond the trampled yard area.

THE GOING was excruciatingly slow for the first several hours, horses and mules having to slog through fresh snow up to their knees, at times shoving through drifts as deep as their bellies. But the air was wonderfully cold and thin, exhilarating, and Big Woodpecker in particular was in high spirits, badgering George's Son about the hundreds of fictional horses he expected to collect when they should reach the Modoc lands.

"I pay you them just as quick as you give Heron his horses," George's Son laughed. "Goddamn Whiteman, you cheat with little square papers. We get home, have hand game."

"Ain't no more White than you are," Big Woodpecker grumbled. "And I ought to warn you about me and the hand game—can't nobody beat me at it. Born to it, I was. No Modoc has ever beaten an Oidoing-koyo Maidu."

He caught Auna-yi's eye, winked. She smiled, and turned her face forward again.

"Tell you what," he continued to Heron, "when we get there, we'll go double or nothing. Hell, make it interesting, we'll throw in our wives and children too."

"You got no children. I don't think you got wife neither, or is that pretty little one back there, one with big. . . ."

Heron's hands described curving breasts in front of his own chest as he grinned at Woodpecker.

"Yeah," George's Son chimed in. "To hell with horses. I take that pretty girl all right!"

"Well, sorry to say she ain't my wife. One of these days, though."

"We got no wives either," Heron confessed, and the three broke out laughing together.

"Is that true, Big Woodpecker? Are you and Yellow Grass going to get married?" Auna-yi asked. "I think it's wonderful. You've known each other since you were little children, haven't you? I suspects she even likes you—to an extent. Likes to kiss you, in any case."

Big Woodpecker shrugged, spread his hands wide.

"She's had me pretty well hog-tied for years, Wahtaurisi—Auna-yi. Ever since I figured out True Bear was the one you. . . ."

"That was such a long time ago. . . ."

Auna-yi's voice trailed off, and she stared out through the trees at a snow-covered plain to the north and below them, squinting her eyes against the glare. Then she spoke again, her tone distant, wistful.

"You've always been in the same place, Big Woodpecker. You were born there, and you will marry a girl you've always known, who has always been your sweetheart. That's how I thought it would be for me, too, but now I can't even imagine such a life. Perhaps I'll go back to Upper Eden when this fight is over. Do you think they really want me there?"

Big Woodpecker studied her face in profile, the thin, high-bridged nose, firm jawline, soft lips set in lines of sadness. He remembered the first time he had seen her, a young girl bringing food to two terrified boys—beautiful, infinitely mysterious, an embodiment of wildness, yes, and of danger too.

In his memory she had seemed supremely confident at that moment, moving surely in a world both strange and terrifying to the two boys from the relative tameness of Oidoing-koyo, but now she was sad, unsure of things, more like a child than she'd been as a child—even though she was, in effect, leading a war party of young men, and had taken them many miles away from their homeland in a quest for desperately needed arms and now was leading them back to join in the fighting.

I'm falling in love with her all over again, damn it. True Bear, you sonofabitch, why aren't you here to keep these complications out of my life? Yellow Grass is the one for me, I've always known that, and you were supposed to marry Wahtaurisi-yi. We worked it all out, you and me. . . .

ONCE THEY EMERGED onto plateau lands to the north of the great uplift that formed the feet of Wahgalu, the going was easier, the covering of snow much lighter here, only a few inches deep, and in places bare patches of earth were already beginning to emerge under the influence of the sun, even though air temperatures were still bitingly cold. The party traveled steadily north, once again skirting ranches and settlements of the Big Valley country, camping without fires at night, spending dark hours individually shivering in blankets and waiting for dawn, sleeping little.

When they approached the area of the lava beds, they began to see evidence of military presence—telltale drifts of smoke from army fires, tracks from reconnaisance parties everywhere, small cities of white tents easily visible as Big Woodpecker and Heron scouted ahead.

"If they haven't attacked yet, and I don't see any sign that they have, they're planning an all-out siege, howitzers and the works," Big Woodpecker said. "We'd better get to Captain Jack fast, let him know what's up."

"He knows," Heron replied, squinting off to the northeast from their vantage point on Little Sand Butte as they peered through a fine, icy rain that touched at their faces, a mistlike precipitation that had kept up all day. "But you're right—we must hurry. Kintpuash will need all his warriors and the extra weapons we're bringing."

The two men returned to Auna-yi and the others, reporting what they'd seen. The party rode down the north slope, moving ahead at a fast trot for a few miles, their pace slowing as the terrain grew rougher.

BUT AS THEY PASSED to the east of Caldwell Butte, they found themselves face to face with a patrol of perhaps twenty blue-clad regulars, emerging suddenly from behind a lava formation, riding three abreast and apparently unaware of the presence of Modocs until they came into sight of them.

The troops were still some distance away—far enough that the order of the lieutenant who led was inaudible, but a volley of rifle fire that followed sounded with a series of distant pops, a couple of the bullets singing among rocks nearby, although most fell far short.

"Scatter!" Auna-yi shouted in the Modoc tongue. "You must get the mules to Kintpuash. I'll try to keep the blue-coats occupied."

The six Modoc warriors, however, had already vanished into some lava rocks to the left, mules protesting but following along on their leads.

Auna-yi, with Big Woodpecker immediately behind her, also rode into cover, dismounted, and worked her way forward toward where the column of soldiers pulled up as the lieutenant in charge decided what to do about this unexpected enemy band.

"He's thinking it may be a trap, an ambush," Big Woodpecker whispered to Auna-yi as they peered over a low lava rim at the troopers.

"That's a good thing for them to think," Auna-yi nodded.
"It'll give our friends time to escape. Let's reassure the
bluecoats."

She raised her rifle to her cheek, squeezed the trigger.
Dirt and rocks kicked up in front of the lieutenant's mount's
hooves, causing the creature to snort and skip back. Auna-yi
quickly scurried to another location, reloading the old flintlock as she moved, then fired off three rounds from her pistol
while Big Woodpecker, immediately catching the nature of
the game, moved away from her, and fired also.

The officer shouted another order, and his troops scattered, heading for shelter in a ravine that led back into the
lava beds. Auna-yi worked her way quickly toward an area
where she expected the troopers to emerge. She ran, stooping low, paused to fire another round from the rifle, and went
on—while Big Woodpecker moved away from her and further
up toward the declivity's end, firing random shots from his
pistol as he dashed along.

He glanced back toward Auna-yi, saw her suddenly stumble and fall, and lie still. He heard the report of a rifle
immediately afterward, distant sounds of several men cheering.

Big Woodpecker leaped out into full view, shrieked and
brandished his rifle, took a shot at a soldier who was climbing
up from the ravine, and then ran off, hoping the troopers
would take the bait and follow him.

*Got to keep them away from her. Maybe somehow I can
circle back later, take care of her. Is she dead? Wahtaurisi-yi
don't be dead, don't be, Goddamn it. . . .*

He was vaguely aware his cheeks were wet with tears, icy
air numbing his damp skin, burning in his lungs as he stumbled over sharp flints, his feet catching in crevices, tangling
in clumps of sage. He was aware, for a time, of pursuit, of
occasional rifle or pistol fire going off behind him, and occasionally he paused to snap off a return shot. And then,
suddenly, he realized that he was alone, unsure of how long
it had been since his pursuers had lost him or simply turned
back.

*Fool. What the hell did I hope to do? How many minutes
since they'd turned back? No sense of time, of anything.
Dumb-fool Injun. I forgot to act like I had a busted wing.*

He retraced his course, circled wide, climbed up onto a low lava rim, and looked over the edge.

Two troopers had already strapped Auna-yi onto a stretcher, a wide white bandage across her chest, and were covering her with coarse brown blankets. The lieutenant, blond and not very old, knelt beside her, speaking in tones too low for Big Woodpecker to make out the words. Then the officer rose, addressing the men in a voice that rang clearly through damp gray air.

"All right, Evans, Higgins, let's get her to Colonel Whitney at the field hospital. On the double. The rest of you men continue with the patrol. Sergeant Daggett in charge."

With aching intensity Big Woodpecker stared at the still form of the girl. He detected a slight movement of one hand as men lifted the stretcher, her fingers clutching and then uncurling by her side.

"Keep an eye to the rocks, men! There might still be enemy there waiting to take potshots. Let's move!"

As Big Woodpecker continued to watch helplessly, the bluecoats trudged back down the ravine and out of sight, carrying Auna-yi among them.

Alive, at least. What will they do with her? Medical care first, that's something. But then what? Prisoner of war? Ship her down to the Indian Territory? You bastards, you take care of her, damn you. Do you hear me, Jesus Coyote? You look out for her, or I'm coming after you too. . . .

He stood watching for a long time after the soldiers vanished, a broad-chested, powerful man, bare-headed in the freezing rain, his hat lost somewhere back among the rocks. Water ran down his face, and his large hands held a pistol and a rifle, these dangling at his sides like useless toys.

At last, when dull gray of afternoon began almost imperceptibly to deepen into twilight, he turned and made his way back through the shadows of a burned-out world, back south toward the edge of the lava beds to a place where his horse stood in near dark, cropping unconcernedly at a stubble of dry grass, Auna-yi's slender bay mare beside him.

TWENTY

Klamath Falls Madam

[January–March 1873]

SHE ROSE GRADUALLY, piece by piece out of blackness, drifting through fragments of dream, flashes of waking, dim awareness of someone standing over her, speaking gently, putting something to her lips, smoothing blankets, other times of pain, probings at a hot center located somewhere in a different land she sometimes recognized as her body, sometimes only as a source of discomfort. Visions—sometimes it was the face of that rancher, Dan Clayton, who'd led the slaughter of her people—other times it was Smoke Woman or Red Turtle who spoke comforting words to her. Once she knew that Tod Bitler leaned above her, saying something she couldn't understand but causing pain, and she was too weak to cry out but swirled down into waiting night. She came back up to see it was not Tod but a round-faced man with glittering spectacles who probed at the area of fire somewhere in her chest. Often she was aware of being feverish, frequently finding herself in Hank Bitler's barn, and it was leaping with flames, horses screaming, nothing she could do about either.

Then she opened her eyes, found her head completely clear, realized she was in a room strangely familiar to her although she didn't remember how she came to be there.

Cold light of winter afternoon seeped in through light cotton
curtains across two windows, touching at a pine chest of
drawers, an oval mirror hanging above it, a pine washstand
with plain white basin and pitcher, a framed crayon drawing
on one wall—a girl in trailing white dress, her arms full of
yellow flowers, two spotted dogs leaping about her, in the
background a big, snow-covered peak that looked something
like Mt. Shasta only more symmetrical, less jagged.

Auna-yi studied the picture, and decided she liked it, liked
the way the girl and dogs were small in the foreground with the
mountain and sky properly dominating most of the space.

She tried to sit up, felt a stab of pain, and reached with her
hands and discovered her chest was wrapped tightly in layers
of white cloth. She searched her memory, gingerly, as one
might touch at a sore tooth, and found clear recollections of
everything that happened before she and Big Woodpecker
tried to draw the soldiers away from the Modoc warriors near
Sandy Buttes. She remembered running, firing her pistol,
and then emptiness, fragments only mixed with dream, long
periods of nothing at all.

On a little table beside the bed, she saw a glass of water
standing among small bottles and jars, green and brown and
blue and containing various liquids and ointments—medicine,
she assumed.

Shot in the chest, she thought as she picked up the glass
and sipped water. *The soldiers must have brought me here,
wherever I am.*

A fleeting memory impression of a face above her, stiff blue
uniform collar, drooping moustache. Vaguely familiar—Lieutenant Biggs, yes, who had been with Colonel Gideon Whitney, not when he came to Bitler's ranch the time he brought
a wagon train over Fandango Pass, but the other time with
the Modocs, when he recognized her and told her the last of
her own people were dead. And now that she thought of
Whitney, she was sure she remembered his face emerging
from time to time during the long period that was mostly
darkness.

What is this place? she wondered. *Am I in prison? A
hospital? I've never been in either, but this isn't the way I
would think. . . .*

She considered rising to go to the windows, but decided the

effort would be too great, sipped again at the water, wincing at the pain—more like stiffness, she realized—in her chest. Her stomach growled as she swallowed, and she felt ravenously hungry.

The door across the room opened and a woman entered, a blocky older woman with Indian features. She wore a dark dress covered in front by a long white apron.

Noting Auna-yi's eyes were open and alert, the woman smiled.

"You feeling better now, Miss Bitler?" she asked, crossing to her and putting a hand to the patient's forehead, nodding. "Fever gone, don't come back today. You look like you feel better, all right."

"I guess I am. I don't seem to have much strength. . . . I don't really remember how I was feeling before, but I think it was bad."

"Plenty bad," the woman nodded. "First we think you die because of the blood you lost, then when you come through that, you start burning up with fever. You talk a lot, then, but I don't think you know what you was saying. Pretty interesting, though."

The woman grinned.

"What is this place? How did I get here? I don't remember much after. . . ."

"After you try to kill Lieutenant Biggs, fighting with damned troublemaker Modocs, you mean?" the other snorted. "Then Colonel Whitney takes you to hospital at Fort Klamath, then when it looks like you gonna live, they bring you here to Klamath Falls, to Mrs. Gold's boardinghouse, and hire me to nurse you."

"Is that where I am now? A boardinghouse?"

"Yes. Colonel Whitney pays for everything. Guess he must like you, even after you try to kill his soldiers."

"Am I a prisoner here? Am I allowed to leave when I wish?"

"No one told me, but you be damn fool to go away now. You want to go back to Captain Jack and troublemakers down there? Hell, you not even all the way alive yet."

"You're Klamath, aren't you?" Auna-yi asked. "Your people and the Modocs don't have much use for one another. I came from the Yana people, down south in the canyons around

Wahgalu—Lassen Peak, I think that's what the Whites call it.
My family, all my tribe was wiped out by White ranchers.
For five years I was married to Red Turtle, a Modoc, and the
soldiers killed him. Now they want to kill all the Modocs."

"Calm down, Pretty Face. You gonna bust yourself open
again an' bleed to death."

"The Modocs can't go back to Klamath Reservation. You
know. You know they can't get along with . . . and yet the
White Chief won't let them go anywhere else. Wouldn't you
fight if the government was doing something like that to your
people?"

"Don't know. Don't worry about wars. Whitney hire me to
look after you, that's all. Time to change your dressing, now."

The woman didn't talk as she worked deftly at removing
the old bandage, dressing the wound, now nearly healed, as
Auna-yi could see, although the flesh was still inflamed around
a small, puckered opening just below her left collarbone. The
Klamath woman applied a large glob of yellowish ointment, a
wad of cotton, and then laced on strips of clean muslin.

By the time she was finished, she seemed to be feeling
kindly toward her patient again, and Auna-yi asked for something to eat. The woman smiled at her, went out of the room,
and returned with a bowl of wonderful-smelling soup.

A birdlike gray-haired lady followed the nurse into the
room and, beaming at Auna-yi, introduced herself as Flor-
ence Gold, owner of the boardinghouse.

"Dolores told me you were feeling better," this lady said,
drawing the room's single, straight-backed chair beside the
bed and sitting down to chat as Auna-yi spooned up delicious
broth rich with scraps of beef and vegetables. "Gideon will be
thrilled—my nephew, Colonel Whitney, that is. He's taken
quite an interest in you, you know. Right now he's down with
the fighting, of course, but everyone expects that to be over
soon."

"What do you mean?" Auna-yi asked, the spoon dropping
to the tray beside the bowl.

"Why, the army's brought in over three hundred troops,
and I understand there are another hundred local volunteers.
Captain Jack has less than sixty men, from all accounts. It's
only a matter of a little time. Then, too, they've sent for

General Canby. He's very good in negotiating with the Natives. Perhaps no more blood needs to be shed at all."

Auna-yi lay back and closed her eyes, a wave of sadness, helplessness, nausea washing over her.

Only a matter of time. Doomed from the beginning. Kintpuash is a good man, a valiant man who only thinks of his people, and now the Modocs will be herded off like so many cattle to some place far away, some place no White settlers want because the land's no good . . . perhaps Kintpuash, as leader, will be hanged as a lesson to others, and the rest will die far from home.

She felt suddenly weary, a fathomless, ancient weariness. Mrs. Gold continued chattering, oblivious to the fact that her audience was no longer paying any attention to what was being said.

As AUNA-YI REGAINED her strength, progressing rapidly now that the crisis point had passed, news that came in from the lava beds was inconclusive. The first attack of over four hundred troops against fewer than sixty warriors had been turned back, the Modocs fighting from a natural fortress in the lava beds, a near-impregnable position.

Colonel Whitney came to visit her once after the battle, and she questioned him closely.

"They had big fires and danced half the night in celebration," he said. "They killed a dozen of our men and managed to gain nine carbines and some ammunition from us, but they can't hold out there forever. I know your heart's on their side, Fanny, and in a way I guess mine is too, but they're throwing away their lives and the lives of our men as well— for nothing. The end result will be the same whether the Modocs surrender today or starve there among the rocks for the next five years."

"Kintpuash is doing what he feels he has to do. What your government wants for the Modocs is wrong. The settlers have stolen their land, and now they want to send them to live among their enemies or to some place far away where they'll all die. When I'm stronger, I'll go back and fight you again, Gideon Whitney, even though you've been kind to me."

"War's over for you, Fanny. You might as well make your mind up to it and find something else to do with your life."

Auna-yi turned her head away, felt tears hot on her cheeks.

The military man stroked at her hair, said, "You know, Fanny, we're not all such evil people. You realize that. You've put yourself on the losing side, and there's no reason to continue fighting for no possible gain. You're not really Modoc anyway. You don't have any family among them. You told me that yourself. When you get better, I can find you a job with someone here in Klamath Falls. You're a beautiful woman. Another man will come along and be swept off his feet. Count on it. Only maybe this time it'll work out better for you in the long run."

Pass for White, snag some banker or shopkeeper or cattle rancher, live easy for the rest of your life. . . .

Matthew Red Turtle's words, so many years ago, before the two of them had gone to his people, before they'd been married, before. . . . Perhaps he had been right, perhaps Whitney was right as well. She felt as if something was dead within her, now and forever.

I'll never let myself love anyone again. That's pain, nothing more. Captain Jack's people will die in the lava beds, and nothing I can do will change that. Even if I die too it won't change what happens. From now on it's only Auna-yi alone, no, only Fanny Bitler, who lives in a Whiteman's world by Whiteman's rules, only me and no one else. Nothing matters, nothing matters at all. . . .

WINTER DRAGGED ON with an endless procession of gray skies, freezing drizzle, occasional spates of snow, although the cold grew less biting, with sub-freezing weather less frequent as February waned.

The woman who'd become Fanny Bitler was now able to go out into the little town that had grown up at the south end of Klamath Lake—neat frame houses in the respectable residential area near Mrs. Gold's, false-fronted saloons and mercantile establishments along a main street, while on the outskirts sprawled a ragtag shantytown inhabited mostly by wary-eyed Indians, children, and lean-sided dogs scuffling noisily in mud streets, chickens scratching in bare yards.

Fanny got into the habit of riding out of town on a road along the shore of Klamath Lake, to a point where she could stand alone at water's edge, and watch mudhens bobbing,

black specks out on steel-gray waves, the surface at times
pocked with raindrops. She gazed across the cold surface
toward a high, nearly symmetrical white cone the Klamaths
called *Yaina*, Mt. Pitt or Mt. McLoughlin to the Americans,
the same mountain as in the crayon drawing. Wawlems Yaina,
the beautiful white lady—or so Dolores had told her.

She imagined Captain Jack, as good as trapped in the lava
beds, supplies running out by now and hunters unable to go
after game, since soldiers were massed all around.

The troubled image of Kintpuash, in her mind's eye, imprinted itself upon the serene and solitary white peak that
rose dreamlike across the broad waters of Lake Klamath.

DURING THE ENTIRE PERIOD of her convalescence, Fanny had a
frequent visitor, one George Livingstone, a Washington attor-
ney and frequent consultant on matters involving delicate and
difficult negotiations with foreign nations, sent to study and
make recommendations concerning the Modoc situation. Livingstone wasn't a large man, very dapper in appearance,
preferring buff and pearl gray suits and silk hats. He was in
his mid-forties, hair streaked with gray and combed from the
sides of his head up over a bald spot at the crown. He was a
well educated and well traveled man, and Fanny found his
conversation both interesting and amusing.

He had come originally to visit Fanny in an official capacity, to glean her impressions of how matters stood with Captain Jack's band, but when the gifts he brought her changed
from coffee and hard candy to a sterling silver dresser set and
diamond earrings, it was clear his calls were of a nature more
social than official.

They continued meeting in Fanny's bedroom long after any
excuse remained for his visits to take place there rather than
in Mrs. Gold's parlor downstairs, partly out of habit, partly
because no one suggested otherwise.

One afternoon when Livingstone entered the room, he was
carrying a white cardboard box embossed with a gold stamp,
his eyes gleaming and face slightly flushed, looking positively
boyish. Fanny watched curiously from where she sat cross-
legged on her bed as he opened the parcel, peeled back
sheets of tissue paper, and at last drew forth a pegnoir set of

nearly transparent pink silk, trimmed with wide ruffles of lace around the throat and sleeves.

"I sent clear to New York for it. I'd dearly love to see you in it, Fanny Bitler," he said, and his usually suave face blushed scarlet, although the quiet gray eyes didn't leave hers.

Fanny couldn't suppress a surprised giggle, and her mirth kept building until she was laughing aloud. Livingstone, blushing more brightly as he smiled, waited for her to get over her fit of humor.

"Am I to gather from this that you'd like to lie down with me, Mr. Livingstone?" she asked, still grinning.

"You put matters very bluntly, Fanny. But yes. Well, I'm a man of few words, though there are many who believe otherwise. Why waste time? *Tempus fugit*. Your wound doesn't trouble you anymore, does it? You're an immensely beautiful woman, the blending of White and Red no doubt, and I like you a great deal as well, so I'll be as forthright as you have been. I'm not offering marriage, my dear. I am afraid I already have a wife in Washington, D.C., one who's at this moment most likely mourning my absence with a tea party or a charity ball. Excellent woman."

"You've brought me many expensive things," Fanny said. "I thought perhaps this was the reason. I'll return them, then, George. I think you're my friend, but I can't. . . ."

"Wait for a moment, Fanny, before you say no. I'm not asking your love, for heaven's sake, only that you share your lovely person with me. You're an exquisite creature. You have something very valuable to men. In this Whiteman's world, as you call it, I'm sure you realize by now that money is power. This is not advice I'd give to an innocent young girl, but you have brains and strength of spirit as well as beauty. If you wish, you can sell your labor. You can become a servant in a White household, perhaps because you can read you might even aspire to be a governess or a schoolteacher, though the latter would require some education. In any case, you'll live on the edge of poverty all your days, dependent on the whims of others, and if there's anything that you wish to do for your people, your loved ones, you won't have the means to accomplish it. You have one supremely valuable asset, Fanny, and it won't last forever. If you learn to use it properly, you can become wealthy, and wealth is always ultimately respectable, no matter how it's gained initially."

Fanny shook her head slightly, trying to figure out a counter-argument.

"I'm asking nothing of you, Fanny. I have more than enough money for my own purposes, so I'm not proposing a *business arrangement*. But I'll set you up in your own home, and I'll pay your bills. All I ask is that you receive me once or twice a week. The rest of your time is your own, to do with as you wish."

Fanny continued staring at Livingstone, frowning, then at last she burst out laughing again.

"I've been trying to come up with a way to explain to you why I don't want to do this thing you ask, George, but truth to tell, I can't think of a single one. So this is how your White world operates, is it? Let me have that nightdress, Mr. Livingstone. We'll see how it fits, hmm?"

"You can wear it for me another time, pretty Fanny. Just now, I'd rather look at you as you are," he smiled, his fingers going to the row of buttons down the front of her blouse, opening them dexterously.

He stepped to the door, turned the key in the lock, returned, and slipped the pale blue cotton shirt back over her shoulders, kissed her throat, touched at the small white scar that remained from the bullet wound, cupped her breasts through the thin material of her camisole.

"Mating in exchange for money, George? I thought Whitemen preferred to rape their squaws."

"A business arrangement is always superior," Livingstone protested—appearing almost shocked at her words. "Come now, Fanny. Nothing will happen without your consent."

She studied his expression—it was almost that of a pleading child. Then she smiled, nodded.

She helped him to unhook her skirt and slip the undergarments off. When she was naked, he took her gently by the shoulders, pushed her away from him, stared at her body in the pale winter light.

"You're making me ashamed—looking at me so," Fanny said in a peculiar fit of shyness, dropping her gaze to the floor.

"You should never be ashamed of anything, Fanny, most especially of your body. You're exquisite in every way."

He ran his fingers lightly up her flanks, rubbed in circular motion at the aureoles of her breasts—and in spite of herself, she began to feel the first tinglings of desire.

He lifted her in his arms and laid her on the narrow, yellow-coverleted bed, turned away, and began to remove his own clothing.

He made love to her slowly, expertly, and she found her body responding entirely against her will, found herself gasping with pleasure—pleasure, strangely enough, that had nothing at all to do with love.

When it was over, he kissed her gently, then rose and dressed, tucking something into her hand as he raised it gallantly to his lips.

A hundred-dollar banknote.

"You're wonderful, Fanny Bitler—wild, and not at all inhibited, just as I suspected you'd be. If a woman doesn't give herself for love, then she must do it for money, not for any other reason. The creation of pleasure is a valuable service, and one should not squander one's labors."

George Livingstone bowed again, stepped to the door, turned back.

"You see, my family's very old money, and we know its uses. We came by it honestly, as they say, stole it fair and square. The first Livingstone fortune was made by privateering under the British. May you establish your own dynasty, my dear."

Then he was gone.

TRUE TO HIS WORD, George Livingstone found a very pretty small house on the waterfront, with a back porch on piers that actually jutted out over the lake itself.

For the first week or so she occupied herself with furnishing and decorating the place, exulting in privacy and proprietorship, regardless of how it was gained. On a whim she bought from Mrs. Gold, the crayon drawing that had hung in her small bedroom, after learning that it had been by a local Klamath girl, who'd actually managed to get an art scholarship to an eastern school and was apparently doing quite well.

On being given this information about the artist, Fanny experienced certain misgivings concerning her own choice of livelihood. There were other ways. But after a period of thought she found reason to suppress her doubts.

Livingstone himself had been called down to the Modoc lands for a couple of weeks to consult with General Canby, who had arrived and was working on a peace commission. Now suddenly, before she'd even finished with her settling-in process, she found herself besieged by Army officers down from Fort Klamath and by wealthy ranchers in town looking for fun as well. The word that Fanny Bitler had set herself up in a house and was living alone apparently had spread like wildfire—so that numerous men were encouraged to try their luck with her.

That Bitler woman, she's the most ungodly beautiful piece of ass I've ever seen! I tell you, she just reeks of it, and it ain't nothing put on, it's just there. Look at her for thirty seconds, and damned if you ain't stiff as any board. . . .

Standing in front of a clothing store and gazing in through panes of glass, she heard the whispered assessment of her body, didn't find the idea terribly appealing. But she remembered Livingstone's assertion that "money is always respectable," and she accepted those who were willing to pay her price—twice as high as that of any other *business lady* in town, take it or leave it. Some left, some took, and it was not very long before the small safe she purchased and kept in the corner of her bedroom held a substantial cache of banknotes and coin, and raw gold as well.

Early in March Colonel Gideon Whitney returned from the battlefield and, after some inquiry about town, found Fanny in her waterfront establishment. He was clearly troubled at first, and shocked to find the sort of life she was shaping for herself, then pitying. She smiled, opened the door of the small safe, and showed him its contents. He went back to being merely shocked.

"Fanny Bitler. I still can't believe it," he said. "I've taken an interest in you, you know, since you were hardly more than a child. I didn't expect it to end this way."

"It hasn't ended yet, Gideon," she laughed. "I'm not dead, you know. Before I'm done, the preacher's wife will be asking me to lead charity drives, and you know that's true. Whether it's my Indian half or my White half, I always learn quickly. First I studied the bad bear's habits, and then I went hunting for it. The method's working, I should say."

"Maybe so, maybe so. I just can't get used to it. Old-fashioned, I guess. Well, I've brought you some news that I think you'll be glad to hear."

"What news, Gideon?"

"The Modoc wars are over. Canby and Meacham and the others offered complete amnesty in exchange for surrender. Captain Jack said he'd think about it, but then in the night Hooker Jim and the others with him at the Tule Lake massacres came to Fairfield's place and turned themselves in. Should be no problem with the rest of the Modocs, now that the murderers have surrendered, since the original sticking point with Jack was that he wouldn't give his people up to be hanged. There shouldn't be any more bloodshed. I thought you'd be happy to hear this, Fanny," he added, looking a little confused at her lack of response.

"Gid, what will happen to Kintpuash and his people if they do surrender?"

"Why, what we've promised them all along. They'll have a reservation somewhere, good climate, plenty of food and supplies, just like any other tribe. You don't think that's good enough for them?"

"I think they'll die before very long. Indian Territory? All they want is to stay in their own lands. Kintpuash even asked that the Modocs be given those lava beds for a reservation. Surely the damned cattlemen don't covet that slag-heap? Oh, hell! I guess it doesn't make any difference in the long run. You bastards won't stop until you've got all Indians stuck in one little corner, and then you can blow up that one little corner with dynamite and not have to worry about the *Indian problem* anymore."

"I didn't realize you felt that way about us," Whitney said, looking hurt. "I thought you'd be glad the killing's over."

"I'm sorry, Gideon. You're only doing what you think you have to, I guess. Would you like a cup of coffee, or perhaps something stronger? I think I want some whiskey."

Whitney nodded. She went to a sideboard, poured them both strong drinks and splashed water into the glasses.

They sipped silently, Whitney looking absently at the crayon drawing.

"I like the picture," he said after a while. "Doesn't seem to fit in a *house of joy*, somehow."

Fanny told him the story of the artist, and he nodded earnestly.

"You see, Fanny, there are indeed other ways to succeed in the Whiteman's world. Let me help you find something else to do. You're plenty bright. Let me see about getting you a scholarship somewhere—there's grant money available to assist promising young Indians. Actually, it would be better if you were scrubbing floors on your knees than this. . . ."

"Would it really? Is that what you think?"

He nodded solemnly, liquor beginning to have an effect on him. Fanny noticed with amusement that he was staring at her bosom, and she purposely leaned forward so the low decolletage of her wine velvet dress revealed even more.

"May I freshen your drink, Gid?" she asked, pitching her voice seductively low. "Are you sure you'd rather see me scrubbing floors? Is it proper for an officer to gawk at a lady's breasts, as you're doing now?"

She wasn't sure why she was teasing him in this way. Perhaps some unconscious hypocrisy in his attitude provoked her, perhaps she really wanted to prove to him, to herself, that what she was doing was after all a good thing.

"Or maybe," she thought, "I just like him. Or possibly I hate him because he's an Army sonofabitch and doesn't understand anything at all, thinks I should be happy that Kintpuash will be forced to grovel in front of the Whiteman's power. No. I promised I wouldn't think of that. . . . Another world gone, and I have this one. Wahgalu itself may blow up, but this girl's going to succeed."

Whitney abruptly raised his eyes, stiffened his posture, and mumbled a negative. Fanny leaned even further across so that the fabric of her strategically designed dress fell away, revealing the swelling mounds even to the nipples. She smiled in the manner of a naughty child and tugged playfully at his beard.

"On the house, Colonel," she cooed. "For old times' sake."

"Fanny? Oh, hell!" he said, and kissed her roughly on the mouth, drew back. "Are you sure?"

She nodded, and he reached for her again.

It was over very quickly, Whitney apparently being considerably more eager than he'd let on. He leaned back on pillows against the brass headpiece of Fanny's bed, and lit a cigar she gave him.

"I guess I wouldn't mind visiting you again from time to time, Miss Bitler, if you don't object," he said comfortably. "My wife took off, went to live with her people back in Ohio. Guess she couldn't deal with Army life anymore. Can't say I really blame her. . . ."

Fanny listened absently, her mind turning again to the Modocs.

"I guess it's over, at least," she said aloud. "Poor Kintpuash. Part of me still feels I should be going away with them."

Whitney grunted a noncommittal reply and squeezed her breast.

Feel nothing. Love is pain. It's Fanny Bitler alone, now, and life is good enough this way. Coyote Man sends each of us a fate. . . . Mine's to lie down with Whitemen and then take their money.

A horse whinnied outside somewhere, and the dull and yet comforting sound of rain on the roof continued.

TWENTY-ONE

Return to the Modocs

[March–May 1873]

THE LITTLE CITY of Klamath Falls celebrated on that night and for two days thereafter, everyone feeling a general sense of relief over the peaceful end of the Modoc dispute—although many of the local ranchers in particular were indignant that Hooker Jim and the whole *gang of cutthroats and cow thieves* should be allowed to escape Oregon justice and the hangman's noose. In fact, several citizens' groups put together hasty petition drives to pressure the governor of Oregon into demanding the captive killers be remanded over to the state's justice system.

But despite these dissenting voices, the prevailing atmosphere was one of carnival. Fanny actually had to turn away business, as off-duty officers and foot soldiers alike from the fort to the north, as well as those returned from the battle site, thronged the bars and competing bordellos.

On the second day after the announcement, a pretty young widow came looking for work, a Klamath girl who lived on the outskirts of town and whose husband had regularly sold her favors in exchange for whiskey—before he'd fallen face down in a drunken stupor one night and drowned in the shallows of Lake Klamath in a spot where the water was less than a foot deep.

The girl's name was Willow, she told Fanny, and she'd happily do anything from housework to sex in exchange for a safe and pleasant place to live.

Fanny hired her on the spot, at a percentage, ordered her to bathe, and put her into the small house's spare bedroom. The girl had a pleasant voice, as it turned out, and she'd learned several old songs, some scandalous, some sentimental, from White soldiers and cowhands as an incidental result of her previous experience. In addition, Willow could play a few tinkly chords on the mandolin to accompany herself, and Fanny found the music her small establishment could now offer drew almost as many customers as other forms of entertainment.

Within a few days after the declaration of peace, George Livingstone returned from Fairchild Ranch with news that Hooker Jim and his band had escaped, returning to Captain Jack, and the entire negotiating process would now have to be repeated.

"Apparently General Canby failed to put them into proper custody," Livingstone explained, "and in their wanderings around camp, they happened upon a good citizen who graciously informed them the governor was demanding their blood and that they'd surely hang—whereupon, of course, Jim's group made their way back to the lava beds and threw themselves on Captain Jack's protection. An absolutely monumental and unforgivable foul-up, Fanny. Oh, hell. . . ."

He leaned back in a red plush armchair and appeared rumpled and weary. Fanny brought him his customary bourbon and soda, sat down on the hassock at his feet.

"Not there, Fan, come here," he said, patting his knee. "You're the only bright spot in this whole sorry business, as far as I'm concerned. With the exception of your delicious person, I'd be just as content to have the whole of the West Coast drop into the sea. Thank God for at least one island of quiet. . . ."

At that moment Willow, doing an enthusiastic clog step and singing "Oh, Susannah" at the top of her voice, emerged from her bedroom, and did a quick whirl in front of the gentleman caller, skirts swirling up to expose a length of rounded leg, head turned back to wink coquettishly at Livingstone. The Washington lawyer was momentarily startled, then chagrined, and then he threw back his head and laughed.

Willow cut off her performance, pretended to sulk, and flopped into a chair, her legs sprawled immodestly from beneath a froth of petticoats.

"Don't tell me, Fanny," Livingstone chuckled. "You've hired a cleaning lady. Where on earth did you find this extraordinary creature?"

"What's that he call me?" Willow asked suspiciously. "He call me a bad name? I cut his gizzard out, by God."

"This is Mr. George Livingstone, Willow," Fanny explained, "and you mustn't cut his gizzard out, for then we'd have to live in the streets. Haven't I told you again and again that this isn't the way to address a gentleman, no matter what you think?"

"Sorry. You want a roll in the hay, Living-stone? Willow damn good. You just don't call me none of those funny names. And you stop laughing at me."

"My profound apologies, Miss Willow," George replied, rising and sweeping his stovepipe in a broad bow while still choking with mirth. "I'm certainly not laughing at you. You're a vision of loveliness, I must say, although your temper may be a trifle uncertain. Still, many men prefer high-spirited lasses, I've heard. . . ."

"Yeah?" she asked, squinting in an effort to follow his meaning, apparently deciding she'd not been insulted too badly. "You want a roll in the hay?" she repeated.

"Thank you kindly, my dear, but I'm otherwise engaged this evening, with Mistress Bitler."

The girl shrugged, addressed Fanny.

"Maybe I go down to Cattlemen's Club, find lonely cowpoke."

"No, Willow!" Fanny snapped, getting up from Livingstone's knee. "We don't solicit men in taverns here, you know better than that. If you can't live by my rules, I'll have to let you go. Look, why don't you just take the evening off? Go visit your mother or something. And lock the front door on your way out."

"Too damned many rules here, but hokay, Fanny. This is the best place I ever live. I won't do nothing bad, I promise."

Livingstone sat back and laughed aloud again after the girl

banged out the front door. He held his glass for Fanny to refill it.

"She's something, all right," he said. "So you're expanding operations, are you? Do you think that's wise? Willow strikes me as being a trifle indiscreet."

"I could have used a half dozen extra girls this past week," Fanny shrugged. "Men like Willow. The local herdsmen call her 'Spunky.' Besides, George, she had no place to go. Her husband left her with nothing but liquor bills and gambling debts when he died. No, she's good for business. . . ."

"Fanny, you don't need to do any of this," Livingstone said. "I'll buy you whatever you need. I'll even write up a contract, put you on a monthly salary, all legally binding, if you'd like."

"What are you saying? You're the one who told me that money was good, was respectable no matter how it's earned. Something like that. You're the one who told me my time was my own so long as I was always at home for you."

"I know, and I meant it at the time. But damn it, Fan, it bothers me to see evidence of your *enterprise* quite so blatantly. I guess I have a jealous streak after all, just like all the other *cowpokes and blueboys and U.S. Gov'mint men*. I don't think I want to share you anymore."

"I can go it alone now, George, if I have to. I thank you most sincerely for the start you've given me, but I don't want to be your property. I'm going to get a new place, I think, something bigger, hire another girl or two. . . ."

Livingstone sighed. He took a long drink from his glass.

"No strings, then. that's the deal we made, wasn't it? I'll live up to my part, Fanny, but please don't threaten me with *going it alone*. You don't want to dump me, do you? Found someone else, true love, something of the sort? No? You're sure? All right, I'll help you with the new place. You can become a genuine entrepreneur. If you have a few girls working for you, then you won't have to. . . ."

"Only when I want to, George. Are you requesting me to save myself for you?" she asked, amused.

"Merely if you find it in your heart to do so, Dearest One. Shall I get down on one knee and hold my faithful stovepipe over my heart . . . ?"

"I don't have any particular appetite for drunken ranchers

and soldiers on leave, George Livingstone. But I have to admit to one other . . . obligation."

"Whitney, isn't it? That backdoor bluecoat. I knew it. The bastard's in love with you, Fanny, the underhanded sonofabitch. It shows all over him when he mentions your name, and the dirty dog talks about you constantly. It's a low trick, Fan, this love business. Surely you haven't fallen for that."

"You know better than to ask me to name my . . . friends. But no, I'm not in love with anybody. You don't have to worry about it. That part of me's gone forever, and I'm a better person for it, too."

"So they all say. Go ahead, then, bed the lowlife scoundrel if you must. But Fan Dearest, don't you even love me just a little? I merely require a very little bit. I'm content with a pittance."

"You're also very silly," she said, leaning over his chair and kissing him on the mouth, "and you talk too much, Whiteman. Let's go into the bedroom. I have something to show you there. Didn't you bring me a present this time? Ah, you're taking me for granted, George Livingstone. I'll make you pay for that."

Her hand moved down, sought his crotch. He groaned, disengaged her grip, fumbled for a moment in his waistcoat pocket, and withdrew a velvet jewelry box.

"Your tribute, Madam," he mumbled. "Now will my lady stoop to conquer? God, I want you tonight, Fan. . . ."

WITH FINANCIAL BACKING from George Livingstone, Fanny bought the Sagebrush Palace, offering a lump sum payment that the previous owner found too attractive to refuse, even though he'd not been contemplating a sale at all. With the Palace she acquired a large barroom complete with player piano and mirrored back parlor downstairs and a half-dozen rooms upstairs—and in addition to the facilities, three girls who elected to stay on with the new owner. These included another Klamath girl named Penelope, a redhead, Samantha (of doubtful natural coloring), and a blonde called Fifi who claimed to be from France, although when startled she often miraculously overcame her Parisian accent.

The business thrived under Fanny's management. She found and hired a piano player to accompany Willow's vocals and to

vary the repertoire offered by the automatic instrument, which
had only one roll of music. She organized her girls into a
dance team, allowing Fifi to teach the others her version of
the cancan. The Palace could now present musical entertainment every evening.

Within a short while, she found it necessary to hire a
bouncer as well.

NEWS FROM THE BATTLEFIELD to the south trickled in every
day, the Palace being one of the town's prime news broker-
ages. Very few shots had been exchanged since the return of
Hooker Jim to the lava beds, and the soldiers, deployed
around the edges of the stronghold for over a month now in
the frequently unpleasant weather, were growing restive. But
negotiations continued endlessly, Canby and Meacham along
with a sub-agent named Dyar and a preacher named Thomas
repeating essentially the same offer of amnesty—although
now Hooker Jim and his group would have to be turned over
for trial on murder charges—with the rest of the Modocs
offered reservation land in Indian Territory.

Captain Jack responded as always—he couldn't give up the
men who'd sought his protection, but the Modocs wanted
peace, would agree to remain in the lava beds without any
government aid at all if only the soldiers would withdraw.

In early March, with the help of his cousin Winema Riddle, who was married to a White settler, Kintpuash wrote a
letter to the commissioners, a copy of which Livingstone
showed to Fanny.

*Let everything be wiped out, washed out, and let there be
no more blood. I have got a bad heart about these murderers. I have got but a few men and I don't see how I can give
them up. Will they give up their people who murdered my
people while they were asleep? . . . I could give up my horse
to be hanged, and wouldn't cry about it, but if I gave up my
men I would have to cry about it. . . .*

Fanny felt tears starting to her own eyes as she handed the
letter back to the government agent, but she forced her voice
to be harsh.

"He'd be better off hanging Hooker Jim than his horse,"
she said. "He has a fine horse. Hooker Jim's no damned
good. I wish there were something I could do. . . ."

"Would you be willing to talk to Captain Jack if the time came?"

"Yes, but if his own cousin Winema can't convince him, then I'm sure there's nothing I can do. In his mind he has no choice."

"I know that. I'm sorry the situation causes you distress, Dear One. I don't see how it can drag on much longer. At least while we're talking, however fruitlessly, no blood is being shed."

FANNY'S BUSINESS continued to prosper, the Palace's reputation as a first-class entertainment emporium spreading throughout the rangelands to the north. Indeed, she discovered a talent for discipline and a business acumen that kept things running smoothly and in an orderly way. Fighting was strictly forbidden inside the establishment, as was misuse of the girls, and guns were checked at the door. The girls didn't attempt to steal from the customers—for Fanny made it abundantly clear that the first infraction of that rule would result in immediate removal of the offender from the premises, minus her earnings. Further, she insisted on absolute cleanliness from her girls, with baths at an additional fifty-cent charge being mandatory for clients as well.

Once it was understood the rules were carved in granite and no infractions tolerated, everyone seemed to accept them without fuss, perhaps even welcomed them. The girls felt safe and protected, the customers were assured of high-quality entertainment and a reduced risk of disease or embarrassment.

Fanny herself presided at the door, welcoming clients, exchanging jokes and banter with the men she knew, but she accepted no visitors to her own room except George Livingstone or Gideon Whitney. She was rapidly becoming a wealthy woman, and as George had predicted, the town merchants, at least, treated her with great respect, dressmakers, furnishers, grocery clerks, and liquor salesmen placing a high value on her patronage.

IN THE MEANTIME, Kintpuash and his band continued among the lava rocks, unproductive acts of diplomacy seeming endless.

In early April, Indian Agent Meacham sent Winema to the

chief's stronghold with a message for all the Modocs individually. Those who wished to surrender on their own, would be given complete amnesty. But Hooker Jim, by now apparently in a struggle for power with the man who had so steadfastly refused to give him up, threatened death to any who might choose to leave with Winema, and so the young woman returned to Meacham and Canby's council tent alone.

"THAT DAMNABLE JIM!" Whitney exploded in frustration to Fanny. "If it weren't for him, this situation could have been resolved long since."

"Not if you send the Modocs to Fort Klamath or off to Indian Territory. Kintpuash will never give away his people's land."

"Even your Kintpuash can see the face of the inevitable," the officer snapped. "But Hooker Jim's a common hoodlum. We have such men in White society as well, needless to say. The best thing for any of 'em, White or Red, is a good stout rope."

Fanny squinted at Whitney, and for a moment terrible memories of the massacre on Mill Creek rose up in her mind—the hate-distorted faces of Daniel Clayton and Robert Anderson, who'd led the carnage. For a moment this horrible vision flamed before her eyes, but then she fought it away, willing it to leave her.

"I think you may be right, Gid. But would you be willing to give one of your men over to Kintpuash to be punished with certain death, no matter what crimes he'd committed?"

"As General Canby's told Captain Jack again and again, the time of Redman's law is past. Only Whiteman's law prevails in this land."

"Yes, and it works only for Whitemen. You'd better go, Gideon. I don't want to get into a fight with you."

Whitney was stunned, then hurt. He rose, stiff-backed, and left the room.

When he'd left, Fanny put her head down upon the table and wept.

LATE APRIL brought the shocking news of murder.

Captain Jack, along with Hooker Jim and a half-dozen other men, had gone to council with General Canby, Agent

Meacham, Sub-agent Dyar, and the Reverend Thomas, Winema and her husband Frank Riddle serving as interpreters.

The Modocs concealed weapons beneath their clothing this time, and at Captain Jack's signal drew pistols and fired point-blank upon the negotiators, killing the general and the preacher and wounding Meacham. The treacherous attack took place, ironically, on Good Friday, and the shooting war resumed with a vengeance immediately following Easter Sunday, batteries of howitzers bombarding the lava bed stronghold, troops storming the breastworks and into the fortress at last, only to find it empty—the Modocs having slipped away during the shelling by means of a network of lava tubes and wide crevices in the stone.

Fanny received the information from Livingstone in utter silence, although he tried to break the news as gently as possible.

"That kind of treachery—not the sort of thing we'd come to expect from Jack at all, is it Fan?" he asked. "I guess if you push a man too far. . . ."

"These are lies," she exclaimed. "I know Whiteman's lies when I hear them."

"Afraid it's the stone-cold truth. I was there—not in the council tent, fortunately, but there with Whitney and Jackson, near enough to see what happened. It was Captain Jack who went into that tent, no mistake, and an hour later he led his men out. He'd stripped Canby of his uniform—he was wearing the general's cap when he left. Canby and Thomas are indeed dead, and Meacham and Frank Riddle and Winema herself are witnesses as to what happened. They all agree Jack spoke with Canby for a long time, asked him over and over to send the soldiers away and let his people remain in the lava beds. Toward the end he was practically begging, and apparently Meacham sensed something was up—he says at the end he himself urged Canby to promise whatever Jack wanted, but by then it was too late. That was when Jack gave the signal and pulled his gun on the general, shot him point-blank."

Fanny sat sunk in silence, trying to put together the Kintpuash she knew, a man of peace, of infinite patience, with the picture Livingstone had just given her of sudden treachery.

*You push a man too far. . . . Is that it? It doesn't fit,
doesn't fit at all. . . .*

"Hooker Jim was there too?" she asked.

"Yes, and Schonchin John and Shacknasty Jim—a couple of
others."

"He's the one. Somehow Hooker Jim pushed Kintpuash
into it. Gideon told me he was trying to shame Jack earlier,
threatening the people who wished to go to Canby for amnesty, trying to take the leadership away from Kintpuash.
Somehow he's behind this, I know it."

"Perhaps you're right, Fanny. It's a tragedy in the making,
and I'm sorry it hurts you so. Come sit here beside me," he
added, gesturing to the bed where he leaned back against the
pillows. "Let me comb out your hair. You like that, don't you
pretty Fan? I absolutely glory in your wealth of curls, a
fragrant cascade to. . . ."

Fanny cut him off with a gesture of her hand, paced
restlessly up and down the room.

"Tell me what else happened," she said. "I want to hear all
of it."

*You said you wouldn't care, would only look out for
Auna-yi—Fanny Bitler. You promised. It doesn't matter,
doesn't concern you at all. . . .*

"There's not a great deal to tell. General Davis, Jefferson
C. Davis, has been brought in to replace Canby, and the
soldiers are searching the lava beds for Captain Jack's new
hideout. The Army's hired seventy-two Tenino Indian scouts
from Warm Springs to help hunt him down. It won't be long
now. . . ."

"I wouldn't count on it too heavily," Fanny snapped.

"You're really not yourself tonight, my dark angel. Here,
come drink some champagne. I sent for it from San Francisco, but it's the genuine French article. I know you love it.
Don't let this thing trouble you so deeply, Fan. I understand
that you care about those people, but there's nothing you or
anyone else can do at this point."

"I don't give a damn about anybody, George," she said
with a quick, half-sobbing laugh. "Don't you know that about
me? Yes, let's have champagne, by all means. We'll make a
toast—to a quick victory by the forces of right. And we know

which side that is, don't we? We know that might makes
right. You told me so once. To the forces of might, then!"

IN KLAMATH FALLS, feelings ran high against Captain Jack and
his Modocs in the wake of the infamous attack on Canby and the
others. Fanny couldn't step out into the barroom of the
Sagebrush Palace without hearing curses of all sorts levelled
against the *Goddamned dirty, slinking sonofabitch savages,
oughta cut all their balls off, by Gawd, then stake 'em out for
the coyotes to eat*, as well as many another equally vitriolic
proposal.

Someone made up a song chronicling the fictitious exploits
of Captain Jack, which ran from raping his own mother and
sons to eating live infants. The tune became very popular
locally, and one man or another was certain to sit down at
the upright piano and bang the melody on the keys, accompanied by a male chorus roaring out the words. Fanny banned
the singing of the "Ballad of Captain Jackoff" from her premises and got into several heated discussions on the subject—
discussions which ended with a number of customers being
escorted out by her six-foot-four, two-hundred-fifty-pound
bouncer, these clients thus informed they were no longer
welcome in the Palace.

Business suffered when the proprietress' views became
generally known, and the ersatz Parisienne as well as the
second Klamath woman quit working for her. Fanny took up
holing up in her quarters, rarely venturing into the bar room
during public hours, and seeing hardly anyone except her
two lovers.

Even local merchants, previously so warmly disposed toward
her custom, treated her coolly now, not going so far as
actual rudeness but certainly not greeting her with the obse-
quious effusions of former days.

Livingstone came to her room one evening in mid-May
with news that the Tenino Indians had indeed discovered the
Modocs' new hiding place—but when the soldiers came in to
capture it, Captain Jack had prepared an ambush and succeeded in nearly wiping out the advance patrol.

"You've got to admire the bloody bastard, Fanny," Livingstone said. "We were sure it was all over a month ago, but
the struggle drags on, and every now and again he gives us a

surprise. Why the hell won't he just give up? Any sane man would. Instead he keeps slaughtering our boys. Damn it! How long can this thing keep on? There are over a thousand troops down in the rocks now. Nothing but useless goddamn bloodshed—from anybody's perspective."

"I'm glad," Fanny said fiercely. "I hope Kintpuash kills all the soldiers. You should have left him alone in the first place."

"Ah, Fanny," the lawyer sighed. "You don't mean what you're saying. They're just boys, the ones that are dying, just babies. . . ."

"Then they should be home with their mothers. Red Turtle was not very old when your soldiers shot him down, and he wasn't making war on them at all. Before this all started, the White settlers killed real babies, shot them to death in their mothers' arms."

"The violence has taken its toll on all of us. Let's not argue, Fanny. I don't know which side is right anymore. Never did, I guess. I'm a peacemaker. My job is to get all the crazy bastards on both sides to stop killing one another. But it's gone too far now. I suppose I'll be called back to Washington before long. Will you come with me? I'm not quite certain I can get along without you now. . . ."

"I don't know," she said, hating him a little, although she wasn't sure exactly why. "Maybe. Can I have a high-society whorehouse back in Washington? Maybe President Grant will come to visit. Would you mind if I fucked the President, George?"

"Why not? What the hell. Have at the drunken sonofabitch. I'm being serious, damn it Fan. Same arrangement as here, only you'd have to be a little more discreet. . . ."

"I'm not interested in your damned Washington. Where's Captain Jack now?"

"You're demon-possessed on this subject, aren't you? Well, it looks like your boys are on the run. No one can hold out forever against the kind of firepower the Army's sent up against them. We think they've broken up into several small bands. They've killed and eaten their horses, we know that much. Some few have straggled in, surrendering in ones and twos. It's winding down. I'm sorry for them, just as you are, but it'll be a blessing when it's over at last. The accursed war's become a lingering disease, and there's relief only when the patient finally dies and can be at peace."

"They'll hang Kintpuash."

"He'll be given a fair trial."

"And then they'll hang him."

"I suppose so. That much seems certain. Come to me, Fanny, let's think of more pleasant things. When we get to Washington, you shall have a big brick house with a grand piano in every room and gilded plaster angels on the ceilings. You'll have a dozen feather beds the size of ballrooms, with red satin sheets, and we'll make love on every one of them in different ways. But now, come here, wench. I want to take your clothes off an inch at a time and nibble at your. . . ."

She pushed him away, suddenly sickened at everything surrounding her.

"You have to go now, George," she said. "I am feeling . . . unwell. If you like, I'll call in Willow or Sammy for you. Sammy has a special thing she does with warm cream. I think you'll like her."

"I don't want any of your whores, Fanny, you know me that well by now. Shall I find a doctor for you? If you're ill, you should lie down. . . ."

"I'll be all right, George, I'm sure. Please. I want to be alone. I have these spells. I want to be alone."

A note of hysteria came into her voice, and Livingstone, after again suggesting a doctor, backed out the door, confused.

ALONE IN HER ROOM, Fanny Bitler quickly changed into a pair of men's jeans and a heavy wool shirt. She emptied the small safe where she kept the take from a day or two, shoving the money hurriedly into a canvas bag. Carrying this with her, she walked through the cool of early evening to a livery stable and rented a horse and a pack mule. Next she pounded on the door of the general store until the owner opened up. She bought two Henry repeating rifles he had in the cabinet behind the counter and five revolvers as well, along with a good quantity of ammunition.

"Don't know what you're up to, Miss Fanny, an' it's probably best I don't ask," the proprietor said, staring at her from behind round spectacles that reflected bright yellow spots from the glow of a kerosene lamp.

"My money's the same as anyone else's, Mr. Jacob," she snapped. "Do you ask everyone who buys a gun what he's going to do with it, or is it only me?"

"Don't get riled, ma'am. Point of fact, I didn't ask. Just seems a little curious, that's all. Hell, I'll take your money all right. None of my business, I guess you let me know that right enough. But if you're plannin' on arming the Injuns, I'm gonna have to let somebody know."

"Rest assured. Now, do I get what I want or not?"

Jacob shrugged, handed her the rifles, placed pistols and ammunition into a wooden box.

She bought foodstuffs as well, sacks of beans and flour, a side of bacon, and some canned goods, paid for her purchases without further discussion, and with the shopkeeper's assistance loaded the whole onto the pack mule hitched to a rail outside, along with her rented dun gelding.

When this task was finished, Fanny mounted her horse and rode away, leading the mule down the main street of Klamath Falls and toward the southern road.

"No point in trying to hide now," she thought. "Jacob will have it spread around town within the next ten minutes, anyway. I think I've gone mad at last."

But it felt good, she realized, when the lights of town disappeared behind her, horse and mule plodding stolidly and rhythmically through early darkness, the air chilly, stars blazing down in vast washes of light.

It seems like years since I've seen stars, really seen them, not just glancing up while going from one building to another, but actually to move, to live in their light. . . .

The air was clean against her face, free and good.

She traveled until morning began to show gray against the eastern horizon, and then she watered the animals at a little stream and moved away from the road, up over a rim and into a meadow beyond, out of sight of the thoroughfare.

She picketed her animals and slept, waiting for darkness before resuming her journey.

She reached the lava beds before dawn a day later, and saw white tents of soldiers pitched everywhere, the troops still sleeping. She circled wide around this military encampment, keeping an eye out for sentries, and then slipped in among the lava flows, on foot now and leading her animals.

When dawn came, she was well into the wild tangle of land
where Kintpuash and his remaining warriors were still hiding—
somewhere.

For the first time since her impulsive departure from
Klamath Falls, she began to question what she was doing.

*Why do I think I can find them when a thousand soldiers
can't? If a Modoc sentry sees me, he might as easily shoot me
as the bluecoats. A fool's mission, Fanny Bitler. No, I am Fire
Woman again—a fool, but Red Turtle's wife.*

LATE MORNING. She picketed the animals, and walked aimlessly on foot. The sun grew uncomfortably hot in the land of
stone and sparse vegetation, and she had brought only a small
canteen of water with her. She found traces of human activity
here and there, numerous small items that, could they have
spoken, might have told her a good deal of truth concerning
the Modoc War—spent brass cartridges in one area, many of
them, empty tin cans in another. Numerous droppings from
horses, scraps of paper, scraps of cloth. A harness buckle, in
one place the bones of a slaughtered horse, scattered wide
now by coyotes and other scavengers.

There were signs of human passing, but no living thing
except vultures circling high up and a few lizards darting
away from her shadow, while a marmot perched on a rock
and whistled warning.

As the sun climbed higher, Fanny began to think she
moved through a ghost land, actually imagining for an instant
that she saw Red Turtle standing beside a twisted juniper
tree, making signs to warn her back.

Then, with shattering suddenness, came the whine of a
bullet bouncing off rocks directly ahead of her, and a moment
later the report of a rifle. She turned, realized that as she'd
been drifting through her half-dream journey a patrol of
soldiers had surrounded her, and stood now with carbines
poised, the leader with his hand in the air.

If the arm dropped, she knew, she'd be riddled by rifle fire.
She thought for an insane instant of dodging behind some rocks
for cover and shooting it out, utilizing the single revolver
she'd brought with her when she left the animals behind.

But then her mind came clear, and she raised her hands in
a gesture of surrender.

TWENTY-TWO

Victory in the Modoc Wars

[May–June 1873]

IT WAS AFTERNOON when Colonel Gideon Whitney rode to the camp where a dozen or so captive Modocs, women and children as well as men, were confined in a barbed wire compound on a treeless expanse of rock and dirt, with no shelter at all from the scorching sun.

Fanny Bitler was among the Indians who sat listlessly in the shade of a hastily erected structure of boards and canvas intended to serve as a barracks, the prisoners with gaunt cheeks suggestive of near-starvation, eyes empty, spiritless, as if the person behind each black, blank gaze had departed and left behind only a human shell.

Outside a wire enclosure a pair of guards paced back and forth, keeping their own eyes fixed on an indeterminate distance, not looking at their charges more than absolutely necessary.

Whitney's face was scarlet, and he perspired profusely beneath his officer's cap as he shouted orders interspersed with profanities at the detachment whose duty it was to guard these prisoners of war.

In a moment he came into the compound and took Fanny's arm, leading her out past the sentry.

"Goddamn it, Bitler, you crazy-ass bitch, what the hell did you think you were trying to prove? Taking arms to Captain Jack again, weren't you? You suppose a couple of repeaters and a handful of revolvers are going to turn this war around? You think that's going to help Jack defeat a thousand U.S. Army regulars? You might have gotten shot, that's about the most that could have been accomplished."

Fanny waited in stony silence while Gideon Whitney sputtered himself out. Then she spoke quietly.

"You'd better put me back in with your other enemies, Gid—because if you let me go, I'll return directly to the lava beds. No, I don't suppose I can accomplish anything, you're right about that, but I've found I can't stand by any longer while you and your army friends wipe out the last of my husband's people."

"Christ, Fan, Jesus Christ, you rock-headed hellion. You're going to force me to lock you up, is that what you're saying?"

"I'm only telling you the truth. I belong with these people, that's all, not in some fancy whorehouse, rolling around in a feather bed with you and George Livingstone, while the blue-coated sonsofbitches hunt down the last pitiful remnant of these poor, starving people in the rocks where you've driven them. I think it's become a fox hunt to you—I think the one who finally drives Kintpuash to earth will be given his ears to hang over a mantel. Don't get close to me, Gid, I'm warning you. If I get the chance, I'll take your pistol and kill as many soldiers as I can before they gun me down. Nothing matters to me, nothing. I've been forced to drink flame in my life, and it's burned out everything that's soft and weak. I may be only a woman, but I know how to kill. Whitemen have taught me that much."

Gideon Whitney stared into a face flushed and twisted with anger, eyes fierce and wild and gleaming with tears. He tried to put his perception of this creature standing before him together with the Fanny Bitler he thought he knew, cool and witty in social situations, strong and warm and pliant in his arms. He failed in his attempt.

Would she really kill me? There are many things about the human heart I don't understand, don't understand at all, and at forty-five years of age, I guess I won't likely ever learn. Fanny, pretty Fanny Bitler, how can I send you back behind that wire with the others, like so many cattle? Wish I were a religious man—I'd ask God Himself what the hell to do and let Him take the blame. Close to twenty years now I've been fighting Indians, from Blackbeard the Shasta to Kintpuash. A man doesn't win against them, can't win. All he can do is kill them, starve them, beat them to their knees, and then put them on a reservation somewhere. You outgun them, outnumber them a hundred to one, and they'll still find a way to make you bleed, inside if not outwardly. Who the hell owns this land, anyway . . . ?

He sucked in a long breath, and made his decision.

"I'll take responsibility for Miss Bitler, Lieutenant," he said to the officer in charge of the guard camp. "I order you to release her into my custody."

Fanny looked at Whitney with something like despair in her eyes, whispered, "Don't, Gid. I don't want to. . . ."

"Quiet," he said with a tone, he hoped, of more firmness than he actually felt. "I don't believe you'll do any such thing. If I'm wrong, then I'll pay for it, won't I?"

Fanny continued to stare at him, looked as if she were about to speak, then shook her head.

A commotion outside the encampment distracted both at that moment, a patrol riding in with a number of Modoc warriors in its midst, and although these men were under guard, they were joking and boasting loudly with their captors in a way that didn't seem in keeping with the situation.

As the group rode up to the barbed wire compound, Fanny recognized Hooker Jim and a number of his band among the soldiers.

"We catch 'em all right," Jim was saying, "Maybe tomorrow, maybe next day. Don't worry none, Hooker Jim know Cap'n Jack better than Jack know self."

Fanny turned a questioning glance on Whitney, hardly able to believe what she was hearing.

"It's Jim, all right," Whitney nodded. "Turned himself in a few days back, asked General Davis for amnesty in exchange for bringing in Captain Jack. The general bought it. . . ."

With a shout of pure rage and a movement so sudden, so unexpected that Whitney had no time to react, Fanny snatched the colonel's revolver from its holster and leaped among the group of horsemen, raising her weapon and leveling it at Hooker Jim.

Just as she fired, an alert horse soldier kicked the weapon from her hand, and in the next instant Whitney had hold of her, his arms wrapped tightly around her waist as she struggled to break free.

A momentary expression of shock and fear on Hooker Jim's face was quickly replaced by his habitual smirk, once the danger was past.

"Red Turtle's woman," he laughed. "Why don't you White boys give old Jim Red Turtle's woman as reward? I tame her down real quick, okay?"

Fanny turned her head up and spat toward his face, and he laughed again.

"What's the matter with you soldiers?" she shouted. "Don't you know this is the man who killed a dozen innocent settlers? Why are you going to let him go free and then hang Kintpuash, who was only trying to protect his own people? If it hadn't been for this man, there would have been no war. If it hadn't been for this man begging Captain Jack's protection from Whiteman's justice for the murders he himself committed, Kintpuash wouldn't have kept his people starving in the lava beds. There are no words to describe how low he is. I'd call him a sneaking dog, but there's no dog that would turn on the master who's fed and protected him for all this time. Hooker Jim was even the one who forced Kintpuash to shoot General Canby . . . I've been talking to the people in the compound. Ask him—how he threw a woman's clothing on Kintpuash when the chief refused to commit treachery, how he threatened to kill the chief and all his friends if they wouldn't murder the general. Do you know these facts, Bluecoats? And yet you'll send this murderer, this traitor, down to the warm lands, will feed him and care for him the rest of his days, and you'll hang the one who always tried to do what was right for his people. My God, it's not the White race I want to quit, it's the human race!"

Hooker Jim and his men sat their horses, grinning through Fanny's diatribe, although several soldiers looked uneasy. Even while she was speaking, a couple of the guards had pulled her, struggling, from Whitney's grasp and handcuffed her wrists behind her back, stood holding her and awaiting the officer's instructions.

FANNY SPENT THAT NIGHT in Gideon Whitney's tent, the colonel taking the precaution, with numerous apologies, of attaching one half of a set of handcuffs to her wrist, the other to his own.

"I hate like hell to do this to you, Fan," he said, not looking into her eyes in the lantern light, "but you're just not yourself where the Modocs are concerned. I hope you won't hold it against me too much in days to come, but if you must, then so be it. More than anything else, I don't want you to get yourself shot, you damned fire-breathing little fool! Fanny, I. . . . Damn it! And Goddamn this whole sorry, stinking business."

"If you try to touch me tonight," she replied, "I'll scream, and I'll kill you when I get the chance."

He gazed into the dark eyes that glittered with reflected yellow illumination and felt a wave of nausea, not physical sickness but something else, something elemental, a kind of cancer whose presence he would have to continue to conceal.

Whitney turned from her, his mouth twisted with hurt, then nodded silently and blew out the lantern.

"Let's get some sleep if we can," he said, his voice not fully under control.

Fanny lay staring into darkness for hours, not sleeping but not thinking either, a confused welter of images coming to her from the past, playing themselves out over and over against blackness. Again she saw Red Turtle lying on snowy, blood-stained earth in the center of the village, a hole torn in his throat. She relived as well the times of their happiness together—one time in late summer when they'd gone off together to pick berries, how they had laughed and smeared each other's faces with purple juice, at last making quick, urgent love there in dry grass near the berry vines. She remembered their good friendship at Bitler's ranch, the time they'd gone woodcutting, and then the terror of that night, Tod Bitler's insane, hissing voice, a barn burning.

Her mind took her back even further, to the massacre of the Yahi village, everyone she'd known since her first infancy, nearly everyone dead, and the ranchers' horses trampling bodies of the dead. Brush lodges burning. And before that, even before that to an innocent time when a young girl and a young boy made promises beside a waterfall, promises that somehow assured the two that their world would always be as it was then, promises neither had power to keep.

When gray light began to filter through the tent's canvas walls, she didn't suppose she had slept at all.

THE FOLLOWING DAY more hollow-eyed, weary Modocs were driven into camp or came in of their own accord, groups of two and three, one band of perhaps a dozen. Fanny was returned to the compound, as Whitney was required to ride out elsewhere, and by afternoon the area was heavy with the reek of frightened, demoralized, and unwashed humanity—that as well as wholly inadequate sanitary facilities. The Modocs spoke little among themselves, ate mechanically, moved mechanically, walked mechanically to the foul latrine in the rear of the compound to relieve themselves. Fanny spoke with some she had known well, but they didn't really hear what she said or even what they, themselves, replied. It was as if a vital element, an individuating spark of personality, had somehow been extinguished, perhaps through despair, or perhaps through simple exhaustion and hunger, she didn't know, but after she'd gained what little information the new arrivals could give her, she ceased in her attempts to make conversation and passed her time standing near the wire, watching activities of soldiers outside, sometimes talking with a young corporal who remembered her from visits to the Palace. He kept apologizing. . . .

This is how they destroy a people, living death. The Saltu ranchers merely killed the Yahis, and perhaps in the long run fate was kinder to us than to these whose spirits are dead but whose bodies go on living ghost lives. I don't know, don't know anything. . . .

Toward evening George Livingstone arrived, furiously demanding Fanny's release, but the lieutenant in charge blandly replied that he couldn't comply without orders from a military commander. Livingstone shouted and threatened in a manner quite atypical of his usual cool demeanor, but with no result. Fanny, unable to muster much interest in the Washington lawyer's personal feelings, assured him listlessly that

she was perfectly content to be where she was and begged
him not to trouble himself. When he had quite satisfied
himself there was nothing immediate he could do, he sat near
the wire, reaching through to hold her hand and assuring her
he'd secure her release in short order. He then began telling
anecdotes, stories of his various travels and of one thing and
another, tales which had amused her in the past and by
which he hoped to cheer her.

"George, for God's sake, shut up," she said finally. "I know
you mean well, but can't you see what's happened here,
what's still happening? Please, please, I can't bear this tea-
room gossip when . . . can't you hear them dying, dying
inside?"

WHEN COLONEL WHITNEY RETURNED with evening, Livingstone expressed violent outrage not only over Fanny's incar-
ceration among the Modoc prisoners but the sleeping arrangements as well. The two men came as close to blows as Fanny
had ever seen either one, with the officer threatening to
heave the lawyer into the stockade, and Livingstone retaliat-
ing by threatening a Congressional inquiry and possible War
Department action on the whole matter.

The two men eventually reached a compromise, with Fanny
sleeping alone in the colonel's tent, the two men standing
guard over both the woman and each other.

IN THE MORNING Livingstone rode out in search of General
Davis, planning to bring pressure upon the commander in
order to facilitate Fanny's release, but he returned that evening without success, and set out the following day to talk
with Meacham to try civilian channels, while Whitney quietly
burned at the bureaucrat's attempts to undermine both his
military authority and his claim to *Miss Bitler*.

Fanny had little interest in the machinations of her lovers.
For her, the two days were a small eternity—more dull-eyed
prisoners and refugees, more crowding, more blank despair.
She began to consider methods of escape, having decided at
last that there was truly nothing for her here, nothing she
could do for these people already vanquished, only the last
agonizing, pitiful scenes waiting to be played out.

But on the afternoon of the third day, an advance horse-

man came into camp, shouting that Captain Jack had been
taken, that he was being brought in under heavy guard. The
soldier spoke with considerable self-importance as well as
genuine awe, almost as the announcer for a wild animal show
might introduce the *man-eating tiger* or *deadly crocodile*.

They brought in Kintpuash in chains, hands and feet shack-
led as he dragged along, a stooped, dirty, and emaciated
figure walking among a dozen or more mounted soldiers, all
with rifles trained on him or at the ready. With Jack were
three more warriors in similar condition, all appearing like
very old men although none in the group was much past
forty.

A loud cheer went up from the assembled troops at the
guard station, many having ridden in from nearby camps at
the news the great chief had been captured.

Kintpuash seemed hardly aware of his surroundings at all.
It was said that at the last, after Hooker Jim led the soldiers
to his final hideout, Kintpuash escaped on foot, leading the
bluecoats in a race for hours before they finally ran him to
ground.

Fanny watched as if spellbound, her eyes fixed upon the
figure of Kintpuash. Even in his pitiable state of humiliation,
the man somehow retained an air of quiet dignity that reflected shame on his captors, who appeared like cruel children, gleefully self-important.

As Jack stepped into the compound, his eyes met Fanny's
for a moment, and his lips curved in a slight, painful smile.

"Red Turtle's woman. I remember you. We got the mules
you sent, Red Turtle's woman. I'm glad you're not dead."

Then he walked to the center of the compound, squatted in
the shade of the barracks, and sat waiting in utter silence—
but waiting for what?

She released the strand of wire she'd been gripping the
whole time, only now noticing a slick smear of blood where a
barb had punctured her palm, the pain coming a second
later.

FANNY RODE NORTH that night, after waiting until both her
faithful guards were snoring outside the tent and then simply
stepping over them. She saddled Whitney's horse and slid
into shadows, giving the sentries wide berth and making her

way one last time through the edges of that wild, lava-strewn country. A half-moon hung above the ragged outline of mountains westward, while Shasta gleamed ghost-white in the distance, sheeted in cold flame.

She was certain of pursuit, and so she traveled all night and well into the following morning, stopping only for a few hours during noonday heat to rest before pushing on. She had no fear either Whitney or Livingstone would try to prosecute her or even to stop her from what she was determined to do. But she wished now most passionately to be alone because human companionship, and particularly sympathetic companionship, would be like whiskey on a raw wound. In solitude, she found, she felt almost nothing, a perfect sense of emptiness, a certainty that something was finished, gone, yet another lifetime ended.

She rode into Klamath Falls late at night, headed along Main Street to the narrow dirt track that led to the Sagebrush Palace. As she drew closer, she detected a faint, acrid smoke odor—no, the smell of burnt wood lingering after a fire has been extinguished.

The saloons, she noticed, were busy, shouts and singing coming through the doors, several men staggering about the streets in knots, apparently celebrating.

News of Captain Jack's capture must have already reached town, she realized, in the way that news has of spreading before it seems possible for any human messenger to have brought word.

One drunken cowhand looked up at her as she passed, then with a whoop he grabbed the bridle of her horse.

"Fanny Bitler, ain't it? Hey, Fan, what do you think now that your lover-boy Jackoff Jack's been caught? You know what they gonna do to him, huh, Fan? They gonna hang his ass, that's what."

The cowhand's two companions broke into loud, appreciative laughter, staggering and hooting with mirth while the first man continued to cling to the bridle of her horse. She recognized him now as one she had thrown out of the Palace and calmly drew her riding whip, slashed it across the drunk's face. He shrieked and let go of the bridle, clutching at his eyes as he stumbled back.

"Bitch!" he shouted after her as she rode on. "Goddamn halfbreed bitch. I oughta. . . ."

Then his voice changed, became gleeful again.

"You got a surprise coming, squaw," he yelled. "A real nice surprise. . . ."

As she turned the corner, she caught scent again of the stale, burnt odor and suddenly knew with an absolute certainty what it was she'd find.

A real nice surprise. . . .

The Sagebrush Palace had been burned to the ground, nothing left but a portion of one wall and a stone chimney rising skeletal in mist-obscured moonlight. She dismounted, kicked at chunks of charred wood in the rubble. There were no street lights here, and only a little lamplight filtered from the windows of a building across the way and the two to either side. Both structures, she noted, were intact, though their walls had nearly touched those of the Palace.

"Damned good job of selective firefighting," she muttered, poking about in the faintly visible ruins for a moment longer. A few shards of glass, broken and partially melted liquor bottles, the wreck of a piano, part of the cabinet and tangled wires, a few dully gleaming keys. Bed frames from upstairs rested on the charred bartop.

"Nothing worth keeping," she concluded after a brief appraisal. "Not a damn thing."

She mounted Whitney's horse again and turned to head back down the street—then sensed more than heard or saw motion from the shadow of a building, a residential hotel across the street. Fanny turned to face the intruder and saw a small form emerge.

"Is that you, Willow?" she asked softly, recognizing something in the woman's bearing or movement.

"It's me. Some mess, huh? Goddamn worthless cowpokers. Burnt it down on purpose, Fanny, and helped the fire department pour water on the buildings next door."

"On purpose? I guess I suspected. . . ."

"Made me an' Sammy get out, and then they poured coal oil all over everything, set it on fire. No big secret, that business."

"Why are you still here, Willow? There's nothing left for either one of us now."

"Figured you'd be back. You been good to me, Fanny. I help you kill the sonofabitches, okay. I show you ones who did it."

"No, I guess I won't bother starting another war over this. I'll camp somewhere tonight, get my money out of the bank tomorrow, and move on. Maybe Reno, I don't know. You're better off if you don't let anybody see you with me, Willow. I gather I'm not too popular here anymore."

"Shit! I don't care. I go with you. Don't make no difference to me how you feel about goddamn Modocs. You been Willow's friend when nobody else was. Anybody want to bother you anymore, I cut his goddamn guts out."

Suddenly, and without warning, tears came, the first time in days Fanny had wept. She had thought there was no more weeping left in her, that everything within had dried to nothing, but at this one word, this one act of fierce and unshakable loyalty on the part of a small, bad-natured creature known as Willow, something released, and she was crying for everything, for Captain Jack and the Modocs, for the life that was gone here in Klamath Falls, yes, and for her own people, dead now, for days of innocence and goodness that in reality never existed.

Willow put her arms around Fanny and cried too, sympathy tears, and then she said, "No, goddamn it, we don't give the bastards no satisfaction. Let's stop cryin' and get the fuck out of here."

THE BANK TELLER was very reluctant to part with Fanny's money the following morning, at first demanding proof of her identity despite the fact that he knew her quite well, and had even been an infrequent visitor to the Palace. He then brought the manager forward, and this individual suavely explained it would take a few days to facilitate a withdrawal of such a size, suggesting first that the funds simply be transferred to a bank in her new location, and, when she insisted upon making full withdrawal, he immediately requested that she accept a promissory note.

"It's really impossible for us to come up with such a large amount of cash on no notice, Miss—ah—Bitler," he explained. "It leaves us dangerously short for our other transactions, you understand."

"You'd best give the young lady her money, sir, and in cash," George Livingstone said, stepping to her side.

Fanny turned with a half-guilty start, but the lawyer, looking unbelievably well-groomed even after what had certainly been the last twenty hours or so in the saddle, continued addressing the intransigent manager.

"If you're truly incapable of coming up with this amount of cash without running short, sir, I believe it would be a matter for the State Bank Examiner to look into. I'll see that he has the information within the week. You know who I am, I believe?"

"Indeed, indeed, Mr. Livingstone. I really don't understand the young lady's impatience, sir," the manager said, "but if she insists, of course. . . ."

"She insists," Livingstone nodded, and the small, well-dressed man, shaking his head and muttering to himself, scuttled toward the vault.

Cash in hand, and with Willow and George Livingstone trailing behind her, Fanny walked quickly to the livery stable, where this time she bought two horses and a pack mule—paying as well for the rented animals she'd not returned. She made arrangements for Gideon Whitney's horse to be boarded, figuring that the colonel would find it there sooner or later, even if George didn't tell him.

Livingstone placed a hand on Fanny's arm as she led her animals into the street, said, "Are you just going to ride off into blue distance, then, not even say good-bye? I did, after all, just rescue your funds from that thieving banker. Surely you owe me a kiss, at least. Madam Willow, you will excuse us for a moment?"

He took off his hat and bowed to the scowling girl who stood beside the horses.

"I didn't need your help to get my money, George," Fanny said. "I would have gotten it with a gun if nothing else had worked. Yes, I'm leaving. Not quite soon enough for the good citizens, it appears. You've seen the Palace?"

"I've seen. Fanny, I'm called back to Washington immediately. I should have left several days ago—in fact, I would have except that I wanted to see you again. Fanny, come with me. It's about as far away from Klamath Falls as one can get. Hell, bring Willow with you if she doesn't have any place

better to go. I'll give you whatever you want. You know I'm
as good as my word."

Fanny felt suddenly like weeping once more, but instead
she touched gently at Livingstone's cheek, then leaned forward and kissed his mouth.

"I don't want to go to Washington, old friend. I think I'd
die there, so far away from . . . everything. You're the one
who travels around the world, and is at home everywhere.
Me, I have only a small circle where I can live. . . ."

"Nonsense, Fan. You've no idea whether you'd like Washington. I tell you, you'd have them eating out of your hand."

"Maybe I don't want that."

"What do you want? I'll. . . ."

"I don't know, don't know. I guess I don't want to be
anybody's woman anymore, not even yours. I'm sorry. . . ."

She unhitched the reins from the rail and climbed up into
the saddle, Willow grinning and swinging up onto the second
horse.

" 'Bye, Living-stone," Willow said. "Come see me an' Fanny
in Reno sometime. On the house, eh Fanny?"

"Come visit us in Reno, George. I'll always be glad to see
you. You'll be West another time before too long. Tell Gideon about his horse, would you? And tell him good-bye for
me."

"To hell with Gideon. Fanny . . ."

She turned, saw George was standing with hands half-
raised, looking helpless. She had a momentary impulse to
dismount, embrace him, say, *Take me to Washington*. Instead, she raised her hand in salute.

"I'll miss you, Fanny Bitler," he called, and then stood
with his arms hanging at his sides, looking after her as she
rode away down the dusty street, with Willow, small and
stolid in the saddle of her tall buckskin, following.

"Goddamn my soul if I won't," he whispered when they'd
disappeared at the end of a row of buildings and into the
silence of a sun-haunted morning.

TWENTY-THREE

Salty Dan Dolliver

[June 1873]

THEY TRAVELED southeastward through a monotonous sameness of splendid weather—nights dropping down cold, skies crowded with stars, days pure blue and warm, tending toward dry heat in the afternoons, but tolerable. They passed beyond Tule Lake and the Lava Beds on the second day, and continued through a land of lava rims, pine forest, shallow lakes, and marshy lowlands, these and hillsides blazing with a profusion of wildflowers. They crossed through the Adin Hills and then followed Ash Creek for a time, passing occasional ranches and even small settlements where the two women traveling alone were looked at curiously but not molested in any way.

Willow began the journey in high spirits, singing obscene ballads into the empty distance, but by afternoon of the first day she was complaining bitterly about the ache in her bones, insisted she was unaccustomed to long horseback treks. Fanny demanded they keep up a steady pace, and by the second day Willow was cursing with most colorful language and fertile imagination—the horse she rode, the land they traversed, Fanny's heartlessness, and the moment of her own birth.

Next the Klamath girl lapsed into a sulky silence, and by

the evening of the fourth day, when they crossed a ridge and headed down a long grade to the considerable cowtown of Susanville, she fairly wept with joy when Fanny proposed they have dinner in a local eating establishment, bathe, and sleep the night away at the hotel in feather beds.

They each consumed large portions of beefsteak and fried potatoes, with dried-apple pie for dessert and quantities of coffee laced with cream and sugar—Willow sweetening her beverage with four lumps as the waitress looked on in mild disapproval.

Other patrons in the establishment managed to avoid staring at the two travel-worn but nonetheless attractive strangers, although whenever either looked up, she was sure to catch a pair of eyes just in the act of peering at something else.

Near the door, an apparently prosperous rancher sat at a table alone, silver-haired and obviously dressed in his "town" clothes—dark woolen jacket, flowered vest, bow tie. His forehead was characteristically marked as he sat hatless—a white streak above the rest of his weather-darkened face—a visage that sent momentary shivers through Fanny, for she perceived a certain similarity to the old haunting image of Big Dan Clayton, massacre-crazed. . . . This individual was more obvious in both his scrutiny and his disapproval of the young ladies. He scowled openly.

Willow began to make faces at the stranger and then, as Fanny was paying for their meal, approached the man, hips swaying in exaggerated fashion, elbows cocked, hands at her waist.

"You want a roll in the hay, mister?" she asked in a loud voice. "Even better than last night, I give you half price."

There was a patter of laughter, stifled guffaws from other tables. The rancher turned away from Willow with a jerk, muttered something about "goldanged hoors."

"Want a knife in your eye, you piss-sucking pig?" Willow demanded, moving to stand in his line of vision once more. "You don't like Willow, don't stare at her like fucking coyote in heat, hokay?"

By this time the outraged rancher was on his feet, and Fanny barely managed to drag Willow out the door of the

establishment as other patrons began trying to talk themselves into intervening in the hullabaloo.

"Goddamn squaw, sure as hell," someone muttered. "Kick
all their tails into the Happy Hunting Ground, somebody
should. . . ."

Fanny pulled Willow, still kicking and cursing, to their
mounts outside, half-boosted her into the saddle, and then
made haste to get out of town as the door to the restaurant
was flung open in their wake. Several customers stood in the
doorway, still obviously debating whether to go into combat
over this insult offered one of their own by a foul-mouthed
Indian girl.

FANNY AND WILLOW headed south by moonlight, an ovoid by
now and riding high above the eastern rims. No one bothered
to pursue them, and they camped on a sage-covered slope
back off the road, a few miles out of town.

Willow cursed bitterly about having to spend yet another
night in the open.

"Goddamn rocks and thornbushes—even rocks got thorns
on them. Rattlesnakes under every fucking bush."

"Your own fault we're not sleeping on feather beds tonight,
my girl," Fanny said. "I wasn't the one who tried to get a
knife fight going with a local in the midst of a whole damned
roomful of his friends. Choose your odds a little more carefully, and I'll back you up."

"Reno better be a damn lot nicer than this place, that's all I
say," Willow grumbled. "Otherwise, maybe I go back to
reservation, find 'nother husband. This time I cut his balls off
if he lay a hand on me. Hokay?"

Fanny drifted into a deep sleep on her own rockpile.
Moonlight shone silver on her face, a breeze fanning chill
against her cheek, and Willow's curses still bumping against
her ears. She didn't wake until dawn spilled rose-colored in
the eastern sky.

IT WAS STILL MORNING when they came to the north end of
Honey Lake, a great, shallow expanse of water, wavelets
lapping gently at the margins, its surface alive with waterbirds—
mudhens like little floating bundles of dark twigs, loons who
would vanish abruptly from their place and reappear after a

few seconds many yards away from where they'd been, flotillas of geese and wild swans, many with troops of small young bobbing after the mother birds, these families staying near shore.

A group of long-necked gray geese who'd been holding some sort of conference among clumps of marsh grass had apparently not noticed the near approach of humans, and took to flight abruptly, rowing their big, ungainly wings and running awkwardly across the mudflats until they managed to launch themselves, honking protests, into the air.

Further along a pair of blue herons stood in the shallows on sticklike legs, one with its neck down, head cocked, peering into the water for fish, the other motionless, its long neck a perfect vertical, even the head tilted back and beak pointed at the sky. These disdained to take any notice of the women and horses on the road above, and Fanny tried to catch a momentary, tickling fragment of memory the sight evoked.

Wilson Lake, eight years ago, a pair of herons fishing in motionless waters. True Bear and I together, watching. . . .

The day hadn't yet really begun to heat up, but the silver-blue water and the soft sound it made against the shore seemed so inviting that Fanny and Willow stopped where the beach was wide but partially screened from the wagon road, undressed, and dived in naked.

The lake was still quite chilly from the night past, but even so it felt wonderful to Fanny to wash off several days' worth of grime and perspiration.

Floating waterfowl drew back when the women entered the water, leaving a wide circle around them. As Fanny and Willow finished their baths and waded out onto shore to dry off, an osprey floated into sight, high above the lake's surface, hovered motionless a few moments, then suddenly plummeted, raked water with talons, and flew back up.

"He missed," Willow laughed. "See? No fish."

The bird circled once more, hovered, dropped in another attempt, and once again came up with empty claws. This time he circled above the women's heads, screaming indignation, then winged away northward, apparently seeking a better fishing hole.

At the raptor's appearance, a mother swan had quickly herded her young into brush a hundred yards up the beach.

Now she reemerged, scanned the sky, and paddled back out onto the water, her little train of dark youngsters trailing single-file.

Fanny and Willow dressed and then mounted again, feeling wonderfully revitalized after the quick bath.

"I feel almost human now," Fanny said. "I think I'm ready to ride straight through to Reno."

"Not me," Willow replied. "I'm ready to sit by this lake for a week—just swim and catch fish and eat and sleep."

A COUPLE OF MILES south along the shore, they found a handsome black gelding with a white blaze on its face and a brownish mule, the two animals browsing on sparse grass among sagebrush on the side of a hill above the road. The two creatures raised their heads and watched the women curiously as they approached, called out equine greetings.

"What on earth?" Fanny wondered aloud. "Who'd turn such a fine-looking horse loose in this country?"

"Maybe they run away, break out of somebody's corral," Willow shrugged. "Maybe they come with us. Get good money for the horse in Reno, I bet."

"I think the Saltus call it horse-theft," Fanny laughed. "They don't take kindly to it. I'd just as soon not hang for a fifty-dollar horse when we can make that much in one night easy, once we get set up in town."

"Hokay, Boss Lady," Willow said. "Too bad, though, when money just askin' us to take."

The road sloped back to the lake, and as they drew near, they noted a tent half-hidden behind a stand of small willows, its once-white canvas now the yellowish color of the region's prevailing dirt. Outside rested a silver-trimmed riding saddle and a packsaddle, the latter partially unloaded and the contents strewn about carelessly, but there was no sign of an occupant in the vicinity.

Fanny decided the wisest course of action would be simply to pass by, but something in the arrangement aroused her curiosity. The women paused, speculating on the matter.

"Black horse, mule, they must belong to tent-person," Willow said. "Probably dead, I think. So nobody chase horse if we take 'im."

"I'm not so sure, Willow. It doesn't quite feel like a death-camp. Maybe the owner's off fishing or shooting ducks or something."

"I sure not leave that saddle just layin' there while I go fishing for damn sure. Some sonofabitch pick 'im up, put 'im on black horse, ride off pretty."

"No larceny, damn it Willow."

A tremendous groan issued suddenly from near the tent, then a second. Fanny and Willow glanced at one another, wide-eyed.

"Let's get hell outta here. Some kinda crazy person in there, or ghost, maybe cannibal spirit."

Another moan, long, heartfelt.

"No," Fanny said slowly, "I think it's only a sick person, or someone who's injured. I'll go see. You stay back. If I get in any trouble I can't handle, you just ride the hell out of here."

"Nope," Willow said, thrusting her jaw forward. "You go, Willow goes."

A figure emerged then, crawling on hands and knees, stopped, and peered up at the women. The face beneath a disheveled mop of wavy, silver hair was haggard, dirt-stained, the cheeks covered with several days' growth of grayish stubble. But the clothes the man wore, despite their rumpled and unclean condition, were obviously expensive, although a trifle flashy. The shirtfront was ruffled above a brightly patterned tapestry vest, a wide silk ascot still half-tucked into place, fastened by a large brooch adorned with what appeared to be an emerald.

Gambler, Fanny thought, and felt reassured. She'd met a number of such men at the Palace, and while they might be more than willing to divest a widow of her last pitiful penny, a gambler was seldom a man of violence—except in self-defense against a sore loser.

"Angels," the man groaned, still staring up at them, his blue eyes watery, fevered-looking. "Am I dead already? Do seraphs ride horses in heaven? Always thought God must surely have steam trains everywhere so a body could travel about in comfort."

Fanny dismounted and let her horse's reins trail. Willow, apparently also reassured by the man's appearance, followed suit.

"Can we do something to help you, sir?" Fanny asked,

ignoring the card-man's melodramatic overture. "Are you injured? We found your house and your mule back up the road—at least I assume they're yours."

"Not injured, no, young lady. I'm merely dying. It seems to be the way of things. This was one time in my life when Madame Fortune appeared to be my faithful consort, and halfway to nowhere the death-worm attacks my guts, if you'll pardon the expression, Fair Ones."

"Why don't you lie down and tell us what's wrong?" Fanny said. "Perhaps we can assist you. . . ."

"I'm afraid I'm beyond help, but the sight of lovely faces would be a comfort to me in my last hours, for I've lain down here to die, and it's been a lonely vigil."

"All men are children," Willow scowled. "Think they die if they get a little ache. Good thing men don't have babies, I say. What you got? Big bellytrouble, eh?"

"Worse than that, far worse. A case of the backdoor trots, except it's been more of a hard gallop, until now, when there's nothing left in my poor dessicated frame at all. I haven't been able to eat or drink for two days—whatever doesn't go down comes up, so to speak. At times I sweat and shake with the ague until my bones are falling apart. . . ."

Willow made a quick sign, went to her horse, and rummaged through the saddlebags, coming back with a small brown bottle.

"Good for the shits," she said. "Cure 'em like that. Make you feel good, too, then you sleep, have pretty dreams. After that you eat, get better."

"Old Indian remedy, no doubt," the gambler muttered. "Well, I'm a dead man anyway so where's the harm?"

"Opium," Willow said. "Better than Indian cure. You drink— not too much. Maybe to here. Too much make you dead man for sure."

She indicated a level with her finger on the bottle, handed the container to the sick man. He drank, sighed, lay back.

"Not bad," he said after a time. "I'm not convinced that you've cured me, but I do think I'll die happier. Now if I could rest my head upon the lap of a fair lady, sleep with gentle fingers like my own mother's soothing my flaming brow, by Gawd I'd thank ye. . . ."

Willow looked at Fanny, shrugged, and took the man's

head onto her lap. He smiled blissfully, began to doze, occasionally muttering in his sleep, at one point awakening with a start, looking around him, then dropping back off.

He was indeed feverish, and Fanny brought water from the lake, dipped a cloth, and mopped at the gambler's face until he began trembling with what appeared to be a chill.

"Swamp fever, I'd guess," Fanny said. "They get that over in the Sacramento Valley. Wonder where he's been?"

When the man began to come around again, she administered a dose of quinine from a bottle of the medication she had found among his things and then let him sleep some more.

"SALTY DAN DOLLIVER'S what they call me, my sweet angels of mercy, and if there's ever anything I can do to make some small repayment for your ministrations, why damn it, I'm your man. Just now I'm flush, as a matter of fact, though before you brought me around, it looked like I was out of tin, out of aces. Not something I'd let on to any stranger, but after what you've done for me, anything I have is yours—and what I've got is a fat stash."

He leaned against his saddle, sipping cautiously at a cup of broth Fanny had prepared while he slept, the emerald brooch on his tie sparkling in the light of their campfire. Indeed, he'd slept most of the day under the effects of the opium elixir Willow had doled out in small doses to cure his dysentery.

"I'm Fanny Bitler, and this is my friend Willow. We're on our way to Reno. Is that where you were headed, or are you going the other direction? We'd be glad of some male companionship along the way, Mr. Dolliver. My guess is that you're a card thief. It could be we can do each other some good. We can discuss matters later, though. You're still not well."

"Good a time as any to palaver, when a man can't do anything else."

Dolliver took a long draught of the soup, cooling now.

"What a blessing this is," he nodded. "The first thing in my gut for days that's felt like it might stay there. You're right, of course, about my profession. Would it be too indelicate if I asked yours? *Business ladies*, as I take it."

"So the saying goes," Fanny laughed. "I don't figure you as

a hypocrite. I had a nice place up in Klamath Falls until I ran
into some trouble. Townspeople burned me out. A long
story. . . ."

"We go back someday, burn down whole damn town, cut
all their balls off," Willow added. "But first we go to Reno for
a while, make big money."

"Think I may have heard something about that," Dolliver
nodded, "the very morning as I was leaving Shasta City.
Burned out for sympathizing with the Redskins. Well, blood's
thicker than water. As for myself, I never pay attention to
such gossip. It's just that one old boy was jawing away about a
certain madam at the Falls, halfbreed, he thought, though
others claimed she were the daughter of a Spanish grandee,
and one version has it she was actually Captain Jack's woman.
However it happened, she went 'renegade,' as they put it,
threw in with the Modocs. The good citizens, in a patriotic
fit, burned down her place. One version of the story goes that
they also rode her and her lover, either a buck Meskin or a
traitorous Washington bigshot, out of town on a rail. Would
that be some version of your own story, Miss Bitler?"

"Not too close," Fanny said, "but I guess it must be me, all
right. So far as I know, I'm the only *madam* to be burned out
in Klamath Falls lately."

She poured a cup of coffee for herself from the pot near the
fire, then told Dan Dolliver the details of her departure from
Oregon.

When she finished, Dolliver nodded his head, drank the
last of his broth, and spoke again.

"I never paid much attention to the Modoc disturbance,
but to tell the truth, my sympathies were mostly with the
poor devils. I've got to admit to a bit of a prejudice, though.
Damned settlers, especially the new ones, cow thieves turned
solid citizen, most of 'em—and a touchy damned lot they are,
too—figure they got a right to everything. If they lose at a
fair game of monte, they'll call it cheating nine times out of
ten, draw a gun on you if they think they won't get shot doing
it. I've seen enough drunken settlers go off on Injun hunts to
last me a long time. They calculate the Indians as predators
and in their way, just like they see coyotes and cougars and
ground squirrels and every other blessed thing that was here
before they come along—as obstacles, varmints to be got rid of

in order to make the world safe for cows, I guess. Hell, the boys aren't all that way, I know it, and you and I'd damned well starve without them, but there's too many that figure they ought to own the world and so stomp everything that gets in their path into dust. My apologies, ladies. I know you didn't want a discourse on my philosophical idiosyncracies. . . . Call it *The Gospel According to Salty Dan*."

"I think we can be friends, Mr. Dolliver," Fanny said, smiling. "Would you like to hear my proposition?"

"Indeed. It's been far too long since I've been propositioned by any young female as pretty as you, and you truly are a striking woman, Fanny. But I think I've guessed the details already. Casino downstairs, cathouse upstairs, something of the sort? You ladies got any tin put by? Like I said, I've got a nice poke at the moment. If I pull through, maybe I'm interested at that. This wandering life is starting to get to me, I think. Busted one day, flush the next—but when a man's flush, the chances are he gets run out of town for his trouble, like as not with a pack of 'solid citizens' howling for his blood. Yeah. Shasta gave me a good welcome but one hell of a farewell. Fever in my guts to boot. Running at one end or the other all the way from Burney. If I don't make it, I want you ladies to have my poke, my horses, everything I got. But truth to tell, I'm starting to feel like I might live, after all. Yes, could be it's time for me to light someplace for a while, steady down a bit. I hear Reno's wide-open."

The gambler was beginning to show signs of tiring again, but Willow insisted that he let her shave him. She found his soap and razor, whipped up thick suds in a tin mug, spread the foam over Dan's face, and wielded his fearsome-looking blade expertly about cheek and chin.

"I dearly hope you like me, Miss Willow," Salty Dan joked as the razor scraped at his throat. "I'm just beginning to get attached to the notion of living again."

Willow didn't say anything, concentrating on the task at hand. When she finished, she washed his face, combed his hair, and then ran her hand over the freshly smoothed cheeks.

"Pretty," she said. "Pretty hair, shiny like lake water on cloudy day. Pretty eyes. Like you plenty, Dan Dolliver. When you feel better, Willow show you good time. Then maybe we go back to that place you talk about, Shasta place, burn it down too."

Dolliver coughed, startled, then grinned, held up his hands.

"I'd truly admire some of the coffee you've got going there, Miss Bitler. It's been years, I think, since I last had a cup of hot coffee. Miss Willow, you make a handsome offer, very handsome indeed. . . ."

QUIET, the moon drifting high among stars, lake ripples of silver. Crickets whirring like musical clockwork, a shrill chorus of tree toads, rhythmic thump and hum of bullfrogs.

Fanny sat cross-legged near the fire's remnant, staring into the tracings of blue and gold flame that from time to time raced across red embers, shadow pictures that formed and disappeared in dying coals. Across from her Willow dozed, leaning back against Dan Dolliver's saddle, the gambler's head once more resting upon her lap. Both snored gently.

A loud, mad, shrieking whoop shattered the night, momentarily stilling all other sounds. Then another sustained cry—like hysterical laughter.

Dolliver sat straight up, and looked wildly around.

"God!" he said. "I've heard that every night I've been here. At first I thought it was the devil come to get my soul."

"It's only Loon Woman crying out for her brother," Fanny said. "I'll tell you the story if you like."

"A damned bird, then? Don't think I want to hear it," the gambler muttered, settling his head once again and winking at Willow. "I take it you mean it's not the devil, then. Don't go telling me any stories about Old Man Death, not with me lying here virtually cut down in the prime of life."

Willow smoothed the hair back from Dan's forehead, her face tender in the dim firelight. The gambler was already asleep again.

"Don't fall in love with him, Willow," Fanny said, "if such warnings mean anything. He's going to be our business partner. The two things don't mix gracefully."

"Me?" Willow said. "Hell, no, I not fall in love with

nobody. I try that once. No damn good. Just think he's
pretty, that's all."

Fanny nodded, got up, and wrapped a blanket around
Willow's shoulders, then pulled one around herself, lay down,
and closed her eyes.

*Loon Woman, her eyes mad and a necklace of dried hearts
around her throat, those of her own family—all dead because
of Ishanahura's incestuous love for her brother. And now she
seeks him, seeks him, laughing and crying through the nights.
See where they fall through a hole in the sky—and their
bones are scattered like stars!*

*The bones of all your people, Auna-yi, burning white in the
canyons, in the lava beds, and you step over them as if they
weren't there.*

*Do you remember one who was like your brother during
the innocent time? Yet he wasn't your brother, even though
his blood is as your own—half-Red, half-White. The myth
changes, and perhaps he's the one you must find. The myth
changes, Auna-yi, and perhaps you join your opposite halves
and step into the future.*

*Long ago, that was a long time ago, and the world was a
different place. . . .*

Fanny Bitler shook her head and then wondered what it
was that she was denying. She stared up at a star-clouded
heaven, momentarily followed the long, broad track of the
Milky Way, and then closed her eyes and shook her head a
second time.

Nine winters had passed since then, almost nine years. The
boy and the girl who had stood together beside a small pool
and felt spray on their faces from a waterfall, what had
happened to them? Would they even recognize one another,
should the whims of Old Coyote Man ever dictate that they
meet once again?

TWENTY-FOUR

The Queen of Reno

[July–September 1873]

"LITTLE HIGHER," Willow called out.

"Whose end, damn it?" Fanny yelled from her place on the ladder where she stood, perspiring profusely in the desert sun of a summer afternoon, holding up one side of a sign while Salty Dan Dolliver, on another ladder, nailed the opposite end in place.

"Yours," Willow replied, then, as Fanny raised her arms a bit more above her head, "Looks good. Damn good."

When the sign was firmly fastened on the newly painted canary-yellow building front, Dan and Fanny climbed down, stepped back to admire their work.

The One and Only SALTY'S EMPORIUM, the legend read, carefully hand-lettered in black on a bright yellow board, the name flanked on one side by a large representation of an ace of diamonds, on the other by a queen of hearts—in subtle suggestion of the Emporium's two primary offerings of entertainment. Tacked beneath the permanent sign was a paper banner proclaiming *Grand opening celebration tonight—free refreshments from 7 to 9. Come one, come all.*

It was a large building, two stories high, with a balcony overhanging the sign, a pair of half-size swinging doors in the

archway beneath, with massive iron shutters to bar entry
when the establishment was closed. In front ran the town's
wide, dusty main street. Two blocks away in one direction a
bridge spanned the Truckee River, while several blocks the
opposite way stood the Central Pacific Railway station, its
loading platform extending out to double sets of tracks and a
big round turntable. Numerous other buildings rose here and
there, many of wood construction, but several of brick or
quarried stone. Others were still in process of being built, a
certain sign that the Athens of the Desert was continuing to
grow.

"Not bad, not at all bad," remarked Salty himself, "though
I think you must have let your end down a tad, Fanny," he
added, squinting critically.

"Like hell," she said. "Looks straight as the Pope's soul to
me."

"That's what I said," Dan laughed. "You sure you don't
want your name up there too?"

"Decidedly not," Fanny replied. "I've had enough of local
fame to know it's mostly good for trouble."

"In that case, then, may I propose a small celebration? A
toast in genu-wine Napa Valley champagne, perhaps? I just
happen to have a bottle cooling inside. Ladies. . . ."

He cocked an elbow to either side, and with Fanny on one
arm and Willow on the other, stepped up onto the boardwalk
and through swinging doors to the interior, relatively dark
and giving at least an illusion of coolness after the full afternoon glare outdoors.

The two women sat at one of the small pine tables while
Dan stepped behind a plank bar and brought forth a silver
bucket filled with cracked ice, a dark green bottleneck thrusting up through.

"God, Dan," Fanny laughed, "you used all that ice? The
wine we can afford, but I'm not so sure about the ice. . . ."

In July in Reno, ice was indeed a very dear commodity,
hauled down from the Sierras in springtime and stored in
underground icehouses through the summer.

"How many times do we celebrate the launching of that
great ship, *Holy Venture*?"

"*Emporium*," Willow said. "That's what you tell me sign
says."

"All right then, that great ship of sacred enterprise, the *Emporium*. How's that?"

"No damn ship, either. You talk funny, Dan, but I still think you got pretty eyes. When we have that roll in the hay?"

"Soon, my duck, soon, and then you'll be sorry."

"Huh. You talk big. Hokay, we toast this silly ship, if that's what you call it."

The three glasses clinked in the air above the table, and Fanny looked around the room. It wasn't yet nearly as elaborate as many of Reno's entertainment palaces, but it would serve, she thought. The walls were plain varnished pine, and the floor was strewn with fresh sawdust, but the gambling area already held three round, baize-covered card tables, another table for billiards, and one for shooting craps—as well as an old roulette wheel and an upright piano. At one end of the room, behind the piano, was a small, raised stage, at the other end the long plank bar and a large, ornate staircase leading to a railed gallery upstairs, and that in turn led to a half-dozen bedrooms in what had been an abandoned flophouse when the partners bought it.

"We'll make it fancier as the money comes in," Dan said, "but I think it'll do for now. You've managed to steal the three prettiest working girls in town away from our competition, and that's worth all the mirrored-back bars and red-flocked wallpaper in St. Louis. We've got first-class liquor and first-class entertainment, and word's sure to get around."

"Not to mention," Fanny grinned, "the best situation we could have dreamed of. That was a stroke of luck, finding this rat-eaten building right on Main Street, a great location and even close to the train station."

"No dude on his first trip west can possibly miss us," Dan agreed. "Ah, think of them all, my flowers, green as grass and with tin burning holes in their pockets. We're providing a real service here, by God, for a whole cross-section of male humanity—stockmen and cowboys, travelers, bankers and other thieves, maybe even a college boy or two from up north of town. The young ones can't spend all their time with books, can they?"

"Young ones?" Willow asked.

Dan pulled a big gold watch on a chain from his vest pocket, and glanced at it.

"Best start moving, I guess," he said. "Just about enough time to get dressed and set the wheels in motion for the party of the century, lasses."

THE GRAND OPENING was a great success, the expense of free drinks served during specified hours more than compensated for by the take from the gaming tables and the activities upstairs. At precisely eight o'clock, Fanny, her shining black hair swept up and decorated with ostrich plumes and her person exquisitely gowned in wine-red satin with velvet trim, led the grand parade of girls, all equally elaborately dressed and coifed, down the big staircase and into an absolute stunned silence in the gaming room, silence quickly overcome by good-natured cheers and whistles.

The girls climbed upon the stage and gave a performance, dancing a variety of tarantella to the accompaniment of a piano player, and then the entire chorus of four sang. After that Willow soloed, and the girls danced again, a rousing cancan.

Fanny, meanwhile, circulated among the crowd, spoke greetings, and dealt a few hands of blackjack, Dan having taught her a number of card games during the period when the Emporium was being gotten ready for business.

When their performance was finished, the girls ran giggling from the stage to a wildly appreciative audience, and all four disappeared almost immediately up the staircase on the arms of men dressed in their Sunday best for the grand occasion, shaved and with hair thoroughly slick with pomade.

Business continued brisk every night thereafter for the first week—their take, even on the worst evening, at least twice as good as the best Fanny had ever done in Klamath Falls— and on Friday she had more business than the four girls could handle, so she determined to hire two extra ladies just for weekend trade.

They closed on Sunday out of deference to the local church society and in order to catch their own breaths, for neither Fanny nor Dan had expected anything like the success they'd enjoyed thus far.

*   *   *

FANNY WAS IN HER OWN ROOM, going over account books, when she heard knocking at the private side entrance. She paid no attention to it, thinking it was likely one of the girls who'd forgotten her key and knowing that Maria, the Mexican woman she'd hired for a maid, would answer.

It was not until a half hour later, when she heard screams down the hallway in the direction of Dan's room, that she realized anything was amiss. As she stepped through her doorway, Willow ran toward her, crying hysterically and shrieking out incoherent syllables before turning and running back toward Dolliver's door.

Fanny followed the girl, and found her partner lying curled against a wall, unconscious and his face beaten bloody.

By now Maria and all the girls had gathered at the door, and Fanny sent the maid for a basin of water and some cloths, one of the girls to fetch a doctor. As they awaited the physician's arrival, Fanny bathed Dan's face and spoke to him until he began to come around, Willow hovering fretfully nearby.

"He be all right, won't he Fanny? Shit, look what they done to that pretty face. I cut their goddamn cocks off and stuff them in their mouths."

The doctor, aged and not particularly concerned, arrived, peered into the patient's eyes, left some pain-killer and ointment for the bruises along with instructions to wake Dan up a few times during the night, and departed. The girls drifted back to their rooms, and Fanny and Willow sat down beside Dolliver, now bandaged and stretched on his bed, while he explained what had happened.

"Fellow came by and wanted to buy our playhouse. Well, I told him it wasn't for sale. Lawyerish-looking sort of a man, said he was an agent for somebody, that his boss was prepared to pay a great deal. I said no deal. He nods, goes out, and by Gawd in come two big sonsofbitches who proceeded to beat the crap out of me, then left. That's about it, Fan."

"Someone wants our place bad, I guess," Fanny said. "How much did he offer?"

"Thirty thousand before he sent in the army."

"Jesus Christ, Dan. You should have sold it to him. At least you might have asked me if I wanted to sell. Aren't we partners? For that kind of money we could set up anyplace we want."

"I like it here. Besides, I don't care to have a man force my hand that way. Stubborn streak, I guess."

"Stupid streak, maybe," Willow grunted. "Somebody rather get beat up than take thirty thousand dollar. Maybe you need sense knocked in."

THREE DAYS LATER, while Fanny dealt faro, Willow jostled her with an elbow, pointing with her chin toward the door. Fanny glanced up and saw a man standing just inside, a stranger, with something about him that arrested the eye, something more than the mere fact he was dressed considerably more expensively than anyone else in the place. He was tall, robust, middle-aged, with hair salt-and-pepper gray and a short-trimmed full beard above his topcoat of flawlessly cut and flawlessly groomed dark wool. His eyes were deep-set, penetrating, and now he was engaged in studying the room thoroughly, assessing it.

When his gaze met Fanny's questioning stare, he halted his surveying movement, looked directly at her for several seconds, then bowed from the waist and moved across the room toward her.

She dropped her head and continued her deal but was acutely aware of the stranger standing to her left as she finished the hand. A high-rolling gambler? Senator Stewart perhaps? Whoever he was, he stood quietly by in a manner calculated to make his presence felt.

Fanny turned the table over to Willow and then rose, faced this newcomer, and curtsied.

"Apparently you wish to speak to me, Mr.—" she said, lifting her eyebrows inquiringly and smiling her iciest professional smile.

"Huntington, madam, Collis P. Huntington. Perhaps you've heard of me."

The blunt announcement caught Fanny by surprise, but she nodded quickly and smiled again.

"Out of three drops of rain that fall in the San Joaquin Valley, two are owned by Collis Huntington," she said, quoting an epigram spoken frequently and usually with considerable dislike when the name of railroad magnate Huntington was mentioned, one of the *Big Four* syndicate who owned Central Pacific and were fair on their way to controlling

California and the rest of the Western states as well. "Are you that Mr. Huntington?"

"Indeed! You flatter me, madam. In truth, out of those three drops, I probably only account for one."

"What may I do for you, Mr. Railroad?"

"You're Mistress Bitler, if I'm not mistaken."

"You flatter me, Mr. Huntington. Yes, I'm Fanny Bitler."

"I'd like very much to speak with you and your associate, Mr. Dolliver, on a business matter. May I also add, quite off the subject, that I find you even more attractive than I was led to anticipate?"

"Thank you, good sir, but I'm afraid my partner and I are rather busy this evening. Perhaps you could come back tomorrow afternoon, before we open. . . ."

"I think you'll find what I have to say to be of sufficient interest. . . . I believe that's Mr. Dolliver yonder, dealing poker, is it not? Please, may we adjourn to your office?"

"How d'ye do, Mr. Huntington," Salty Dan said when the stranger introduced himself. "Sit down for a spell—do you some good, and the house as well. Five-card draw. A friendly game. I think you'll enjoy it. We can talk later."

Huntington smiled, sat in an empty chair, and when the first hand was dealt, counted out ten one-hundred-dollar bills onto the table.

"Fifty-dollar limit, Collis, old boy," Dolliver said, pushing the pile of bills back at the financier. "That's your name, isn't it?"

Huntington nodded, staring steadily into the dealer's eyes.

"Fifty dollars? Well, I'd prefer higher stakes. What do you say we take off the cap?"

Dan stared back at him for a moment, then nodded.

"All right, Mr. Huntington. You the one who sent over the gorillas? Gentlemen, you're welcome to take back your wagers. I'll be here later if you wish to continue the game. C.P. Huntington, eh? Would you like me to have my associate bring the cashbox—just so you know you're covered?"

"Your word is pure gold to me, Mr. Dolliver. Let's play cards."

Dan wrote out a chit, placed it on the table with Huntington's banknotes.

"Cards, sir?" Dan asked, and Huntington waved his hand in negation.

"Dealer takes two. Your wager, Mr. Huntington?"

The railroad baron peeled off another five one-hundred-dollar notes, and then drew out a checkbook and wrote a draft for an additional five hundred.

The onlookers gathered about the table sucked in a collective breath.

Dolliver studied his opponent for a moment, smiled, and then wrote out a chit for another thousand.

Fanny, sitting next to her partner, unconsciously reached over and gripped his thigh, her fingers biting into muscle. The Emporium had been making money, right enough, but not this kind of money.

"Call," Dan said, spreading his cards on the table. Three tens, the ace of spades, and a four of diamonds.

Huntington hesitated and then turned his own cards over. He grinned.

He had nothing at all.

"Two thousand dollars on a hand like that?" Fanny asked, incredulous. "I don't understand you at all, Mr. Huntington. I thought rich men were careful with their money."

"The investment principle, madam."

"Guess the gentleman wanted to get our attention," Salty Dan grinned. "What's on your mind, Huntington? You send over those boys, or not?"

"I'd like to buy your establishment, Mr Dolliver. I'm prepared to pay quite handsomely. . . ."

"I had an offer of thirty thousand the other day," Dan said, still smiling but with a glint of hostility coming into his eye. "You hear anything about that?"

Huntington held up one hand as Salty Dan started to rise from his chair.

"Yes, it was my offer, Mr. Dolliver. But I'd like to add that my . . . ah . . . agent's choice of persuasion was not mine. I came tonight partly to apologize, as a matter of fact, and to offer thirty-five thousand instead."

"As I told your so-called agent, the place isn't for sale. But if you'd care to play another friendly hand of cards, Huntington, I'll be happy to take your money. Hell, I wouldn't mind owning a railroad."

The millionaire leaned back in his chair, drew a gold cigar case from a breast pocket, and offered it to Dolliver. The gambler drew out a long Havana, sniffed appreciatively, nodded thanks, and flicked a match into flame with his thumbnail, offered Huntington a light. Then Dan bit off the end of his own smoke. The two men eyed one another through clouds of fresh blue haze, puffing silently for a moment.

"What I'd like to know, Huntington," Dolliver said slowly, "is why you're so all-fired eager to get your hands on the Emporium. You know it's not worth anything like thirty-five thousand dollars—to you or to anyone else."

"Such being the case, why not simply profit from a rich man's folly?"

Dolliver shrugged.

"Say I'm naturally suspicious. Curious, too. And I don't take well to being 'railroaded,' as the expression goes."

"What do you say to all this, young lady?" Huntington asked abruptly, shifting his attention to Fanny. "I understand you're an equal partner in the enterprise. Where do you stand on the matter? I'll buy out your share for half the amount I'm offering for the whole."

"First I'd like to hear the answer to Dan's question," she said, looking Huntington in the eye.

"Very well. It's not all that complicated. I like to have things connected with the railroad under my own control. Your business is close by, and to a certain extent, you derive profit from our operations. I think Central Pacific should have a share in those profits. Call it a whim if you like. So. I believe you suggested another appeal to the great god Chance, Mr. Dolliver. That particular deity has usually been kind to me. Miss Bitler—are you interested in selling your half or not?"

Fanny glanced at Dan and then, tight-lipped, shook her head.

"All right, then," Huntington shrugged. "Let's have at it."

As THE GAME CONTINUED, most of the casino's occupants drifted over to watch the high-stakes contest. Three girls stood in a group close by, not even pretending to work, and Willow sat beside Fanny, clutching her fingers tensely when a hand went against Salty Dan, relaxing and smiling when the gambler raked in a pot.

Gradually, however, Dan's winnings began to pile up, and at the end of an hour he'd milked the railroad tycoon of the incredible sum of ten thousand dollars and change.

"All right, Salty Dan," Huntington said, "if you're truly a gambling man, we'll have one last throw. Double or nothing, all to be decided on one cut of the deck. High card wins."

"Too rich for my blood, Huntington," Dan shrugged, preparing to rise. "No skill in cutting cards—it's blind luck, nothing more. Let you off the hook on the turn of a card? That's a fool's game. Besides that, you know damned well I can't cover the bet without mortgaging the farm."

"Exactly. You have something I want. Your claim to Salty's Emporium against my twenty thousand. How can you refuse? You have ten thousand dollars of mine and a fifty-fifty chance to take C.P. Huntington for a total of thirty thousand. You'd be famous, Dolliver. You'd be known all over the West. The way I see it, you have to give me a final chance. What kind of gambler are you?"

Fanny swallowed at a dryness in her throat.

Huntington's right, of course, Dan can't really refuse— whether it's turn of the card or another hand of something. He can't refuse with everyone watching. . . .

"Just a moment, gentlemen," she said aloud. "Mr. Dolliver has no claim to my half of the business. He can't put that up as stakes."

"Quite right," the millionaire tipped his hat to her. "We'll play only for Mr. Dolliver's share, then, as I suggested. I'd be more than delighted to have you as a partner, Miss Bitler. More than delighted."

"What the hell am I going to do with a railroad, Huntington? The way I figure, you're going to want to keep going double or nothing until I own the whole shooting match, Pullmans and all. Well, I'll hire you on as a conductor to show my appreciation, then."

Huntington grinned, winked at Fanny.

"And if I win?"

A fresh deck of cards was brought out, seals still intact, and presented to Huntington for inspection. He glanced casually at the cards and passed them to Salty Dan.

"I have implicit faith in Mr. Dolliver's honesty," he said, smiling slightly, "for I believe him to be a gentleman. Proceed, if you will, sir."

When the gambler had shuffled several times, he handed the deck to the tycoon. Huntington also shuffled and then passed the cards to Fanny.

"I'd be honored if my new partner would draw for me, lovely lady. Remember," he added, his deep-set eyes fixed on hers, a trace of a smile nearly hidden in the stern beard, "my fate rests entirely in your charming hands."

She glanced at Dan, nodded, and spread the cards onto the table. Then she touched her fingers to the deck and closed her eyes. A mist of perspiration broke out on her palm. Without looking, she lifted a card and turned it up on the table.

"The queen of hearts!" Collis Huntington chuckled. "How appropriate."

He reached out, raised Fanny's hand to his lips.

Good God, what have I done? she thought. *A queen. Damn it, Dan, why didn't you teach me how to cheat? I hope you've got the ace up your sleeve. . . .*

"You've made it tough for me, Fan," Dolliver mused. "You sure it's me you want for a partner? Well, let's see what the goddess of fate's got waiting for me. . . ."

He studied the table, showed his teeth in a faint grin, reached, and turned over one card.

Fanny let out her breath in a long sigh. The ace of clubs lay face-up beside Huntington's queen.

The spectators cheered. Dan leaned back in his chair, drank off a shot of whiskey. Willow threw herself into his arms and kissed him on the mouth, then turned and kissed a tall cowboy who stood nearby.

"Drinks on the house!" Dan called out, and the group of spectators broke up, heading for the bar and talking excitedly among themselves. "Collis, would you do me the honor of having a drink with me? Willow, bring this gentleman a—whatever he'd like."

FANNY, Salty Dan, and Collis Huntington sat alone at the table, sipping champagne. The other gamblers had resumed their own games, and Willow had disappeared up the staircase with a tall cowhand. The railroad man lifted his glass in salute to the partners, drank.

"Now that you have thirty thousand of my dollars in your pocket, I'd like to make one more proposal, Mr. Dolliver, Miss Bitler," he said. "I'll add to that another thirty-five—not to buy you out, but to buy the controlling share. I'll own fifty-one percent, the two of you will have forty-nine between you. I propose to change nothing about the way you run your business. You remain in complete charge. I'm quite frankly impressed with the two of you. No one at all need know, in fact, that I have any part in your operation. I'll merely provide capital and expect my fair share of the profits."

Dan and Fanny glanced at one another.

"Wait. Hear me out. In the past several days I've managed to purchase your competition—that's correct, I own all seven of the other pleasure houses in Reno. Tomorrow the prices go up. I'm convinced the rates you charge here for . . . services . . . are unnaturally low. Miss Bitler, I'd like you to take control of all these operations. You strike me as a woman of uncanny acumen for one so young and, if you'll pardon me, so strikingly beautiful. Mr. Dolliver, of course, will run the gaming operations. It's an opportunity neither one of you is likely to come upon again. You will, in effect, be running the show in this town."

Dan looked at Fanny again, hesitated. But she was staring at Huntington, on the verge of a realization that she and Dan actually had no choice. One way or another, Huntington would be able to squeeze them out—have the two of them murdered if that were necessary for him to accomplish his purposes.

"Sold!" she said decisively. After a moment Dolliver shrugged, laughed.

"What the hell?" he said. "All right, Huntington, you've bought yourself a gambler and a madam. Now what do you do with us?"

"For the moment, only this," he smiled, staring at Fanny again. "I would be more than rewarded if Miss Bitler—Fanny— would do me the honor of joining me for dinner in my private car?"

Fanny looked into the millionaire's eyes, glittering under

dark brows, glanced at Dolliver, then threw her head back and laughed.

"Mr. Huntington," she said, "for thirty-five thousand dollars it's the least I can do."

THE STREETS OF RENO were deserted near dawn, this being perhaps the only hour when most of the little boomtown's inhabitants slept. September chill was in the air, breath down off the Sierras cold with promise of winter to come. Fanny walked alone, following the railroad tracks to a trestle bridge over the Truckee, leaned against a railing, and stared down toward water rushing invisibly into darkness. During the past two months, things indeed happened as Huntington promised. She possessed effective control of every brothel of any size in the city, and she was rapidly becoming wealthy beyond her previous imaginings of wealth. She owned gowns made in Paris and shipped west directly from New York shops. The Emporium sported a back bar of carved mahogany and Venetian glass, handsome murals on the walls, brass and gilt everywhere—in short, it had become the premiere establishment in town and was rapidly developing as a legend, all with an infusion of railroad money.

For her own part, she was aware of the scrutiny of people wherever she went about town, looks of envy or of admiration, often the two mixed.

She was called "The Queen of Reno" by some—a title half-derisive, half-awed. That, and "Huntington's Woman," this spoken in whispers, in rumors, in prurient speculation about *what she does for him.* In fact, as a lover he was quite conventional, not particularly demanding, often contenting himself with talk, endless talk about financial speculation, empire building, and himself. She was merely required to seem impressed. Sometimes she acted it out, while at other times, taken by a demon of perversity, she refused. Her independence of mind often maddened the man, but she suspected it also kept him interested.

In all, this was not a bad life.

But tonight she was restless. Out over the desert a pair of coyotes sang to one another, fine, lonely, quavering notes slicing through predawn darkness, and she felt an aching, intangible wish for something she could no longer define.

Behind the great barrier of mountains, the sky was beginning to show light.

"Damn!" she whispered, striking her palm against the railing. "What's the matter with me, anyway?"

She heard footsteps on the bridge now, turned. Dan Dolliver came up and leaned on the rail beside her.

"What do you think I want, Dan?" she asked without preliminaries. "Why shouldn't I be content? It's a long way this halfbreed kid's come up in the world. What the hell's wrong with me?"

"Maybe you haven't got the hang of being a kept woman, Fan," he said lightly. "You've got to learn to relax and enjoy it."

"Yes? And why aren't you sleeping right now, Salty Dan Dolliver?"

"Itchy feet, I guess. Could be neither one of us can stand too much prosperity."

"I don't think that's all of it. Listen to those coyotes out there. Lonely as hell, but I wish I could join them. Crazy, huh?"

"Mad as March Hares, the both of us," he said, putting an arm around her shoulders and squeezing for a moment, then releasing her.

They watched the light growing stronger behind the black bulk of mountains in silence, a few birds beginning to sing.

"Did you cheat that time?" she asked abruptly.

"What are you talking about?"

"The big game with Huntington. Did you have the ace up your sleeve, Dan?"

Dolliver laughed.

"Thing about coyotes is that there's a pair of them. Maybe what you're missing is love, Fan," he said. "Did you ever think of that? You play it tough, but I've heard women can't live without l'amour."

"Don't be an ass. You're changing the subject. What the hell do you know about it, anyway?"

"Oh, me, I manage to stay in love most all the time. Right now I'd probably tie Miss Willow over my saddle, but I'm too old to change, and she's too damned cantankerous. Too fond of bedding young 'cowpokers' as well. I'm serious, Fanny. You say you don't need it, but I don't believe you. You ever been in love? I know you have. Figured it hurt too much, or I'm dead wrong. You cut yourself off, after a while you start feeling like an amputee. Maybe that's what your trouble is."

"Not going to tell me, huh?"

"Tell you what?"

"Whether you had a damned ace up your sleeve."

"Oh, that. Sun's about to come up, Fan. Look at it. Clouds as pink as a lady's. . . ."

"Fuck you, Dolliver. I don't give a rat's backend, anyway."

III

✠

When Eden Burns

[July–October 1874]

TWENTY-FIVE

A Letter from Ben

[July 1874]

AT AGE TWENTY-THREE, William True Bear McCain was an impressive figure of a man. His six foot six inch height was further enhanced by a stovepipe hat he commonly wore in public and by an entirely black costume of boots, trousers, vest, and greatcoat that were his nearly inevitable attire. Shirt and bow tie provided the only deviation from the overall monochrome he'd adopted two years earlier, and these were usually red or white, sometimes in combination. His mustache and chin whiskers were kept neatly trimmed, in accord with accepted custom—but in contrast to long black hair, sometimes worn braided in yet another quiet affront to the polite society in which he found himself.

From the beginning, McCain's classmates at Harvard College dubbed him "The Savage," though only one or two close friends ever used the term to his face. True Bear was aware of the sobriquet, however, and from time to time he actually attended seminars while wearing a gull feather woven into an Indian-style topknot, his general appearance more than once eliciting reprimand from the Provost.

In fact, young McCain took quiet joy in offending the sensibilities of those around him, making no secret of his halfbreed heritage. Nonetheless, he paid strict attention to his studies in history and literature, passed his examinations with distinction, and gained first-class honors at graduation.

In his spare time he frequented taverns along Boston's waterfront, occasionally drank excessive quantities of ale or rum, and sometimes indulged in fistfights with stevedores, cod-fishers, and lobstermen. In this alternate world of rough, working-class individuals, he was known as "Books Billy," and he gained both their acceptance and their respect. Fascinated by the sea, he spent two summers on a fishing vessel working the shallow waters of Cape Cod Bay and Nantucket Sound, allowing his strength to catch up to his size.

Bare-chested and wearing canvas trousers, he took delight in days of sunlight and rain, heaved at woven-cord nets, and mastered the subtle art of rigging sail. With the other hands, during leisure moments, he dived or leaped whooping into salt water, scrambled up a rope ladder onto the foredeck, and dived again.

"Books, ye look like a Gawddamned Injun, no two ways around 'er!" the Irish and Italian sailors were fond of saying—grinning broadly and pleased with their wit. A halfbreed college boy he might have been, but he was willing to learn from them and *was* one of them.

Autumn, however, would find him back at his room in Cambridge, and once again he'd blunder ahead into the perplexing world of human knowledge—with an energy that surprised his professors and created envy among fellow students, who saw him as a creature delivered to them from the mind of Jean Jacques Rousseau. McCain's thirst for information was immense, and in some way peculiarly appropriate to his herculean physical proportions.

By the end of his second year at the college, he was known not only as "The Savage" but as "The Walking Encyclopedia" as well.

But now that life was behind Books Billy, just as was, he supposed, his former existence in Wahgalu's shadows in the mountains of Northern California, a land from which he had come to feel himself an exile. Nonetheless, among his things, carefully wrapped away, were the rifle and pistol his father had given him, curious relics of a previous existence, unused but not to be discarded.

Ahead of him lay a new kind of life, one that would require a more standard haircut and no doubt a final farewell to his cronies along the waterfront. The long rite of passage was essentially complete.

He was, in short, engaged to be married—to Miss Harriet Collins, a schoolmistress four years his senior and an "old maid" by common reckoning, the daughter of one B.J. Collins, a highly successful Boston lawyer with several junior partners and an office on Atlantic Street. True Bear and Harriet had been engaged for nearly a year, in fact, the result of chance meetings, first in a restaurant, later at a lecture one of his professors gave at nearby Radcliffe College, and again at an opera in Boston. On the third occasion, Harriet demurely agreed to yet another meeting, this time in more private circumstances—and the trysts continued, with True Bear renting a flat not far from the river, within walking distance of both their residences.

Harriet Collins, tall for a woman and quite thin, soon took the role of sexual aggressor, and the two of them explored one another's anatomies quite thoroughly—each acquiring a healthy lust in the process.

At length the relationship had to be owned up to, but Harriet's parents weren't pleased, particularly B.J. Collins himself, pillar of the community and concerned for his *little girl*'s reputation and future well-being. After all, who wanted to have a wildman for a son-in-law? But eventually B.J. gave in to what appeared to be inevitable, and after that the lawyer began to encourage True Bear to read for the law, perhaps thinking of the novelty of having this half-breed giant as another of his junior partners as well as a son-in-law, since there seemed to be no cure for the latter.

When young McCain announced his intention of accepting the offer of a low-level teaching position at Massachusetts Agricultural College, B.J. once again began to attempt to persuade Harriet of the folly of her proposed marriage to the "California Halfbreed."

By this time, however, both True Bear and Harriet began to have second thoughts of their own. Harriet, terribly fearful that continued lovemaking would result in a child being born less than the prescribed nine months after her scheduled marriage in September, first insisted that True Bear satisfy himself with oral copulation only and later decided that all sexual activity would have to cease until after the enactment of formal union.

True Bear shrugged, agreed, and shortly thereafter began to patronize the brothels he'd discovered the year before his initial meeting with Harriet.

The marriage remained scheduled, but William True Bear McCain contemplated the possibilities of spending his life somewhere away from the restricting confines of New England society.

THEY SPENT AN AFTERNOON on the beach at Lynn, riding out from Cambridge in a rented one-horse shay. Harriet had packed a lunch, complete with fried chicken, French bread, creamery-fresh butter, several kinds of cheese, gherkins, and a bottle of red New York wine.

True Bear set up a tan-and-white beach umbrella a few yards back from where inward-rolling gray-green waves were slushing against sand, and then spread out a large blanket for the two of them to sit on as they ate.

A number of boys were playing close by, running full tilt into the waves, sputtering to the surface, and dog-paddling back to shore.

McCain used a corkscrew to open the wine bottle, tilted the container to his lips, and drank.

"William! I did think to bring glasses, you know. Sometimes I suppose you'll never change."

"Isn't that why you're fond of me?" he asked.

He handed his betrothed the bottle, winked, and grinned. She shook her head, pretending disapproval.

"There's little point in changing what works, is there?" he asked. "Harriet, you're getting stodgy in your old age. Let's see you do it—chug-a-lug, my girl."

She ignored him, brought out the oilcloth-wrapped chicken, untied cross-laced strings she'd secured the morsels with, and placed the food on the blanket between them.

"Would you like bread and cheese first, William?"

"How about a leg? A breast, perhaps, or a thigh? I think I'll devour the cook—worry about the food later."

"The Philharmonic is performing the *Eroica* by Beethoven this weekend," she said, ignoring him. "Do you think you could get us tickets? There's a guest conductor from New Haven . . . what's his name? In any case, he's supposed to be quite good."

"Filbert Flutterwrist, the boy wonder," McCain replied, breaking off a section of the loaf of bread. "Whatever my lady wishes. . . ."

"That's not his name at all. Oh, why can't I think of it? Do you suppose it's likely to rain tonight? The clouds out over the ocean look very dark."

True Bear glanced toward where the boys were playing, lifted an edge of the blanket so as to shield himself and Harriet from view, and leaned forward to nuzzle at the ribbon and lace of her blouse.

"William!"

"You look stunning today, my dear," he grinned. "How could I resist? Why don't you take off that silly little hat and comb your hair out? I love to watch while you're doing it."

"Eat the lunch I brought with us, you great lout. It took me two hours to prepare all this. Here's a breast, since that seems to be what's on your mind. You must learn the virtues of patience."

"Three months?" True Bear groaned. "Perhaps we should just drive up to Danvers and find an obliging justice of the peace."

He ate the chicken Harriet offered, reached for the wine bottle, and took another long drink.

"I like it when you get chicken grease all over your mouth," he laughed. Then he stood up, removed his hat, took off his coat, and began to unbutton his vest.

"What are you doing, Mr. McCain? Act decent, for heaven's sake."

True Bear stripped off his shirt, removed the wallet from his trouser pocket, and sat down on the sand to pull off his boots.

"Those kids don't own the ocean," he said. "I'm going out for a swim."

"You'll have cramps! Put your hat back on—when are you going to have that hair cut to look. . . ."

"Proper New Englandish? Maybe in September—I'll do it as a wedding present. I'll be right back, Harriet Slim. It's not a good day for a trans-Atlantic crossing at any rate. But it's a hell of a shame to waste this sunlight. Miss my fisherman friends, I guess. Must have got addicted to saltwater."

He ran toward the waves, past where the boys were now engaged in impromptu wrestling, and dived into an incoming surge.

He swam a long way out, began to tread water, and then gazed back toward the tan-and-white umbrella and the girl sitting under it. Beyond the beach stood a row of houses, and to the south stretched the long landspit of East Point and another cluster of houses, the small village of Nahant.

True Bear took pleasure in the rise and fall of swells as they passed under and around him, and for one reason or another he began to think about his old friend Big Woodpecker—the day they cut their wrists and allowed oozing blood to mingle. Then came to mind the time he and Woodpecker were captured by Chief Wolf Tracker's Yahis. With this memory appeared the image of a girl named Wahtaurisi-yi.

Massacre, and she had been stolen by cattle drovers—raped, no doubt, used until the men grew tired of her.

Miraculously, the girl had avoided being dispatched with a pistol shot, as he was later to learn. For a long time he hoped she might somehow manage to return to Upper Eden, but the current of Fate was not so inclined—not until after he himself was sent East, partly as a consequence of a dispute he'd had with two of Dan Clayton's cowhands over a little brand-altering on McCain cattle. One of cowboys pulled a gun, and before the confrontation was finished, True Bear had shot and killed both, interring their bodies in a lava cave. That incident marked an utter, ragged end to boyhood, and his mother and father escorted him to Reno and put him on the recently opened transcontinental railway.

Two years later Wahtaurisi-yi, using the name of Fanny, actually had returned to Upper Eden, after allying herself, so Ben reported in a letter, with the Modoc Indians, who were then attempting to fight off the United States Army. Was it possible that Wahtaurisi-yi, Fire Woman after her emergence from the woman lodge, was still alive? Big Woodpecker had gone north with her, and reported seeing her badly wounded, since he'd been unable to do more than watch as soldiers took her prisoner. The Modocs were eventually defeated, of course, their leaders hanged—and the tribe's remnant sent to Indian

Territory, Oklahoma. Perhaps that's where she was, then, if she had been fortunate enough to survive both her wounds and a thousand-mile journey, with the Indians being shipped like so many cattle to market.

What, in all his reading over these past four years, now sufficed to render such a black reality palatable? In this best of all possible worlds, war and violence seemed common denominators.

SHORTLY PAST FIVE, with cloudbanks having drifted in off the waters of the Atlantic and a thin drizzle beginning to fall, True Bear McCain delivered his bethrothed to her parents' home in Chelsea. Feeling vaguely annoyed with the way the afternoon had gone, and particularly with Harriet's professed unwillingness to relocate anywhere away from the Boston Hub after their marriage, possibly to upstate Vermont or New Hampshire (the idea being ". . . utterly unthinkable, William . . you simply can't be serious . . . No doubt it's different for you, but I have a family, responsibilities, my teaching post . . ."), True Bear declined to have dinner with "B.J. and the Mrs.," electing instead to return to his own room in Cambridge.

He took the horse and shay to the neighborhood livery stable and quickly walked a half-mile to his boardinghouse residence. Back within doors, he paced nervously about the room, at one point delivering a hard straight right to a paper-covered lath-and plaster wall, leaving an oblong dent in its surface. He shook his fist, assuring himself that he hadn't in fact broken a knuckle, lectured himself in the most colorful language, opened a tin of sardines, and sat down with these and a box of oyster crackers and ate.

Directly he rose, lit one of his two lamps, placed it on a stand beside his reading chair, and strode over to some makeshift bookshelves that held, along with a number of boxes, many of the various books he'd ingested while a student at Harvard. He considered browsing through a volume of Spinoza, decided against that, and selected a copy of Emerson. He sat down and began turning pages.

The great man's "nature," True Bear concluded after a few minutes, was altogether too tame to be worth reading about—

and besides, he'd half set the piece to memory three years
earlier.

He went back to the shelves, fussed with one book or
another, and finally sat down with Joaquin Miller's *Life Among
the Modocs*, a used volume he'd purchased a week earlier
and hadn't yet gotten around to reading.

It was past midnight when he finished, and as he rose to
replace the volume on the shelf, he realized his hands were
trembling.

*California . . . the great white cone of Mt. Shasta . . .
half-crazed gold miners . . . young Joaquin living among the
Shasta Indians . . . in love with Paquita but not marrying her
. . . Paquita's death, her body riddled with bullets, the crimson of her blood glwoing on her brown skin . . Joaquin
riding away at last but leaving his soul behind . . . yes, a
belated tribute to a place and a people . . . written because a
Modoc chief named Captain Jack had chosen to fight desperately against crushing odds, and had held off numerically
superior military forces, only to be betrayed, captured,
executed. . . .*

Joaquin revealed himself as a renegade, and his pro-Indian
sympathies, True Bear concluded, were almost certain to
destroy his reputation as a poet. Indeed, that had largely
already occurred during the brief interval since the book's
publication. Miller had been attacked as liar, renegade, and
Indian lover.

But for True Bear McCain, the figure of Joaquin Miller had
just emerged from that of a mere poseur, elemental show-off
and second-rate poet, and had been transformed into *great
man.*

Was it partly because the dying Paquita had also been
transformed—into the figure of True Bear's first love?

McCain put on a pot of coffee, paced about impatiently,
and then turned to one of the closets. He began to dig
through things—found what he sought: a Hawken cap-and-
ball rifle and a Navy Colt pistol he'd once used to kill two
men. Each Christmas since his arrival at Harvard, he had
carefully oiled the weapons and then rolled them back inside
a wrapping of canvas. He undid the fastenings, took the
weapons to his bed, and laid one beside the other.

"To hell with B.J. Collins and his ilk," True Bear grumbled. "Why in the devil should I be obliged to live the kind of life I just ain't got no stomach for?"

He listened to his own voice, and shook his head.

Ain't doin' 'er right, ye dumbass idjit. Try 'er again, like this hyar: The kind o' life I jest ain't got no stomach fer. . . .

"Bully O'Bragh," True Bear mused. "Dead now, in all likelihood. How old did he say he was? A hundred and twenty-nine. And that was . . . nine years ago. Well, nobody lives forever, not even Bully O'Bragh—my dad's words. Goddamn it to hell, McCain, what are you doing here? Alaska—that's where I'm going. Maybe it's 'Seward's Icebox' and maybe it isn't, but by heaven it's preferable to eating dinner with Proper Bostonians! Or maybe Bolivia—I'd like to see what the Andes Mountains look like. . . ."

IN THE MORNING he rose late, dressed, and walked downstairs to the boardinghouse's dining hall. Old Mrs. Elmore was doing dishes as True Bear entered the kitchen area, nodded, and headed for the pantry to see what leftovers might be available. He found a portion of cheese omelet, saved no doubt for neighborhood cats, and ate that. Then he drank half a quart of milk and fixed several slices of toast and jelly.

"You're going to starve to death, William, if you don't start rising in time for breakfast," Mrs. Elmore said, not looking up from the large pan she was scrubbing.

"Dumb Injun go shoot dog, eat that," True Bear replied—using the same line he always used when he missed breakfast, a line Mrs. Elmore was expecting, even anticipating. She laughed, as usual.

"You'll do no such a thing, young man," she said—again, as usual.

He left the boardinghouse kitchen, walked out through a glass-paned front door, and crossed the street—decided to take a stroll over to Somerville, maybe throw pebbles out into the inlet, a pastime he commonly resorted to on occasions when he felt a need to sort out his thoughts.

On this day he found it necessary to hurl stones for half an hour or more, and even then matters did not truly fall into place. Whether to go through with his marriage to Harriet Collins? Indeed, he was thinking seriously of terminating the relationship. Something had gone out of it, and that something, he surmised, no doubt had to do with their earlier secret meetings in the run-down flat he'd rented for the precise purpose of an illicit affair. Secrecy, yes, the two of them *getting away with something*, their lovemaking unknown to those with whom they were in daily contact. That part of it was over, then. From now on they would have to be both discreet and proper, enacting all socially approved rituals. Maybe it would be better for both of them if he did some kind of disappearing act. Possibly there was a need for a schoolmaster in Colorado. . . .

But at this point in his musings, True Bear became aware of having an audience—half a dozen ragtag-looking children of indeterminate background. The boys were sizing him up, wondering if they could hurl stones as far as "the big bloke."

For a moment True Bear felt he should explain what he was doing and why. Instead, however, he merely gestured with his hands, turned, and began to walk back toward Cambridge.

As he reached the street's brick pavement and crossed, he heard a firecracker go off—then several others, followed by a good deal of childish whooping.

The Fourth of July, 1874, True Bear thought. *In two more years, the Grand Experiment will be a century old. In that small space of time, we've mastered a continent, killed most of the Indians, fought the British twice, fought the Mexicans, fought ourselves, killed every wild animal we could set our sights on, buffalo just about gone, grizzlies are going, the wolves. . . . We've by Gawd done good, when you think about it. A parade downtown—probably over by now. Harriet and her parents are there, all dressed up and solemnly watching Civil War veterans march past. Independence Day— has a nice ring to it, by cracky! And today's supposed to be the day when they open that big steel-arch bridge across the Mississippi itself. Be something if the trains started across, and the whole kaboodle fell into the water. Well, if that designer, Jim Eads, did his job right, the bridge'll probably hold up forever. The thing was already in the building when I got sent East, into exile. . . .*

HE DIDN'T RETURN directly to the boardinghouse in Cambridge, but instead walked south to Watertown. He picked his way along the shore of Charles River, its tidewater channel low and far more than the usual number of gulls swooping along, even a couple of herons and one pelican. True Bear passed by a solitary Colored boy, net in hand, staring intently into the murky water and waiting for a crab to nibble at some scrap of stale meat fastened to the end of the line. Further upstream a pair of Irish youths (judging from freckles and red hair) were engaged in the same elemental activity, while their younger sister was engrossed in teasing fiddler crabs out of their holes in the mudbank.

It was midafternoon when he arrived at the boardinghouse. Mrs. Elmore was in the anteroom now, reading. She looked up as he entered.

"William," she said. "It slipped my mind this morning—a letter came for you yesterday. I see it's still in your cubbyhole. Mail from California—your father, judging from the handwriting. Is your mother dead, William?"

"No, she's still not dead," he replied, winking. How many times had she asked that question?

"She never writes, though," Mrs. Elmore persisted.

"That's true, that's true. . . ."

He reached for the envelope, stuck it into his coat pocket, and walked up the stairs to his room.

The letter had been postmarked in Reno, Nevada, three weeks previously. True Bear opened the envelope and unfolded tightly written sheets of paper.

Upper Eden
June 12, 1874

Dear Son,

Today marks your graduation from college, and your mother and I send our most sincere congratulations! In all your letters to us, you've never mentioned the manifold difficulties you must have gone through, for Harvard College and Plumas County, California, represent rather extreme manifestations of two utterly dissimilar worlds.

What I'm saying is—we know you've often been homesick, and we're hoping you still feel that way at times. In truth, we have great need of your presence here at the ranch right now, and have had for the past several

months, though I haven't mentioned the matter in previous letters.

Son, my health is failing, and I have so little eyesight
left I'm virtually an invalid on that account alone. Either
I've read too many books during my life or not nearly
enough. Oh, I'm still capable of overseeing operations
here on the ranch, with the able assistance of those
Maidus who remain with us. As I've told you before,
there's been a general exodus from Upper Eden over
these past four years—indeed, it was going on even
before you went East. Big Woodpecker, faithful soul
that he is, has been an infinite help to Ooti and me, and
I daresay that he's nearly as knowledgeable with regard
to raising cattle as anyone I know. His own herd pros-
pers as well, and that's as it should be. He and Yellow
Grass were married finally, and we had quite a celebration. That was in April—but I think I mentioned this
news before, in an earlier letter.

Back to the point at hand. What I'm worried about is
simple enough. In the event of my death, an attempt
may be made to dispossess your mother and the other
Maidu people of their lands—on the grounds that she
and everyone else still at Upper Eden is Indian and
should therefore be removed to a reservation at Hoopa
Valley or Fort Bidwell. You alone can inherit the land,
while Ooti, as a fullblooded Indian, cannot. Such are the
remnants of barbarism in our laws.

Our old enemy Daniel Clayton has greatly increased
his operations over these past couple of years, and he's
made fruitless attempts to lease a good portion of our
land as summer pasture. Clayton has friends in the
county government in Quincy and influence in Sacramento as well. If something should happen to me, there's
little doubt in my mind that he'll attempt to have the
Maidus removed and to take over our land—on one
pretext or another.

I anticipate no problem with regard to those two
burials you presided over down in Mill Creek Canyon.
Whatever suspicions Clayton may have had at the time,
the entire matter has long since been forgotten. You
may set your mind at ease in this regard. The bodies

were never found—at least we never got word of such a discovery.

Your mother and I know, of course, that you and Harriet plan to be married in the fall, and we couldn't be more pleased than we are. A trip to California now might well result in postponement of your union, and that would be regrettable. Is it possible you might be able to return to Upper Eden and then, in the fall, go back to Boston? Perhaps, after a honeymoon, you might ride the transcontinental railroad to California yet again, this time bringing your wife with you. I think there are ways of solving the Clayton problem, but your presence is required. Ooti and I would delight in meeting your chosen mate, needless to say, and it's even possible she might like it here—as primitive as things are in comparison to the world she's lived in.

We look forward to seeing you once more, Son, and I wish this present missive were not so filled with a tone of desperation. But truth is truth: I'm not as young as I used to be, and there's too much at stake for me to be other than blunt about it.

Please send a wire to Reno. I've already made arrangements for someone to deliver the telegram when it arrives.

Your father,
Benj. McCain

TWENTY-SIX

To Reno, by Pullman

[July 1874]

HARRIET COLLINS, as was to be expected, didn't wish him to
go. His father, she said, was simply overreacting and being
melodramatic into the bargain. In short, it was outrageous for
Benjamin McCain blithely to suppose his son should put behind
him a new life that was truly just beginning, board the railway system, and cross an entire continent. What the elder
McCain actually needed, Harriet insisted, was a good lawyer.

In the face of Harriet's resistance to his proposed journey
westward, True Bear, pausing only a moment, made his
decision.

"And what you need, my lady," he said, "is a good lawyer's
son. Well, I'll return when I'm able to do so. What kind of a
man would I be if I didn't go? Responsibility to family doesn't
begin and end in the state of Massachusetts, no matter what
you may suppose. The problem is—there are no damned
mountains to speak of around here. You come West—climb
to the top of old Wahgalu with me. Perspective changes in a
place like that, and a whole lot of things come remarkably
clear. Maybe it isn't just that my father has asked me—perhaps
I have to go back there for my own purposes. Left something
up on that mountain, I think. . . ."

"You left something? William, you're being absurd. What could you possibly have left that's so important—and what makes you think it would still be there after all this time?"

"It'll be there," he replied. "I left a dream up there. Yes, that's what it was. Everything's changed for me since then, but I've got to go pick up that dream, hold it in my hands for a while. Probably doesn't make any more sense now than it did then, but I've got to take another look at it. Could be I need to kill two or three more people. . . ."

"Don't you ever get tired of playing your Wildman role? It might once have helped you to adjust to civilization, but now. . . ."

"Never did adjust," True Bear said. "You do what you think best, Harriet. I have to do the same. In truth, there's no reason why you should wait for me. But right now I've got some other fish to fry. Say good-bye to your mother and father for me, but I don't think B.J., at least, is going to be too damned disappointed. I'll be back in September or October, by the first of the year in any case, if the stick's floating right."

"What stick? You're not making the least bit of sense, William McCain."

"Name's True Bear," he replied. "And that's another problem. . . ."

THEN HE WAS ONCE AGAIN listening to a steady *clack-clack-clack* as the iron wheels of his Pullman rolled away, this time westward, in some inexplicable manner nullifying his previous journey—or perhaps completing that journey.

Day and night blended into one as a series of different trains made their way across Connecticut and through New York City, then on to Philadelphia, Pittsburgh, Columbus, Cincinnati, and across the new steel bridge that now spanned the wide, lazily running Mississippi River to St. Louis, that onetime gateway to the American West.

His trip East four years earlier had been punctuated by a steamship voyage from railhead in Omaha on down the Missouri to St. Louis, but now all of that was changed, with the Kansas-Pacific Railway slicing completely across the plains to Denver and finally to a junction with the older Union Pacific route at Cheyenne, no boats required.

Two hundred miles beyond Kansas City, however, the train screeched to a halt, inasmuch as a sizable herd of buffalo was very slowly moving across the right-of-way. Men in suits, previously content to read newspapers and talk idly among themselves concerning the great drought that was crippling agricultural endeavors on the plains, drought complicated by the previous year's terrible grasshopper swarms and the grave likelihood of an even more severe insect plague as summer wore along, were now galvanized into immediate action.

Sharps rifles and Henry repeaters appeared as if by magic, and the men spilled out of the train, intent upon killing big brown wild cattle. The atmosphere was transformed to one of celebration, and men took bets with one another, firing at will. Blue-gray gunsmoke drifted up in prairie air, and numerous buffalo bellowed, stumbled, fell, or moved away, bleeding from wounds that would prove fatal within an hour or so.

At length the herd's dominant cow began to plunge away southward, the remainder of the herd pounding after her.

The men in suits raised a cheer and then, their faces red as though they had stood too close to a big brushfire, they moved back into the passenger car.

No attempt was made to do anything at all with the animals that had been slaughtered. One or two creatures, dead upon the tracks, were dragged to one side, and after several blasts of a steam whistle, the 280 locomotive began to move forward once again, bell clanging enthusiastically.

True Bear experienced an intense sense of revulsion, of disgust, and when the train stopped at a wayside inn for dinner, he had no heart for eating. Instead, he resolved to purchase a Henry repeater of his own, for quite a different purpose, and buried his nose in a copy of Mark Twain's *Roughing It*, sometimes smiling and sometimes scowling as he read.

All in all, he concluded, America was hell-bent on destroying not just wilderness but the very idea of *wildness*, a state reserve of Yosemite in California and a recently established national park of Yellowstone notwithstanding. If, indeed, old Bully O'Bragh were dead by now, why, that was probably just as well, for the land that had created him and given him both his identity and his purpose for continuing to exist was dying. No, it was being devoured alive.

Cattle empires had been created, and the new railroads served to ship millions of animals to the East. Range wars were in progress, sod-busters against cattlemen, with both sides conspiring against the remaining buffalo herds and the Indians as well, the latter doomed to reservation life and slow extermination, the former to massive and immediate slaughter, for fun and profit.

Cowboy, a new symbol for America's vaunted freedom, half-myth and half–shit-kicker.

Were not the McCains, in fact, among them? That was the life he himself grew up living—that was the thing he wanted to be, would have been had he not become a bit too proficient, too confident with a Colt pistol and so faced down a pair of cattle thieves and killed them. Then the bubble burst.

If he had it to do over again?

True Bear relived the incident. Once again he was nineteen years old and by-God ready to take on the world. He saw one of Dan Clayton's drovers go for his gun, saw himself leaping sideways, pistol instantly in hand, firing, firing. . . .

McCain grinned, stared out the window, and observed seemingly endless prairie lands through which he was passing.

Somewhere ahead, the Rocky Mountains—that's where reality begins. At least, I think it does. . . .

When the train finally reached Cheyenne and a transfer to Union Pacific, entailing a six-hour layover, McCain strapped on his holster and pistol, though without having any particular reason for doing so. Once he was aboard the U.P., other passengers looked on askance, noting the weapon. A pretty young married woman pursed her lips in obvious disapproval and nudged her husband's arm.

But with the Navy Colt in place, True Bear felt unaccountably better about things.

THE TRAIN was running well behind schedule as it puffed and snorted its way across Salt Lake Desert and on into the silver-mining state of Nevada, clack-clack-clacking along beside the slow-flowing Humboldt River.

True Bear wondered if his father would even be there—in Reno, at the appointed meeting place. With his son's train some ten hours late, perhaps the elder McCain had given up and begun the ride back toward Susanville and on through the mountains to home.

The 280 finally reached Truckee River and steamed on toward Sparks and Reno. True Bear caught sight of the still snow-draped Sierra Nevada Mountains dead ahead and breathed a sigh of deep-felt relief. It had been a long five days from Kansas City, and, late or not, the sight of genuine California topography was a welcome one.

"Five days, hell," he mused. "Four years, and they've vanished just like that—spun out from under me and gone, nothing more than a blur of books and faces, one face in particular. Harriet's."

He had a distinct feeling he'd never again see her. Human life, he had long since concluded, was much like riding a river down—everything was change, occasional danger, chaos moment-by-moment. In some ways God (call it Old Man Coyote) had played a grand practical joke on his two-legged sapient creatures. He had given them just enough wit to realize their time was limited and death was their destination, as well as enough foolhardiness to get them into all kinds of hell. Lovers spoke of "forever," but the term was meaningless. At this moment his feelings toward Harriet Collins, for instance, however intense they might have been only a few months earlier, were now fairly well a numbness—like a memory of some part he'd been obliged to play, and now the role was finished. She would without question be better off with a lawyer's son, but he himself? God only knew about that, and God wasn't tipping his hand.

WHEN THE TRAIN pulled into Reno, and True Bear descended from the Pullman onto a wide board platform beside the tracks, his father was there—Ben and Big Woodpecker as well, the latter now a powerful man wearing chaps and a cowboy hat, thick-chested and short-necked as always, and grinning from ear to ear. Ben, however, was indeed changed—he'd lost weight, and despite his great size, the man appeared almost—what? *Frail.* He was seventy-two now, True Bear reflected, but somehow the change came as a surprise. When True Bear had anticipated the reunion with his father, the man was still the giant he'd always been, with arms like the limbs of oaks.

True Bear strode forward, embraced Ben—and was pleasantly surprised to find that, despite appearances, a very considerable strength remained in his father's grasp. The two pounded each other on the back, and for one fleeting instant True Bear realized that he felt like a child once more, a young boy overwhelmed by this man who had sired him.

He felt, also, a flicker of disappointment that Acorn Girl hadn't come down to Reno to meet him, though he really hadn't expected it.

He turned to Big Woodpecker, and the boyhood companions clasped hands, hesitant for a moment, and then hugged one another.

"Congratulations, you old married hawg!" True Bear said. "So you finally talked her into it. Well, Yellow Grass'll have a long time to regret that decision. Save my soul, but it's good to be back—even if we do have a long ride ahead of us. Pop—did you bring my horse? How's Mom—she's all right, isn't she? I was hoping. . . ."

"Your mother's in good health, Son," Ben said. "It's your father who's wobbling in his boots. Big Woodpecker has to lead me about these days, my vision's deteriorated that much."

"He lies, naturally," Big Woodpecker grinned. "I don't know about the glasses, but Ben still sees right through me. I can't put nothing over on him, hard as I try."

"I suppose there must be a restaurant here in Reno," True Bear said. "The food coming across was terrible, and now I think I could eat half a cow."

"You've grown as large as a whole cow," Big Woodpecker said, shifting from one foot to the other. "I think you're taller than Ben."

"No question about it," Ben laughed, "now that I've started shrinking. Let's just hope the boy hasn't inherited his father's proclivity toward premature blindness. Yes, in fact, the Woodpecker and I, we've discovered quite a satisfactory dining establishment, but after that. . . ."

Big Woodpecker laughed.

"I think Ben wants to go to the Emporium," he said, reaching down to grab hold of one of True Bear's two suitcases. "Lots of pretty girls there in low-cut dresses. Gambling too, and drinking—they'll even serve Indians. What's wrapped in the canvas, True Bear? Is it your old rifle?"

"Of course," True Bear replied. "That gun's my link with home. Lead on, reverend Father. I'd admire to wet my whistle with you two gents—but first, I insist on having something to eat. I'm starved, starved. . . ."

THROUGHOUT DINNER Ben talked with grand enthusiasm, attempting to detail the entire four years of True Bear's absence from Upper Eden—and eliciting as well a great deal of information from his son, most of which True Bear had dutifully included in the many letters he'd written home.

"I gather your lady friend, then, is not totally sanguine about the prospects of living in our wilderness with her husband—I speak prospectively—no matter how much she loves him. True Bear, if you're genuinely in love with Harriet Collins, then perhaps you'll have to live where she wishes to. New England isn't such a bad place, after all. You seem to have survived. It's crossed my mind to take a trip back there myself—a continent away isn't all that much, not with the modern miracle of a railway. When I came West, I traveled the canals and rivers to St. Louis, then took another riverboat to Independence. That's where I first ran into my old friend Bully O'Bragh, God rest his crooked soul. Haven't heard a word from him since . . . well, since just after the Yahi massacre. And then he disappeared without so much as a fare-thee-well. Love, True Bear. A man can't live without it, and that's the truth. But see if Harriet will come out for a visit. With the Palace Pullmans and all, the journey might not make such a bad honeymoon. I wish I hadn't had to summon you home this way, but we've got some legal matters that simply have to be attended to, and time may be running short."

Big Woodpecker drank several cups of coffee, occasionally winking at True Bear as he did so. Of late Benjamin McCain had been moody to say the least, given to uncharacteristic spells of conversational brevity. It was good to see life come back into the man.

"Your father hasn't talked this much in two months," Big Woodpecker chuckled. "I think he's happy to see his son again."

"Of course I am, of course I am—you fool. But not nearly as happy as Ooti's going to be when we get back to the ranch. For the past four years all I've heard from your mother, True Bear, is how she's concerned about her 'little boy' being so thin. She's certain you never eat enough, certain you've wasted away to nothing while you've been at college. When she sees the size of you, then she'll have to find something else to worry about. Damn it, Son, it is good to have you back, even if the return to Upper Eden isn't permanent! Big Woodpecker here has been virtually as bad as Acorn Girl—he's certain he can beat you at rock-tossing now."

"I never said that," Big Woodpecker replied, shaking his head. "True Bear always could throw farther than I. As strong as he looks now, we couldn't even have a fair contest."

True Bear swallowed the last portion of roast beef, wiped his plate with a piece of bread, and drained his coffee cup.

"Now I'm feeling half-human again," he nodded, "I'm up to practically anything. Woodpecker, you don't mean to suggest that Father's been looking at young women again? And you, of course, are a married man as well. Since I'm the only single male present, you two will have to act as chaperones, so to speak. I may not even be engaged anymore. I left Boston in a bit of a hurry, and without my lady's blessings. Nonetheless, I suggest we visit this Emporium you mentioned. At the very least, we can have a drink or two. The gambling and the ladies—those I can manage to survive without."

"He talks just like you do, Ben," Big Woodpecker laughed. "I guess he's your son after all."

Benjamin McCain took off his thick glasses, polished the lenses with a handkerchief, and stood up.

"That matter was never up for debate, Mr. Woodpecker. Gentlemen . . . ?"

BEN PAID the tab, left a two-dollar gold piece as a tip for the smartly dressed young blonde woman who'd waited their table, and nodded to the cashier.

"My boy William here—he's just returned from Harvard. Graduated with First Honors, by heaven."

"Good luck to you, then," the cashier said, extending a hand, first to the father and then to the son.

The three men exited the restaurant and walked on down Main Street to a bright yellow, two-story frame building whose front was emblazoned with a large sign neatly painted in yellow and black: The One and Only SALTY'S EMPORIUM.

A player piano clanked away inside the main room of the place, while various groups of men—some cowhands, some miners, some businessmen—sat at the plush bar, drinking, or around several card and craps tables. Women in brightly colored and tight-fitting attire brought drinks to the gambling tables, these attended to by clean-shaven men clothed in maroon suits.

"Three young fellows out on the town," Ben laughed. "I see several empty seats at the blackjack table over there— why don't you two sit down? I'll cover fifty dollars apiece, but when you've lost it all, then we'll have to go back to the hotel. Go on, now, sit down. Here's money. I'll get us each a mug of beer—be right with you. We'll see who's bossman at the gambling table. . . ."

THEY DRANK and played a few hands of twenty-one. Big Woodpecker turned up an ace and a queen of hearts on the first deal, drew in his winnings, and grinned broadly.

"Beginner's luck," Ben growled. "Or else the dealer's asleep at the switch. Come now, the battle's not yet fairly joined. . . ."

Big Woodpecker's luck continued, however, and he was seventy dollars ahead of the game when Ben put out his last fifty-cent piece and a moment later watched the dealer sweep it in.

"Ask the plutocrat for a loan, Father," True Bear suggested.

"Not fitting, not fitting at all. I'm already in debt to him for many things that money won't cover. At this rate, he'll soon own Upper Eden, lock, stock, and barrel."

"Five-dollar side bet?" True Bear challenged his boyhood pal. "What do you say?"

"Side bets aren't allowed," the dealer intoned. "Ante up, gentlemen. The house takes on all callers. . . ."

Two hands later True Bear lost the last of the fifty Ben had given him. He pushed back his chair, shrugged, and finished off his second mug of beer.

Big Woodpecker, still with more than seventy dollars on

the table in front of him, clucked his tongue and glanced at Ben.

"Tonight I beat both McCains," he said. "Now I will bet everything on just one hand."

"Don't do it," Ben cautioned. "This dealer's just been waiting for you. Keep your winnings—buy Yellow Grass a new set of dishes or something of the sort—clothes, maybe. It's free money you've got right now. Don't squander it."

"Trust my luck, Ben," Big Woodpecker said. "Oidoing-koyos have a special relationship with Coyote Man. You'll see. . . ."

"High stakes," the dealer said. "You going for it?"

"Deal, card-man."

The first card came down. Big Woodpecker flipped the edge up, nodded.

The second was a nine of spades.

True Bear glanced at Ben, then at the dealer, who already had a ten of clubs showing.

Eight of hearts.

"Can't hit it," the dealer said. "What have you got hiding?"

Big Woodpecker, savoring the moment, hesitated, then turned over an ace of spades.

"Death card!" he laughed. "Only this one wins for me. . . ."

The dealer frowned, counted out seventy-three dollars, and pushed the money across the table.

"Now I quit," Big Woodpecker grinned. "Maybe I'll buy Yellow Grass a little something in the morning before we head north. Am I the champion?"

"No question," True Bear laughed. "Let's have one more beer. What do you say, Dad? Woodpecker, he's buying."

THEY'D BEEN DRINKING and talking for a couple of hours, and Ben had just said for perhaps the fourth of fifth time, "The old man's getting sleepy. You young fellows sure you can find your way to the hotel if I leave you on your own? True Bear, you make certain our friend here doesn't fall into the clutches of one of the professional ladies. . . ."

"Hey, Injun," a newcomer to the bar growled, "I don't like your hat. You pretending to be Lincoln's ghost, or what? Probably a Gawddamned Reb to boot, ain't you? Don't figger it's right for no Injun to be makin' fun of Abraham Lincoln."

True Bear glanced at the thickset, bearded individual who'd just sat down beside him.

"Have a drink on me, cowboy," he replied. "Just do it quietly—we're having a private discussion here. It's a home-coming, you might say."

"You one of them Washoes from Virginia City? What kind of place is this? Ain't no Gawddamned Injuns is supposed to get served alcohol. Two of you bastards? Who's the old man—your keeper?"

"Maybe we all better leave," Big Woodpecker said, standing up.

"You ain't leavin' until I'm done talking, Black Kettle. . . ."

"My friend," True Bear replied, turning to face the more-or-less intoxicated man, "you keep shooting off your mouth, and I'm going to stick my fist into it. We've no quarrel with you. Hell, I might even like you if you weren't sotted. Go make friends with one of the whores—get yourself bred. You'll feel a great deal better afterward."

"Son, it's time for us to leave," Ben said. "Buy the man a beer, and let's go."

"Don't drink with no damned Injuns. The old guy—he's your pa? Squaw for a momma, then. . . ."

True Bear grinned, shrugged.

Then, twisting on his stool, he drove his right fist into the center of his antagonist's face, knocking the man backward onto the floor, the head hitting with a dull thud.

The stricken man didn't move.

"Jesus Coyote, I think you've killed him!" Big Woodpecker exclaimed, staring about as the customers in Salty's Emporium suddenly became ominously quiet.

"Outside!" the bartender commanded, a short-barreled shotgun appearing in his hands. "Rest of you—just keep your seats! The guy had it coming. . . ."

The drunk on the floor began to stir, turned over, pressed one hand to a split lip and apparently broken nose.

"We were just leaving, young man," Ben McCain said. "Enough excitement for one night. . . ."

At that moment a vision in red silk and lace and black ribbons descended the stairs from above. True Bear was oblivious, but Big Woodpecker stared as if not believing.

"Goddamn," he whispered, "it's her—or else her twin sister. True Bear, look!"

The younger McCain was standing now, staring about the gambling hall, his right hand open, ready to draw the Colt revolver at his side. He heard what Big Woodpecker said, and slowly shifted his gaze toward the stairway. No name was mentioned, but somehow, intuitively, True Bear understood the meaning.

He stared at the astonishingly lovely and elaborately dressed dark-haired woman as she approached, her face set in the expression of a young mother attending to a band of unruly children.

"Wahtaurisi-yi!" he cried out. "Where the hell have you been for the last nine years?"

The woman stopped in her tracks, as though dealt a stinging and totally unexpected blow. Placing both hands on the rail, she searched the crowd to find the one who'd called out the greeting.

A long silence followed.

"Jack," she said, addressing the bartender, "whoever the troublemakers are, get them out of here! There'll be no brawling in Fanny Bitler's place. One round on the house for everyone else."

A moment later she vanished back up the stairs, with Ben, True Bear, and Big Woodpecker being unceremoniously ushered out the door.

TWENTY-SEVEN

Madame of the Emporium

[July 1874]

THEY STOOD under a gas street light on a board sidewalk outside Salty's Emporium, were quiet for a moment. A waning moon hung low in the sky eastward, out over the desert, while to the west loomed the high black shadow of Mt. Rose, a single remaining stripe of snow faintly visible. The air was filled with an odor of sage, borne by wind from across the dry reaches of Nevada—that and smells of beer and dust. A few clouds streaked the summer sky, and night was hot—almost oppressive, saved from that by the movement of air.

Ben grumbled about "drunks in public places," but neither True Bear nor Big Woodpecker could think of any appropriate response.

The men turned, glanced back at the doorway through which they had just been escorted, and began to walk in the general direction of The Desert Oasis Hotel.

"That was her, wasn't it?" True Bear asked. "Woodpecker, you recognized her first. I haven't seen her since. . . . But you did. You rode north to the lava beds with Wahtaurisi-yi, and that was. . . ."

"Near Christmas, about a year and a half ago. We all saw her then—Ben, Ooti, Yellow Grass, everybody. She was with

342

six Modoc warriors, and they were trying to get help for Kintpuash. Captain Jack trusted her, I guess. She'd been with him for a while. Anyhow, Ben rounded up pistols, rifles, and ammunition, and we set off north—up Warner Creek and then across to Bunchgrass Valley. Way beyond there, at Sand Buttes, we ran right into a patrol of damned bluecoats. Fire Woman was shot and. . . ."

True Bear nodded.

"Dad wrote me about the whole thing. Christmas before last? You were actually with her, then, for a week or so. Was that her back in the gambling hall, or wasn't it?"

"It was Auna-yi, all right. Looked a lot different in them pretty clothes, not like last time. I couldn't forget her face any more than you could, but I don't understand what in hell she was doing there. I saw her taken prisoner, I heard the lieutenant order her sent to Whitney. I figured she ended up in Indian Territory—if she pulled through."

"It was our friend, without question," Ben nodded. "I may be blind, but I'm not that blind. I can still see fairly well at a distance. The girl's a survivor, like the coyote. So's old Wolf Tracker, apparently. Big Woodpecker's certain he caught sight of the chief's little band over near Brokeoff earlier this spring—probably Smoke Woman and two or three others."

Big Woodpecker nodded.

"Might have been a different bunch," he said, "but I think it was Wolf Tracker. Tried to follow, but they got away, just like that time when we. . . ."

"If her mother and grandfather are still alive, then what's she doing here in Reno?" True Bear demanded. "I don't get it at all. She came flouncing down those stairs as though she owned the place—as though she were damned well in charge. You both heard her give orders to the barkeep. And who the hell's Fanny Bitler? That must mean Wahtaurisi-yi—Auna-yi—is working for the woman, one of her prostitutes. Jesus Christ!"

"It was certainly a surprise to me," Ben said. "Big Woodpecker and I had no idea—otherwise we'd have gone to a different gambling hall. It wasn't supposed to be part of the reunion, True Bear, believe me. I guess I know a bit more than I ever told you, though, and in all likelihood one or two things Big Woodpecker hasn't heard about either."

"Now's probably a good time to turn the cat out of the bag, then. Let's hear it, Dad. I think I've got a right, and I don't need to be protected from anything as innocuous as truth."

"Okay. Very well, Son. That's our hotel four or five blocks ahead, next to the livery stable. Well, it goes this way. I met a man named Hank Bitler over at Red Bluff about a year ago. Nice fella, raises horses. I bought three animals from him, a new pair of Clydesdales and one other. Don't be impatient— I'll get to the point directly. Anyhow, we got to talking, and he asked me when it was that I'd been Auna-yi's teacher— just that simple question, out of the blue, as it were. Turns out she'd been a housemaid to Bitler and his wife for a time. Then there was some trouble, and the girl ran off with a Modoc youth named Matthew, also known as Red Turtle. . . ."

"She told me she was married to a man named Red Turtle," Big Woodpecker said. "But she claimed he'd been killed by the soldiers."

"Yes," Ben nodded. "She gave Ooti the details of that tragic happening. You ready for all this, Son? Afterward, she was Captain Jack's woman, though whether they were companions or lovers, I don't know."

"You should have told me. I. . . ."

"There's more. Bitler had been up to Fort Klamath, and he'd caught sight of her there—did some asking. Fanny Bitler, that was the name Hank's wife had given her, became Gideon Whitney's mistress and then turned professional—hired some girls of her own. It's just hearsay, of course, though Bitler struck me as an honest sort. Still, I didn't pass the information, such as it was, along to you, Son, because you were in the process of getting yourself engaged to Miss Collins at the time, and Acorn Girl figured gossip couldn't do anything better than cause you anguish, to say the least. We all loved that little girl, True Bear, but people change, and I guess we have to accept things the way they are. Circumstance is a difficult master, and events often don't go the way we'd like them to. It's necessary to walk a mile in another man's moccasins before. . . ."

"I know," True Bear replied. "You got our room key, or is it still at the desk?"

"In my pocket," Big Woodpecker said. "Sometimes Ben forgets where he puts things."

They entered The Desert Oasis Hotel and trudged up the stairs to a room on the second floor.

"Fanny Bitler's place," True Bear mused. "No brawling in Fanny Bitler's place. That means. . . ."

"Our little friend's no doubt the madam of the Emporium," Ben finished his son's sentence. "By God, when a man considers everything that's happened to her, she hasn't done so badly. Indeed, if our surmise is correct, her accomplishment's remarkable. It's not up to us to pass negative judgment, as the Good Book tells us."

ONCE IN THEIR HOTEL room, the three men talked for a time about potential difficulties back at the ranch—and what might happen if, for instance, Ben's position as unpaid Indian agent were revoked. Legal title to the land was clear, the original portion by virtue of homestead rights, but that after all was only a very small hundred-and-sixty-acre tract. Everything else came to the McCains via purchase from the state, and from one or two adjoining ranchers as well—Ben's initial fortune having been expended in this fashion. A majority of the profits over the years, from cattle ranching and breeding horses and logging and sawmill operations, had further gone largely into land acquisition. Six hundred acres of the total, however, could conceivably be reclaimed by the state of California, for that was the designated rancheria site for Oidoing-koyo village, lying almost dead center among the other holdings. Since at least half the Maidus had subsequently drifted away from the village, a good case might be made for relocating the remainder south to Walker River or west to Hoopa Valley.

And in the event of his death, Ben insisted, the entirety of Upper Eden might well revert to the state, inasmuch as Ooti's right of inheritance was vulnerable, since her legal protection in being married to an American citizen would vanish. True Bear, however, could legally inherit the lands, but enforcing a claim from across a continent would have proven difficult in the face of demands by the likes of Anderson and the Claytons and whatever sort of alliance or ranchers' cooperative they might be able to put together.

Hi Good, at least (Ben noted), was no longer among their enemies. That worthy, who along with Anderson, Clayton,

Henry Curtis, Billy Sills, and a gang of their cowhands, had massacred what they presumed to be the last Yahis, more than forty Indians under the leadership of Big-Foot Jack, had now gone to his eternal reward. Four years earlier, and only a month or so after True Bear had been dispatched eastward, Good had embroiled himself in a dispute over wages with a Wintun lad who worked for him. Good made threats, thinking to silence the young man's demands, but a few days later the Wintun stuck a hunting knife into Good's abdomen and fled on foot. Captured two days later, he was hanged on the spot, not far from the town of Chico.

One further group of Yahis had also been butchered—in 1871, thirty of them, nearly all children. J.J. Bogard, Jim Baker, Scott Wellman, and Norman Kingsley had cornered the Indians in a cave and then proceeded to murder the lot of them. These four Whitemen, drinking and carousing in Red Bluff afterward, had made no secret of their heroic exploits at *Injun hunting*.

Such men would, along with Clayton, Anderson, Curtis, and Sills, in all likelihood attempt to enforce claims upon the lands at Upper Eden—owing to a clear need for summer pasture for their various operations.

"So I called you back," Ben said. "The ideal thing would be for you to marry your Boston lady and bring her to Upper Eden to live. In the face of that, your simple and established presence, the jackals might howl until their lungs fell out, for all the good it would do them. I could imagine B.J. Collins hotfooting it out here to protect his daughter's interests, from what you've told me in letters. I've done some checking, True Bear. Your potential father-in-law is quite a well-known barrister, as it turns out. My sister Elizabeth is living in Hartford now—actually, she's been there for some time. No doubt I should also have told you about that earlier, but there were complications I wished to avoid and. . . ."

"Father, what is it exactly that's wrong with you? You act as though you're going to die next month, next year. Goddamn it, you seem healthy enough to me. You've lost weight, yes, but. . . . I think maybe you've kept me in the dark about far too many things."

"Ain't sick at all," Big Woodpecker said. "Ben's always complaining about one thing or another, but I guess he'll live to be a hundred. Even his eyesight isn't as bad as he says. We went deer hunting last fall, and he took a blacktail at more than a hundred yards, first shot."

"Pure luck," Ben laughed. "Blind luck, you might say, if you'll pardon the jest. Well, perhaps I have kept a few things from you, son. What the hell? Tonight's a good enough time for revelations concerning the past, and I may not always be around to supply such information. I've got a journal at home—Ooti has it and is to give it to you in the event . . . All right. First, my boy, our last name isn't actually McCain at all. 'What was your name in the states?' the old gold rush tune used to run. As a matter of fact, ours was Goffe. It's there as one of your middle names, True Bear. William True Bear Goffe McCain. After your mother and I blew hell out of a mining camp near Grass Valley, we were obliged to make a hasty retreat northward. When we reached Oidoing-koyo, with no inconsiderable assistance from one Bully O'Bragh, we decided to start over. At that point, a new name seemed appropriate—inasmuch as my identity was known in the Mother Lode region, and it would have been just a matter of time. Our ancestor, Judge William Goffe, fled to America after the Restoration, incognito, since his life wouldn't have been worth a half-penny if he'd stayed in Jolly Old England. In Cromwell's time, Goffe was signatory to the death warrant for the king. As a Harvard graduate, I gather you're familiar with the story."

True Bear nodded.

"I guess I'd already pretty much figured the matter out, Father. The puzzle wasn't actually so difficult to decipher. I knew about Aunt Elizabeth too, but I didn't realize she was still alive. Yes, you should have told me about that minor detail. Now I'll make a point of visiting her when I. . . ."

He didn't finish his sentence, the interior voice changing "when" to a highly conditional "if."

Ben gestured with open hands.

"Actually, I've been trying to get her to move to California," he said. "She's alone now, since Tom died."

True Bear withdrew the slim flask he carried in his coat pocket, took a sip of rum, and offered the liquor to his father and Big Woodpecker.

Ben shook his head.

"You young fellows can stay up all night talking if you like, but it's time for me to go to sleep. Tomorrow we head for Upper Eden. Ooti'll be worried—we're a day behind schedule as is."

"I'll have a drink," Big Woodpecker grinned. "What kind of stuff is it?"

TRUE BEAR SLEPT at last, but fitfully. If the railroad trip had been somewhat physically exhausting, and had followed directly upon the making of a decision and a severance he now believed to be permanent, the events and revelations since his arrival in Reno were somehow even more taxing on a psychological and emotional level.

His sleep was filled with a melange of inchoate images— not really inchoate except in sequence, fragmentary pieces of some large puzzle that was beyond his solving.

He woke once, saw that it was still quite dark outside, and turned over.

The mountain shuddered, with steam and sulphur gasses venting from huge cracks in its sides. Above even the roarings of an earth in upheaval, violin music was strangely audible.

He climbed, only gradually realizing that someone, someone unseen, walked beside him as he labored the high slopes of Wahgalu.

"Who are you?" he asked. "I came here to be alone, I came here to watch the end of the world."

"Fanny," she said—and in that moment became visible. Only it wasn't the beautiful woman in crimson who descended the stairs in the gambling hall, it was a child. She wore a cedar-bark skirt, moccasins, and a headband of white deerskin. Her breasts, small and finely shaped, were bare.

"Wahtaurisi-yi! Years have passed, years, and yet we're both children again. Look—I'm still short and too skinny. What's happened to us? It should never have happened this way. . . ."

A long moment of silence, and then the mountain itself shuddered, hurled itself outward. A tide of rock, dust, fire bore down upon them, covered them over, and carried them harmlessly away.

Fire. Everything was aflame. The forest was burning, red-

yellow cones of flame engulfed entire trees, passed, left standing black skeletons, smoking and steaming.

Animals fled—thousands of creatures, uncountable numbers—deer, bear, elk, rabbits and squirrels, porcupines scuttling along, wolves, marmots, skunks. . . . Then bands of Indians on foot, their heads bowed, expressions blank, numbed, like the creatures that hurried along before them.

"Not even rattlesnakes are safe down among the boulders where they sleep," the girl said. "Olelbis the Dreamer, he's changing everything around. Watch, True Bear. Next will come the Saltus, your father's people. All will be changed, nothing can resist such forces as these. Once long ago there was smoke and fire everywhere, and that's why we call this place the land of burnt rocks, the hot pitch land. Deserts form, and lakes vanish in sunlight and flame. You and I will soon be alone, you and I together. That's how we dreamed it once, and that's how it will be."

"We never dreamed all this! Acorn Girl's bear spoke to me once, but now I see grizzlies lying dead in the forest—so many animals dead!"

"Dreams change too. One Above makes up His own rules. No, we must protect ourselves, we must do what we have to do. . . ."

HE AWOKE, gasping for breath.

Stars still burned outside the open window of the hotel room, and True Bear sat up on the edge of the bed.

"Need another drink," he whispered—and then thought better of it.

Instead he rose unsteadily, fumbled in darkness for his coat and hat, strapped on the pistol, pulled on boots, stole from the room, and descended a stairway.

Outside, he found the street deserted, and the solitary witness as he relieved himself in front of the hotel was a horse someone had left tethered to a hitching rail, the animal asleep on its feet, head and neck draped over a horizontal beam close by a watering trough.

Gas street lamps were still sputtering, would not be extinguished until a tender walked his rounds just after sunrise.

True Bear strode along a board sidewalk, his steps creating hollow, clumping sounds that echoed faintly. At the first cross street, he left the boardwalk and continued down the middle of the dusty roadway, more comfortable now in silence.

He made his way toward a railway bridge spanning Truckee River, a stream, like the Humboldt, vanishing into the desert, in this case into Pyramid Lake, one of those places the Whites had given the Washoe Indians and other Paiute Peoples for a reservation. But while the Humboldt rose among desert ranges four hundred miles to the east, the Truckee fed down from the Sierra Nevada, from a great deep body of water originally called Lake Bigler, though the Indian name of *Da-o*, Sacred Water, had now gained general usage in the form of its White transliteration, "Tahoe."

The two rivers flowed toward one another, but they never met, one vanishing into the brackish Humboldt Sink, the other into Pyramid, a desert lake as large as Da-o itself.

He reached the railroad bridge, stood beside it and stared down into the river's dark eastward flow. The moon was long since gone from the sky, and stars burned across midheaven, paler now with approach of dawn. Already a thin sensation of grayness appeared to the east, out over the desert.

Crickets were singing along the river's margin, and the current moved with a soft rushing sound.

TRUE BEAR MCCAIN WALKED quickly back toward the main part of the railroad town of Reno, Nevada, not to the hotel where his father and friend were sleeping, but rather to Salty's Emporium.

Only one or two stars yet remained in the sky, now a dull silver-gray, as he stood in front of the gambling establishment and whorehouse, its great iron double gate closed and no doubt barred from inside.

From an alley door a man emerged, a gentleman dressed in suit and top hat, a gold chain dangling from his watch pocket. He took note of True Bear, nodded without speaking, and stumbled away down the board sidewalk.

A lamp, True Bear observed, continued to burn behind a second-story window. Was it her room? The fine old gentleman who'd just left—was he one of her customers? Fire Woman—Fanny Bitler—she was his age, perhaps a few months older, not more. If she were indeed the madam of the establishment, as Ben had concluded, then perhaps she'd ceased having customers—at least enjoyed the luxury of being exempt from the "take your pick, gents" routine.

Who was Salty?

After all, it was virtually inconceivable that Fanny could have amassed a fortune sufficient for her to own this place, apparently the most prosperous joint in town. The establishment was ornately built and well furnished within, and that suggested an owner with genuine money.

Perhaps "Salty" was a nickname used by one of the more successful silver mine owners in Virginia City, perhaps even Senator Bill Stewart, the great Nevada entrepreneur who had once, back in the sixties, faced down Bad Sam Brown in a court of law, drawing a pair of pistols when the outlaw entered his chambers. In a fit after this humiliation, Brown proceeded to murder one man too many and was subsequently blown apart by two blasts from a shotgun.

Another possibility was that they'd all been mistaken—it was simply a matter of remarkable resemblance. Years had passed since he had even seen Wahtaurisi-yi, a girl then just reaching womanhood, and it was true that appearances could change greatly in the course of nine years.

No.

Big Woodpecker and Ben were both with her, had conspired with her only a year and a half earlier, an adventure ending with the young woman falling, critically wounded, taken prisoner by a military officer named . . . Whitney. the other stories . . . ? Too many stories—and the whole thing was almost beyond belief. But a year and a half from neardeath in an Indian war to being proprietress of a thriving and well-financed gambling hall and whorehouse? Such a transformation in fortunes would surely have required the intervention of someone with wealth and power.

If Whitney indeed took her as his mistress, then. . . . But military officers assigned to Indian campaigns in the West, unless they were generals, like General Canby whom Captain Jack had killed, weren't likely to have that kind of money. Perhaps Meacham, the Indian Agent. Or perhaps some wealthy Oregon rancher whom Fanny Bitler had for a customer, one who found her particularly pleasing and so had. . . .

None of it made sense, and True Bear shrugged and began to walk away.

Then he stopped, turned back to face Salty's Emporium and the single lantern still burning behind an upper-story window.

"Goddamn it, Wahtaurisi-yi!" he shouted. "Is that you up there? This is True Bear McCain!"

His words echoed down the length of Reno's dusty and deserted main street.

TRUE BEAR RETURNED to the hotel and roused Ben and Big Woodpecker—insisting that they make tracks toward Upper Eden, that he was eager to see his mother, to be home at last.

They ate a quick breakfast of ham and eggs, specialty of the Central Pacific Railway station, drank coffee, and left, Ben paying the tab. The three men walked to the livery stable, where the elder McCain presented his son with a red stallion, also purchased from Hank Bitler. True Bear's old saddle was ready as well, its complementary but empty rifle scabbard in place.

"A fine-looking animal," True Bear grinned. "He's got a name, I take it?"

"Bitler called him 'Renegade,'" Big Woodpecker said. "But Ben liked his looks, and I figured I could tame him down. The name was a good one, all right. Damned near broke my neck before I'd gentled him. You won't have no trouble unless you've forgotten how to ride. Maybe we'll have a race when we get back, like old times?"

"Renegade, eh? With this horse under me, Woodpecker my friend, you're as good as beaten already."

"Don't think so," Big Woodpecker said, swinging up onto an Appaloosa that looked every bit Renegade's match. "You been reading books for four years, I've been riding. Besides I'm the one who trained your horse. Whatever he figures i the finish line, he pulls up just short of it."

"I suppose you two will grow up one of these days," Ben said, winking, as the livery man brought out his buckboard and pair of matched Clydesdales. "Gentlemen, let's direc ourselves toward Hallelujah Junction. This desert air isn't good for old men like me. . . ."

They rode out, past new brick buildings of the small Uni versity of Nevada campus, True Bear having some difficulty with Renegade for a few miles until the horse decided its rider knew what he was doing. North from Reno they crested a rise and continued along the wagon road toward Honey Lake and Susanville.

Noon found them at a roadhouse at Hallelujah Junction, where the old Beckwourth Trail turned westward to cross one low ridge before entering into Sierra Valley and on down Feather River to the Sacramento Valley at Marysville, a road they themselves would follow to Quincy, and then on to Chester and the North Branch and home.

After a welcome lunch, Ben got involved in a discussion with the owner, and while the men were talking, True Bear took note of several weapons the man had for sale. Among these was a beautifully tooled Henry repeater, an iron-frame model with adjustable leaf rear sights.

"I want this gun," True Bear said to the proprietor when he and Ben finished their discussion. "How much is it?"

"Seventy-five dollars—a high price, but she's a beauty. Don't think they'll ever manufacture a better one. Only iron-frame I've ever had for sale—not many around. Takes forty-four rimfires, just like the regular model."

"A new horse wasn't enough," Big Woodpecker laughed.

"This I can pay for myself," True Bear replied. "Two boxes of ammo. . . ."

Transaction complete, the men walked out to the buckboard. True Bear thrust the Henry rifle into his empty scabbard and mounted.

"Dad," he said, "I can't get Wahtaurisi-yi—Fire Woman—out of my thoughts. If that was her, and I guess it was, then I can't just let the thing pass by. I've got to see her again. I want to talk to her, damn it. The whole business is crazy, but I'm not going to be able to rest easy until I've at least done that. She saw us. She had to recognize at least you and Big Woodpecker, for Christ's sake, unless she's suffering from a complete loss of memory and doesn't even know who the hell she is. No, she knows all right. Just held a straight face and escaped back up those stairs."

"So what are you telling me, Son? We weren't exactly in a position last night to grab her and throw her over our shoulders and disappear into the night. Even in Reno, the law frowns on such behavior."

"What I'm saying—I've got to go back to Sal' 's place. At least I know where she is right now, and otherwise I might never see her again. Got to do it. You tell Mom what I'm up to and that I'll be home just as quickly as I can make it. With Renegade here, I'll probably arrive at Oidoing-koyo before you do—since Big Woodpecker's horse seems to have difficulty keeping up with the Clydesdales."

"He talks a good race," Woodpecker mumbled.

"Mom will understand. And maybe that's not such a bad idea."

"Namely?" Ben asked. He squinted and adjusted his spectacles.

"Kidnapping," True Bear grinned.

TWENTY-EIGHT

True Bear Meets Fanny

[July 1874]

THE YOUNGER MCCAIN tethered Renegade to a hitching post in front of a combination trading post and card house just south of Nevada's small university campus, the latter's three brick buildings reminiscent of those at Harvard but incongruous in a setting of empty sage-covered hills rising to either side—almost grotesque, almost ridiculous.

"One mountain whose innards were crammed with silver," True Bear reflected, "add a few thousand miners—and Lin-

coln in need of a couple more antislave senators. Presto, a
sagebrush state emerges. Drop in a railroad, gambling houses,
the requisite number of hookers and thieves, plus a citadel of
higher learning. . . ."

"Help you, stranger?" the typical merchant behind a
glass-topped counter asked.

"Want to trade in this hat."

"Give you four bits for it. Truth is, I won't be able to sell
the thing for any more than that. Not much call for stove-
pipes out here—except the railroad people, bankers, and
doctors. Men like that, they generally buy new anyhow. You
want something more Western, I take it?"

True Bear nodded.

"An Oregon felt," he replied. "Black if you've got one
that'll fit me."

"Could be. Gather you're partial to black. You some down-
East bounty hunter, or what? Here, try this one on. . . ."

"Texas Ranger, as a matter of fact. Chased a procrastinator
all the way from Abilene—or was it Dallas?"

The merchant raised one eyebrow but said nothing. His
eyes were bloodshot, the left not quite in tandem with the
right.

"Fits," McCain said, winking. "I'll take it. Don't need any
poison arrows or warpaint today, though. Just the hat."

"Be ten dollars."

"Too much. Nine-fifty, not a penny more."

"Nine-fifty with the trade-in."

"Deal. The girls in the card room—they professional ladies
by any chance?"

The merchant rang up his sale, handed True Bear a fifty-
cent piece in return, and grunted affirmatively.

"Clean," he said, "all of 'em. We got a doctor comes in
once a week. See a female as interests you? Go buy her a
drink, get acquainted, stranger."

"Truth is, I was told to go to Salty's. Supposed to be the
best place in town."

"Hell," the merchant said, "here in Reno it's all the same.
Six of one, half dozen of the other, if you get my drift. The
whole operation's controlled by the railroad, C.P. Huntington himself. That little Injun gal standing by the bar, for
instance—she works the Emporium usually, but Fanny sent

her up here as a fill-in. Name's Willow—cusses like a cowboy, and the trail riders love 'er. They take to a filly that sasses back, I guess. Turns out she's the boss lady's right-hand man, so to speak. But every one of the girls is checked out by a company sawbones. Prices stay pretty much the same, so there's no competition and no rough stuff. Things are a hell of a lot better since Huntington took over, I'll tell you that much. From what I'm told, this town used to get pretty wild at times—girls being cut up, cowhands shooting one another, that sort of thing. Made it damned bad on respectable citizens. Now the ladies don't have to take on no one they don't want. Cowhands come in, and by God they're required to have a bath first, which is an extra three dollars. Of course, Reno still has its gunfights every so often, and occasionally a hanging comes of one. Townsfolk seem to enjoy seeing some poor sonofabitch getting his neck stretched."

"Fanny Bitler? Is that the lady you're talking about? As I say, I just rode in from El Paso, but I've heard of her. Wanted for bank robbery in St. Louis, if I'm not mistaken."

The merchant raised one eyebrow again, accentuating his skewed eye.

"You enjoy playing with words, I take it. A gambler then? Most of 'em like to fool around with the lingo as well as the deck. Not that it's any of my business, actually. . . ."

True Bear grinned. He'd begun to think he wasn't going to get a rise out of the man.

"So who's Fanny? Come along, old fellow, us Injuns has got curious natures."

"Figured you were—at least part," the merchant responded. "Don't know what your gig is, but you've got the name right. She's Huntington's woman, that's the gossip. Or else Salty Dan Dolliver's. Keeps to herself mostly, and one hell of a looker. But whoever she's bedding down with from time to time, she's a fine businesswoman, no two ways about that. Well, there's more than one man in Reno who'd give his left marble for a drop of Fanny's sweat. Some say she's an honest-to-God Bolivian princess, but I don't know that for true. I've only been in town three, four months as a matter of fact. Well, word has it that Salty Dan whipped C.P.'s tail end in a poker game, and after that him and Salty and Fanny Bitler decided they had something in common. So Huntington bought out every whorehouse in Reno and put Fanny in charge. She's an institution around here, you might say. Stranger, it sorta looks like I got a couple more customers coming in—anything else I can do for you?"

"One thing," True Bear grinned.

"What might that be?"

"Remember to quote accurately when you're employing proverbs. It's *half of one, six dozen of the other*."

"That don't make no sense. Well, it's good talking to you. . . ."

LONG CRIMSON BANDS of cloud hung off to the west, causing the remaining snow high up on the side of Mt. Rose to shine faintly. Half a dozen bullbats streamed down Reno's main street, perching atop the false front of Oliva's Mercantile Palace in apparent anticipation of the gas street lamps being lit for the evening, the glow from these attracting all manner of flying insects.

True Bear McCain entered the Emporium, the establishment already busy with evening trade. A different man was behind the bar, and to one side stood a neatly and expensively dressed gentleman, his wavy white hair slicked back. He wore what appeared to be a large emerald brooch in the middle of a broad red tie, the latter tucked carefully beneath a foxfur vest.

"If that's not Salty Dan," True Bear mused, "it sure as hell ought to be. Professional gambler strikes it rich, thinks he owns a railroad baron, though I imagine it's the other way around. . . ."

McCain adjusted the angle of his new felt hat and walked casually across the gaming hall to the bar.

"You're Mr. Dolliver, I take it?"

The man with the emerald brooch nodded.

"That I am, but not playing poker tonight. Plenty of seats open at the tables, though. There's a five hundred limit unless I say otherwise. You get real lucky, and I'll lift the cap and sit in. Take your pick, Mister."

"Not a gambling man—not with cards, at least. My name's Arnold Geldman, one of Mr. Huntington's accountants. He sent me up from San Francisco to give your books a quick check. Actually, I'm on my way to Denver, so I don't have a great deal of time. I gather you're busy here on the floor, so perhaps you could let me talk with Miss Bitler. I believe Mr. Huntington said she handles the accounts in any case. . . ."

Dolliver looked puzzled.

"C.P. was just here last week—didn't mention nothing about an accountant. Don't think he did, anyhow. What was that handle again?"

"Arnold Conroy Geldman, at your service. It's just a formality, Mr. Dolliver. Huntington likes to keep the paperwork on all his ventures in good order, but of course I don't have to tell you that."

"True, true. How'd you get here, Geldman? Train's not due back until day after tomorrow."

"Blackhawk Stage. I'm on my way to the Reese River silver mines tomorrow morning, first thing. After that the stage takes me to Elko where I catch the eastbound express. I'm really pressed for time, so if you'll just guide me to Miss Bitler's suite. . . ."

Dolliver shrugged.

"Your name sounds Jewish, but you look Injun to me. How long you been with C.P.?"

"Mr. Dolliver, if you please . . . My grandmother was Shawnee, not that it's relevant. If you don't wish to show me the books, both sets of them, I'll simply be obliged to report the matter to Mr. Huntington."

"Have at it," Dolliver said. "Up the stairs, turn right, end of the hallway. Fan's probably getting dressed just about now, so don't go barging in. Geldman, you sure as hell are the biggest damned pencil-pusher I've ever met up with. Shawnee, you say? Don't get touchy, we've got nothing to hide. In this line of work, it pays to be cautious, that's all."

True Bear tipped his hat to Dolliver, turned, and made his way across the gambling hall to the stairway, resisted a temptation to go bounding up, and climbed one step at a time, as befitted a professional accountant.

HE KNOCKED SOFTLY, three times, and waited.

No response.

He rapped again.

"Dan?" the female voice called out—and for a moment True Bear wasn't at all certain he even wished to answer. Just one syllable to make a judgment on. Memory traces flared inconclusively.

"You decent, Fan?" he asked softly in a not-altogether-satisfactory imitation of Dolliver's voice.

"Enough for family. Come help me lace up this damned corset. Door's not latched."

Her voice—cadence changed, tone somewhat different in full womanhood—but it's her, her. . . .

True Bear opened the door, stepped inside, closed it behind him.

On the far side of the room stood a woman, lustrous black hair trailing down her back. She was barefoot and clothed in pale pink bloomers and a camisole—was struggling with a white corset.

Then she saw his reflection in the full-length looking glass before her, turned to confront him, eyes blazing.

"Who the hell are you, Mister, and what do you want?"

In her hand was a shiny thirty-two caliber Deringer revolver.

The sudden movement startled McCain momentarily, but he held out both palms in a gesture of placation, and grinned.

"Hello, Wahtaurisi-yi," he said. "Thought perhaps you'd like to hike up to that little pool with me. I need some good black obsidian, as it turns out."

Their eyes met, locked for a long moment. There was as yet no change of expression on Fanny Bitler's face.

"You called out my name last night," she nodded. "You were with Big Woodpecker and Benjamin McCain. Who are you?"

But already she knew—already she'd mentally transformed this black-clad, hulking stranger before her into the likeness of a fourteen-year-old boy, and they were riding somewhere together among the hills above Upper Eden, destination indeterminate and unimportant.

"William True Bear Goffe McCain," he replied, taking off his hat and making a sweeping bow, one executed in proper Eastern fashion. "You said you were decent enough for family, and so I took the liberty of entering."

The Deringer dropped to her side, but there was still no change in her expression.

"True Bear? It's really you? I. . . . I'm. . . . Go into the other room and wait—let me get dressed, for God's sake!"

"Thought you needed help with the corset."

Then all hesitancy broke down on both sides, and the two stepped closer to one another, closer yet, stopped perhaps two feet apart.

"True Bear?"

"It's me—I arrived on the train yesterday. After I saw you last night, I. . . . We got as far as Hallelujah, Woodpecker and Dad and I, but I had to come back. Goddamn it, girl, I just had to see you again, that's all."

He glanced down, noted the pistol still held firmly in her hand.

"But how . . . ?"

"Told Dolliver I was an accountant Huntington sent up to check your books. Not easy to bluff an experienced gambler, but I got past him."

"Then . . . you know about me? Things didn't exactly turn out the way we once hoped they would, did they? You've graduated from your college now I suppose. Ooti and Ben told me what happened—why you had to go away. And I'm . . . well, I run this place. I'm a prostitute, True Bear, and a damned good one. One thing led to another, some of them terrible. Then I met Salty Dan, and we—that is, he. . . ."

"Cleaned out C.P. Huntington's wallet in a card game. I managed to pick up some of the particulars, at least."

She nodded, and as he stared down into her face, he was nearly certain he detected tears about to form.

McCain, this is a damned delicate moment—almost anything could happen next, including that gun going off. I feel like a tongue-tied kid standing here in front of a half-clothed woman I ran around with nine or ten years ago, before everything got twisted about, and I haven't the slightest idea what to do next. . . .

He reached down, placed one big hand to either side of her waist, and lifted her up over his head.

Taken by surprise, there was a moment when Fanny didn't resist. Then her body went tense, and she began to struggle, actually thrust the pistol toward True Bear's face.

"Put me down, you overgrown loon! True Bear, if you don't put me down, I'll. . . ."

"Marry me," he said and began to laugh. "Goddamn it, it's

going to be the way we planned after all—just took a long while in coming, that's all!"

"Crazy sonofabitch Saltu!"

He set her back on her feet. He was grinning, shaking his head.

"Not me. I'm as much Injun as you are, and I demand the right to pay a bride-price for the woman I love."

Then she was crying, clinging to him, her face against his chest, holding on to him in a way that momentarily erased a passage of nine years of struggle and terror and desperation, so that in some utterly insane way they were both once again fourteen years old and in love in the way that only children on the verge of growing up can be. No matter if the moment couldn't last, that present reality would reassert itself directly.

They held one another in what seemed almost an embrace of death, she sobbing quietly and he nearly unable to breathe, a tightness in his throat that he'd never before experienced.

But when he attempted to kiss her, she turned her head to one side.

"Dearest one," she managed to whisper, "no, don't spoil it. Didn't you understand what I told you? You mustn't play with my feelings, I've cherished them too long."

"I don't care about any of that," he said, half-stammering, "I want to marry you—Auna-yi. . . ."

In uttering the words, in hearing them, their truth was borne out—he had never for an instant supposed he would make such a proposal—that wasn't why he'd ridden back from the junction. Only it was, and now he knew it, knew that he spoke from the absolute depths of the human heart.

She pulled away from him.

"You sonofabitch!" she exploded. "You came up here to buy my favors for an hour or so, didn't you? You just want some sack-time with Fanny Bitler. I hate you!"

She struck at him, her free hand stinging against his face.

And then she realized he hadn't felt the blow at all. She was still holding her Deringer, but now she relaxed, dropped the weapon carelessly onto the red-carpeted floor, reached up, and placed her fingers against McCain's forehead.

"I'm sorry," she whispered. "It's just that I never in the world expected you to come in through that door. . . ."

He embraced her again, slowly, gently, and each felt a

terrible sense of panic, of things being out of control. But their mouths somehow inevitably sought each other, their lips touched hungrily, as though this single act might change everything from what it was to what both felt, however irrationally, ought to be.

"Make up your mind, Fan," a voice issued from across the room. "You want me to shoot the coyote or just close the door and be back about my business? Don't be taking too long, though. Gal, we got customers downstairs, and you aren't even gussied up yet."

It was Salty Dan. He had a revolver leveled at McCain's back.

TRUE BEAR TIGHTENED the strings of the corset for her and then went, as directed, into a small anteroom, sat down, picked up a folded copy of *The Sagebrush Gazette,* and tried fruitlessly to concentrate long enough to read a paragraph or two. Then he laid the paper aside, stood, paced back and forth, taking time out to study the intricacies of flocked indigo design on the wallpaper.

When at length Fanny entered, she was fully clothed in a petticoat-buttressed organdy dress, its neckline plunging dangerously low and setting off a simple gold necklace highlighted by a single large diamond. A wide silk belt hugged her waist, a huge bow hanging on one hip. Her hair was neatly pinned back into a chignon and accented with a gold comb.

"For an Injun kid from Mill Creek Canyon," he said, "you're by-God gorgeous. Not practical, though. We're riding north to Wahgalu tomorrow. Well, I'll pick up some denim britches for you."

"Crazy man," she said, smiling. "I've got a business to run. Perhaps one day I'll visit you and your family—I owe a great deal to all of you. Tonight, however, you're my guest. We'll sit together and talk. Salty Dan can take care of business. I can't get over how big you've grown, True Bear. You must be taller than your father by now, and I always supposed he was the largest man in the world. Shall we go downstairs?"

"Too crowded," McCain said. "Would my lady care for a stroll about town? I know a fine spot next to the railroad bridge."

"Come along, Goose," she said. "I've a few things to attend to. After that we'll see about this . . . stroll . . . of yours. Reno's a bad place for a woman to be wandering about after dark, but with a giant to protect me, I suppose I'll be safe enough."

THEY DID EVENTUALLY FIND their way to the railroad bridge, and True Bear spread out his coat for the two of them to sit on, placing it over the sandy earth of an embankment next to the river. Half a mile away, lights of the small frontier city glowed feebly against darkness, and a waning moon rose over the desert as they talked. Bullfrogs moaned and groaned from faintly visible river water, and an owl hooted, its cry answered half-audibly after a few moments.

"We were only children who had dreams," she said, "and we have to remember that. The world we lived in, you and I, it's gone forever. I'm partners with Salty Dan and Collis Huntington. That means I'm C.P.'s woman when he wants me, True Bear. Well, I can live with it—and I owe him a great deal. He's provided the money for everything—not just the Emporium, either. We own every house in Reno. Salty's in charge of gambling operations, and I have control of the girls. It's a very lucrative business. One day soon, in perhaps two or three years, I'll have enough money put aside to retire from the profession. Yes, that's what it is, and I'm not ashamed of it. It's a Whiteman's world now, and I have to play according to Whiteman's rules. By then Huntington'll no doubt be tired of me and have found another mistress. He's got one in Sacramento now and another in San Francisco—he's told me about them. In his own way, he's a very honest man, though I don't suppose you'll believe me. I know—he steps on weaklings whenever he can, and I guess he takes delight in it. But if you stand up to him, he admires you."

"As long as a man doesn't get too obvious about standing up, I gather. Look, Fanny, I'm not concerned about any of that. It's altogether possible I'm not quite the innocent soul you take me to be. You know why I was sent East. Dad decided I needed to be civilized, and of course he didn't want me getting hung. You listen to me now. . . ."

"Why?" Fanny asked. "You'd talk forever if you had the chance. You were always that way."

"Pot calls the kettle black. I proposed marriage back there, didn't I? Didn't know I was going to—never even thought about it ahead of time. But I meant it, Wahtaurisi-yi—excuse me, Auna-yi."

"Fire Woman died when the soldiers shot her—I know Big Woodpecker must have told you. In the Whiteman's world, I'm Fanny Bitler. I've decided I like the name. At least, I think I do."

"Hank Bitler's alive and well," True Bear said. "Ben bought some horses from him last year. He remembers you fondly, or so I'm told."

"You know about that, too?"

"Partial information, nothing more. You lived with his family for a time. That much, anyway. But here's something I'll bet by God you don't know. Give me another kiss, and I'll tell you."

"Friends don't need to be bribed. Tell me the great secret."

"Will you go to Upper Eden with me? Answer that first. Perhaps you'd like to visit Smoke Woman and Wolf Tracker. . . ."

Fanny was silent for a long moment.

"I think you have a cruel streak now. You didn't used to be that way, True Bear. My mother and grandfather are both dead, long ago. . . ."

"Matter of fact, you're wrong, Miss Bitler. Big Woodpecker saw them near Brokeoff just a few months ago. Wolf Tracker and your mother and a couple of others. They had a boy with them, thirteen or fourteen years old maybe. Woodpecker tried to catch up to them, but they gave him the slip. Nevertheless, he says he's certain who they were. Not likely he'd make a mistake about something like that, now is it?"

"Just not possible. . . . all the Yahi people are dead now."

"You aren't. And unless Big Woodpecker was having visions, they aren't either."

Fanny placed one hand on True Bear's arm.

"Could it really be possible? I cannot believe that."

"Come to Upper Eden with me, Auna-yi. One way or another, we'll find them. Then I'll have someone to pay my bride-price to."

"Talk sense, True Bear McCain. Maybe we should stroll

back to the Emporium. You're forcing me to remember things that I tried for years to forget."

She started to rise, but McCain grasped her arm and gently restrained her.

"We've waited nine years for this conversation, Wahtaurisi-yi. The sun won't be up for hours yet. We deserve that much time at least."

"The Yahi boy," she mused. "He'd have to be Wood Duck, the son of Broken Willow and Salmon Man. Yes, he'd be about that age now, the age we were when. . . ."

"Your grandfather's men tied Big Woodpecker and me to a tree, and you brought us food."

"It was so long ago, and yet it doesn't seem that way at all. Time runs too quickly, too quickly. Life's like a long dream. Do you suppose we ever wake up?"

"Ben thinks he's dying," True Bear said after a long silence. "That's why he asked me to come home. He's afraid Clayton and Anderson and those people will find a way to get the land away from my mother and the other Maidus—through the state's Goddamned inheritance laws. Personally, I'm not sure he's sick at all. Woodpecker doesn't think so."

"What does Ooti say?"

"Don't know. I haven't been home yet."

"That's right. I'm sorry. My mind was drifting. . . . Do you hear how that horned owl keeps calling and calling? It's a very sad sound."

"He's calling for his mate, Fanny. It's always sad when a man calls for his woman, and she doesn't answer."

"You'll find someone," she replied, understanding his drift immediately. "What you asked me—I'm very honored, but you spoke out of impulse. What we had long ago was very special, and you and I will always be friends, I think, even though we may not see each other for years at a time. When we grow very old, maybe we'll climb Wahgalu together and then just step off into the stars. Now I'm speaking foolishly, aren't I? You cause me to do that."

"I accept the engagement," he said. "We'll be a stodgy married couple by then and have grandchildren all over the place."

Fanny shook her head, gazed up at a waning moon.

"I'm sitting on something hard. What do you have in your coat pocket?"

"Let me look. . . ."

She moved to one side, and True Bear reached into the pocket, withdrew his rum flask.

"Would my lady like a sip? It'll be a wedding toast."

"Yes. No. I'm not sure whether you're joking, but you must stop. I'll bet you had women when you were in Boston, perhaps even someone special? Tell me whether it's true."

She sipped from the flask, handed it to True Bear, who also drank.

"Yes, but that's over. We were engaged to be married, in fact. I thought you were probably dead, Auna-yi. I don't suppose I'd have gone through with it, though, even if Dad hadn't written to ask me to return to Oidoing-koyo. She's a lawyer's daughter, and altogether too damned civilized for my taste."

"Did you . . . make love to her? I shouldn't ask. That's private—not like what I have to do. Do you want to know something? For a woman, if she doesn't care, it's almost as though it never happened at all. Was she pretty—this one you were going to marry? You should marry a pretty woman, but one who's pretty inside also. That's most important, I think. Men are very stupid about women. They fall in love with legs or breasts. But women are stupid too, in a different way."

"Harriet Collins," he said, "that's her name. Yes, I guess so. But Harriet wasn't the right woman, and it's got nothing to do with fancy clothes or cosmetics. She's pretty enough, as far as that goes, but she's not the one I want to be with. You are, and I guess I've known it ever since that first night. I've never stopped thinking about you, Auna-yi. Even your new name doesn't sound right. Maybe I'll change it—a husband's got the right, hasn't he? Wahtaurisi-yi has a nice ring to it."

"Foolish. You're a foolish young man, True Bear McCain. Now you come back wearing that gun. It's safer not to have one. . . ."

"Unless a coon knows how to use it. Never carved two notches on the handle, but maybe I should. From what I hear, there are men with a dozen or more. I can think of a few Gringos that need killing, so maybe I'll end up with a fair collection after all."

"You really shot two of Dan Clayton's men? Ben told me no one ever found the bodies. But you mustn't think about shooting anyone else. Too much of that, too much. The soldiers hung Kintpuash and his friends. There was no justice, there is never any. . . ."

True Bear took Fanny into his arms, and when he tried to embrace her fully, she didn't turn her face aside. They kissed and clung to one another for a long while, but when he placed his hand on one of her breasts, she pushed him gently away from her.

"The sun isn't up yet," she said, "but we must go now. I'm feeling . . . strange. I don't want this to happen, True Bear. I'll tell you something when we get back to the Emporium. That will have to satisfy you, and I. . . . I'm confused. I don't know what I mean to say."

When they reached the gambling hall, she turned to him.

"A year from now," she whispered, "maybe you'll wish to come back to Reno, but not before. I'm glad this happened— very glad. You go away now."

"What is it? What were you going to tell me?"

Fanny shook her head, smiled, and turned from him. Then she stopped.

"I loved True Bear when he was a boy. Maybe I love the man also. Who knows? Fawns lose their spots, but they don't forget. . . ."

She was gone, vanished into Salty's Emporium.

True Bear gazed after her for a moment and then walked off into thin gray light of false dawn.

TWENTY-NINE

Inca Courtship Ritual

[July 1874]

TRUE BEAR ANTICIPATED it might take a day or two to kidnap
Fanny Bitler, and for this reason he'd rented a room at the
Desert Oasis. The sun was on the verge of rising when he
entered, took off his hat, boots, coat, and pistol, lay down on
the squeaky bed, and tried to sleep.

But too much was coursing through his mind. Events, he
decided, were running ahead either far too rapidly or with
glacial slowness—which, he wasn't prepared to say.

He sat up, fumbled into the coat for his rum flask, drank
what remained, resolved as one of his first priorities to get a
refill, and then lay back down, letting his thoughts wander.

He slept till midday, went to the railway station for something to eat, walked to the livery stable, and ended up telling
Renegade his problems. The horse stared at him, one visible
eye brimming with ancient and unspoken wisdom. True Bear,
appreciating his animal's patience, withdrew a small cloth bag
from a trouser pocket, poured a bit of sugar into his hand,
and offered it to the stallion.

"Compliments of the railroad, big fellow," he said.

Now fully awake, he paced the board sidewalks to Salty's,
glanced inside, did not enter.

I need some kind of strategy, he thought. *Never have* *en very good at this courting business*.

He did a good deal of walking that afternoon, every so ten returning to the gambling hall and each time deciding t to enter.

Come back to Reno in a year? What the hell kind of ggestion was that? Hadn't he offered to make an honest oman of her? Hadn't he been sincere, intense, even courtly?

Perhaps wisdom lay in murdering the railroad baron—who as, unfortunately, not even in town.

At length McCain sat down on a bench across the street om Salty's place, retrieved a pen knife from his pocket, and scribed two notches on the rosewood handle of his Colt. In s mind's eye he could envision at least one more—for Dan ayton himself. Another for Anderson? Ben had mentioned few others as well.

Perhaps, when one got right down to it, half the Whitemen California would be better off resting comfortably in lava ves.

As a boy, he'd practiced endlessly with the pistol—until en finally decided to limit the amount of ammunition he lowed his son. But by that time, True Bear was already a ack shot. Thereafter he'd spent much of his time practicing quick draw. It wasn't necessary to expend ammunition to do at.

Had he possibly lost his skill? During the preceding four ars, he'd not so much as fired a single round—having made rtain promises to his father.

McCain rose, strode to the western limits of the small city, lected a gray-red rockface with pale green lichens growing pon it, and paced off twenty steps. He aimed carefully, red. The shot missed its target by no more that a few ches, but such, he decided, was hardly adequate. He proeded to empty the cylinder, and when he finished, four ray-white marks were clustered tightly together, the reaining two close by.

He nodded, set himself into position, imagined Dan Clayn standing in front of the boulder, went for the pistol, red. . . .

* * *

AN HOUR LATER he was back on the bench across the dust
roadway from Salty's Emporium. He'd acquired a recent cop
of the *Gazette* and now read it through—a smattering
national news, a brief account of legislation permitting farm
ers to be absent from their homesteads or preemption land
until May of the following year—without losing their right
due to residence requirements (a gesture acknowledging th
severity of problems with drought and grasshopper swarm
on the plains), another article about an act fixing the tot
amount of greenbacks in circulation at $382,000,000, th
hanging in Elko of two Digger Indians for murdering a pro
pector and butchering and eating his mule, a glowing foreca
of prosperity to come for the Reno area (owing to favorabl
shipping rates allowed by the railroad for baled hay sent t
California).

He was perusing the paper for a second time when Fann
Bitler and Salty Dan Dolliver walked out of the Emporiu
and proceeded up the street.

True Bear waited until they'd covered perhaps fifty yar
and then stood up, folded his paper under one arm, and se
out to follow the two.

Numerous people were moving about despite late afte
noon's oppressive heat—a scattering of businessmen, sever
gangs of cowboys in from the rangelands, delivering cattle t
the Reno stockyard for shipment either to California or to Sa
Lake Basin in Utah Territory, wherever the market was be
ter, local ranchers and hay farmers and their wives and chi
dren, as well as a scattering of sullen-eyed Washoe Indian
Horses were hitched to rails lining the main street, an
buckboards, carriages, and solitary riders sent up gray spira
of dust as they moved one way or the other.

True Bear kept his distance, not precisely certain why h
was following but determined not to let his quarry get out
sight.

Somewhere, several blocks away, a gun went off, and ye
no one seemed to notice.

Tired-looking men, their faces grimed with dust beneat
brims of battered Stetson hats, sat on benches, talking an
making casual observation of those who passed before them

The Canterbury Pilgrims, True Bear reflected, *a virtu
cross-section of the human portion of the State of Nevad*

*But where are the Knight, the Pardoner, and the Second
Nun?*

Salty Dan and Fanny Bitler paused in front of a clothing
store, and Dan was pointing at something behind the glass.

True Bear stopped, leaned against a brick front of one of
the more permanent buildings, and quickly unfolded his
newspaper—not reading but keeping a close eye on Fanny
and Salty Dan.

Half a dozen cowboys were riding in a group down the
street's center. One man let out a whoop and reined his
mount to a halt.

"Anna!" he shouted. "Goddamn my soul, it's you, ain't it? I
never forget a face. . . ."

True Bear let his copy of the *Gazette* drop and began to
walk quickly toward Fanny and Salty Dan.

Books Billy to the rescue—a dumbass drunken drover. . . .

"Don't turn away, you little bitch—I wondered what the
hell happened to you. Run off from that dirt-farmer, did
you?"

The cowboy nosed his horse to the edge of the street,
dismounted, and vaulted over a hitching rail, stumbled forward, and caught his balance.

"By God, look at them clothes! You've come up in the
world since I hauled your naked young tail into Shasta City—a
damned wonder I recognized you at all."

"Move off, Mister," Salty Dan said, placing himself between Fanny and the half-intoxicated individual who was
attempting to impress himself upon her.

"Who the hell's this—you caught you a White husband?
Damn it, Anna, don't you remember me? I saved your life
that day on Hat Creek. . . ."

She turned to face the man now.

"I remember you, McLaughlin," True Bear heard her say
as he bolted past the other cowhands, still mounted, crossing
the street to where Salty Dan and Fanny were standing.

"Well, Goddamn! I should hope so. You in business here,
or what? The old white-haired guy, he's your keeper?"

"I said *move off!*" Salty Dan growled, reaching under his
vest and producing a Deringer precisely the duplicate of the
one McCain had seen in Fanny's hand the previous night.

The stranger backhanded Dolliver across the face, the force

of his blow sending the gambler sideways against the frame of
the clothing store entryway. Dan's pistol clattered along the
board sidewalk, spun about, and lay still.

"Next time you pull a gun on Wes McLaughlin, Whitey,
I'll kick the lights out of you. This Injun gal's an old friend of
mine."

McCain chose not to vault over the rail. Instead, as though
he were a casual observer, he walked around. Pretending to
pass by McLaughlin, he put the crook of his elbow about the
man's throat and twisted him backward, hurling him headfirst
into the street.

The remaining trailhands had dismounted now, and rushed
to where Westley McLaughlin was picking himself up, brushing dust from his clothing.

"What in hell?" McLaughlin sputtered. "Ain't no damned
mudskin's gonna'. . . ."

"Pull that gun," True Bear said, "and I'll drill you on the
spot. The lady made it clear she didn't want your attentions."

"Gun be damned," McLaughlin replied, squinting. "Don'
need no gun to whip your ass. . . . You want a fistfight,
youngster, you got it."

He unbuckled his weapon and handed it to one of the men.

McCain nodded, removed his own pistol.

"True Bear!" Fanny said, a great deal of indignation in her
voice, "What do you think you're doing? I can take care of
myself. You. . . ."

"Better pull off that coat, kid," McLaughlin grinned. "Ain'
no sense in gettin' it all dirtied up. Boys, stay back—don'
want you all endin' up in the Reno hoosgow. Won't take me
long to put this oversized Meskin in his place, by God!"

McCain slowly and deliberately slipped under the hitching
rail and walked toward McLaughlin—a large man in his own
right but suddenly dwarfed by the young giant who stood
before him.

"I serve at your pleasure, sir," McCain said, half-bowing to
the man.

Wes McLaughlin grinned, put up his fists, spat, and made
a wild swing at True Bear, the blow striking nothing but air
as its intended target took a quick half-step backward.

Then the trail boss was out cold, cruciform on his back,
nose bleeding, mouth wide open, one leg twitching.

The other cowhands appeared ready to close in, but Salty Dan had retrieved his Deringer.

"Pick him up and get him out of here!" the gambler said. "When he's sober, there's a free drink for him at the Emporium. But if he bothers Miss Bitler again, I'll kill him myself. You trailhands make Goddamned fools of yourselves, you know that? Now get the hell out of my sight!"

A NUMBER OF TOWNSFOLK and passers-through had gathered by this time and were standing about in anticipation of yet further excitement—almost as though they expected some sort of virtuoso performance by a Lotta Crabtree or Calamity Jane or possibly the ghost of Bad Sam Brown. But when the trailhands hoisted Weasel McLaughlin, still groggy, onto his horse and led him away, the spontaneous audience quickly dispersed.

Salty Dan, Fanny, and True Bear returned to the gambling hall, entered, and sat down at one of the tables.

"A bottle of the good stuff," Dan called, "and three glasses."

The house was already about half full. A wire dice cage was turning, the wooden goose was laying eggs for keno, and half a dozen men stood about the faro table. Poker and blackjack were already under way as well, and one of the more ambitious girls was sitting at the bar, conversing with three well-dressed land speculators.

"True Bear, you sonofabitch!" Fanny said after she finished her first drink and poured another. "The one thing I don't need is you following me around and acting like my protector. Maybe I was a fool even to talk to you last night. Go home and see your mother, for heaven's sake—and don't be hanging around Reno like some great lovesick buffalo! I can handle myself very well, thank you, and all you've done is antagonize potential customers. Get on your horse now and go—it's a wonder those men didn't kill you. . . ."

True Bear was astonished at Fanny's response to what had happened, for he was of the opinion that he'd dealt with matters in quite an effective way.

"I'll be happy to do exactly that, Auna-yi—if you'll come with me. I know that's what you want to do anyway, and. . . ."

"True Bear McCain, you don't know a damned thing. What's happened—it'll be all over town in an hour or so. It isn't that I'm not grateful, but I don't want you getting yourself killed."

McCain stared at Fanny, immediately finished his drink, and rose from the table.

"It's altogether possible I've made a great mistake," he replied. "Salty Dan, it's been good meeting you. My apologies, Miss Bitler. Well . . . have a good life. I'll pass your best wishes on to Dad, Woodpecker, and Acorn Girl."

He tipped his hat, turned, and strode toward the door.

BUSINESS WAS BRISK that evening, and a few patrons openly admitted they'd come to the Emporium in simple anticipation there'd yet be some outfall from afternoon's excitement on Main Street—possibly even a shoot-out between the cowboy and the tall kid in black. Rumors of a love-triangle had spread, while some toyed with the idea that Fanny Bitler's long-lost brother had showed up. But everyone wanted to get a glimpse of beautiful Fanny Bitler and to be present just in case something further did happen.

Despite the crowd, however, Fanny didn't make her expected appearance.

At length Salty Dan went to her rooms, rapped on the door.

"Fan—okay if I come in? Gal, the floor's buzzing. They all want to see you. . . ."

When she opened the door, Salty Dan could see that she'd been crying. Her eyes were red, and the vermilion blush on her cheeks was streaked.

"Problems of the heart, I take it," he said. "Listen. The way I've got it figured, young Hercules'll be back. You were kind of rough on him, considering. . . ."

"Dan, I'm confused. . . . This whole thing's crazy. There's no reason why I should be feeling the way I am. Goddamn it, I put all that behind me. I stayed Indian too long as it was—I watched my people die, I got raped and mauled and abused, saw my husband killed, my Modoc friends hung or sent off to a place where they can never be at peace. . . ."

She put one hand over her eyes and began to sob—then reached out to Dan, who embraced her, held her in his arms.

"Still no need to turn on the big kid," Dan said. "Ben McCain's boy, eh? From all the time you've spent talking

about that family, I'd say they . . . he . . . was pretty important to you, Miss Fanny. A fellow doesn't act as impulsively
as he has unless he's either loco out of his mind or set on
courting a wife. You're no innocent schoolgirl—you know
what I'm saying is true. True Bear McCain's got marriage on
his mind, that's my guess. He doesn't hold it against you that
you've been whoring for a spell, and that might even be part
of the attraction, who knows? In any case, you two were
kid-sweethearts, and sometimes that's the best kind of match
there is. He's been trained as a gentleman, and his family's
well off. The kind of life you're living right now, it can't last
forever. We both know that. We'll make enough out of this
arrangement with Huntington so we've got a good stake to
play with when we move on, but in the last analysis, C.P.'s
holding all the high cards. Men like him always do. Bad on
his reputation when word gets out what he's got going here in
Reno, and then he'll cut and run. Or else he'll just get tired
of the game. I took a few chips from him, and that got him
interested. But it's sure as hell nothing to count on. Right
now it's fun running our own little empire, but we've got to
remember it really isn't *ours* at all. We rake in some tin,
don't get foolish, and we'll come out of this just fine. But
there are limits to everything, gal."

"What are you telling me?" Fanny asked when Dan's spiel
was finished.

"For a smart hooker, you're dumb as a post, Fan Bitler.
The son of a wealthy rancher makes a pretty fair catch, and
besides that, the damned fool's in love with you. A man
would have to be blind not to see it. Sometimes it happens
that way—the snap of a finger, so to speak. There's no explaining *love*, since it doesn't make sense in the first place.
But that's just an old man's brain talking. Fact is, I'd say
maybe the professional lady's feeling close to the same thing."

"Passion," she said. "I swore to God I'd never let myself
feel anything like that again. It's not safe. It hurts too much.
You and I, Dan, we're friends. We trust each other, and
together we make a fine team. We're partners."

"True enough, Fan. But if I was you, I wouldn't trust
me—not all the way, anyhow. I've got a history of moving on.
In any case, owning the game ain't got quite the appeal of
breaking the house. A gambler's like a prospector. A strike's

fine, but then he gets to thinking about some rockface or
another he should have checked out a little more closely—
might be back in Colorado or even up in Alaska, for that
matter."

"So what should I do?"

Dan kissed Fanny on the forehead, patted her on one
shoulder, stood back, squinted.

"Why, take a vacation, I guess. Go visit the McCain clan
for a week or two, get your mind straightened out. If the big
boy appeals to you, then have a *roll in the hay*, as our pal
Willow says. Just because you do something for a living
doesn't mean you can't have fun with it too. One thing's
sure—being all teary-eyed isn't going to appeal to Huntington when he shows up, interested in getting his ashes hauled
and then counting up how much money we've made for
him. If you're not back when he comes calling, I'll fuck him
at blackjack and then turn him over to two or three of the
girls at one time. If that program don't produce a fatal heart
attack, nothing will."

"Well, it sounds all right, but I suppose True Bear's halfway to Mt. Lassen by now. I'm sure he's already come to his
senses. When I got angry, that probably shattered his last
illusion about me. . . ."

"Damn fools like McCain, they spend their whole lives
chasing illusions. You may have scratched the window, but
the glass isn't broken, not yet anyhow, And he doesn't strike
me as someone who gives up right off."

"I could go visit, I suppose. No matter how I've been
making a living, they'll be glad to see me, I think. Dan, I
need to be by myself tonight. I have to do some thinking.
Can you handle the floor by yourself?"

"Imagine so. By God, I don't blame the big horse."

"What are you talking about?"

Salty Dan walked to the door, looked back at Fanny Bitler.

"Guess I love you too," he said, "in my own peculiar way,
that is."

Fanny gave a choking laugh.

"Don't let on to Willow," she said. "I'm too young to have
my gizzard cut out."

*   *   *

IT WAS CLOSE TO MIDNIGHT when True Bear McCain once again entered Salty's Emporium, and business, as he could plainly see, was booming. He actually toyed with the idea of doing some gambling himself, but once inside the swinging half-doors, he realized that wasn't at all why he'd come.

He scanned the room, perceived that Fanny was nowhere in sight, and walked directly to Dan.

"Upstairs?" he asked.

"That she is, Mr. Geldman," Dan winked.

True Bear nodded, made his way to Fanny's second-story rooms. He reached for the white porcelain knob, realized the lock was set, and felt a momentary flash of anger take hold of him.

One heavy thump with his shoulder sent the door banging inward.

Fanny was sitting in a blue velveteen chair, next to a table with a fancy glass-globed lantern and an open whiskey bottle sitting on it.

She looked up, momentarily puzzled.

"What are you doing here, Mr. McCain? I told you to go home to your mother."

"Stubborn little bitch," he said as he crossed the room. "I'm tired of the games. You're coming with me."

Fanny turned, apparently searching for her pistol, and accidentally sent the whiskey bottle bouncing to the floor.

"See what you've made me do. . . ."

Then he had hold of her, lifted her from the chair, slung her over his shoulder.

"True Bear, put me down! I'll have you horsewhipped, you big sonofabitch!"

She beat at him with both fists, kicked—but he was oblivious.

"We're riding north," he said. "You stop struggling or I swear to God. . . ."

Then they were out the door and on their way down the stairs.

Gambling hall patrons looked, and for a moment all activity whatsoever ceased.

Inexplicably, once the men realized more or less what was going on, a cheer went up.

When True Bear and the still-struggling Fanny Bitler were across the wide room and out through its swinging doors,

Salty Dan stood up from the table where he'd been amusing
himself with a game of cards.

"Nothing to worry about, boys. It's—well, you might say
it's an Inca courtship ritual, kind of like the waltz, you might
say. You come here to see Fanny, and now you've by-God
seen her. I hereby order one round of drinks on the
house. . . ."

"ALL RIGHT," Fanny said when they were halfway to the
livery. "I know when I'm beat. Put me down. It's not digni-
fied with my rear end up in the air this way."

"You going to be nice to me?"

"As much as you deserve. Put me down now."

When he set her feet to the ground, she slapped him
across the face.

True Bear grinned foolishly.

"All right, hellcat. Back over my shoulder. . . ."

"I said I'd go with you. Keep your hands off me, True Bear
McCain. You've got horses, or do we have to walk all the way
to Wahgalu?"

"Yes," he replied, "but I should have bought you a mule—
except a mule's got a better disposition."

"Flattery will get you everywhere," she said, falling into
step beside him.

He began to laugh, softly at first, and then louder and
louder.

"What's so funny?" she demanded, suddenly realizing that
she, too, was laughing.

She took his arm, and the two of them walked quickly
between pole-mounted gas street lamps about which spotted-
wing bullbats were darting, intent upon catching moths and
mayflies.

True Bear awakened the livery attendant, placed a ten-
dollar gold piece in his hand, and waited for the man to bring
out Renegade and a Palouse mare, complete with saddle and
bridle, an animal he'd purchased late that afternoon, shortly
after exiting angrily from the Emporium in the wake of his
street brawl with the man named McLaughlin.

Then they were riding away from the city of Reno, Nevada,
heading north toward Hallelujah Junction.

Somewhere out in a star-filled and sage-smelling darkness,

three or four coyotes were singing their hearts out and giving the distinct impression that at least half a hundred brush wolves had entered into sustained chorus.

A waning quarter moon rose above treeless rims to the east.

THIRTY

A Notch for Weasel

[July 1874]

MORNING SUNLIGHT found them asleep together, side by side, beneath the covering of a single saddle blanket. The two passed by Hallelujah Junction before dawn and continued to the crest of Beckwourth Pass before exhaustion overcame them. With no real place to make camp, they simply rode a few yards back into sagebrush, found a small clearing splatched with clumps of dry desert grass, tethered the horses, took a sip or two apiece from McCain's pocket flask, and lay down to doze for an hour or so. Predawn chill drew them closer together, however, and they fell asleep with Fanny's head pressed in against True Bear's chest.

Midmorning brightness awoke them, penetrating heat of mountain summer drawing them groggily alert.

The horses were stamping about, uneasy, thirsty.

"I'd give half my soul for a cup of coffee," True Bear said as he cinched the saddles.

"That's all you've got, maybe. What in God's name am I doing out here, anyway? Kidnapped by a madman—I suppose you'll demand ransom from Huntington. It won't work, True Bear. He'll just find someone else to take my place."

"Quit being a grouch, Wahtaurisi-yi . . . Fanny . . . Fire Woman . . . whoever you are. What happened was fated. Old Man Coyote wrote it all down in the Book of Life long ago. In the final analysis, you wouldn't have come with me if you hadn't wanted to. By God! It was wonderful making love to you last night. . . ."

"What are you talking about, McCain?"

"Don't you remember? You woke me up and insisted—said you had to have me or you were going to die. Naturally, with a situation as serious as all that, I did what any gentleman would have done."

"Nothing of the sort happened. You've gone crazy since we were children. . . ."

"Bad memory. I suppose you were so tired that. . . ."

"Let me borrow your pistol. I'm going to shoot you now. I don't feel very good, True Bear. How far is it to the next way station?"

"About fifteen miles, I think. Jim Beckwourth's old trading post is up ahead—a man named Ramilli runs the place, owns a big chunk of the valley there. Turner and Dotta and a few others have pretty much divided the flatland among themselves. Dad explained the whole thing to me four years ago when we were on the way to Reno. You know who Beckwourth was?"

"Some Saltu sonofabitch, I guess. Quit talking and let's get going—either that or I'm heading back to Dan Dolliver and the girls."

"A Black man, half-Black at least. I read his book. His father gave him a writ of emancipation, and he went west from St. Louis fifty years ago—became a great war chief with the Crow Indians."

"Then why was he running a trading post in California?"

"Long story, long story. If you're not interested in the rudiments of Western American history, it's agreeable to me."

"All right, then, let's go. But I have one more question.

This man Beckwourth—does he have a restaurant? True Bear, I'm not going any farther until I've had something to eat."

"Ramilli probably does, if he's still there. Things change in four years. Beckwourth, he's dead, I believe. Or else he's off in the mountains somewhere with Bully O'Bragh, each one determined to out-lie the other."

Fanny snapped the reins along her mare's neck and began riding toward the valley floor. McCain laughed, mounted Renegade, and followed.

They passed through the ranch settlements of Chilkoot and Vinton and proceeded to Beckwourth, reaching that outpost just before noon.

Tom Ramilli's wife was tending the cafe, her husband and his men chasing down cattle that apparently had strayed somewhere up onto the slopes of Beckwourth Peak, to the southwest.

True Bear and Fanny Bitler drank several cups of coffee and dined on steak and eggs, in the aftermath of which both wished to sleep some more. They had to resist the temptation to find a cool spot beside the barely moving waters of Feather River's Middle Fork, that stream rising from an infinitude of springs oozing from the floor of Sierra Valley.

Instead, they rode onward, through the village of Portola and into a steep-sided canyon beside the now cascading little river.

They spoke quietly, almost as though something were actually settled between them. Being together this way—it was almost as though nine years and more had never passed and they were still children, the two of them riding their ponies across Ben McCain's high meadows, exchanging bits of information, simply enjoying one another's company.

When True Bear attempted to draw Fanny out as to what had happened following the Mill Creek massacre, however, she either protested that she didn't wish to talk of it or merely changed the subject.

Weasel, Hank, Eleanor, the wretched and insane Tod, the good interval of years when she was wife to Red Turtle, then Whitney, Klamath Falls and George Livingstone, a trail south to where she had found Salty Dan beside Honey Lake, on the verge of death, Reno. . . . The whole passage of time swirling about her, unreal, like an insane dream from which one

*awoke still uncertain whether the events within that dream
had occurred or not. . . .*

Her rational mind silently insisted she was doing no more
than taking a few days off from business operations in Reno.
She would visit Ben and Ooti McCain, as well as Big Woodpecker and Yellow Grass—True Bear had told her about the
marriage. That relationship, at least, had come to something.
Perhaps Big Woodpecker was right—perhaps Smoke Woman
and Wolf Tracker and the others were still miraculously alive.
She and True Bear would search the area around Wahgalu
and the canyons of Mill Creek, Deer Creek, and Battle Creek
as well. It wouldn't be easy to discover the whereabouts of so
small a group, particularly if Wolf Tracker didn't wish to be
found.

If any Yahis had survived, it was only because Wolf Tracker
knew all that land so well he could simply vanish into it. A
small level grassy area down under a volcanic rim, perhaps, a
cave with a trickle of water running out—a few people on
foot, ever alert as they hunted and fished, never building a
fire except after darkness fell. . . . It was possible, after all,
and Big Woodpecker wouldn't have claimed such a thing if
he hadn't at least seen some group of Indians. Who else
might it have been? Maybe a few of Big Foot Jack's Yahis had
escaped *that* massacre. Maybe those people had even managed to find Wolf Tracker.

During the few times when Auna-yi became uncommuni-
cative, True Bear sensed she saw their present journey together merely as an interval in a life she'd already established
in White society. He himself toyed with the idea he might
yet return to Boston, to a marriage with Harriet Collins, a
quiet life the two of them might lead if only he could convince Harriet they should move away from the city, possibly
to the woods of Maine.

But then conversation would begin once more—simple talk
about trees and animals and the effects of light upon still
water, hawks and eagles drifting against remarkable blue
California sky, an old black bear wallowing about in a shallows at river's edge, a mother raccoon and six young ones
trailing along behind her as the animals crossed the dusty
wagon road.

And things seemed just the way they should be.

*   *   *

ON THE THIRD DAY of their journey, they passed beyond Quincy to where a bridge spanned Feather River, a pair of hundred-foot-long Ponderosa pine logs laid over with sawn planks, and here they turned upstream along Indian Creek toward a cattle and logging town called Greenville, where Peter Lassen himself lay buried.

Darkness caught them well beyond the town, along Wolf Creek below Keddie Ridge. A cold rivulet poured from the mountain, and at this spot they made camp, complete with several blankets, a couple of pots and pans, and food—all purchased in Quincy.

True Bear tethered their two horses where the animals could get at both grass and water.

"Tonight we're damned near civilized," True Bear chuckled as he brought in an armload of firewood, set it down alongside the small blaze Auna-yi already had going.

"Tired," she said. "How much farther do we have to go? I've gotten out of the habit of lying on the ground this past year and a half. When we get to Upper Eden, I'm going to sleep for about two days."

"We're both out of practice, but I can't say it's all that bad. Something damned comforting about having the earth itself under one. That coffee ready yet?"

"Almost," she replied, at the same time using a metal fork to turn a full-cut round steak that was happily sizzling in a cast iron frying pan.

They ate, arranged their blankets, lay down, and stared upward through a break in the pines at clear mountain sky, an infinitude of stars splayed across heaven. A faint odor of smoke in the air, and not from the dying campfire—perhaps lightning had started flames up on the high ridges.

After an interval of conversation, mostly True Bear talking about his summers with the cod fishermen, as well as details of one or two tavern brawls he'd been involved in, Auna-yi turned onto her side, groaned softly, mumbled something about pebbles beneath the blanket, thought longingly of her big feather bed at the Emporium, and then was silent.

True Bear reached over, placing his hand on the side of her face.

Then the hand began to move, sliding downward, cupping one of her breasts, moving further.

He leaned over her, kissed her.

For a time she responded to his advances, but when he slipped his hand inside her clothing, she sat up.

"I agreed to sleep with you," she said, "and that means 'sleep.' Don't spoil things, McCain. Maybe when conditions are right, then I'll consider it. Now behave yourself and turn over."

"I'll be damned," he muttered, "a genuine frigid lady of the evening. Who'd ever have thought it?"

There was no anger in his voice, and Fanny realized he had not actually taken offense. What he wanted from her now—it was not so much, it was nothing she hadn't done many times before, and with strangers, with men she barely knew, for money. But what, after all, would he think of her if she let him have his way?

Part of her, she knew, wanted precisely the same thing he did. No sense to it—not even a matter of desire. Yet desire was there also, a strange kind of yearning that hardly seemed sexual at all and was something she had in fact never experienced before, not even with Red Turtle, her husband. She had loved him, and they had sought and found pleasure together, but this was something strangely different—and perhaps that was why she found it necessary to resist. When close to this man who both was and was not the True Bear she'd loved desperately nine years earlier, she had a deep feeling of not being in control.

Emotions, she had resolved long since, were simply to be kept in check—for otherwise the result was pure chaos. One might agree to something and later realize a promise had been made blindly. The possibility of becoming pregnant had nothing to do with it. If new life had never managed to implant itself within her after all this time, then it was likely she was simply a *barren doe*.

Once she and Red Turtle wished for children, and none came. Instead, a soldier's bullet had. . . .

"I want you on my own terms," she whispered.

"And what does that mean?"

"In a real bed, you damned fool. You make me ride all day and sleep in a rock patch, when you let me sleep at all, and

en you want to ride me. That's not the way Fanny Bitler
oes things, True Bear McCain."

"Stop thrashing around and let me sleep, in that case," he
eplied.

Within moments he was snoring peacefully, but she wasn't
all certain whether the whole thing was not pretense.

Now she couldn't sleep. She even thought about reaching
ver and fondling him, arousing him—since he'd wakened
er in the first place. At length she decided against this
ourse of action, took a few deep breaths, and felt herself
rifting into welcome darkness.

RUE BEAR ROUSED HER early, pointed northwestward to where
angry-looking broad gray plume of smoke was boiling into
e sky.

"Forest fire," he said. "Can't tell how far away it is—maybe
n miles, maybe more. Might be on the ridges beyond Ches-
r, and that's not all that far from Oidoing-koyo, if I haven't
tally forgotten the lay of the land. Why don't you fix us
me breakfast, Wahtaurisi-yi? I'm sorry, Fanny Bitler. Haven't
tten used to that name yet. You have too many damned
ames. I'm going to ride up the mountain a couple of miles—
e if I can get a better look at things. I like my bacon crisp,
oman. And three flapjacks, please."

"Cook your own when you get back, Growling Bear. Just
n't go wandering off the way you used to and forget about
e, damn it."

"Be right back, Fair One. You can count on me. . . ."

Auna-yi rose from the blankets, turned her back on him, and
alked to the campfire. At least he'd been thoughtful enough
fix that before vanishing into the forest.

"Just like some wild Indian," she heard herself saying
oud—and then was shocked at what she'd uttered. But a
oment later she began to laugh softly.

She stood by the warmth for a moment, listening as McCain's
allion thumped away upslope, wished desperately for one of
alty Dan's bad-tasting cigars, which she sometimes smoked
private, turned, and walked to a fir where True Bear had
ashed the canvas bag containing their supplies. She un-
ooked the container from a broken-off limb, sorted through
e contents for a slab of bacon and a white cloth sack

containing flour, a small bag of baking soda stashed insid
that.

She dipped a pot full of water from the stream that gurgle
past their camp, measured out a few large pinches of groun
coffee, stirred these in, and set the pot against the flames.

Next she walked a few yards from the fire, found a shel
tered spot, and relieved herself.

Pulling up her bloomers and buttoning the jeans McCai
had bought for her in Portola, she moved to the stream
rinsed her mouth and splashed cold water on her face. She'
forgotten her comb, so she used spread fingers to untangl
her long hair.

*Alone again, alone in the forest morning, away from th
tyranny of watches and clocks and all the busyness of th
Whiteman's world. . . .*

She felt tears starting to her eyes, and smiled as sh
wiped at them. A bluejay was shrilling—a sound that migh
have meant warning in the forest near Wolopti village.

Her morning ritual finished, she walked back to the camp
fire. She could smell coffee beginning to boil, an aroma, sh
had always thought, much finer than the actual taste of th
drink.

Then she heard a voice.

"By God, Jake, would you look who's here? Seems like
man don't see someone for years at a time, and then all of
sudden he starts runnin' into her every time he turns aroun
That is you, ain't it, Anna? Where's your friends now—th
old one an' that big Greaser?"

"It's her, all right," the blue-eyed, wiry man said. "Look
different though, not all painted up. What's she doin' way th
hell out here? Guess she ain't the famous Fanny Bitler afte
all, no matter what that guy from Winnemucca told you afte
you come to. . . ."

"Horseshit she ain't. I sold her to Bitler myself, an' that
just too damned much coincidence. All right, Miss Anna, yo
tell us. You Fanny Bitler or not? And what the hell you doin
here?"

"Hello, Wes," she replied. "I'm *the* Fanny Bitler, all righ
If you boys are paying a social call, I'm afraid I don't have m
girls with me at the moment. Perhaps next time you ge
down to Reno. . . ."

"Next time, hell," McLaughlin said. "Actually, we saw our camp smoke and rode up the hill to see if whoever it was might have coffee cookin'. Turns out you do. Where's the big guy?"

She shook her head, smiled.

"He was just a stranger on the street, Wes. A knight in shining armor, as they say. You were being a bit pushy, and I suppose the man thought he was helping. He certainly did a job on you."

She laughed, then shook her head in apology.

"Bastard blind-sided me, that's all. I was drunk, but I was just tryin' to be friendly. You sure he ain't around here? What about the old fella—that was Salty Dan, wasn't it? I take it he's the one that owns you now."

"No one owns Fanny Bitler," she replied, "and there's no one here but me. Take a good look, if you want. I'm on my way to Ben McCain's ranch, but I'll be happy to share the coffee."

"Jake," McLaughlin growled, "you and Tom take scout round. Anything moves in the brush, shoot it. Anna here, she's a trained whore, an' I figure she owes us something. Owes me, at least. Guess I'd like a little ass with my coffee, if you don't mind, ma'am."

Maybe I can get this over with and have them out of here before True Bear gets back. With that temper of his, there's bound to be trouble. I'll play the game. McLaughlin's pride not hurt, and if I'm not very careful, he's going to hurt me.

"Not exactly good working conditions," she said. "But I'll be happy to provide you with free drinks and a girl apiece— any house in Reno you like. My partners and I control the entire operation, and. . . ."

"Shut your fucking mouth, you little whore! I should of put a bullet in your head years ago, right after we found you. Now you got airs, like you really *was* somebody. Just a damned little Yahoo tramp. Shit, I actually sort of liked you before, but now you just rile me. What you need's a damned trained mule."

"Calm down, Wes McLaughlin. I'll do whatever you like. Here, let me get you some coffee. I think it's about ready."

Then light exploded behind her eyes, and she felt herself

stumbling backward, falling, the wind knocked from her, and she was trying desperately to breathe, but couldn't.

"Get my own coffee, you slut. Woods are burning—maybe when we're done, we'll start another little fire. That way ain' no one's going to recognize the body, if they ever find it in the first place. Ain't nothin' I know of worse than an Injun that starts thinking she can jack a White man around, an' that means Wes McLaughlin in particular. I done give you one chance to turn out decent. . . ."

"No one around, Weasel," Jake called out. "She's tellin the truth about that, at least."

McLaughlin ignored the nickname beyond glancing balefully in Jake's direction, kicked the pointed toe of his boo into Auna-yi's side.

"Get up, Miss Anna," he said. "You ain't been hurt at all not yet. Maybe I'll let the boys here work your tail end ove first while I'm drinking that coffee you offered. Jakey, yo wanted first poke at this mopful of black hair nine years ago when we caught her over on Hat Creek. Well, have at it then. Older I get, the more I'm content just to watch. Don' take so much energy that way."

Wes McLaughlin turned toward the bubbling pot full o coffee, and Jake, grinning and shaking his head at the same time, lunged toward Auna-yi and with one snake-quick move ment ripped open the red-and-white cotton blouse she wa wearing, exposing her breasts.

"You sonofabitch!" she said. "Keep your damn hands of me until you get permission, or I'll. . . ."

"Do what?" Jake demanded, backhanding her to the groun once more.

Then the grin faded from his face, and, clutching at hi midsection, he turned toward McLaughlin, half in appea staggered, and fell face forward.

The sharp snap of the Deringer echoed among the grove of pine and fir, and a thin trace of smoke coiled up from th pistol's short barrel.

"You dumbass tramp!" McLaughlin yelled. "You've kil Jakey. . . . Tom, Goddamnit, git on over here—she's got gun!"

"I was defending myself, Wes," she said, "and I've got tw shots left. That's one for each of you. Take your friend . .

get back on your horses . . . ride out. Sometimes a woman's
not so helpless, eh? I've got no grudge against you—maybe I
even owe you something, I don't know. But right now I'm
not in a mood for your company. Sorry about your friend,
but. . . ."

McLaughlin had begun backing away, hands held up at
shoulder height. Then he dived for the protection of a pine,
in the same motion drawing his pistol.

"Tom's got you covered from the rear, you worthless whore,"
he called out. "Throw down the sneak gun, or by God we'll
riddle you where you stand, Squaw Anna."

*So. They're going to rape you and kill you after all, just
when everything was beginning to go right. Your luck's finally run out. . . .*

She tossed the pistol onto the ground. She was, as Salty
Dan might have said, "out of tin," and she knew it.

Then the crack of a Henry rifle—once, twice.

Tom screamed, let out a long, pitiful wail, and then was
silent.

"McLaughlin," True Bear shouted, "you want someone to
shoot at, I make a lot better target. Get on your horse, like
the lady says, or I'll drill you, so help me God!"

Big Wes recognized the voice—it was not one he was likely
to have forgotten.

"Your pet bear was off in the woods taking a shit, huh? Tell
him to walk out into the clear, or I'm going to give you
another hole to sell."

*What to do? Stall. Give True Bear the time to get around
behind him. Weasel McLaughlin isn't going to shoot me, not
now. I'm the only chance he's got. . . .*

"Forget how to say in English. Stupid squaw, can't remember. You come down to the Emporium, Wes, and I'll give
you free whiskey and the two best-looking girls in the house.
Whatever you want from them, all night long. Two girls,
they'll make you feel like a young man again. Believe me, it's
amazing what two women with professional training can do
for a man. You ever heard of what we call the *straight flush*?
Just like in poker, it's a winning hand. McCain—he's over
behind you, Wes. Think about what I'm offering. . . ."

"Shut your yap, girl, or by God's green bung I'll. . . ."

"Turn around, Mister. I've got no heart for nailing a man in

the back. The game's over, whatever it was. This is Books
Billy talking to you."

"Shoot, then. I'll plug the squaw one way or the other."

"Wahtaurisi-yi, he's bluffing. Do what I tell you now,
damn it. Just turn around and walk—keep going until you
get to the little fir grove. Westley here thinks he ought to be
given a fair fight, am I right, McLaughlin? Forget about the
girl. I'll give you an honest draw, if that's what you want. Or
you can ride on out, and the matter's closed. Other than the
fact that you keep trying to ride herd on my woman, I've got
nothing against you. I gather she's not interested, and that
means hands off. Wahtaurisi-yi, do what I tell you!"

Fanny Bitler turned slowly and began to walk, almost
certain the next moment would bring a bullet in the back.
But it didn't come. She breathed deeply, continued moving
slowly toward the fir grove.

The sky to the north was now filled with a huge yellow-
gray plume, and the sun itself began to go amber. Wind was
driving the smoke cloud eastward, filling the sky.

She reached the fir trees, stepped between two of them,
and immediately fell to the ground. A sensation of absolute
numbness passed over her, and then a jolt, as of a fist striking
her in the stomach.

Not gunshot—herself, stomach knotted, heart pounding,
teeth chattering.

She struggled to hands and knees, gazed back into the
clearing.

"Get on your horse," she heard True Bear say. "You can
come back later to fetch your two friends, if you're of a
mind."

"All right, all right," McLaughlin replied. "Kid, things
kind of got out of hand, that's all. The squaw was coming on
to Jake, and he just took her up on it, that's all. A Goddamn
mistake. . . ."

True Bear stepped into the clearing, rifle clutched in one
hand, revolver in the other.

"Watch out!" Fanny screamed.

There was a sudden blur of movement and the reports of
two pistols at nearly the same instant, McCain dropping to
one knee, McLaughlin standing still, taking a step backward,
crumpling.

"It's over," True Bear called out. "But the sonofabitch put
hole through the top of my new Oregon felt. I've got to do
ome more practicing, I can see that."

Fanny walked out into the open area where two men lay
ead. Behind her, in the fir grove where she'd taken cover, a
hird man was sprawled, a portion of his neck blown away,
lood still oozing into the duff of dead needles and twigs.

Death. The Yahi village, Tod Bitler, Matthew Red Turtle,
`aptain Jack and the other Modocs, and now this—this, and
` never should have happened at all. No purpose, no rea-
on. Old Man Coyote having a good time, that was it. . . .

Like one who sleepwalked, she went straight to McCain,
eached out toward him in a gesture of pleading, and then fell
ito his bearlike embrace.

She was sobbing, sobbing, unable to control herself—and
et dimly aware that the powerful male arms which held her
vere but a boy's arms, and the boy himself trembling like
ne who'd stayed too long in a cold, still pool in a stream in
ummer twilight.

"Auna-yi, Auna-yi, my God Fanny, are you all right? We've
ist killed three men and. . . . Your clothing torn, nothing
iore? McLaughlin, when did you meet him? Some time
fter the massacre, I take it—or was he there with Clayton
nd Anderson?"

To the north, great torrents of smoke poured up into the
ky, and heat of day was only beginning.

Vultures drifted overhead, their long, dark wings casting
hadows upon the ground below, and air was thick in the
ellow light.

THIRTY-ONE

Return to Upper Eden

[July 1874]

SMOKE POURED OVER the northern flank of Keddie Ridge and southward across Almanor Basin like some strange, acrid midsummer fogbank, enveloping the forest and sending long, trailing bands of grayness horizontally among the trees. Fire was visible now, high up, sputtering along the slopes of the mountain and occasionally igniting entire stands of trees, transforming them into minute-long flares.

Sun hung in the air as if it were a disc of faintly pulsing red-gold, and wind flowing down along Wolf Creek became a gale of hot, almost unbreathable dryness.

"The damned thing's alive," True Bear said, "and we're in its way. We've got to retreat—keep going—or we'll get cooked sure as hell. I've never seen anything like this before. If vultures find our three friends when the fire's passed by, they'll have roast pig to dine on. Goddamn it, Auna-yi, I was going to let your old acquaintance off the hook, but he wasn't having it that way. He's not exactly the one I had in mind, but some men are better off dead, and that's a fact—like the whole bunch that murdered your people, for instance. Coming across country I had the opportunity of watching a number of *good citizens* engaged in mindless slaughter of buffalo

392

I decided right then that one day I was going to go buffalo
hunter hunting. Well, this is no time for me to be shooting
off my mouth. What's done is done, and I'd say McLaughlin
and his two friends pretty well bought it. You're not bad with
that purse-pistol of yours, incidentally. Right now we'd best
get moving, or there are subject to be five chunks of steaming
hog meat out in the woods."

In the throes of a numb awareness that she'd actually killed
a man—not just a man, but someone she'd known, someone
who was more than simply a faceless entity—Fanny was all
but oblivious to the immediate danger of forest fire. Now,
however, the very real threat to their safety became apparent
to her.

"Which way can we go, True Bear? I'm hardly able to
breathe with all this smoke."

"We turn around and ride like hell, that's which way we
go—back to Greenville, maybe. Better yet, there's a big
saddle in the ridge up above. I think we can get across, then
down to the valley on the other side, Pinetown. . . ."

They retraced their steps for perhaps two miles, wind-
driven smoke swirling about them as they rode, and then
turned north, upslope, and made for the saddle in Keddie
Ridge. Behind them the forest was a wall of flame, and fire
had leaped across to ridges southward as well, creating a
second substantial blaze.

The two horses labored upward through a small ravine and
finally emerged at the saddle below Keddie's summit, bare
rock where fire had nothing to feed on.

True Bear and Fanny looked back, saw what appeared to be
an inchoate gray river of immense proportions flowing above
and completely obscuring the settlement of Greenville and
on into Indian Valley, finally washing up against the flank of
Mt. Hough to the south.

Yet more fire was burning northeasterly, along ridges below Coyote Peak, visible now for the first time.

"My God, this is something!" True Bear said. "Half the
world's blazing, and the other half's hidden by smoke. But
here we are, above it all, standing in clear sunlight. A general
downpour will put it out, nothing less. And if that damned
wind keeps driving the thing, it might even take Quincy.

Who knows how far it's spread? In its own terrible way, the monster's beautiful as hell."

"Will Oidoing-koyo be safe? How far are we from the ranch?"

"I'm not sure—twenty-five miles, maybe thirty. With wind coming from the north, Upper Eden's probably been spared. But wind blows whatever direction it wants to. I'm tempted to stay right here until she burns herself out—out of our way, at least. But maybe we'd best keep going opposite to where the fire's heading. If we can make it to Pinetown, then Chester's due east, and from there we follow the North Branch home. . . ."

They urged their nervous horses downslope into sparse pine forest that seemed, as they rode through it, almost to be calling out to the fire—almost desiring a red baptism.

BY LATE AFTERNOON they had reached Chester, the town as yet unscathed but lying beneath a dull gray pall through which sunlight, heavy gold-yellow, barely penetrated.

A mule train loaded with supplies and apparently headed for Susanville to the east of the mountains, was untended in front of Tumbleweed Till's Eatery & Hardware, the dozen mules stamping about nervously in their traces.

True Bear and Fanny walked inside, and sat down at a table. The only other patrons were the two muleskinners, crouched over their plates, eating and drinking beer—one man with a red bandanna wrapped about his forehead, the other in a black slouch hat. They were talking in low tones.

Tumbleweed Till walked to the table, nodded casually, and then recognized True Bear.

"Billy McCain!" she said. "Is it you? My heavens, you're as big as your father—they must have fed you good back in Massachusetts. Ben said you'd be riding through in a day or so, but I figured with the fires and all. . . . This your lady, I take it?"

Till was a permanent fixture in Chester, and True Bear had known her since just before his twelfth birthday—when she and her husband Jack put up the building—and Jack, that first winter in town, attempted to shovel snow from the roof, slipped, fell, broke his neck, and died sprawled over the front porch—a story that spread, in several variations, throughout the area.

"I'm back," True Bear replied, "just in time to see the whole damned place burn up, from the looks of things."

"Lad, you ain't just whistling 'Dixie.' The wagon trail to Susanville's closed—fire all over Fredonyer Summit. Fred Samsel come over from Pinetown this morning—gave us the word. Guess we just have to wait for it to burn itself out, and hope the wind don't shift this direction. Can I get you two something to eat? There's a big pot of beef stew simmering, and fresh-baked muffins to go with it. Wild lettuce salad, just gathered down at the swamp this morning. The Ebersole kids bring it in for me—you know the family, more likely than not."

"Sounds good, real good. Coffee as well, *s'il vous plaît*. And fill this pocket flask with whiskey, if you'd be so kind, *tout ce qu'il y a de mieux*, your best. We'll have to eat and run if we're going to make Upper Eden by nightfall."

Tumbleweed Till laughed.

"Your young fella sounds almost like a gentleman, don't he?" she said to Fanny. "Guess education's got something to be said for it after all."

Till winked, turned, walked away toward the kitchen.

"What kind of language was that?" Fanny demanded. "You sound funny when you talk that way."

True Bear shrugged, grinned.

"Damned if I know," he said. "*Le professeur*, he never told me what it was."

"Whiteman not speak truth," she said, staring out the window and into grayness that rose up like cold fog over an endless chaotic tumble of lava beds in midwinter.

THEY DIDN'T REACH Upper Eden that night.

Staying to the wagon road rather than following the course of North Branch, they made their way to Childe's Meadows and turned onto the McCain Trail. Darkness began to set in, and overhead great mounds of thunderhead loomed, while other banners of cloud obscured Wahgalu itself. Sunset came in a rush of crimson, and thunder could be heard roaring high up on the mountain.

"It's officially Mt. Lassen now on all the maps," he remarked as they approached Wilson Lake, where True Bear had spent many childhood hours observing geese, mudhens, loons, and the resident pair of blue herons. "Call it a final indignity, the official conquest of the land. Names, Gringo names. *Wahgalu*, the Yahi word—but now your people are gone, and the name drifts out of human memory. *Tehama*, the Maidu word—that would vanish also, but it became the name of the Goddamned county, and so is officially and forever recorded on all maps of the state. *Wawlem* handles on everything, and even the Oidoing-koyos have forgotten their old terms—never use them anymore. Well, the mountain will blow up one day and cover all of us. Pardon McCain's minor diatribe, Fanny. It's been a long while since I've killed two men in one day. . . ."

Lightning, close by, spitting bark from a sugarpine on the hill above. A blast of sound.

Then rain—sudden, hammering drops of moisture, lashing down out of the sky.

"Dad's wrong!" True Bear called out. "Ben always says I don't have enough sense to come in out of the rain, but I've got it figured out this time. By God, woman, let's take shelter—you remember that grove of firs on the other side of the lake? Inform your mare that it's time to make tracks. . . ."

They thumped their heels to the horses' sides and went galloping through rain-filled dusk, rounded the lake, and drew up beside the thicket.

Laughing, both of them laughing, they led their animals back under overlaced branches of the fir tangle, turned to one another, and embraced.

"You're crazy, True Bear McCain! And I'm even more crazy for being with you. We've murdered three men, and now the Whiteman's law is going to come after us. Do you realize what's happened today?"

"Law?" he grinned. "That's nothing to worry about. In the first place, we were just defending ourselves, and in the second place, no one's ever going to find the remains. Just hope their horses had sense enough to get out ahead of the flames. Nothing to worry about, I suppose—horses are amazingly intelligent in certain situations. They *know* fire's dangerous. Well, the day started out all right. The first half hour wasn't bad. . . ."

"We need some fire right now. I don't think this thunder-storm's going to ease off. The noise—it sounds like Coyote's waking up."

"About time, too. I was beginning to lose faith in the Old Gentleman. The duff's still dry. Matter of fact, we're going to have to be careful not to burn the grove down. A big green tent, that's what we've got."

"Your parents' ranch—it's just the other side of the little ridge. Maybe we should go. . . ."

"And miss another chance to sleep on Mother Earth? Light the fire. I'll break off some dead twigs. Hell, we'd have to beat the horses to make them venture forth."

"Talk English," Fanny said.

"Of man's first disobedience, and the fruit of that forbidden tree, whose mortal taste brought death into the world, and all our woe, with loss of Eden, till one greater Man restore us, and regain the blissful seat—or so expatiated one Johann Von Milton—and thus hath it gone, from that day unto the present."

"What in heaven's name are you babbling about?"

"Home," he replied. "It's good to be home—the Prodigal Son returns from his exile and brings his true love with him. Light the fire, Fire Woman. I shall trek through *Sturm und Drang* to fetch us coffee water."

"Books Billy? *Crazy Bill*, that's a better name."

FULL DARKNESS came on, and after an hour or so beneath shelter of the fir copse, the storm continuing unabated, pre-cipitation began to work its way though—heavy drops hissing in the fire and spattering on their faces and clothing. Rene-gade and the mare nosed their way in through close-grown firs and stood, looking expectant, at the edge of firelight, the two equine heads appearing almost disembodied in the thin, flickering glow.

"We need another tent," True Bear said.

He unrolled their blankets and, using a length of cord, fastened one in place, its corners lashed to four saplings.

"That'll keep the wet off for a time, at least. You horses stay back! There's room for humans, no one else."

True Bear and Fanny lay down side by side, talked a little, and listened to storm noises. Occasional lightning flashes brought moments of blue-white illumination so that boles of firs stood out, and then darkness rushed back.

"It's almost like being born all over again, True Bear McCain . . . I mean . . . I don't know what I mean. But I'm glad we're here together."

Fanny turned toward him, pressed her face against his chest, and clung to him.

He stroked her hair, and lay staring out at the faces of two disconsolate horses.

"Something's fouled up the Master Plan, but perhaps we've made the right adjustments now. This is the way things should have been all along."

"I think you're right," Fanny whispered. "Will it last forever—this way? I think I'd like that."

"Makes no difference. Change is a powerful force, Auna-yi. We can't stop it, can't even really alter it. Yet perhaps individual human beings, if they've once perceived the drift of nature, can manage to live their lives in accord with that and in accord with their own desires as well. We have this little space of time together, and if we're very clever and don't fight the river's current, then perhaps. . . ."

"I think I can alter something," Fanny said, her voice lower, more throaty than he had heard before.

She reached down, placed her hand between his legs, cupped his maleness, and squeezed softly.

He groaned, clung to her.

"You've got troubles if you keep doing that," he whispered.

"Only a little trouble," she laughed, "but it's growing larger. I wonder how big it will get. . . ."

She unbuttoned his trousers, grabbed hold, laughed again.

Then they were mad to get free of their clothing, and the garments came off.

Male and female, their mouths joined, hands grasping, exploring.

Fanny attempted to pull True Bear onto her, but he slipped from her arms and slid down so that his face was pressing against her womanhood.

"You mustn't do that—nobody does that. . . ."

"Yes they do," he murmured, and then she felt his tongue searching, touching. Small flames of sensation ran through her. For a moment she relaxed and let it happen.

Then she tried to wriggle away.

"Hold still, Wahtaurisi-yi. Give in, let go, listen to the rain. There's something I want to do. . . ."

She closed her eyes, placed her thumb between her teeth— and ceased to resist what was happening.

It lasted, lasted, and the part of her mind that was still consciously aware began to worry that his tongue might be growing tired.

Then the flames became more intense, wave after wave, rising and falling.

Her entire body was shuddering, and she heard an odd moaning wail, a cry she dimly recognized as her own.

She gasped for breath, rolled her head from one side to the other.

Darkness washed in over her, and she spread her legs, raising her knees as he entered into her, gasping for breath as male strength penetrated, penetrated, and after a time shuddered, trembled, collapsed forward, covering her.

"Wahtaurisi-yi . . . I. . . ."

They clung to one another, droplets of water blowing in, burning against their skins.

"What happened," she whispered, "never before . . . I thought I was dying, True Bear McCain. No one has ever . . . touched me that way before . . . no one has ever. . . ."

His weight was heavy upon her, and dimly she realized that he had passed into sleep.

Withdrawing, slowly, slowly, I can feel you, True Bear, I can feel you drawing back out of me, I don't want that to happen, not ever. . . .

He mumbled something she couldn't quite hear and then rolled over, pulling the blankets away with him.

She reached for the heavy cloth, pulled it toward her, and covered both of them. She still wished to tell him something when sleep took her.

An indeterminate passage of time, and then sensations of light and cold dampness. Fanny awoke. Water had pooled on the stretched blanket above and was dripping steadily.

"It's morning!" she said, pushing at him, momentarily resenting this great lout of a man lying beside her. But she began to laugh, couldn't help herself. She stood up naked,

searched about for her clothing, and found that her garments
were also wet.

True Bear yawned and rubbed at his eyes.

"Has the world ended yet?" he asked. "There seems to be
a goddess standing over me. Artemis, call off the dogs. I
promise not to look next time."

"Wake up, you damned fool. The rain's stopped. It's time
to get going."

He sat up.

"Why is it time?" he asked. "Come to me, sleek vixen of
the forest. My member's all swollen again—I can't go waggling home this way. I need help, Auna-yi. Is that really your
name? Take a look at my problem."

She stood over him, hands on hips.

"All right," she said. "Lie back and close your eyes. I'll
give you some . . . medication."

She dropped to both knees, straddled him, at the same
time wondering idly where the horses had gotten to.

But just before he groaned, quivered, and reached out to
pull her down against him, she heard one of the animals
crashing about through a tangle of brush.

"NOW WARRIOR SLEEP some more," True Bear said as he lay
there grinning. "Squaw humps real good."

"Get up and get dressed, you lazy bastard. I came here to
visit, not to spend all my time tending to your needs. Get up,
True Bear McCain, or I'll whip you with a fir branch."

"An interesting idea," he replied. "We'll have to try that
some time when we can't think of anything else. Even the
bullfrogs are applauding—listen to them. You're all sweaty,
Auna-yi. What have you been doing, anyway?"

"I'm going to go get a fir branch. Our clothes are wet,
naturally. Big warrior makes very poor lodge. Why didn't you
attach one end lower than the other?"

"Why didn't you point out the potential difficulty last night?"

He got to his feet, and the two embraced. They stood
together naked, kissing.

"I'm getting another . . . idea," he said, blowing into her
ear.

"To hell with your ideas."

"Get your mind off mating, Wahtaurisi-yi, Auna-yi, Fanny.

I mean—let's go for a swim. What do you say? Why should the frogs be the only ones to enjoy themselves? They're going crazy out there. Storm's over, the rainstorm at least."

She reached up, pulled at his hair, and nodded.

Then they were at the water's edge, and the frogs went quiet.

"We've disturbed them," Fanny said. "They were happy, and now we've ruined it all."

"It's not us," True Bear said, pointing. "Look who's come to pay a call at the Great Frog Pond in the Sky."

Across the small lake, a blue heron was in the process of wading stiff-legged through lily-pad shallows, its long, heavy-looking beak poised above the water. On the bank another heron stood, one wing raised at an odd angle, preening feathers.

Fanny smiled.

"Herons live a long time, True Bear. Perhaps they never die, I don't know. But I think maybe those are the same birds we used to see sometimes when we came here years ago."

She waved to them, but the birds seemed singularly unimpressed by two featherless creatures standing together across the water.

"They're also not particularly friendly," he said, hardly listening to his own words, instead staring at Fanny, the lithe curves of her bronze body that seemed to be glowing in morning light that refracted through wisps of steam rising from the lake's still surface.

When the man and the woman dived into the water, the herons flew, great wings driving the big birds upward through mists and toward the forest beyond.

True Bear and Fanny glided beneath the surface, moving as if in unison, and then emerging several yards from shore. They stood up in water to her chin and his chest, and once more they began kissing.

"I think we've left a couple more worlds behind us," he said as they waded shoreward, "but they weren't very good worlds in the first place."

"This one's much better," she agreed. "Maybe we should keep it."

*   *   *

THE SKY WAS CLEARING rapidly as True Bear McCain and
Fanny Bitler reached the top of the low ridge overlooking
Oidoing-koyo, and steam-banners were trailing westward from
Wahgalu's summit. A heavy odor of smoke remained in the
air, however, either not expunged by a single night's rainfall
or replenished in the aftermath of storm—from fires still
burning twenty-five or thirty miles eastward, near Fredonoyer
and Coyote Peak.

McCain turned in his saddle. He gazed about.

Two great smoke plumes marked the horizon, one east and
the other southeast.

He shook his head.

"We had a downpour, but maybe the clouds never got to
where they were needed. In any case, it looks like the devil's
still at work. Wind's shifted, too. One or two real hot days,
and this whole damned area could be one big, black, smoldering forest of skeletons. I don't like the looks of this, not at
all."

"Everything's wet right now, but. . . ."

"Right. With wind and heat both working. . . ."

Fanny recalled vividly a lightning-caused fire that had burned
out of control far down in Mill Creek Canyon one summer—
how it had raced to the ridgetops and along basalt rims to
either side of the stream, spilling over the top beside the
crags at *huk-umi* and then burning sluggishly downward but
exhausting itself without scorching the *an-sxa*, the hollow
area along the creek. And for one terrible moment, she could
actually envision fires raging across the ridgetop they were on
and spilling down to ranch and village below.

They urged their horses forward, downslope to the place
Benjamin McCain had long ago named Upper Eden.

THIRTY-TWO

Gideon Whitney's News

[July–August 1874]

TRUE BEAR AND FANNY RODE directly to the McCain ranch house, tethered their horses, and climbed the front steps. True Bear hesitated for a moment, actually thought about knocking on the familiar door, then opened it—allowing Fanny to pass in ahead of him.

No one was in the house.

"Maybe they went out with Big Woodpecker, to check cattle. Jesus—surely they wouldn't have come looking for me, not with fires burning all over hell."

"You're not a good detective," Fanny laughed. "There's a fresh pot of beans and bacon on the stove—still simmering, from the smell of it."

"Right, right," he said. "Just testing you, that's all. I smelled the beans immediately. Well, where the hell are they?"

He tossed the black felt hat with the bullet hole through its crown onto a cushion of one of the chairs, moved aimlessly about the big front room, examining things that seemed to have instantly emerged and materialized directly from his memories of them—including a framed copy of Lincoln's portrait and next to that a similar likeness of the great Puritan poet and theologian, John Milton, a man the elder McCain sometimes referred to as *the god*.

403

"Overgrown liar," Fanny said sotto voce, "Men never notice details."

True Bear walked to the back door, opened it, gazed off
toward barns and village beyond.

"Mom! Dad!" he bellowed. "I'm home!"

Fanny began to laugh.

"Now you sound like the True Bear I remember, only your
voice is much louder."

Then he saw them walking toward the house, Ben limping
slightly and using a cane—something he hadn't done when
they were together in Reno just a few days earlier.

Acorn Girl pulled at her husband's coatsleeve, let go, and
then began to run.

True Bear took a few strides toward her, and then she was
in his arms—or he was in hers.

He kissed his mother on both cheeks, and Ooti, wiping at
her eyes, immediately reached up to brush the hair back out
of his face.

"You are truly grown up now," she said. "I should be very
cross with you—why didn't you come straight home? When I
saw Ben and Woodpecker riding in without you, I was afraid
something awful had happened. Well—did you bring Fire
Woman with you? Or didn't she wish to come?"

"She's standing over in the doorway," he replied, turning
suddenly as if to assure himself Fanny hadn't disappeared.

"Ben told me . . . where you found Auna-yi," Ooti said.
"Sometimes women as well as men do what they have to in
order to survive, but now I think perhaps she's embarrassed
to meet me. We must be very careful to see that she's made
to feel welcome here, the same as always."

Benjamin McCain walked to where his son and wife were
standing, extended a big, calloused hand.

"Glad you found time to stop by, Son," he said, winking.

Ooti turned and proceeded to the house, met Fanny, and
embraced her.

Father and son watched as the two women hugged and
began to talk.

"By God!" Ben said, pushing his spectacles back onto the
bridge of his nose, "from this distance I can't tell which one's
the kid and which one's the sedate old married lady. Your
mother carries her years well, doesn't she? But hell, she's

still a young woman, after all—made the mistake of marrying
a curmudgeon. I was actually four years older than she is now
when we started helling around together."

True Bear squeezed his father's hand and grinned, aware
perhaps for the first time of the intense pride Ben felt for his
wife. The son nodded.

*A well-preserved woman, doesn't look like someone in her
mid-forties, and that's a fact. An unusual union produced
me, unusual all the way around.*

"You must have gotten a look at the fires—the world's
parched, Son, even North Branch is running low. Dry lightning, and we're going to have a jolly time. Woodpecker and
the boys spent all day yesterday sharpening every tool we've
got on the place, and we've had the kids cutting fireline
through the grass around all the buildings. It's not much in
the way of preparation, but what is? You and Auna-yi come
up through Quincy, or over the Susanville Trail?"

"Quincy. When we got to Chester yesterday, and Tumbleweed Till said the Fredonyer was closed—the whole mountain's burning. Rained like hell at Wilson Lake last night, and
I was hoping. . . ."

"Our Wilson Lake? What in hell's name were you doing
there? Why didn't you ride on down?"

"Seemed like a good place to sleep—back in under the
firs."

"If that don't beat all! True Bear, if you're trying to court
the lady, and that's my guess, then. . . . Son, you and I are
going to have to have a man-to-man talk. She's used to
feather beds, as I gather."

True Bear slapped his father on the shoulder.

"Peculiar methods, Dad, but they work. Trust me. By the
way, we had to kill three trailhands down toward Greenville.
You ever heard of a man named Westley McLaughlin? He
and two others were roughing Fanny a bit and . . . well, she
shot one of them."

Benjamin McCain scowled.

"You pulling my leg, or have you forgotten why it was we
sent you East in the first place?"

"There wasn't any option, I'm afraid. It was a fair fight, as
these things go."

Ben glanced in Ooti's direction.

"Not a word of this to your mother, now, you hear me?"

SMOKE STILL HUNG heavy in the air for the next several days, and heat continued unabated. Afternoon clouds formed up and down the range, obscuring Wahgalu's summit, but no more rain fell, and what lightning occurred was restricted to the peaks.

With Ooti presiding, the Oidoing-koyo Maidus held their traditional summer celebration, despite the gathering sense of doom precipitated by smoke-filled air, the older people dressing up in costumes of Spirit Impersonators, but the younger people, now generally *civilized*, were not much interested in ancient Kuksu rituals, most preferring square dancing to the accompaniment of fiddle music, the latter supplied by Big Woodpecker's father, Blue Loon.

Despite the return of her son, and Fanny Bitler with him, Acorn Girl was saddened. The last remnants of the magic rites deemed so important both by her own father and grandfather, Kuksu Man and Hurt Eagle, had lost their potency with the youths of the village. Two older people had died during the previous few months, two Panos who'd undertaken the revenge-quest with her a quarter of a century earlier, Crane—the widow of Hurt Eagle, and Goose Leader— whose Kulkumish village had been massacred. Who now would gather acorns, since everyone had ground wheat flour? And who would oversee the placement of *Ustu* poles at the autumn grieving time? Who would worry about *the burning* when the entire world was on fire?

And then it appeared almost as an omen—like a being out of the Spirit World, a great male grizzly, *Pano*, her own totem.

While Blue Loon made music with his fiddle, and the young people stepped lightly back and forth in a square dance, the bear, growling and coughing, came lumbering through the village. There were not very many grizzlies left in the mountains, and the people, more curious than frightened, drew back on either side to allow the creature to pass through their midst.

He had come from somewhere out of one of the fires that

continued to burn throughout the area. His fur was clearly singed, and he smelled very strange.

Was this an omen of some catastrophe that would soon be upon them? Once, when Ooti was hardly more than a girl, Pano had come to her, had spoken to her. But now the great bear itself was fleeing.

Other things vexed her mind as well.

Her son True Bear, she realized, was deeply in love with Fanny—that was plain enough. What was not clear to Acorn Girl was how Fanny felt about matters. As part-owner of a fancy Reno whorehouse, Fanny was much changed from the child who once shared their home—or from the young woman who came to them in desperate need of help—weapons and supplies for the Modocs who'd taken refuge in the lava beds to the north and who fought the bluecoats and lost, were now dead, executed as though they'd been horsethieves or murderers. Fanny had turned completely away from the world of her childhood and young adulthood. She was now playing by Whiteman's rules and was on her way to becoming wealthy in her own right.

Acorn Girl feared her son would suffer heartbreak, a final loss of and severance from his own boyhood. The education he'd received at the Whiteman's college did not make him less emotionally vulnerable. Even as a child, the range and intensity of his feelings had always somewhat frightened her. Such a person, as big and strong and healthy as he was, could be hurt—and hurt badly.

She listened as Ben and True Bear talked about what might be done to protect the McCain and Maidu lands in the event of Ben's death—a subject her husband seemed literally obsessed with of late, though beyond the usual problems of old age, she could detect no real illness in him. Indeed, these past few months Ben had become genuinely amorous once more and was forever tweaking her on the rear and wishing to make love, sometimes even in the mornings.

She understood the legal problems concerning the land, but what use would she have for a cattle ranch in the event that her husband passed into the Spirit World? The difference in their ages was not important. If that did happen, she was resolved to join him immediately. She would have to speak of this plan to True Bear—somehow make him understand. However, some men lived to be a hundred winters old, Hurt Eagle, for instance. And Benjamin McCain, she firmly believed, was simply too strong, too committed to life itself to sicken suddenly and die. No, he was one of those who forever prepared for the worst while quietly continuing to hope for the best. This man of hers, he would never die easily. As Acorn Girl assessed the matter, the two of them still had many years to be together.

Was it possible that she might yet bear him a second child? Other women her age had sometimes managed to have a late birth. Perhaps she would begin to calculate the number of days from each of her moons, just as she had read in one of Ben's books. The woman-moons still came with regularity.

A WEEK LATER Big Woodpecker returned from chasing strayed cattle, and he rode directly to the McCain house, wanting to see Fanny.

He'd met the missing band of Yahis just down from the wagon road that now crossed over one shoulder of Wahgalu. They'd come to the mountain to drink sulphur water but had not fled when he approached them.

"Part of the news is bad," he said. "Wolf Tracker died in his sleep three weeks ago. Smoke Woman speaks a little English, and she told me how it happened. Yes, your mother's alive and well—she would like to see you, Auna-yi, but she's afraid to come to the ranch, even though I told her you were here. Perhaps she didn't really believe me, I don't know. The boy Wood Duck is becoming a man—it will not be much longer. Salmon Man is sick, but Broken Willow is able to take care of him—something's wrong with his foot, it swells up sometimes. That's why they were at the sulphur springs. They've searched everywhere for some other group of Yahis, but now none remains. A few more years and they'll all be gone, unless they're able to find a wife for Wood Duck—but where can they go?"

"So," Fanny nodded, "little Wood Duck is about to become *Ishi*. Salty Dan tells me some Yana people are living outside of Red Bluff, where the men work for orchardists and cattle ranchers. Those Yanas are cousins to the Yahis, so maybe Wood Duck could go there to look for a wife when the time comes. But that will never happen, it cannot happen.

Those who are left will die in the forest—Dan Clayton or Bob Anderson will find them one day and kill them. I am childless, and my blood is half-White. Wolf Tracker's people are doomed—soon they will all vanish. Grandfather's dead? He saw the end coming and taught me English—he said that I alone would find my way into the future. He wanted greatgrandchildren, but I could not give them to him, and now. . . . My heart grieves for Wolf Tracker—I owe my life to him. All this time I believed he was already gone, and now I'm too late. My mother's well, though?"

"The three of us will go looking for Smoke Woman and the others," True Bear said. "Perhaps among us we'll be able to convince them to come here, to Oidoing-koyo."

He put his arms about Fanny, and the moment he did so, she began to sob. She clung to him with an intensity that he both understood and did not understand at all.

A WALL OF GRAY CLOUD drifted in from the west, and rain began to fall—softly at first and then gaining in intensity, soaking dry ground and hissing through already yellowing leaves of oak and maple, droplets clinging to curling barkpeels of manzanita and madrone.

The fires that raged throughout the area died, leaving only a smoking snag here and there by the time the storm passed.

Bluejays cried out, mocking the voices of hawks and eagles, and nighttime music of coyotes drifted down from the ridges above Oidoing-koyo.

Then the weather began to heat up once more, and already there were reports of small fires burning, one of these on Jenne Mountain, not far from Pinetown.

Colonel Gideon Whitney and twenty soldiers rode in to Upper Eden, the military officer accompanied also by George Livingstone, the dapper middle-aged lawyer from Washington, D.C., emissary and negotiator for the Federal Government.

Benjamin McCain greeted the officer and the government lawyer, invited them into the house, and introduced them to Ooti.

"We've never met before, Mr. McCain," Whitney said, "but I know a great deal about you—probably more than you'd like to be the case. For instance, I have it on good

authority that your last name is actually Goffe and that at one
time you taught literature at Yale College. In your capacity as
acting Indian agent here at Oidoing-koyo, however, you've
been a genuine blessing to us. In all these years since your
appointment, we've had not the slightest bit of trouble with
your band of Maidus. But everything comes to an end
eventually—the state's growing rapidly, and the governor, as
well as President Grant himself, wishes to have the remaining loose ends of the Indian problem tied up. Things elsewhere aren't as quiet as they are here. In Kansas the
Cheyennes are still causing trouble at times, and troops have
now been dispatched to Dakota Territory to protect railway
surveyors and gold miners from the Sioux tribes. There's
some talk of an Indian confederation, and we don't even
know positively which way the Crows will go, though they've
been helpful in other matters."

"Goddamn it, Whitney, get to the point. So you know
who I am, and you've come to arrest me, is that it?"

"Quite the contrary, Mr. McCain," George Livingstone
said, rubbing an open hand over his bald spot. "The Government owes you a great debt, all things considered—after
certain early irregularities following your arrival in California,
you've been a model citizen and an exemplary Indian agent,
unpaid except in terms of authority, but an example for
others, nonetheless. Besides, officially speaking, Benjamin
Goffe is dead. As a matter of fact, we've discovered records
indicating that a Peruvian miner, unable to speak English and
thus defend himself, was lynched for having murdered you—in
Grass Valley it was, nearly a quarter of a century ago."

"Then what do you gentlemen want?"

"Nothing, actually," Whitney replied. "But as I was saying,
situations change and. . . . Well, most of the rancherias are
going to be disbanded. I'm certain you've already been informed of this policy. Most of the land surrounding the
Upper Eden rancheria is already in your name, and the government herewith cedes the Maidu holdings to you as a way
of expressing its gratitude for a job well done. The Indians in
the village, however, will be given new land on the Round
Valley Reservation, with the Covelos, over in the Coast
Mountains— they'll be provided with housing and, of course,
food and supplies."

"You're forcing them to leave, then, even though I'm willing to have them remain for as long as they wish? Jesus, Colonel, you don't understand the situation here at all. These people have created a profitable settlement for themselves. You yourself admit they've never caused anyone any trouble. . . ."

"No one will be forced to leave," Livingstone said. "I'm instructed to explain what it is that the Government's offering and then to hold an election. If some choose to stay with you, that's fine. But the Government will provide new housing, a medical facility, a B.I.A. school, allowances for food and clothing. I don't mind telling you that the whole concept has been partially generated from the example of what you've accomplished here, Benjamin McCain. You're in your seventies now, and we could hardly expect you to keep on much longer. . . ."

"There's another matter," Whitney continued, "and that's pressure from the ranchers at Vina, Oroville, Chico, and other Valley towns. They want the Indians moved away from mountain pasture areas because of a sustained pattern of predation against their herds, or so they claim. My own experience is otherwise, but old notions die hard. Daniel Clayton has made certain complaints against your Indians, I have to be honest with you, Ben. He's just purchased the Childe Ranch to the south of you, and my map tells me his land now touches corners with yours at the edge of the wagon trail. We must avoid trouble wherever we're able. In short, George will meet with the Maidus this evening, and an election will be held tomorrow. . . ."

THAT AFTERNOON True Bear, Big Woodpecker, Fanny, and Yellow Grass returned from their second unsuccessful attempt to discover the whereabouts of Smoke Woman and the remaining Yahis—were astonished to find bluecoats camped in neat rows of tents beside North Branch, not far from the McCain sawmill.

If that were not surprise enough, the news of what was about to happen was stunning, and Big Woodpecker and Yellow Grass went immediately in search of Blue Loon, Goat's Head, and the other village leaders. Many Maidus, as they saw, were already assembled in an empty corral, engaged in heated discussion and awaiting the arrival of the Washington lawyer, who would "explain everything."

A far greater surprise for Fanny Bitler was the presence at Upper Eden of both Gideon Whitney and George Livingstone.

Her two former lovers were astonished to see her as well, and each in turn hugged her warmly—then entered into what appeared to True Bear to be a quiet contest as to which man was more adept at paying Fanny compliments.

True Bear shook hands with the officials, mumbled something about having to tend to horses, and quickly left the house. He cooled out Renegade and Fanny's mare, took them to the barn, and then wandered out to survey the soldiers' encampment.

From a basalt formation to the immediate north, he concluded, he could in all likelihood utilize his Henry repeater to remove at least half the troops. There was a certain amount of comfort in the thought.

FIRST GIDEON WHITNEY TOOK HER ASIDE, and the two of them walked together for a brief inspection of the sawmill, now standing idle because the Maidus were involved in a conclave.

Whitney took note of a big waterwheel Ben McCain had designed as a means of providing power to a steel axle and flywheel that operated a long belt-drive to a shining and carefully filed buzzsaw. Sections of log, the colonel observed, were apparently skidded in by means of mules, levered to the sawyer's platform, and there cut into planks and beams. At the far end of the operation was a small shingle mill, hand-operated.

"McCain's a clever old bastard," he said, "always thinking. I'm told his Herefords usually bring top dollar at the stock auctions in Red Bluff. The amazing thing is that the Indians work for him so happily."

Fanny nodded.

"It's simple, Gid," she replied. "They're working for themselves mostly. The Maidus are all well-off, as these things go. Had there been someone with vision among the Modocs— had *your* government not chosen to force Captain Jack's people onto Klamath Reservation, where they were obliged to live among people who'd always been their enemies, there would never have been a war at all. Kintpuash didn't want to fight you, and you know it's true. Well, I understand things much more clearly, now that I've been 'emancipated' for a time—but the main thing I've learned is how stupid, how blind most of you are. Oh, not you personally, of course—you realized all along what the problems were, but you had to follow orders."

"Yes," Whitney scowled, gazing off across meadows to where a hundred or so fat-looking cattle grazed, "my orders. Fanny, I just learned two months ago that you were in Reno. You've got a partnership with Huntington himself, or so I've been told. . . ."

Fanny smiled, gazed into Whitney's eyes—noting, not for the first time, a softness, even a sense of melancholy that must occasionally have troubled the man greatly. She felt very kindly disposed toward Gideon Whitney—who, after all, had not only saved her life but had made arrangements necessary for her to shift quietly from the doomed world of the Redman to the at least temporarily prosperous world of the Whiteman.

"I intended to come see you, Fanny, even though last time you stole my horse and went off without even saying good-bye," Whitney complained.

"Didn't George give you my message? You must surely have found your horse. . . ."

"Yes, the sonofabitch gave me the message, and gloated over it like Lucifer. That was the hardest thing of all. But you're prospering in Reno? I understand that. . . ."

"Yes, Gid. I'm still a whore, but now I'm a wealthy whore. You don't like me to say that, but it's true. I have no apologies. One must do what one is able, and I had only a woman's body and my wits to work with. Then I met Salty Dan Dolliver, the gambler, and together we ran one hell of a streak of good luck. We'd have accomplished our purposes with or without the railroad man, but Mr. Huntington certainly gave us a boost. I'm very good at what I do, as you'll recall."

Whitney grimaced.

"My wife back East, she's applied for a divorce. I don't blame her, actually. She's from a wealthy family, and soon she'll be free. But the other side of that coin—I'll be free as well. I've never been especially pleased with your choice of professions, Fanny, but in the final analysis, it makes no difference. I've loved you for a long while now—you know that. I don't think you ever felt the same toward me, but that's not important either. The reason I intended to come to Reno to find you was . . . is . . . to ask you to marry me. I'll be retiring from the military soon, and I have numerous profitable business interests. We could move to San Francisco, if you'd like. There would be respectability, security. But most important, I love you, damn it. You don't have to answer just now—yes, I see the doubt in your eyes. But I want you to be my wife, Fanny Bitler."

"Dear Gid," she replied, shaking her head at the same time, "no. It would never work, and you know it. When you come to Reno, we'll talk some more, if you like, but you deserve better than a runaway halfbreed like me. I'm uneducated, and you'd never be able to forget what I've. . . ."

But she could see that Colonel Whitney wasn't really hearing what she was saying.

BACK AT THE McCAIN HOUSE, she found George Livingstone on the rear porch, hurriedly making notes on a pad of paper—a revision of the outline for his speech to the Indians.

Whitney walked past, into the house, and Fanny sat down beside Livingstone.

The lawyer adjusted his glasses, reached for his hat.

"I've been called 'that bloody long-winded barrister' more than once in my life," he said, "so this time I'll be a man of few words, albeit words carefully chosen. Nothing to do with what I've got to say to the Indians. Damn you, Fanny Bitler! I had a mistress once, and she became far more important to me than I ever realized at the time. I even set her up in her own house and encouraged her to go into business, which she did, with what's turned out to be astonishing success, according to all reports. In the process, she left me broken-hearted, quite painfully aware of what I'd lost, what I'd had and never valued properly. In truth, I've been one lonely sonofabitch ever since. Now this woman owns part of the Central Pacific Railroad, or so Colonel Whitney's story runs, and my beloved former mistress has long since forgotten her old patron, the long-winded barrister. I leave off the 'bloody' in consideration of brevity, you understand. So now I'll get to the point.

Whitney's been telling me all the way up here that he was of a mind to venture down to Reno to find you and to ask you to marry him. Has he already done that?"

"Yes, George, but that's between me and Gideon, I think."

"Don't be coy, Fan. This is George Livingstone you're talking to. We've never had secrets before—an open and honest relationship, I'd say. So what was your answer to the estimable colonel's matrimonial proposal?"

"I'm not sure why I ever liked you," she said, smiling and leaning forward to give him a pecking kiss on the mouth. "The simple fact is—you're a terrible person, and not an ounce of romance in you. If you must know, I declined. This girl just isn't the marrying type."

George Livingstone nodded and winked.

"Precisely as I thought," he said. "Well, then, since you're not otherwise engaged, may I propose that you return to being my mistress? Don't answer. Listen. I haven't Huntington's millions, but I do have a considerable fortune, as you know. And I'm not a tightwad. Whatever the railroad baron's providing you with, I'll double the offer. Goddamn it, Fan, do you want me to grieve my soul away in utter loneliness and black despair? After having made love with you, it's absolutely *nothing* with anyone else."

"That's a lovely compliment, George, and I know I owe you a great deal, far more than I'll ever be able to repay. I don't wish to be anyone's wife, and not anyone's mistress either, I'm afraid."

The lawyer nodded, and coughed discreetly.

"Well, I've got to go convince the savages of their best interest. What about Huntington, though?"

"A business proposition, George, nothing more than that."

George Livingstone picked up his notes, rose to his feet.

"Fanny Bitler, I miss you more than you'll ever know."

He turned, stepped into the house to get Whitney. His mind, Fanny realized, had already addressed itself to the matter immediately at hand.

THIRTY-THREE

Miss Bitler's Decision

[August 1874]

LIVINGSTONE PUT THE BEST POSSIBLE FACE ON things, and when he was finished with his presentation, he graciously answered questions for some time.

"Is the Government telling the people of Oidoing-koyo that they must leave their lands and go to Round Valley?" Blue Loon demanded. "You say we must vote, but why may not each person decide for himself? And will we be paid for the lands that we have right now?"

"That's at least three questions, Chief, so let me take them one at a time. Yes, the Government would be pleased if everyone went to Round Valley—and, of course, the people will not have to work so hard as they do here. Nonetheless, I've secured a special dispensation for those who wish to remain with Agent McCain. They may do so, if they wish. So that answers your second question—the vote isn't binding upon all. If you have compelling reasons for remaining here, then you may do so. The third question. No, you're not going to be paid for the land you presently occupy. Instead you'll be given new land, forty acres to each household and an additional forty acres to each male of marriageable age. As I say, houses will be provided, school for the children, an infirmary—livestock, clothing, blankets, a supplemental allowance of foodstuffs each year."

"But we own this land," Blue Loon argued. "If you take it from us, then you must pay for it. For myself, I intend to stay here, on land that is mine."

Livingstone shook his head.

"This land was never yours—it belonged to the United States Government all along, though it was yours to use. Now the Government has given it to Agent McCain."

A murmur of angry disapproval went up.

Benjamin McCain had been sitting to one side, occasionally tapping the corral railing with his cane. Now he stood.

"My friends," he said. "I've had nothing to do with all this. According to what I'm told, your lands will in fact be deeded over to me. I could refuse to accept them, but then they'd simply be sold to someone else. So I will accept. For anyone who wishes to stay here, things will go on exactly as they have in the past. You've known me and trusted me for a long while. Trust me now. You're my friends, all of you, and just as I have looked out for your interests in the past, so will I in the future. What the Government offers you seems fair—reasonably fair. You must now decide among yourselves what to do."

With these words, Ben turned and walked away toward the ranch house, Ooti following half a step behind him, her face set into a mask of troubled anger.

Blue Loon rose again.

"We will talk among ourselves now," he said.

BY MIDMORNING the following day, the matter had been settled, but not to the overwhelming satisfaction of George Livingstone and Colonel Whitney, who suspected the area ranchers would continue to press for total removal.

A vote had been taken, in accord with official instructions, but it turned out to be a vote to stay. Less than a dozen of the younger people expressed a wish to go to Round Valley, however, and so Livingstone, Whitney, and the soldiers conducted these people over the ridge past Wilson Lake and on down the road westward, toward Chico and a new beginning somewhere across the Great Central Valley, to reservation life in the Coast Mountains.

In the aftermath of this sudden dislocation, Blue Loon and Goat's Head proceeded directly to the McCain ranch house.

Ben opened the door, and motioned for the two men to enter.

"I don't understand what has just happened," Goat's Head shrugged. "Now you own our lands, Ben? How can the Government do this to us?"

"I don't know. But at least this much is true—they can't take the land away from me, their own law prevents them from doing it. One way or another, I'll discover a means of deeding everything back to you and the others who've chosen to stay. The law will change within a few years, perhaps even sooner. Then things will be better for all of us."

Blue Loon scratched his head.

"Our people have always trusted you because you've been honest and fair with them—more than fair. You've given us the means to protect ourselves, and after all these years we are still here, even though many other tribes have been killed off or forced onto reservations. We'll continue to trust you, Benjamin McCain."

BIG WOODPECKER, True Bear, and Fanny rode off in search of Smoke Woman and the other Yahis, combing the ridges beneath Brokeoff and following down Digger Creek toward the butte of the same name—all without luck.

On the third day, however, they caught sight of an Indian boy not far from Battle Creek. Big Woodpecker called to him, but the lad immediately disappeared into a tangle of brush and basalt boulders.

Their attempt to follow the boy's trail proved fruitless, and they rode on toward Mill Creek Canyon, dropping down to the stream well below the old massacre site that had once been Wolopti village.

Here they came upon an Indian hideaway, but the residents had apparently seen them coming and had fled.

Fanny called out in the Yahi tongue, announced her name as *Fire Woman, daughter to Smoke Woman, granddaughter to Wolf Tracker.*

"We must wait now," Fanny said. "They've heard me, and you've already told them that I was at the ranch, Big Woodpecker. If they wish to see me, they will come."

"Wolf Tracker taught them the magic of vanishing into nothingness very well," True Bear nodded. "We've ridden fifteen miles, perhaps more, since we caught sight of the boy, and we haven't detected so much as a sign. It's simple luck that we came here, nothing more than that. Was the boy— Wood Duck, is it?—off hunting, or do you suppose they were all together in the first place? Whatever the case, our instinct brought us here."

Fanny shook her head and stared into a tangle downstream from where they sat on their horses.

"I hear something behind us," Big Woodpecker whispered.

They turned around slowly but still saw nothing.

Then a woman appeared, her hair streaked with gray and pulled back behind her head. She was very thin, and her face was weathered.

"Hello, Smoke Woman," Big Woodpecker said in greeting. "I've brought Fire Woman and True Bear to visit you. We have ridden a long way. . . ."

The woman approached to within a few steps, halted.

"Auna-yi? True Bear McCain—we could not recognize you from a distance. You are both grown now, you've changed greatly. My daughter, is it truly you?"

Fanny dismounted, walked slowly toward Smoke Woman.

Then the two embraced, clinging to each other for a long while and not speaking at all.

As True Bear and Big Woodpecker watched, other Yahis appeared from out of the brush along the creek—Wood Duck, Broken Willow, and Salmon Man, the latter with a mat of pounded cedar bark wrapped about one ankle, laced on with strips of deerhide.

"I AM THE LEADER now that Wolf Tracker has died," Smoke Woman said, speaking to Fanny in the Yahi tongue. "Salmon Man and Broken Willow insisted that I should lead, for I had shared Wolf Tracker's mind for many years, and he taught me as much as he could. We no longer speak Man Language and Woman Language—it was not necessary any longer. Now it's all the same language. I have taught the others a little English, because that's all I know."

"Mother, you must bring the people to McCain's ranch. You'll be welcome there. Several houses are empty now,

because a few Oidoing-koyos have left. Salmon Man needs
the Whiteman's medicine, I can see that. Big Woodpecker
told me he had met you at the sulphur springs on Wahgalu.
Wood Duck will be a man soon. He needs to learn English—he
needs to learn how to read and write. There are other children in Oidoing-koyo. I think you'll all be happy there—and
safe. Mother, I'm rich now—rich the way some of the Whites
are rich. I can pay Ben McCain for everything that you and
the others will need."

Smoke Woman glanced at True Bear, who was standing
with Big Woodpecker some distance away.

"Have you married him?" she asked.

"No. I was married once to a man named Red Turtle, but
the bluecoat soldiers killed him. Now I live among the Whites,
in a city to the east of the mountains."

"You will marry True Bear eventually. When I saw you two
together, I knew that you still loved each other, just as you
did when you were merely children. You've been apart for a
long while, Auna-yi, and now there's still strangeness between you, perhaps. But that will go away soon. Maybe when
you and True Bear are married, then we will come to visit at
Oidoing-koyo. That is possible. But not now. No, we have
chosen to follow the vision of Wolf Tracker, and his vision is
still alive, even though he has gone into the Spirit World."

"Tell me of the vision, Mother."

"It's not a good one, but we must follow it. Wolf Tracker
dreamed that we should remain in the lands that have always
been ours until we go into death. When we wandered beyond
Wahgalu, that was when you were stolen by the Saltus. It
was after that when Wolf Tracker left his body and went to
see Gray Squirrel, Lizard, and Rabbit. They told him what
he had to do. The fires in Wahgalu are coming to life again—
we've been up on the Sacred Mountain many times, we have
seen the signs. One day the mountain will explode, just as it
did in the time of the Ancient Ones, and fire will cover
everything. The Communicators did not tell him when this
would happen, did not say whether we would be alive to see
it. But it makes no difference. After the Fire Time, then Old
Coyote Man will create a new world, and things will once
more be as they were before the Saltus came to dig for gold
and raise cattle."

"Do you believe this, Mother?"

"Believe?" Smoke Woman asked, smiling as she might have smiled when Wahtaurisi-yi was only three winters old and had asked a foolish question. "I do not have to 'believe' what is true. This vision is all my people and I have left. There is something, Auna-yi, that I intended to tell you when you were old enough—but then the terrible thing happened, and I couldn't speak. You asked me once—do you remember the time?"

"What is it? I don't understand you. . . ."

"Floating Hawk was my husband—that was long ago, before you were born. The Saltus killed him, and afterward I was left for dead. But I didn't die. I got up and ran to *Nem eyoo*, the Big River, and its water carried me to safety. Then Wolf Tracker found me and brought me home. After that I learned I was with child, and I prayed the child belonged to Floating Hawk. But when you were born, I saw that your blood was half Saltu."

"And so I was named Wahtaurisi-yi. Yes, I know the story. You told me. Wolf Tracker told me. Everyone in the village knew I was different, but Wolf Tracker protected me and taught me English and even showed me things in the White Medicine Book. Why do you repeat it now, Smoke Woman?"

"There is something else, my daughter, something I never told you, and that is the name of your father. I heard his name called out when he took me. Other men were standing round, and they shouted at him and laughed. Perhaps now that you live among the Saltus, you will wish to go to him and ask him to help you. It has been many years, and perhaps he will do that. The man who is your father hates the Yahis, but how can he hate his own flesh? He has done many terrible things, but always Wolf Tracker would find a way to strike back. Now that Wolf Tracker is dead, perhaps you should be told."

Fanny stared at her mother, uncertain what was to come next.

This is not something I want to hear, this is not something I will ever need to know. . . .

She shook her head.

Smoke Woman studied her daughter's eyes, did not speak for a long while.

"Is it better for me to know, Mother?"

"I cannot be sure. Perhaps I should wait until after you've married True Bear. I give my word—I will come to visit you then."

"I cannot marry him. How can I explain so that you will understand? I cannot marry him because I love him. Yes, it's still the same as when we were children, but I cannot both live in the Whiteman's world and love anybody. It's too dangerous—does that make any sense?"

"No, but maybe you will think more clearly after a time. I have kept my secret from you because I wished to protect you, Auna-yi. Do you understand what I am saying? And now I don't know how soon the path I follow may end."

It could not possibly be Ben McCain—for otherwise my mother would never have allowed—would not speak of my marrying one who would be my half-brother. It isn't that I've known many Whitemen—is it possible that I've actually lain with my own father? No, that's madness—madness to think such a thing.

"What is . . . this man's . . . name? Yes, I think I need to be told now."

Fanny took a deep breath, waited.

"He is Clay-ton," Smoke Woman said. "He is the one who raped me that day near Table Mountain, close by the Big River."

It took a moment for the information to sink in, to register fully.

"Daniel Clayton, the rancher who led the massacre of our village? The one whose barns Wolf Tracker burned, whose cattle he killed? The one who has always been our greatest enemy?"

"Yes," Smoke Woman replied, "Clay-ton."

BIG WOODPECKER OFFERED to give his Jennings short-barreled cap-and-ball rifle to Wood Duck, supposing the outmoded weapon might still prove of great service in hunting. Though Woodpecker had a fine New Haven Volcanic repeater, he continued to carry the ancient Jennings, complete with supply of caps, rounds, powder, and wadding. Occasionally he even fired the weapon.

But Wood Duck either didn't comprehend English suffi-

ently to understand the offer, or perhaps, with no present to
ve in return, he simply pretended ignorance and continued
hold tightly to the yew-wood bow that he'd evidently made
mself and was quite proud of.

"Wood Duck is a fine hunter," Smoke Woman said. "He
rings us game when we're hungry, for Wolf Tracker and
almon Man have both given him instruction. We appreciate
ig Woodpecker's generosity, but we don't need a rifle. Guns
ake noise, and we are obliged to live in silence. . . ."

TRUE BEAR, Fanny, and Big Woodpecker returned to Upper
den, and upon their arrival, Ben McCain reported that a
umber of cattle had been stolen—primarily animals belong-
ng to the Maidus. Fences had been cut.

"Range hands, no doubt, men working for our new neigh-
or over the hill. The animals hadn't been branded as yet,
d that was invitation enough, I guess. Woodpecker, I think
e're going to have to convince your people that branding's
ssential. Maybe it wasn't before, but now's a different mat-
er. I presume Clayton will put a foreman and his family into
e Childe place as permanent residents, but summer's the
me when we're going to have to keep closest watch on the
nes. He'll probably be bringing up three or four hundred
ead, though perhaps not that many this year. The season's
rawing along."

Big Woodpecker nodded, his jaw set.

"Perhaps I should get some of the men from the village.
Ve will all ride over the hill and pay a visit—inspect our
eighbor's cattle. Branded or not, we know which animals are
urs."

"Sixteen heifers in all, as close as I can tell," Ben said.
Cattle have a habit of coming home on moonlit nights. . . ."

"Perhaps that can be arranged. True Bear and I will look
ings over."

"Maybe it's time for a few more cave burials, Dad. You
an't just ignore what's happened—that makes it hunting
eason."

Acorn Girl stared up at her hulking son, and when she
poke, her voice carried a tone of genuine authority.

"You are not, under any circumstances, to start a range war
r us, True Bear. The time may come, but it's not here yet.

You've just come back to us. We're not ready to lose you
again."

"I be good," True Bear grinned—and then tweaked hi:
mother's nose. "Not kill bad rancher until little warrior tell:
me to."

"Don't be playing with fire, Son," Ben said. "Now look—
maybe we can work out a plan. Something subtle. Like
said, cattle get lonely for their home pastures. It's a fact
Cows are good people—more loyal to their humans thar
we've got any right for them to be, considering their fate."

True Bear glanced from his father to his mother an
shrugged.

"We're not planning to ignore anything, Son," the elde
McCain continued. "If there's one thing I don't believe in
it's letting anyone push me around. That's Blind Ben's firs
rule of procedure. The bastards let my cows alone, though
Clayton's been told that most of the Oidoing-koyos are stayin
on, and I figure he's trying to give them second thoughts
Well, there's more than one way to handle the situation.'

"Is Dan Clayton at the Childe Ranch now?" Fanny asked.

Ben shook his head.

"Half a dozen cowhands, that's all. Ooti and I rode dow
there yesterday but didn't say anything about missing cattle
Talked with the foreman for a time—fella named Bob, not
bad sort, all things considered."

"Like being a cattle thief, for instance?" True Bear asked.

"Things like that," Ben replied.

"I'M GOING to have to go back to Reno," Fanny said. "Salt
Dan's probably wondering what's happened to me. He's no
strong on bookkeeping or riding herd on the girls. They ca
wrap him around their little fingers, and hardly a one's ver
good at keeping her room neat or at getting out of bed befor
early afternoon, for that matter. As long as I'm there t
enforce some kind of discipline, things run well enough, bu
Dan's mind runs to gambling tables and a smoothly operatin
bar. I suppose he actually sees my girls as a secondary enter
prise, and that's true in some way. But I need to retur
before any of my more ambitious ladies decide that it's tim
to go into business for themselves."

True Bear nodded, and made a gallant show of kissing her
and.

"I don't want you to go," he said. "We haven't had a
hance to visit Wilson Lake since we've been here."

She winked at him.

"Strange man, a very strange man. There are better places,
rue Bear, than a leaking, makeshift tent in the middle of a
ownpour. Harvard College may have educated you, but it
urely didn't provide you with much in the way of common
ense. The stolen cattle, for instance. You'd like to ride down
here alone, confront Clayton's men, and wave your pistol at
hem—wouldn't you? It's not reasonable. You can't just keep
hooting people, no matter what they've done."

"Captain Jack was willing to take on the whole United
tates Army, and he almost pulled it off. What's happened to
ou, Fanny? You were with him. You rode south to Upper
den to get guns—you were ready to sacrifice yourself in
rder to help your Modoc friends. Now you seem willing to
urn the other cheek—you've gone Christian on me, I think.
he best way to handle a bully is to let him know that what
e wants to do is going to cost him, cost him dearly. Some
en are of the opinion that they don't have to act decent
ntil they've had their jaws broken. Yes, I'm going to get
ose cattle back—and I might just burn down the damned
nch house while I'm at it. It's a far better thing to die like a
an, with dignity, than to live like a coward, always having
buy someone or another off. Learned that from my fisher-
an friends—if I didn't already know it. I understand com-
letely why Wolf Tracker kept striking back at the ranchers,
ven though his people—your people—were on foot and
med with bows and lances, nothing else."

"Are you through with the lecture, True Bear?"

McCain stared at her. The self-generated anger drifted
way, anger that had been occasioned, in any case, not by
olen cattle but by something else.

"I want you to stay here," he said. "Auna-yi, I want you to
e my wife. We dreamed that once, both of us. You know
hat I'm saying is true. The dream was right, it was the
orld that got turned around, not us. You love me. Try to
ide it all you like, but I can tell. You love me, damn it, you
ways have."

Fanny smiled, touched her fingers to her lips, and then pressed them against True Bear's cheek.

"What's that supposed to mean?"

"You're right, True Bear. I do love you. And that's precisely why I have no intention of marrying you."

He gazed into the dark eyes, scowled.

"Well, I'll be a sorry sonofabitch!" he said.

TRUE BEAR RODE to the upper pastures, turned Renegade loose to graze as he would, and set up a long line of pinecones along a more-or-less horizontal shelf of lava rock.

He stood back twenty paces, set himself, drew, and fired.

The pinecones stared at him, unmoved.

"All right, you little bastards. . . ."

He replaced the pistol, set himself once more. . . .

He squinted toward the ledge as one of the cones, barely touched by his shot, spun off and bounced against the rock behind.

"Need bigger pinecones, maybe. Bigass sugarpine cones. Or else some cow thieves in front of me. . . ."

He repeated the ritual, and this time a cone exploded upward, leaping into the air.

McCain grinned momentarily, then forced a serious expression back onto his face.

The hand whipped down to the revolver, and an instant later gunsmoke drifted from the barrel end. Another pinecone hopped into the air.

"Do I get to shoot, too?"

McCain turned about quickly, gun in hand.

"Easy, True Bear. Don't go blasting away at your blood brother, for God's sake. I didn't steal any cattle."

"Woodpecker. . . . Didn't hear you walk up. Guess I was concentrating on my targets over there."

"Great Hunter got to listen," Big Woodpecker laughed. "Otherwise gets shot in the back while he's killing pinecones. Well, let me try it."

Big Woodpecker deliberately drew his own pistol, aimed and fired, the shot thudding against basalt, two or three inches low. He aimed a second time, squeezed the trigger, and sent one of the cones flying.

"All right, Peckerwood, do it with a fast draw. When the war comes, we've got to defend ourselves."

"Not very good at that," Big Woodpecker laughed. "That's why I sneak up behind people. Easier to shoot them from close range. Then by Gawd scalp 'em. True Bear, I've got some bad news for you, I'm afraid. That's actually why I came out to find you. Fanny—she's gone. On her way to Reno. Don't think her heart was in it, though. She started crying like a kid, cussing at herself all the while for doing it."

True Bear heard the words, shrugged, holstered his pistol, and then drew and fired, the shot running high and missing completely. A second shot struck one of the targets. McCain nodded, snapped out the cylinder, and ejected spent shells. He reloaded and then holstered the weapon.

"You talked to her?"

"Yep. She came down to my house after you rode off. I was over at the sawmill, so she spoke with Yellow Grass for a time—not about anything in particular, as I gather. When I got back, though, she really unloaded on us."

"For instance?"

"I guess she'd just told you she didn't want to get hitched, is that right? Well, it was like she had to explain to someone, someone other than you, True Bear. And so she came looking for me. Sometimes things get complicated as hell, you know that?"

"It's crossed my mind. What did she tell you? The truth is, I'm feeling like a gray fox with its foot pinned in a number four. It ain't a good feeling, Woodpecker."

"Love's a bitchkitty. Never does make sense. When snow flattens the brush lodge, though, you rebuild the damned thing, that's all. Fanny says that . . . well, she thinks in the long run you'd never be able to forget how she's earned her living for the last couple of years. I don't know how else to put it, True Bear. She says she's slept with a lot of men, and she's been raped and mauled and generally abused. You killed one of the bastards on the way up from Reno—that's why he was after her again. McLaughlin was the sonofabitch that caught her years ago, when you and I were trying to trail Wolf Tracker's people and lost them up on Wahgalu. Then he got sold to Hank Bitler, the same Bitler your dad's been buying horses from, including Renegade out there. The guy's crazy son hog-tied her and—well, Matthew Red Turtle saved her from that and killed young Bitler. Afterward she married Red Tu: e, and he was killed by soldiers. Colonel Whitney and the lawyer that came here to roust out my people, she was with both of them at one time or another, after she got shot when she and I tried to take guns to Kintpuash. The lawyer, Livingstone, he actually set her up in a house, got her started as a. . . ."

"Whore," True Bear said.

"Yes, I guess so."

"Both of those bastards? Talk about bad luck! What crazy kind of fate would bring not just one, but both of them here? Jesus Christ, Woodpecker, how in hell did all of this happen? One day we took her back to the Yahi village, and then everything ruptured, just blew apart."

"I don't know, but Fanny wanted me to tell you all this. I promised I would. Don't get angry at me, True Bear. I loved her, but I never touched her—I swear to God. I could never have done that. For one thing, Yellow Grass would have killed me—and then you'd have killed me too. Even dumb Injuns get some things figured out."

"Been a lot better if you had, maybe. Kept her here at the ranch—married her. At least we'd all still be together, and the rest of that never would have happened. I guessed at most of it, actually. She's got something that . . . draws men, I guess. More power to her."

Big Woodpecker gazed off toward the crown of Wahgalu, whose remaining snowfields had been diminishing rapidly during the past few days.

"Dan Dolliver, the gambler—she's just friends with him. She wanted you to know that. The railroad millionaire, that's mostly business, with a little sex thrown in to keep the pot boiling. She doesn't dislike him, doesn't particularly like him either."

"Then why in hell does she sleep with him?"

"Same reason as with all her customers, I guess—only now she doesn't have to do that anymore, not since she's in charge of everything. She says love's dangerous—that the only way she can succeed in the Whiteman's world is by not loving, keeping her emotions under lock and key."

True Bear drew his pistol once more, sighted in on some

imagined target high up on Wahgalu, clucked his tongue, and then holstered the weapon.

"There anything else?"

"A couple of things. The colonel asked her to marry him when he was here—and Livingstone offered to set her up as his mistress again. Fanny has a powerful effect on men, that's certain. She turned both of them down, just like she did you. And there's one more thing. When we met up with Smoke Woman—her mother told her who her father is, the Whiteman who. . . ."

"Good God—the sonofabitch is still alive, or not?"

"Alive."

"So who is it?"

Big Woodpecker shook his head.

"Fanny wouldn't tell me his name," he replied.

THIRTY-FOUR
A Time of Lightning
[August 1874]

WORLD MAKER HIMSELF SEEMED INTENT upon blasting his creation into shards as dry lightning screamed across the mountains in late August. A hot wind came on shortly before midnight, and True Bear, tormented by memories of Wahtaurisi-yi and what might have been, dozed fitfully until repeated white flashes through panes of window glass, a few sufficient to illuminate outlines of buildings and trees, caused him to sit up, rise, dress, and finally slip out through the rear door of the house.

He felt his way through shadows to North Branch, waded across the shallow, summer-low stream, stumbled up a bank, and continued toward a basalt rim beyond the high meadows.

Once there, he sat atop the rough, cracked formation and gazed toward Wahgalu, waited for snapping lightning to reveal the big, domed mountain's form.

Thunder poured across heaven, rattling and echoing through an oppressive darkness—no, not oppressive—it was filled with intermingled odors of grasses and sage, juniper and pine, buckbrush and cascara.

McCain thought about Harriet Collins, asleep in her apartment three thousand miles eastward, a continent away. He recalled how she sometimes mumbled in her sleep or made small squealing noises, almost like those uttered by a jackrabbit caught by a fox. A wave of tenderness went over him, and he resolved to complete the letter he'd begun perhaps half a dozen times in the wake of Fanny's departure.

He tried to envision Harriet beside him, the two of them sitting close here on a basalt rim this night of exploding light and booming noise. He imagined himself describing various odors, identifying them for her. Surely, once she set foot in the California mountains, perceived their stunning beauty, all thoughts of returning to New England would vanish.

It was true that the one thing sufficient to draw Harriet away from The Hub for a weekend excursion had been the wonderful colors of Massachusetts woods in October, orange and crimson and burgundy and yellow, as though the hardwoods were all burning a slow and exquisite fire brought on by first chill nights of autumn, hoarfrost that covered whole fields, turning grasses to crisp yellow-white, to glitter with morning sun.

Would rich gold of aspen groves and low-growing, fiery blushes of bush maples provide adequate recompense for the loss of those New England woods?

Would Wilson Lake and Emerald and Helen Lakes high up beneath Wahgalu's dome be able to replace those dark green ponds in the Massachusetts countryside?

No perpetual smell of saltwater, no winter fogs replete with occasional clanging of bell buoys.

No ballet, no opera, no lectures on various abstruse theological and religious topics.

To McCain's great surprise, he realized he was actually feeling a kind of regret at having left New England—almost a species of homesickness. And he missed those secret meetings with Harriet, missed the run-down flat he had rented so they might have some place of their own to meet, to cling to one another, to investigate the possibilities of sensual pleasure, something Harriet greatly desired and yet feared at the same time.

Well, if she was going to be his wife, then she was going to have to accept his world, that was all. And his world lay at the foot of a sleeping volcano—not really sleeping at all, just dozing fitfully, as he himself had been doing this night before bursts of white light summoned him into summer darkness.

Then he thought about B.J. and his faceless wife, the stuffy, crabbed, cramped-up odor of their home, old, carpeted, adorned with marble fireplaces.

Several lightning flashes in a row, leaping from clouds to the high rock and waning snowfields of Wahgalu, and a torrent of noise poured down, long, rumbling, sustained noises—as though Pano the Spirit Grizzly, perhaps, and Old Coyote Man were having some sort of profound disagreement—Emerson and Thoreau yelling across the room at one another, something about theory and practice and perhaps even about philosophical hypocrisy.

Raindrops spattered onto the surface of the basalt rim for a minute or two and then ceased. A world of new odors welled up around him, intoxicating, wonderfully alive. . . .

McCain rose, worked his way carefully down from the rim, and began to stride toward the ranch.

Suddenly and precisely, without question, he knew exactly what he was going to do.

FOR THE FIRST TIME since the McCains had been in the cattle business, Ben elected not to make the late summer drive downcanyon to the auction at Red Bluff. Big Woodpecker, as operations foreman, knew the fifty-mile Battle Creek Trail perfectly well, and with True Bear and half a dozen Maidu

men as drovers, the elder McCain could foresee no problems
that couldn't be dealt with.

True Bear, devastated though he'd been at Fanny Bitler's
departure and presumed return to her former way of life,
accepted responsibility for the necessary venture and even
took notes in proper Harvard fashion as Ben covered details
of what needed to be done after the herd of two hundred
steers reached the stockyards.

"Truthfully, Son, I hate missing the cattle drive—I've always looked forward to it. But I'm not as young as I used to
be. It'll be your ranch to tend to one of these days in any
case, and you may as well make your presence known to the
other stockmen. They're good old boys, most of them, and
the sooner they get used to dealing with you, the better.
Gives you something to take your mind off Auna-yi, as well."

The latter, True Bear reflected, was the actual reason Ben
had chosen to stay at the ranch. *Give the kid something to do,
keep him busy. . . .*

The cattle were selected and brought in from pasture, fed
heavily for three days, and then moved out—to the whooping
and yipping of drovers and cow dogs.

They crossed the ridge past Wilson Lake and down to the
wagon trail near Seth Childe's old place, broad meadows now
grazed upon by Clayton's Herefords, and on over the pass
beyond Circle S Ranch to Nanny Creek, headwaters of the
South Fork of the Battle.

From there the trail was easy enough, the only difficulties
lying in a ten-mile passage through Battle Canyon, for the
stream went through a series of cascades, and the way was
narrow, in places allowing for passage of no more than two
animals at a time.

With Big Woodpecker's expert guidance, they managed to
navigate the difficult stretches without incident, and by sundown the second day were out of the huge defile and down
into rolling hills, areas of brush and grass interspersed by
stands of black oak, blue oak, liveoak, and digger pine.

By noon of the third day, they were back on the main
wagon road, coming up beneath Soap Butte, and thereby
avoiding any trespass onto the Clayton Rancho near Table
Mountain.

"We've got easy going from here to Red Bluff," True Bear said. "A virtual Appian Way, by heaven. What is it—another fifteen miles? First we hit Dales at Paynes Creek, if my memory serves me, and then past Tuscan Buttes and on into town. That's the butte, off to the southwest. . . ."

"Just like clockwork!" Big Woodpecker chortled. "Ben turns the cattle drive over to us kids, and by God we make better time than he does. We'll have to ask for a raise in pay."

"Maybe we'd better see what we get in the way of prices first," True Bear laughed.

"To hell with that, True Bear. I'm Buffalo Bill, and you're Kit Carson—except maybe we're tougher and meaner than both of those guys put together. Me, I don't believe what's in those Beadle books you brought with you from Massachusetts. It was fun to read them, though. Easterners will buy anything, that's what I think."

True Bear grinned. As a matter of fact, Big Woodpecker had devoured nearly half a dozen of the dime novels, having discovered them when one of True Bear's suitcases fell from Ben's buckboard during the trip up from Reno.

ELIAS GRANGER, San Francisco cattle buyer, arrived in Red Bluff three days earlier. He and Ben McCain had been on close terms for the past five years, and Granger now made a point of being in the North Valley when McCain's herd arrived, a rendezvous set well ahead of time via the United States Mail.

Visibly disappointed at Ben's absence, Granger shook hands with Big Woodpecker and was introduced to True Bear.

"So you're the new generation? Well, I'd say you're actually bigger than your old man, if that's possible—taller, anyway. Must be something in the mountain water, same thing that puts meat on the bones of the whitefaces. Whatever it is your dad's been doing all these years, young man, don't change it. My buyers in San Francisco, the restaurants that is to say, are what you might call 'addicted' to McCain beef. Well, let's see what you've brought me. Times are bad, and prices are down everywhere. Can't give you what I did last year. . . ."

Dad knows this old bastard well enough, I guess. Predicted

*that speech almost to the word. No surprise to learn that
prices are down, though. We anticipated that all along.*

True Bear and Big Woodpecker watched the buyer go
about his business, moving in practiced fashion among the
cattle, pinching at hides, patting here and there, occasionally
even resorting to a fold-out measuring stick, though for what
purpose True Bear wasn't sure. Something about proportion,
as he gathered, but the application of that to the quality of
beef wasn't clear.

The sale was made a penny a pound higher than other area
ranchers were getting, and the men shook hands.

"You tell Ben I expect to see him down here next year.
You tell that old hypochondriac I don't want to hear any
excuses. I probably could have cut the price on you boys, and
you wouldn't have known any different. Besides, Ben and I
usually make a ten-dollar bet to see who's closest to guessing
the overall weight. Gentlemen, it's been a pleasure doing
business with you."

With a draft from California Livestock Acquisitions in hand,
True Bear and Big Woodpecker proceeded to the Red Bluff
Bank, cashed the note, deposited a portion into the general
McCain account, and took the remainder in greenbacks.

The buckboard they'd brought with them as a chuckwagon
was now put to a new purpose—becoming a freight wagon for
the trip back to Oidoing-koyo.

True Bear and Big Woodpecker purchased several hundred-
pound sacks of flour (cheaper here than at Chester prices), as
well as quantities of coffee beans, sugar, and a shiny new set
of kitchen knives for Ooti. In addition, they acquired two
dozen rifles of various manufacture—some cap-and-ball, some
cartridge models—and a good supply of ammunition.

"Setting up your own private army?" the gun merchant
asked. "You're Ben McCain's boy, I take it. Yep—there's a
certain family resemblance, no question. Haven't sold this
many guns all at once since the lads cleaned out the Chinese.
Now you've by-God cleaned me out. Sure you don't need
howitzers and a couple of Gatlings? Old Captain Jack, he's
not going to be thieving any more cattle, you know. . . ."

The merchant, pleased at his own wit, nevertheless had
rifles and ammunition loaded into the McCain wagon. He
accepted payment in folding money fresh from the bank.

* * *

As True Bear, Big Woodpecker, and the Maidus made their return trip to Oidoing-koyo, they stayed to the main wagon road—since the route was both quicker and easier on the animals.

But at the top of Soap Bluff rim, they found the way blocked by a dozen riders led by Daniel Clayton and Robert Anderson, the two ranchers now well into their fifties and, from all reports, quite wealthy men.

True Bear immediately pulled Renegade around sideways, in front of Big Woodpecker.

"Mr. Clayton and Mr. Anderson, cattle barons of the North Valley, if I'm not mistaken. Don't believe I've seen you since you murdered the Yahis, though I did have a brief conversation with a couple of your men. Gentlemen, this is a public road, and you're in my way. If you'd be so kind as to allow us to pass through, I'd appreciate it. President Grant's having tea at Upper Eden, you understand, and we're running a bit behind schedule—otherwise we'd be pleased to stay and talk."

"These are McCain's vaqueros—I know Woodpecker over there," Dan Clayton said. "Who the hell are you? And where's McCain?"

"You're looking at him. Don't remember me, eh? I tried to put a bullet in you once, Mr. Clayton, sir—but that was nine years ago. I've been thinking about it ever since. I've got a long, long memory, and some have said I'm a tad bit monomaniacal. Get out of my way."

"True Bear," Big Woodpecker said, "take it easy, for God's sake. This is no place to get us all shot."

"You're the kid?" Anderson asked. "You look like McCain's pup, but I heard you were back East."

"Bad pennies always turn up," True Bear grinned, winking at the ranchers. "They let me loose for good behavior, as it turns out. If you've got something on your minds, gents, let's hear it. Otherwise, move."

"Looks like the halfbreed kid's worse than the old man," Anderson said to Clayton. "Stupid, too. They sent him to some kind of school, but he cain't even count."

"No time for a range war right now, Young McCain," Dan Clayton said, "but Bob's right. We got you boys outgunned,

an' I don't think the Injuns are up for gettin' killed today. So
you listen to me, you damned upstart. I want you to tell Ben.
Them Injuns of his was supposed to get sent over to Round
Valley, an' your old man weaseled his way past the government somehow. Well, there's twenty ranchers who want
them out of there. I lost enough cows to Injuns in my life to
stock the state of Texas, an' I'm not having any more of it.
I've got the Childe spread now, an' Anderson's in the process
of picking up the Circle S. Your old man can hire Whitemen,
just like the rest of us. I mean it, Kid. The first time one of
my Goddamned animals gets butchered, me an' the boys are
going to take matters into our own hands, just like we've
done before. If the government don't protect our interests,
then we'll do it ourselves. You get my drift?"

"You gentlemen are in my way," True Bear insisted. "Either you move, or I'm going to put holes in half a dozen men.
Clayton first because he's an ugly sonofabitch. I think maybe
you picked the wrong man to bully. Let's see what happens. . . ."

A moment of silence followed, and then Dan Clayton reached
casually toward his pistol.

True Bear's revolver was in his hand instantly, the weapon
pointing directly at the rancher.

"You so much as twitch, you're a dead man, Clayton. It's
going to come between you and me anyway, soon or late. If
one of your men goes for a gun, I'm going to gut-shoot you.
Easy, easy, boys. I'm crazy as a shithouse rat, no doubt about
it, and touchy as a rattlesnake with a toothache besides. You
men—toss your weapons onto the ground, take off your boots,
and start walking west. The bossmen are coming with me.
Maybe I'll turn them loose later, or else I'll take them to visit
this cave I know about."

"THAT WAS A DAMNED FOOLHARDY thing to do, Son," Ben
laughed, "though I like the way the tale runs. There's trouble
ahead, but that's not news. I figured it all along."

"It was good to watch," Big Woodpecker grinned. "I tried
to calm him down, but he's always been that way. All of us
thought the shooting would start any moment. I've never
seen anyone draw a gun that fast—Dan Clayton hadn't either,
I guess."

"I lost my temper, all right—wasn't using my head. Something about that worthless sonofabitch just sitting there, blocking our way. . . . Once it got started, I just blundered ahead. Jesus, I could have gotten all of us killed—because of an old grudge, that's what it comes down to."

"Clayton and Anderson," Ben said, "they're not going to forget, of course. But maybe it's better if they don't. They didn't get a look at what you boys had stowed in the wagon, did they?"

True Bear shook his head.

"Range war, indeed. It's usually sheepmen and cattlemen—not an argument about making the hills safe for stray cows. But a couple dry years like the last two, and Valley ranchers get panicky. *Summer pasture*, that's all they can think of. And every stillborn calf's the work of thieving Indians, even after they've butchered the last wild Redman in the state."

"I wish I'd been there." Acorn Girl said, smiling. "Maybe we should have killed Dan Clayton years ago. Then Wolf Tracker's people would still be alive. He's the one who's crazy—he wants to own everything. I would have led my people on a revenge-taking after the massacre, but everyone thought it was only the Yahis Clayton and Anderson were after. Now we begin to see a truth that should have been visible all along."

"Woodpecker, old fellow," Ben McCain shrugged, "I think maybe we'd best mosey on over to talk to your pa and Broken Wing and Goat's Head and the others. Pass out the new armament and ammo. It sounds to me as though our Valley friends don't take very kindly to the Oidoing-koyos declining to make that trip to Round Valley in company with the colonel and the lawyer."

THE MOON was nearly full.

True Bear pinned a note to the wooden topbeam over the stones of the fireplace, walked quietly out of the house, got Renegade, and rode to some offshoot meadows just south of Childe's Ranch.

The stolen Maidu cattle were still there, twenty of them, herded for the night into a brush corral he had discovered two days earlier—as the result of an extensive covert survey of Dan Clayton's new holdings.

A single cowhand was in charge of the stolen cattle, and he was dead asleep under his blankets, a few feet away from some still-smoking embers of a campfire.

McCain tethered his stallion, gave the horse strict if useless instructions to remain perfectly quiet, and then crept toward the sleeping cowboy.

A single blow to the head sufficed to cause the man to sleep even more deeply than before, and McCain worried for a moment the slumber might well be permanent. But Clayton's cowhand was still breathing, and True Bear nodded. He hadn't meant to kill the man, after all, though the thought had crossed his mind.

He fetched Renegade, opened a makeshift corral gate, and began to work the animals out and over a rim toward the lower end of Childe's Meadows.

It was two o'clock in the morning, according to the barely visible hands on his pocket watch, when he managed to get the balky cattle to pasture below Oidoing-koyo.

He'd intended to complete his retrieval mission and then get some sleep, but something about a big white moon dropping westward toward the dark shadow of Turner Mountain caused him to urge his horse in the opposite direction.

His saddlebags were already packed, in any case, and a return to the house might serve only to awaken Ben and Ooti an hour or more before they normally rose. Then he'd have to explain the whole thing, listen to his father's arguments and counterarguments, his mother's solicitations and appeals for caution.

Ooti, he thought, *my strange, half-mythic mother, who's never been cautious in her life—who's still of the opinion the Maidus ought to declare war on the State of California and the United States Government as well. . . .*

The moon disappeared as he rode along streamside in the direction of Stump Ranch, the old Rawlings place, recently sold (according to rumor) to none other than Henry Bitler, the horse-breeder. Bitler's wife had died of consumption the previous year, so the story went, and now the man was selling his own ranch in the Warner Mountains and moving south—apparently wishing to distance himself from haunting memories.   •

Three questions crossed True Bear's mind as he skirted

past the unlit ranch house, keeping well away so as not to rouse any dogs and thereby awaken whomever might be inside.

First, why would a man who'd spent years building a ranch, eating and drinking its earth, wish to leave—no matter what tragedies had befallen him?

Second, had Bitler been more than a substitute father to Fanny? What was the nature of that former relationship—if, indeed, it was "former"? She would have been no more than a girl at the time—but was she a mistress as well? Significantly enough, she used Bitler's last name, and he'd given her a first name also. Or was it the wife, a simple corruption of *Auny-yi*? Ben spoke warmly of the man, but was he yet one more discarded lover of the Queen of Reno?

Finally, if push came to shove in the inevitable confrontation with Clayton and the Valley ranchers, was Bitler a likely ally or yet one more enemy?

The questions remained without answers, musings and nothing more as True Bear McCain rode past and continued toward Chester.

The sky darkened and was now brilliant with stars, but Renegade moved ahead, confidently surefooted.

Soon the east would lighten to false dawn, and stars would begin to vanish.

HE RODE across Fredonyer Pass and late in the afternoon reached Susanville, nestled at the foot of the mountains just where the country began to merge into desert. He urged Renegade down the steep main street of the settlement, crossed Susan River, and continued southeast along a wagon road to Janesville and the wide, shallow waters of Honey Lake beyond that.

Darkness found him camped on the big lake's edge, fire burning, and a full round steak sizzling, meat flopped over a section of lightweight steel rod he'd found along the trail.

He ate nearly the entire steak, wrapped the remainder into oilcloth for morning, leaned back against a section of weathered stone, lit a cigar, and sipped a mouthful or two of bad whiskey from his pocket flask.

After a time he stood up, visited with Renegade, and spent a while rubbing the big horse about the ears.

"How many times do I have to tell you not to eat a lit cigar?" he demanded. "You'll burn hell out of your fat tongue."

The horse continued to make attempts to lip the cigar away, and True Bear gave in, extinguished the stogie, and presented its remains to the insistent animal.

"Satisfied? Well, it doesn't take much to please a horse, I guess. Cigars, sugar, grain and grass, water, and once in a while a lady who's in the mood. Don't care whether it's the 'right' lady or not, do you?"

Lips fluttered, jaws continued to grind.

"You up for a midnight swim? Moonlight out over the lake—look at it. A man can't catch the moon, even if a horse can. What's that? You say you don't like to swim? Hell with you, then."

McCain stripped off his clothing, walked over a few yards of mushy lakebed exposed this drought year, and waded into the shallows. When the water was knee-deep, he pushed forward and began to stroke.

The moon's reflection, he noted, was no closer to him than it had been when he started swimming.

He stood up, his feet touching bottom, head and shoulders above the glimmering surface.

"So what am I going to do, Madame Artemis, if you'd be so kind as to tell me? The way things stand, I'm no good to anyone. Dad brought me home to save the ranch, and what do I do? Cause more trouble than was already there. Put manure on a weedpatch, and more weeds sprout. If Bully O'Bragh were still alive, he wouldn't have been satisfied with a lot of bluffing and posturing and hauling back some pilfered bovines. Hell no, the old bastard would have gone straight to the heart of the matter. He'd have ridden back to Table Mountain, waited until Dan Clayton was alone, and then blasted a hole in him and probably scalped him as well. I need better strategy, a clearer sense of direction and purpose. . . ."

Soft wind across the water, causing patterns of ripple to fragment the image of the moon.

"Artemis, Bully, Renegade, Coyote, whoever's listening . . . this is True Bear talking. What about that other halfbreed, Phyrne of Reno, the one who's become a Goddamned obsession with me? What in hell am I supposed to do about her?

he stupid little Yahi bitch can't even own up to what it is that
e's wanted ever since we were dumbass kids together. . . ."
But the only answer was a sound of wind across the surface
the big shallow desert lake.
He waded to shore, shook water from his long hair, dried
mself on a blanket, got back into his clothes, and lay down.
'ithin moments he was deep in the sleep of exhaustion.

IRES WERE BURNING in the mountains west of him as he rode
ong, and True Bear reflected that whatever Being it was
ho threw down lightning bolts was persistent but, in gen-
al terms, working with an unpredictable kind of fire-starter.
t the present rate, years might pass before every forest and
ge-dotted slope had been consumed, and by then new
rests and new expanses of sage would have sufficient time
regenerate. There had been so damned many fires sending
smoke plumes since his return to the West that True Bear
rdly took the situation seriously anymore.
Nonetheless, dry heat held on, day after day, and what had
ready occurred could well be as nothing compared to what
ight be coming.
"Coyote, you fur-faced sonofaporkypine!" he shouted as he
de along, "can't you whip up a genuine rainstorm? Nobody
ants everything turned black. Birds need places to roost,
u dumb bastard of a god. . . ."
He passed Hallelujah Junction, stopped for a quick meal,
ank off two mugs of beer with his roast beef and potatoes,
d hit the saddle once again, his sense of anticipation and
ustration and hopelessness growing as he drew nearer to
eno.
"What the hell you going to do, McCain? There's no point
trying to reason with that hard-headed female, and noth-
g's to be gained by pleading, either. So what's the plan, my
ave philosopher? What did Marcus Aurelius have to say on
e matter of courting the Western World's most Gawddamn-
eautiful courtesan? Kidnapping worked once, but I don't
ink she's going to buy it again. What exactly have I got to
fer? Not even Wilson Lake in a rainstorm figures to provide
e proper sort of allure."
Ahead, under a heavy curtain of accumulated smoke, lay

the city of Reno, Nevada, complete with stockyards, railroad
gambling dens and whorehouses, and small brick college.

True Bear checked his pistol and repeating rifle, uttered
a mouthful or two of profanity, and headed for Salty'
Emporium.

"Nothing ventured, nothing gained," he said, leaning for
ward and muttering into Renegade's ear.

THIRTY-FIVE
True Bear Goes Courting
[September 1874]

SHORTLY PAST NOON the following day, True Bear entered
Salty's Emporium, stood tall in the doorway, and looked
about the already crowded gambling hall. Neither Fanny
Bitler nor Salty Dan was present.

One or two men glanced up, made note of a large man in
black, and returned their attentions to card game or crap
table.

A keen sense of disappointment ran through him—but
what, after all, had he expected? Had he supposed Fanny
would see him immediately and come walking across the
room to him, her arms open?

True Bear made his way to the bar, recognized the man
behind it as the barkeep who'd been present that first night
back in Reno.

"Shot of whiskey," he said, placing a small gold dollar on the counter.

The barkeep poured, returned a fifty-cent piece, and automatically ran his damp white towel across the polished wood to either side of where True Bear was sitting.

"I've got an appointment with Fanny Bitler," McCain said. "Supposed to meet her here at twelve o'clock."

"Can't help you, I'm afraid," the man replied, motioning to a gaudily dressed and rather good-looking Indian woman a few feet away. "Willow, this gent says he's got an appointment with Fanny. You know anything about it?"

The name rang a bell, and True Bear remembered the girl from the day he bought his new hat.

Willow came sidling over, raised her petticoats so as to reveal one well-formed leg, and sat down next to him.

"Hokay, Big Spender. Fanny, she's busy as hell now. Don't roll in the hay no more anyway, not with regular customers. You like Willow? I ain't busy—you buy me a drink, then come upstairs and show me what you got. Maybe you set house record or something, huh, Black Hat? Hey, somebody shoot at you? Bullet hole. . . ."

"You're Willow—Fanny's top floor-woman."

"That's me, hokay. See, you know all about me. I'm damned good. You any good?"

"No question in my mind," True Bear grinned, "on either score. Pleased to meet you, Miss Willow. Fanny's told me a number of things about you, all good."

"You shitting me, Black Hat? Hey, you the one she went to visit—True Bear McCain? Don't look half-Injun to me. You him?"

"The very man, Fair One. Now tell me where the hell Fanny is."

"No cussin' in this Goddamn bar. You act nice. Come on, buy Willow a drink."

"Be glad to. Bartender? Whiskey for the lovely lady."

This gesture momentarily placated Willow. She sipped, but her drink down.

"You talk like good-for-nothing lawyer, you know that? Well, Fanny told me about you, too," she said in a whisper. "She ain't expecting you, though. Goddamn! She's upstairs with Salty Dan an' the railroad hotshot. Talkin' big business

today. Gonna buy out Carson City, maybe. We better not g[
upstairs after all—don't want Fanny to get mad. She's good
friend to me."

True Bear drank the remainder of his whiskey, turned the
shot glass upside down on the counter.

"So, the entrepreneurs are at work, scheming up new
acquisitions. . . ."

"What's that suppose to mean? You call Fanny name, you
sonofabitch? I cut your little pecker off, give to the birds to
eat."

HENRY EDWARDS HUNTINGTON SAT next to his uncle, C.P.
directly across the table from Fanny Bitler and, of course
Dan Dolliver, whom the younger Huntington considered
little more than a weasel in disguise, an opportunist who'd
somehow gotten his hand into C.P.'s pocket.

For the moment, however, Henry Huntington was not at
all interested in Salty Dan. It was the exquisite Miss Bitler
from whom he couldn't seem to take his eyes. She was, he
concluded, absolutely and without question the best-looking
whore he had ever met, though with relatively limited experience, he didn't actually consider himself an expert.

Fanny Bitler, he gathered, was no doubt within a year or
two of his own age. He could understand her interest in
C.P.'s money, of course, but how could she bear to have
sexual relations with a man in his fifties, such as Uncle Collis
As a junior partner in the railroad operations these past three
years, he'd been made privy to several of his uncle's favorite
brothels, but Fanny Bitler was the first such woman who'd
ever seemed genuinely attractive to him.

Uncle Collis would grow tired of her eventually, but that
might take two or three years—too long to wait. There had to
be, Henry supposed, some way of speeding up matters. Miss
Bitler would make an ideal away-from-home-woman, but he
would have to proceed carefully. With a full, soft-looking
mouth, smoldering eyes, and utter sensuousness of her every
movement, she was, Henry concluded, a dark-skinned incarnation of some Greek goddess or another. His own youth and
patience would win out, he was certain, but patience was
going to be difficult.

"I admire you two thieves," Collis was saying, "I truly do

But you have to learn a basic principle. If a man robs a bank, someone's going to figure it out. Yet if that same man can find a way of getting all the banks to give him a dollar an hour, then it's just a matter of time—and if the thing's managed correctly, the banks all end up supposing they've been done a great favor. You see my point? When Mark Hopkins and I started out, we had little more than a pot to piss in. After a time, we had the factory that made the pots. . . ."

Dan and Fanny listened, and they were both translating Huntington's anecdote in the same way.

Not going to move on Carson City, not with us as partners, at least. . . .

Fanny was avoiding young Henry's fixed gaze, but now she looked directly at him, smiled, and winked.

The young man flushed, averted his attention.

"God damn it, C.P.," Salty Dan said, "I tell you we can handle it from here—and turn a hell of a nice profit to boot. You don't have any complaints on the Reno houses, now do you? The fact is, we're holding a handful of hearts."

Someone was knocking at the door—three soft raps.

"That's Willow," Fanny said. "If you'll excuse me a moment, gentlemen. . . ."

Henry took note of the movement of her hips as she walked quickly to the door, opened it, and stepped outside.

"Someone downstairs you want to see, Fan. You talk old fat wallet into buying Carson City? We go down there, I get the government first, hokay?"

"Who is it, Willow?"

The girl grinned.

"Big guy in black—say he's going to shoot up the place if you don't marry him. But first he's going to kill railroad man, then scalp him."

Willow laughed hysterically, and Fanny took a deep breath.

"True Bear—and at just exactly the wrong moment. . . ."

As Fanny descended the stairway, pointedly following behind Willow, she experienced a momentary difficulty in breathing—and mentally cursed herself for acting like a damned fool. But her heartbeat was racing, and she felt perspiration on her forehead.

She mumbled the words ". . . big, lovesick puppy dog
. . ." as she glanced around the gambling hall.

"Willow, are you playing a little joke on me? Negotiations
upstairs were just getting to the critical point. . . ."

"No shittin' jokes, Fanny. McCain, he was here just a
minute ago. Talked me into comin' up to get you. We was
sitting right over there, havin' a drink. Ain't no way that big
guy could hide—where'd he go?"

"Left you a letter, Miss Fanny," the barkeep said, handing
her an envelope.

Inside was a quickly penned note and a poem written in
carefully drawn and very neat script.

"What's it say?" Willow demanded. "Goddam. I'm going to
learn how to read too, one a these days. Maybe you teach
me, huh?"

Fanny momentarily ignored her friend and read what True
Bear had written:

> Dear Auna-yi,
>
> I was here—left when Willow went up to tell you—no
> doubt overstepping myself once again—or maybe just
> not certain what it was I wanted to say—you're busy
> just now, and I shouldn't interrupt—be back later if
> I can get my wits together. I composed the prose-
> poem by firelight last night, out along the trail. Perhaps
> it says what I've never had the grace to tell you in
> person.
>
> —True Bear

Fanny turned the sheet over, continued to read:

> We live in a time when earth is boiling with flame,
> And yet the flames in our hearts may be dying:
> We met in a moment of innocent wildness, in a dark
>   canyon yet darker
> With mystery. But the fear I knew on that night
>   vanished
> When a girl's eyes met mine—yours, O my dearest one.

*   *   *

Our time together was short, and we were but children:
Then forces beyond our control drew us apart and hurled
    us
Into realms where the sun burned black in the sky
And died—all that we knew, all that we cherished
    withered and died.

Coyote Man (or whatever mad Force we call God)
Brought us once more together—as if simply to show us
How deeply we'd changed, and yet magic caught us and
    bound us
In the silk ropes of love, and we kissed in the darkness
As rain fell, as lightning flashed, and we could merely
Know for a moment the deep promise whose fulfillment
We once believed was certainly ours.

Auna-yi—Fanny—I cannot write anymore—I cannot
    control my feelings,
The deepest and most precious I've ever known—
But I can go into death with full knowledge I've known
    love,
A love more precious than breath or the soft singing of
    blood.

Fires burn everywhere. Great conflagrations sweep the
    mountains,
But a greater conflagration surges within me, this
    miserable man
Who pledges his faith and still desperately wishes
The slip of a girl he loves might join him in pilgrimage
In a time of the dying of things, in a time when earth
    boils with flame.

"Well," Willow repeated, "what's the note say, Fan? He
goin' off to shoot himself, or what?"
Fanny shook her head slowly. She gave thought to reading
the missive as Willow asked but was unable. She swallowed
hard and used a handkerchief to dab at her eyes.

SALTY DAN and young Henry adjourned to the rear rooms,
leaving Fanny and C.P. Huntington together—the potential

business arrangements for Carson City still not concluded.
C.P. had come around somewhat, but he remained doubtful
that Fanny and Dan would indeed prove successful in overseeing operations a day's ride away from Reno.

"Oh, hell!" Huntington said at last. "Fanny Bitler, I think
you could talk the devil himself into turning preacher. . . ."

Fanny smiled, leaned across the table toward the railroad
baron.

"I'd never ask you to take up spreading the Word, Collis.
Letting me have Carson City's another matter."

Huntington chuckled and was pouring himself another drink
when Willow once again knocked at the door—this time not
waiting for it to be opened.

"Big guy's back," she said. "Want him to wait?"

Fanny stood up, used her fingertips to press a kiss to
Huntington's forehead.

"I'll be right back, C.P.," she said. "Pour me one while
you're at it. . . ." She turned then, followed Willow out of
the room.

"MR. McCAIN, for pity's sake, I'm busy right now. Look—I'll
make arrangements to see you tomorrow night. Huntington
and his nephew will be gone by then, and. . . ."

"I'm busy too, Wahtaurisi-yi. You see, I've got a little
problem, and—well, it's an armful."

Before she could say anything else, he grabbed hold of her
and slung her over his shoulder and managed to hold her in
place with one hand, despite some surprised kicking and yelling.

Everyone in the gambling hall turned to see what the
ruckus was about—observed the odd predicament Madame
was in, and began laughing.

"Gettin' to be a habit, ain't it Fan?" someone yelled out.

Two bouncers started forward, stopped. True Bear was
shaking his head, and he had a pistol leveled at them.

"Kidnapping in progress," he said by way of explanation as
he backed out the double half-doors and into the street.

Renegade and a handsome sorrel mare, the latter with a
silver-embossed saddle and trimmings, stood ready at the
hitching rail. Four brown equine eyes looked up, questioning.

"You want to ride along peacefully, Auna-yi, or do I have

to gag you and tie you over the saddle? I've thought it over. You're not getting away again."

"Put me down, you sonofabitch! What in hell gives you the right to come storming in and . . . humiliating me this way? I have to maintain the respect of those men."

"You want to ride, or get tied? Up to you."

"You're a lunatic—you know that? I'll ride without assistance, thank you, but only to some place where we can talk. I'm absolutely, positively *not* leaving Reno—not now. A damned badger's got better manners than you have, I swear to God!"

"Squaw make too much noise. Let's go."

They rode out of town, followed the swirling gray-green Truckee River upstream for perhaps a mile to a small grove of quaking aspens that grew in a grassy area beside the stream.

"This is far enough," Fanny said, drawing her mount to a halt. "All right, then, now what's so damnably important that you had to put me through all this?"

True Bear nodded, and the two dismounted, sat down perhaps a yard apart on a shelf of gray-black stone.

"You know as well as I do," he said. "We're getting married."

"I see. I have no choice in the matter. Even though I said 'no,' you think you can leave me a poem and then bull your way in. . . ."

"You didn't really say it to me, Fanny. You just bent Big Woodpecker's ear and then rode off. Didn't even bother to shake hands, for Christ's sake. So I figure that actually means yes."

"I was wrong to leave the way I did, I admit it. I just didn't have the strength to see you again, that's all. Too much was going on all at once. Whitney and Livingstone both showing up that way. . . ."

"I know. You explained the whole thing to Big Woodpecker. Fanny Bitler, Auna-yi, I humbly request the honor of being your husband until death do us part, and maybe after that as well."

"Perhaps college makes men stupid, True Bear. It teaches them how to write poems but not how to use their heads. What happened between us was a long time ago."

"Wilson Lake in the rain—not exactly ancient history."

"True Bear, listen to me. I'm a whore, do you understand?

Right now you say that doesn't make any difference, but it would. All right, Goddamn it, I love you—I won't deny it, even if you do make me furious. But I am not going to leave my business interests behind—not now—not when things are just starting to go so well."

"Think I got lost there. Does 'all right' mean you'll marry me?"

"No, it means I want you to go back to Upper Eden. It means I'll ride up there with Willow in about two weeks— that way you and I will have plenty of time to talk things over when we're both in our right minds. Why can't you say pretty things the way you did in the poem? I'm glad it doesn't rhyme—it sounds more real just the way it is. Damn it, True Bear, I get so confused when I'm around you that I can't think straight. Hold me, please. I need to be kissed. My heart's pounding so badly I can barely breathe. You're crazy, and you make me crazy, too."

McCain stood up suddenly.

"So," he said, "it's business as usual, with me as a possible sideline? It hits me now that perhaps, just perhaps, Fanny Bitler, I'm not interested. Damn you anyway! Come with me today—or not. It's up to you."

Fanny stared at him, his face strange now and hard with anger. Tears came to her eyes and she found it impossible to speak.

He observed her for a long moment and then turned, swung onto Renegade.

"Keep the horse and saddle," he said, his voice softening. "They were presents. . . ."

Then he was riding away.

Don't go you miserable Goddamn sonofabitch True Bear, can't you see I don't want you to go, can't you see that I love you even though I swore I would never love anyone again, never . . .?

HE STOPPED at Smoky Joe's, just north of town, explained to Renegade that a man had certain needs just like a horse's, and walked inside, banging the door behind him.

The bartender looked up, scowled, and motioned to a yellow-clad prostitute seated on top of the bar. She slid down, walked toward True Bear. The girl was, he realized, ess than five feet tall—more or less the size of a child, hough endowed with fully adult female breasts.

"No need to break down the door, Big Guy," she smiled. "You're the only customer we got this afternoon. You inter-sted in buying me a drink, maybe?"

McCain stared at her, felt whatever need for a woman he'd ust had leave him, and nodded.

"Truth is," he said, "what I need to do—is get drunk. How he hell'd you get so little, anyhow? Bet you don't weigh ighty pounds dripping wet."

"We could try it and see," she said, kissing at the air and aking him by the hand.

"What'll it be, Abe?" the barkeep asked. "By God, all you eed's a different hat. Ain't that so, Jackie?"

"Got rid of the stovepipe after that tomfool actor shot me."

"Looks like he put a bullet through your Oregon sombrero, hough. Let me guess—you just robbed a bank and came in ere to spend it all. So what's your pleasure?"

"Jackie, is it? Give her the usual. Me, I'd like a shot of nud."

"Which is?"

"Mud, you dumb bastard, just plain mud. Got in the habit ack in '24, first time I went up-country with General Ashley. ou bring it, I'll drink it, by the blue balls o' Gawd."

The barkeep shook his head and poured two whiskeys.

"This stuff do any good for a man with a broken heart?" rue Bear demanded.

"Couldn't say. Jackie's more of an expert in such matters."

"You had a fight with your girlfriend?" Jackie asked. "I've ot music to soothe your savage beast, if you're interested. Nobody plays it the way I do."

McCain drank off his whiskey, coughed, blinked his eyes.

"Quote accurately," he said, shaking his head. "If there's ne thing I can't stand, it's improper quotation. Music, by God, is supposed to soothe the savage breast. I've been to Harvard—I ought to know."

"Whatever you say," Jackie laughed. "What's your girlfriend's ame? Tell me about her."

"Another drink. Well, that's the problem. She's got too nany names, and she isn't sure who the hell she is. Fanny's ne of them."

Jackie placed a tiny hand on McCain's arm and looked genuinely sympathetic.

"My boss is named Fanny," she said. "I guess it's a common name."

"Too damned common. I know. I'm talking about your boss. Miss Fanny Bitler, my truelove. What the hell did I come in here for anyway? I'll tell you something, Jackie, the first thing you absolutely have to do is grow up. Children shouldn't be in places like this. Go on now, tell me you're twenty-five. I'll bet you aren't more than—what?—sixteen or so."

The girl laughed.

"Big Fella, I think you were drinking before you ever came in here. Don't breathe a word, and I'll tell you a secret. I'm twenty-eight. Been at this for a long while, though, mostly back in St. Louis. Journeyed west to seek my fortune last year."

McCain stood up, gestured with open hands.

"Came in here to get drunk and then get laid," he complained. "Then I find out you don't serve mud—and all you've got in the way of companionship of the feminine variety is a midget. Barkeep, I'm telling you, this child ought to be in school. Holding down an extra job this way, she's subject to miss half of her fourth form work. Reading's important, and I most devoutly recommend it to one and all. Good afternoon, folks. I'll be on my way to Quincy now."

He paid for the drinks and turned to leave.

"Some like 'em tight," the bartender mumbled. "Ain't that right, Jackie?"

True Bear rode on ahead a mile or so up the dusty wagon road, nodded to a couple of trailhands traveling the other direction.

"If you're heading north, Mister," one said, "don't take the Junction road if you can avoid 'er. We just come down from Sierra Valley—the whole damned swamp's on fire. Half the valley, anyhow, and all the hills off toward Yuba Pass and Sierra City. It's a damned inferno."

"I see the smoke," True Bear replied. "Wondered where it was coming from. Thanks. I'll head for Susanville."

When the cowboys had passed, he pulled Renegade about,

gazed back toward Reno, and then turned onto a dimly marked trail leading into the sagebrush.

Once out of sight of the road, he dismounted, gathered a few scraps of dead sage, and set them up in an area of open ground. From twenty paces he began shooting, grinned each time a target leaped up like something alive.

After half an hour of wasting ammunition, he kicked at the dirt twice, holstered his Colt, and got back into the saddle.

"Friend Horse," he said, "I wonder if they serve mud at the Junction. Tell you, I've got a *powerful dry*. You never met Bully O'Bragh, did you? That old bastard filled my head with dreams—said 'True Bear, go climb the mountain. When ye come back down, everything'll be clear to ye.' Well, it has been—clear as mud. Let's go see what's burning."

LATE AFTERNOON HEAT, and the sky to the northwest a virtual wall of smoke that rose up to take on the appearance of summer thunderheads—and the sunlight glared down an almost red-gold hue.

True Bear reached the wagon road and turned north.

Half a mile farther on he caught sight of a buckboard pulled by four horses, the driver pushing his animals forward at a fast clip. Beside the man sat a woman, her long hair trailing down her back.

"Well I'll be a fat coyote! Friend Renegade, do you realize who that is?"

He thumped his boot heels to the stallion's ribs, pushed the big roan into a gallop.

"Fanny! Where the hell you going?" he yelled as he drew up on them.

The buckboard came to a halt, and True Bear could see the horses were blowing hard, thankful their run was over for a time at least. One of the animals in traces had a saddle on, the sorrel mare he'd bought earlier that day.

Salty Dan Dolliver threw back through his mane of graying hair and then brushed his fingers lightly over the surface of the emerald brooch that was his trademark.

"Dust's enough to choke man and beast alike this time of the year," he said. "Well, young fellow, Fanny came back from wherever you hauled her, and she burst into tears, couldn't by-God stop. I could see she wasn't in any condition to conduct business, so I said, 'Fan, you want that McCain or not, make up your mind. Can't put up with a partner whose face is all blotchy from bawling. Throw the dice and ride with whatever comes up. I reckon I can handle the Huntington boys, and if not. . . .' It went something like that. Anyway, we came riding after you."

"Do you still want me?" Fanny asked, her face a strange configuration of dust smears. "I'll go with you, if you want me."

True Bear grinned. He felt weak inside, suddenly tired, tired the way one gets after running a very long way.

"Wash your face," he said, "and I'll give the matter some thought."

Fanny stared at him.

"You sonofabitch—we damned near wrecked half a dozen times trying to catch you, and then you come up behind us!"

True Bear turned toward Salty Dan.

"How you going to get back with just three animals? Makes for an awkward team."

"Unhitch one and trail him, of course. I think maybe Fan's right about you being a tad bit thick between the ears. Well, you're what she wants, and once a female goes crazy, there's just no curing the disease. Fan, best you take the extra horse. I didn't figure you needed those two suitcases in the first place, but since they're here, you might as well haul them with you. Don't be worrying now. Willow and I, we'll handle things just fine. Neither one of us has any sense, but between us we make a fair team. If you're not back in a month, we'll come looking for you. Fifteen miles west of Chester, turn right? With directions like that, you're as good as found."

Fanny got down from the buckboard, glanced at McCain, and began to unhitch her mare.

He dismounted as well, stepped hesitantly to her side, fumbled at the lead lines.

Then he turned to her. They embraced and clung desperately to one another.

"Oh, hell!" Salty Dan called out. "Kiss each other, you damned fools."

SMOKE POURED UP from the west as they rode north, smoke drifting downslope from the Sierra as well, causing their eyes to water and the horses to shy suddenly and to make soft, nervous, whickering noises.

"Range fire in Sierra Valley," True Bear said, gazing upward at gray-black, wind-driven clouds.

The sun, a pale yellow blur but half visible through the plumes, dropped lower and then disappeared behind a wall of mountains, and sunset came in strange glowing hues of orange and red arching toward sky center, as though a monstrous late-summer aurora were in progress.

It was already past dark when True Bear and Fanny Bitler reached Hallelujah Junction, and the moon, now full, rose large and red-tinted over desert ranges to the east.

Several horses were hitched in front of the way station, and half a dozen men were inside, all of them drinking beer and exchanging tales of what the fires had done that day—animals suffocated, barns and stacks of hay ignited, even one ranch house destroyed near Loyalton, at the mouth of Smithneck Creek. To the west of the valley, the fire was working its way through heavy timber, crowning halfway up the mountain toward Yuba Pass and closing the road to Sierra City and Downieville.

True Bear and Fanny sat down at a small table across from the bar, and the locals, engrossed in what was happening in the world about them, at first paid little attention to the tall halfbreed dressed in black or to the finely featured woman with him, clad in men's denims and a green plaid flannel shirt several sizes too large for her.

The owner brought two cups and a coffee pot.

"You're Ben McCain's boy—how you getting along with that Henry I sold you? Damned fine rifle. Miss—you ain't Fanny, are you, from Salty's? No, of course not. By God, you look like her, though. You folks be wanting something to eat? I got bean soup and sandwiches, that's about all."

"Sounds good. Auna-yi?"

She nodded, and stared across the room at the cattlemen.

"Coyote Man's striking back," she said. "This is the summer of fire—I've never seen anything like it. Things have been burning for more than a month now, ever since we rode north last time."

"Might be another month before the rains come," True Bear replied. "California's subject to look just like Nevada before all this is over. Let's take our chow with us and keep riding. Is that all right with you? We've got a long way to go. and I'm starting to feel nervous as hell. . . ."

"The famous kidnapper of helpless women gets nervous? You mean I've agreed to marry an actual human being?"

"I don't know. Have you?"

"Yes," she said. and then began to laugh.

THE MOON had reached midheaven when they finally stopped for what remained of the night, and placed their blankets in an area of bunch grass close beside the small desert stream called Long Valley Creek. For a number of minutes they lay side by side, not even touching, not speaking at all.

"A strange wedding night," Fanny said at last. "I guess it's not part of my fate for anything to happen according to custom."

"You want custom?" True Bear asked, turning over upon her and kissing her. "By God, I'll show you custom."

"No you won't, True Bear McCain. Here I am again, off beside some godforsaken trickle in the middle of miles and miles of sagebrush. If there are any cows around, they'll probably shit on us in the middle of the night, and. . . ."

"It's already the middle of the night, my love. At least it's not raining cats and dogs, you've got to grant me that much."

"Like hell I do, McCain. Besides, it never does that. Just water, that's all, and I'd welcome it right now. Kiss me some more, and then I'll tell you what's going to happen."

True Bear complied, cupping her breast with one hand and drawing her to him with the other.

Then she bit at his ear.

"Take your britches off," she whispered. "I've been riding a horse all day, and I'm starting to like it. Now I'm going to ride a different kind of horse. Shut up and do what I tell you, True Bear. You insisted on this, and you may as well find out right now what you've gotten yourself into."

McCain laughed.

"I'm hungry," he said. "May I eat first?"

"Shameless sonofabitch. Don't you realize the horses are watching?"

"Equines understand these things."

"If you get to eat, then so do I. But after that I'm going to ride you until you beg for mercy. . . ."

WHEN THEY AWOKE, all three horses were standing in the shallow creek. Fog lay everywhere about them, only it wasn't fog at all.

THIRTY-SIX
Fire Woman
[September 1874]

AFTERNOON SUN was waning when True Bear and Fanny reached Upper Eden two days later—arrived to find a mourning in progress and the Maidu people moving about slowly, stunned and defeated. Small Ears, Kauda, and one or two older women had even slashed themselves with knives and hacked off their hair.

Big Woodpecker came forward, his hands held out in a gesture of helplessness.

"The day after you left—that's when tragedy struck, True Bear. How can I tell you this? Death comes suddenly, and afterward there's nothing any of us can do to alter what's happened. One Above and Old Coyote Man take joy in human pain, I think."

"What is it, Woodpecker, for God's sake! What's happened? Where are Mom and Dad?"

"My friend, True Bear. . . ." Big Woodpecker managed, his voice choking off as he embraced McCain, clinging to him almost in the manner of a drowning person, "it's Ben and Ooti—they're dead, dead. I was there. The three of us were riding our south boundary—just stopped to watch a doe mule deer and three fawns—little ones that didn't know enough yet to be afraid of us, and the mother wouldn't run off without them. Dan Clayton and four or five of his men came up— they started yelling. Then Clayton pulled his gun and began to shoot. Even one of his own tried to stop him, but it was too late. Just like that, both gone. My God, True Bear, what are we going to do? *Hammu, hammu.* . . ."

McCain heard the words his friend spoke, but the syllables hardly registered—didn't seem real at all. Utterly insane. What was Woodpecker telling him? Was it some sort of crazy practical joke—the way the two of them had sometimes attempted to startle one another when they were still boys, crying out that a cougar or grizzly or wolf or rattlesnake was nearby?

Fanny turned to True Bear, her eyes wide in disbelief, lips parted as though she were about to speak, and yet no words formed.

An instant of strange, pellucid silence when everything about him moved, shifted, sought out some new and more stable position.

Then utter numbness, his mind still attempting to deny what some deeper, darker center of intelligence had already taken in and even accepted.

"They're buried already. We didn't know what else to do, True Bear. We didn't know how long you might be gone."

Gut-shot. A buck bounding forward, arching through air at the top of its glide, hit—then earth rushing upward, no strength for a next leap, darkness covering the clear eyes. . . .

"Where?" he asked in a voice that sounded nothing like his own.

"The Ustu grounds . . . we dug one grave, placed them together, just as if they were sleeping. Small Ears said they would never wish to be apart, and we all realized it was true. We carried stones up the hill from North Branch, from that small pool where Ooti liked to bathe. I feel helpless, True Bear—how will any of us be able to live without them? We're nothing now, only Indians. We have no one to show us how to live in this Whiteman's world. . . ."

Strength. Call upon whatever strength you have, William True Bear Goffe McCain. Their love gave you life, their wisdom created you and turned you into a man. This is why Ben called you back—somehow he knew, knew, and yet he didn't know, never for one moment supposed he wouldn't step into darkness alone, not even dreams could have told him. But he called you back, and now it's up to you to save whatever remains of this Eden—these are your people now, yours and Big Woodpecker's and Fanny's as well. There will be time for grieving. Se-meni moon will rise, and then the Ustu poles must be raised, cleansing fires ignited, a final tribute to the spirits of a man and a woman who found each other from opposite sides of a continent and walked together from that moment onward. They've gone to Upper Meadows now—yet how could they? No, they look back, they tarry, they cannot set foot onto the Spirit Trail until they've seen what will happen next, what becomes of everything they strove to create—this frail bridge into the years ahead. How much strength is yours, William True Bear Goffe McCain? Are you strong enough to lead? For that's the role they prepared you to play. . . .

Fanny clung to him, her head pressed against his chest. She wept silently, didn't speak.

Pain. Omeya. Hard even to take the next breath. Emptiness, loss. Mother and Father, don't leave me now. You've stepped into darkness while your son lingers behind, but now I need you so that I may do what comes next. Yaaw-huy-eni, don't go away, just circle around. I'll hear your words in sounds of the forest, in shifting motions of air. . . .

"It was my fault," True Bear said. "I should have been here. I. . . ."

"No," Big Woodpecker replied. "I should have realized what was going to happen. I should have warned them. Dan Clayton went crazy—even his own men realized that. But the forest was so still, so peaceful until. . . ."

"Will you lead us to the graves?" Fanny asked. "We can do nothing when people we have been close to leave us, but. . . ."

"Yes," Woodpecker said, staring numbly at those before him, his own voice choked with pain, futility, helplessness. "Let us go . . . there . . . now. Ben and Ooti are waiting."

Then he too closed his eyes and attempted to control himself.

THE ENORMITY of what had transpired swept over Fanny. Ben McCain was the White father she'd never known, not a crazed killer but a good man. And the fierce, mystical Ooti was somehow a second mother, a close friend she'd not truly known well, but who was important to her, often in her thoughts, protectress, a kindred spirit, she thought, but much stronger, much more certain which path was proper, which actions were needful, which to be avoided. Now this—her own blood father, a man she'd never known as a person but only as threat and finally as killer of her people, a world-destroyer, a man she hated beyond all others—he had reached out and in one instant of senseless rage had slain True Bear's parents.

A moment after Smoke Woman had revealed her father's name, Fanny had resolved that she'd eventually find some means to kill him—to kill him before he was able to destroy whatever fragments remained of a time of mystery and warmth, her own mother's gentle embrace, the smells of cooking fires, bats flitting through twilight above alders along Mill Creek, a time of acorn-gathering, old Wolf Tracker teaching his bastard granddaughter Saltu tongue, English, the language of her enemies but also the language that might somehow enable her to survive during the years after the sun grew black in Yahi skies. . . . *Dan Clayton. Fanny Bitler. Fanny Clayton.* Even the secret conjunction of those syllables was hateful to her. And now this guilt, obscure and twisted and deformed, it was also hers, even as the old name *Wahtaurisi-yi, Sits-by-the-ladder, Bastard Child* had been hateful. Yet Wolf Tracker had reformed the meaning and nearly succeeded in turning it into a name of honor. But who now could help her transform secret shame into something that was not hateful?

Auna-yi.

Yes, that was her name, a name given to her and in some way she never understood presumed to reflect her actual nature. She might well have grown into the name, she thought, but Whitemen stole it from her—changed her into Anna, into Fanny, into a paid woman for the likes of Gideon Whitney, George Livingstone, Collis Huntington—and many others, nameless, faceless, expunged from memory as soon as they'd left her rooms.

Now, after all of it, and even after vowing that never would she risk *loving* any man again, she nonetheless found herself beside True Bear. She was his woman, and she loved him desperately, beyond her own will. It was insane to think, but she knew now that she'd never loved any other man. A sacred bond formed the moment she'd been told to take food to two captive Saltu boys who were not Saltu at all, and one of them became an unquestioningly loyal friend, the other her mate. How, at that instant, could she have guessed such a thing? *Yet she knew it, knew it deep inside long before conscious mind ever considered even the wildest possibility.*

Now they stood together before a cairn of heaped stones— the three who had first seen each other that night in Mill Creek Canyon. Others came up the path behind them, Maidu people—including some of those who once rode with Ben McCain and Ooti, avenging Panos, set upon and ultimately exacting revenge from the Whites during days when gold was first discovered near Kolo-ma village. Small Ears. Kauda. Raccoon. Little Basket. Crooked Knee. Broken Wing. Slow Rabbit. Grasshopper Man. And others from Oidoing-koyo itself, the two groups long since merged utterly: Blue Loon, Goat's Head, Waima, Sumi-Tawaal, Wet Coyote, Big Woodpecker's wife Yellow Grass, more. . . .

True Bear kneeled before the cairn, and whispered something that no one could hear.

Then Small Ears, Ooti's closest friend from young womanhood onward, stepped forward, held out her hands, and chanted:

> *Aawpawpawkawm aawm yoo-oolooshkit, Acorn Girl, Bear-who-cannot-see-well. Continue to guide us, even when white rock all falls to pieces. We will honor your names at the Ustu burning, but we will not forget you. Hammu, hammu, hammu. . . .*

*   *   *

THEY COULD SMELL smoke in the air shortly before sundown, and a thin haze drifted upcanyon along North Branch, apparently blown from some distance away, perhaps near Chester.

A bubble of memory rose to the surface of True Bear's mind, and for a moment he could almost hear the Pano Spirit's voice issuing from the mouth of a dream of a grizzly his own mother had once raised. Fire licked about everything and then faded, the bubble bursting against consciousness.

His mind drifted, drifted through numbness, but he turned to listen to what Big Woodpecker's father was saying.

"Life has been too easy for us," Blue Loon said. "Now we've been harmed, all of us, in a way that cannot be healed. I keep thinking Ben will tell us what to do next, and yet he's no longer here. True Bear McCain, you're in charge of the ranch now. You're the only link we have with the Whiteman's world. They speak of their justice, but will anything be done? Will Dan Clayton be arrested and put on trial for murder? Or will Sheriff Bannon in Quincy simply write some letter to a sheriff in Red Bluff, and that will be the end of it?"

True Bear shook his head.

"I don't trust Whiteman's justice either—no more than you do, Blue Loon. It's hard for me to think at all right now, but something has to be done, and I'm the one who must do it. I could have killed the sonofabitch last month—he started to draw on me. But then hell would have broken loose. Where's my horse? I'm going to ride down to Childe's Meadows. If Clayton's still there. . . ."

"Not alone, you won't," Big Woodpecker said. "Ben almost convinced me the law could be made to work for us instead of against us, but now I don't think so. I'm ready."

"True Bear, use your head!" Fanny protested. "How many men are down there? You two can go riding in, of course, maybe even get Clayton between you, but against odds like that—it doesn't make sense. Kintpuash fought that way, but he had no choice. Your people, the Oidoing-koyos, they're all armed. Their village is safe for now, and there are those who have far more influence than Dan Clayton. Perhaps my friend Huntington would like to go into the cattle business. In any case, he'll speak to Governor Newton Booth if I ask him to—at least I think he will."

"The Governor's not a likely source of protection or justice, either one, not if you ask me," Big Woodpecker said. "I don't trust any of those bastards. True Bear—you remember how we used to sneak up on deer? I come in from one side, you hide on the other. It'll work with Dan Clayton too."

True Bear nodded.

"Yes—but deer are stupid, and Clayton isn't, not unless he's completely lost his mind. When I brought those damned cows home, that's what triggered him. Ooti would have called for a 'revenge-taking,' and I'm the one who has to take it. If I'm killed, it's no great loss. Damn it, I have to face him— he's got to know who's putting lead into his guts."

"You're not going down there!" Fanny cried out. "I won't lose you, True Bear, no matter what's happened. There's got to be a better way. We'll post a reward. I have money to do that. George Livingstone will help us—he understands how to use the law. . . ."

Then conversation stopped, the four people in the McCain house listening intently.

"Rifle fire!" Blue Loon said. "It's happened. Son—we have to protect our wives . . . we're being attacked by the Wawlems. . . ."

True Bear burst across the room, grabbed for his Henry rifle, and flung open the door.

In near darkness, riders were spilling out of the woods, skirting about the McCain ranch house, and heading for the village itself. Horsemen were shouting and laughing and seemingly shooting at random.

McCain fired, and a trailing rider spun sideways in his saddle, slipped to the ground, rolled over, and lay still. Those ahead of him apparently didn't even notice what happened.

True Bear jacked another cartridge into the chamber and fired a second time, but without effect.

THE RAID was over within minutes, and in its aftermath several Maidus lay dead, old Grasshopper Man and one four-year-old girl among them. Two big haystacks burned brightly, and half a dozen Oidoing-koyo houses had been set afire. Nearly all of the cattle pastured beyond the sawmill had been driven off.

Sporadic rifle fire from Clayton's rear guard, stationed on

the rim above, continued to whine down toward the village for perhaps ten minutes or so after the main band of cowboys passed through on their mission of terror, and then, by full darkness, the forest grew quiet once more, punctuated only by wailings of Maidu women and the five-noted calls of a great horned owl.

The wounded were given immediate aid and then brought to the ranch house, where Fanny and Yellow Grass and Kauda, working together, utilized bedding, pads, cushions from the furniture, and whatever else was available to make those who'd been shot as comfortable as possible.

Then Fanny Bitler nodded to her two companions, turned, and walked out into the big front room where a number of the Maidu men were assembled.

She looked about, and saw masks of stunned confusion, indecision, and even terror. She observed True Bear and Big Woodpecker, standing apart from the others in a far corner close by Ooti's prized large window, the two friends engaged in heated discussion. Even in their faces she could see doubt, uncertainty.

Then her world changed again, a transformation that occurred in less than an instant—perhaps had already occurred on the day when she saw Smoke Woman after so long a time apart, saw young Wood Duck, bow in hand and his eyes sullen, saw Salmon Man, one leg swollen and wrapped. Or perhaps it was when Weasel McLaughlin showed up, first in Reno and again as she and True Bear were riding north and everything was aflame, hateful words presuming to give Jake permission to rape her, but she drew out her Deringer and pulled the trigger.

Whenever it happened, she knew full well the transformation was complete.

You are like lizard, lizard who sheds one skin each year and emerges new and whole. How long can you go on changing, Fanny Bitler? How long until there is no more skin to shed, and only raw flesh remains, muscle and nerve and unending pain?

"I don't know," she whispered as she pushed her way through to the big stone fireplace, "but I know I have walked a fool's path, and yet that path has gone in a circle."

She raised her hands high, just as she'd seen Ooti make the gesture on several occasions.

"Maidus!" she called out. "There is blood on this grass. You have lost those who gave you protection, but now you must hear what I'm saying! Ben McCain and Acorn Girl are gone, killed by your enemies and mine. I'm not some woman True Bear found wandering about in Reno. I am Auna-yi, a Yahi, and Wolf Tracker's people were my people. They are gone now, slain by the Whites—yes, Whitemen led by Daniel Clayton, the one who murdered Ben and Ooti McCain. Listen to me! I stood beside Kintpuash the Modoc, who fought the soldiers until he was betrayed by his own kind and captured and hanged. His people were sent far away, never to see their own lands again. Is this what you wish also—to be sent off? Or will you now defend what belongs to you? I came first as a guest to Oidoing-koyo, and I was made welcome. I am only a Yahi woman, but I will help you to fight for this land. I'll kill Dan Clayton myself, for that's a debt I owe him. Will you fight beside me, or will you wait here until he's burned all your houses and killed your women and children? He'll do that if he's able. He doesn't need any reason to hate you. Then those who are left will be taken away. There's no justice for the Redman, but there's still honor. Kintpuash died, but he died with honor even though the Whites tried to disgrace him with hanging, and the rightness of what he fought for will still be remembered many years from now. I'm not afraid of dying. Ooti wasn't afraid of dying, and neither was Ben. They risked everything. . . ."

She stood there, intending to say yet a few more words, but now her wits had deserted her, and the room was filled with heavy silence, silence like ice on the surfaces of shallow pools at winter's end.

The Maidus began to applaud, and their voices rose up in anger.

True Bear and Big Woodpecker made their way across the room toward her, and for one terrible moment she was afraid they were vexed with her—that she'd intruded into the matter at hand in a foolish, impulsive way. But then she saw their eyes and knew if they were shocked, they were nonetheless intensely proud.

True Bear was beside her, one arm draped about her middle as he gazed out over the faces before him.

"I'm Ben's son, Ooti's son. Perhaps my own hot temper caused all this, I don't know. But I'll ride with Auna-yi. Life's worthless to me so long as the one who killed my parents still breathes. Some of you have lost loved ones as well. . . ."

· "I ride too," Big Woodpecker said. "Ben and Acorn Girl trusted me, and I owe them more than I can ever repay. Clayton's death begins to even things."

Blue Loon called for silence, stilled a rising tide of voices.

"It's been many years since such words were spoken," he said, "and I never thought I'd live to hear them again, certainly not from my own tongue. Maidus, I call for a war council. Auna-yi has said it for all of us. We've lived quietly and tried never to offend, but we've also kept our weapons ready. Now we must use them, for honor demands it."

The men spoke in rapid succession now, and the group quickly coalesced, its purpose made certain.

There would be yet one more revenge-taking. The Maidus would strike the Childe place at dawn—would proceed from there to Table Mountain on the Sacramento River, should such a course of action prove necessary.

Grim-faced men filed out, walking away under moonlight toward their village.

Beyond Oidoing-koyo, a number of boys stood close to burned-out haystacks, shovels and rakes in hand. Smoke hung in the air, but most of it did not come from either burning hay or the houses that had been set afire and subsequently extinguished.

As Big Woodpecker, Yellow Grass, and Blue Loon walked away, True Bear and Auna-yi nodded good-night. They continued to stand together, staring upward at dim stars and breathing an odor of drifting smoke.

"I don't know if we'll see stars tomorrow night," True Bear said. "Death's a final kind of business, but I intend for it to be *his* and not mine. What comes after that, only God knows."

"There will always be stars, William True Bear Goffe McCain." Auna-yi replied. "Even if everything on this strange little planet of ours burns up, stars will remain as they've always been."

"We can't sleep in the house—not yet—not for a long

while, perhaps. We should sleep, though. Even the last dawn comes early, and we need to be rested."

"Maybe we shouldn't wait for dawn then. . . ."

True Bear didn't speak for a long moment.

"Yes," he said finally, "you're right, Auna-yi. I believe we should go pay our neighbors a visit. I gather you've changed your mind in the last hour or so."

THE SMOKE grew thicker, wind-driven—hot, dry desert air sucked in from the great Nevada desert some eighty miles to the east. The moon, still bright but now somewhat deformed as it began to wane, hung in the sky like a ten-dollar gold piece, its light diffused and refracted through drifting, acrid air.

Yet another kind of light, glowing orange-red, was visible downcanyon, half a mile beyond the sawmill, in the direction of Stump Ranch.

"Bitler's place now," True Bear said. "Probably his upper meadows—and the fire's headed this way, directly at us. Clayton's boys are playing all their cards tonight—or maybe your old friend Hank's in on it."

"Hank Bitler? What are you talking about, True Bear?"

"Didn't I tell you? Word has it the horse-breeder's bought the place. Not sure whether he's actually moved in, however. Most likely Clayton's taking advantage of the wind—figures fire'll have time to turn into an inferno, as dry as things are. Wipe us out slick as a whistle, and no questions asked, not with half the damned state burning."

"Why would Bitler wish to come here? He's got a fine place north of Alturas. . . . I don't understand."

"Can't say. Can't say. Right now it looks like Blue Loon and the boys are going to spend this night cutting some kind of fire line, and that's what Clayton's schemed. Tomorrow, with everyone exhausted, he'll hit us again."

"What will we do, then?"

"Visit Childe's Meadows, naturally, stick to our own plan. Fire burns more than one direction, that's what I'm thinking. It's time for a counterattack. Everything's drawn up into a kind of Gordian knot, and it's up to us to untangle the damned thing. . . ."

True Bear put on Ben McCain's pistol and a pair of over-

the-shoulder cartridge straps as well. He handed his own
weapon, ammunition belt and all, to Auna-yi. She nodded,
pulled the belt as tight as she could, cinched its buckle,
placed her right hand on the gun's handle, and realized she
liked the feel of a Colt low against her hip.

They mounted their horses, Ooti's new lever-action Win-
chester carbine in a sheath on Auna-yi's mare, and moved off
into smoky moonlight, angling upslope and avoiding the
McCain wagon road. They ascended a forested ridge and
dropped down behind Wilson Lake, where they took note of
a campfire burning at the water's northern margin.

"Sentries," True Bear said. "Probably two or three men—
just in case we attempt some kind of night reprisal raid.
Look—there they are, standing at the edge of our fir grove.
Trespassers on McCain land, by God. Time to shorten the
odds. Your friend Dolliver could give us advice, perhaps.
Well, let's take a little lakeside walk, what do you say?"

They tethered their horses, crept close, and watched for a
minute or so. One man was squatting by the campfire now,
the other two standing.

True Bear handed Auna-yi his Henry repeater.

"Get the one by the fire. Don't miss now, and don't shoot
until I do. I'll be in the fir grove."

He slipped away into shadows, and a short time later two
shots echoed through the trees.

A cowboy beside the fire stood up, and spun about, gun in
hand.

Auna-yi squeezed the trigger—watched her man double
over and fall facefirst into the flames.

THEY CAME DOWN to Childe's Meadows a quarter of a mile
east of the ranch house and barn, close by a big brush corral
containing perhaps fifty head of cattle apparently brought in
off the range so their brands might be altered from the
former owner's rocking-C to Clayton's circle-C—a simple
enough operation, as True Bear surmised, with or without a
bill of sale.

"A bonfire all ready to go," he said.

"Not with the cows in it. . . ."

"Of course not. These yearlings aren't guilty of anything.
Gather some dry grass, Auna-yi, and we'll make a torch. Set

it off at the far end—wind'll do the rest for us. As soon as the Whitefaces start bellowing, I'll open the gate. Old Seth's varmints are going to add to the confusion more than a little. Clayton's got men posted at the foot of the wagon road no doubt. They'll rouse the rest of the gang, and then the party begins. Are you ready, Fire Woman?"

He put his arms about her, and they clung fiercely to one another.

"What's a nice girl like you doing in a place like this?"

"You're crazy, True Bear McCain. Do you think we'll hold each other like this again, or . . . ?"

"I don't know. I love you, Auna-yi. It's no matter—not anything that's happened. This world wasn't created for us, but for one instant, at least, we're together—and that much at least has turned out right. We've got a job to do, though, and maybe we'll make it through the next couple of hours, maybe not. Will you definitely marry me if we're still alive in the morning?"

"I've already told you that, but perhaps you wouldn't have asked if you'd known. . . ."

"I want you even if I have to fight God to get you. Ben and Ooti wanted it to happen—ever since we were kids—and so did Wolf Tracker. He told me all about how to bring gifts and the like. I'm not thinking right. Jesus, it's all pulling apart from the center, but. . . ."

"Maybe we'll walk the Spirit Path with them, True Bear. But I'm your woman, if you want me."

"No Spirit Paths until Dan Clayton's dead and on his way to hell. Christians keep that place just for people like him. I hear someone calling, or is it just the wind? Let's go."

They tethered their mounts in the woods above the Chester Road and walked quickly to where the cattle were penned.

A fire was set, the flames sputtered, then caught in heaped rows of dead brush, fanned by a continuing current of air from the east. Within minutes the cattle, now bunched to the corral's west end, began to bawl and push toward the wired-off gateway.

When fire was close enough to make the animals decidedly uncomfortable, True Bear pulled down the wire and jumped back out of the way as milling Herefords streamed out, plunging off wildly and blending with wind-driven smoke.

"Auna-yi! Bring the horses around from above," he said. "I'll be waiting in that clump of willow. . . ."

He set off jogging, rifle in hand, in the wake of the stampeding animals.

After a minute or two, lamplight appeared in a ranch house window, then in the bunkhouse.

Men emerged, pulling on shirts and buckling belts. Some rushed to their horses in the corral beside the barn, while others grabbed for shovels and mattocks, and ran toward the fire.

True Bear, muzzle of his Henry resting on a chunk of basalt, waited until the would-be fire fighters were directly in front of him and no more than fifteen yards away, and then he started shooting.

Three cowhands were hit almost immediately, while two others threw themselves flat upon the ground and began to use their pistols. But within a matter of moments, these men also lay still. They did not move as flames leaped ahead toward them.

Nine men dead already, and the night's still young. . . . But there's just one I want, just one I'd like to cut apart slowly, slowly, so the sonofabitch can enjoy it. . . .

Flames blew with the wind, leaped ahead in long waves, slowed through stubble, and jumped onward where ground cover was sufficient to feed them.

Two riders were coming toward him, then veering away as they saw dead men lying ahead and realized the nature of the ambush. True Bear pulled off another shot, then another. One rider fell, but the second turned about and spurred his horse in the direction from which he'd come. McCain fired again, and the shot struck home, in the back, dead center.

What's keeping her? I'd better get the hell out of here, back up into the cover of the pines. . . .

Then he saw flames licking at the base of a haystack, clawing their way up over the big pile's surface.

She didn't go to the horses at all. . . . How'd she get to that hay without them seeing her? Get moving, Books Billy!

He sprinted to where their horses had been left tethered, stumbled about in confusion for a moment, and then found the two animals. He left Auna-yi's mare behind, mounted

Renegade, and rode up the wagon route in the general direction of the ranch house.

Rifle fire ahead—who the hell was shooting, and at what?

He thought of Auna-yi, pinned down, a ring of armed men about her, and urged his stallion to a full run.

No.

Many shots, back and forth. Clayton and his men were under siege from the far side, close to where the McCain Trail came down the drainage from Wilson Lake.

Only one explanation possible. . . .

He turned his horse upslope, crashing through low brush, hit the trail, and shouted his name.

"True Bear?" came the reply. "Down here, we're down here!"

Big Woodpecker.

"Don't shoot me, old hoss! I'm coming in. . . ."

"What the hell you trying to do, you dumb Wawlem bastard?" Woodpecker demanded. "You think you're going to wipe them all out yourself? True Bear, you got less brains than any damned possum. Where's Fanny? My God, she isn't . . . ?"

"Don't know. She slipped off by herself, must have lit that haystack afire. . . ."

BIG WOODPECKER BROUGHT a dozen men with him, and now the Maidus moved forward, keeping to cover, four managing to slip around to the far side of the ranch house. Once in position, they opened fire, signaling Woodpecker's group to begin their own fusillade.

Smoke welled up, obscuring even the moon at times, and flames worked their inevitable way toward the house until they licked at the front porch.

Clayton's men were returning pistol and rifle fire, but when the house itself whispered to the blossoming heat and embraced it, several ranch hands bolted to the corral, stumbled onto horses, and galloped away westward—in full flight.

The men from Oidoing-koyo continued to pour in lead at the least sign of movement within an ever-increasing swirl of smoke and flame, and within half an hour another band of men broke from cover and made for their horses.

Still no sign of Auna-yi, and True Bear was half-crazed with dread. He hoped against hope she had somehow managed to find her way back to her horse and was safe—away from the Goddamned gun battle.

Old Man Coyote, damn your pointed nose, this is no way to finish the drama. There's been enough goat-song already, endless centuries of it. . . .

"The hold rats are leaving the sinking ship," True Bear said. "Don't know how many are still there, but probably the bossman's not among them. Cease firing, damn it, quit shooting! I'm going down. . . ."

"Not alone, you ain't," Big Woodpecker said, reloading the magazine of his carbine. "Don't argue—you're not about to outtalk me on this one, True Bear. Let's move."

The two men slipped forward, kept to cover as well as they might, and worked their way through long trails of blowing smoke and dancing red flowers of flame, passed by the barn and now-empty corral.

Cattle bellowed, lowed mournfully, and a big whiteface bull, momentarily trapped by flames, charged through the fire and thundered past them. Hogs, penned beside the barn, screamed in fright, and an indeterminate number of banty chickens, half-running and half-flying, went by in a whir of wings.

McCain placed a hand on Big Woodpecker's shoulder, pointed to where flames issued from a second-story window in the house.

"Circle around—I'll go the other way, but for Christ's sake let's not shoot each other when we meet. Take Clayton unharmed if you can. Maybe he's still here, but more likely not. If Auna-yi's alive, she must be in the brush, close by the creek."

Big Woodpecker nodded, moved off into the smoky night, and True Bear rounded the front of the blazing building.

A figure directly ahead, pistol in hand, nearly obscured by low-blowing silver grayness.

True Bear flung down the Henry, reached instantly for his Navy Colt.

Don't shoot, ye dunghead idjit, ye cain't tell who ye're gunning down. . . .

The figure turned and pointed a weapon in his direction.

"Auna-yi!" he called out. "It's me, damn it! Don't shoot."

"True Bear? It's over, it's over. . . . They've all gone, those who aren't dead. I shot a pig by mistake. It's bleeding to death, I think."

McCain approached her, then saw the form lying at her feet, gasping for breath, blood dribbling from mouth and nose.

Not a pig. A man. His mouth was open, as though he was attempting to say something, but if any syllables were uttered, they could not be deciphered.

"I emptied my pistol on this thing," she said, "and then I reloaded. Maybe I'll shoot it again. . . ."

Fire danced up all around her, gleamed back from her eyes.

On the ground before her lay Big Dan Clayton. His hands shook, and his head wagged back and forth.

Flames began to slither around his sprawled legs.

EPILOGUE
Atop Wahgalu
[September–October 1874]

FIRE HAD SWEPT upstream from Henry Bitler's Stump Ranch, but damage was held to a minimum—the only things harmed being some outbuildings close by the sawmill. The Oidoing-koyos, working through the night of the gun battle with Clayton and his men, had managed to keep flame away from both the village and the McCain ranch house.

Dry sections of pasture land, however, were a different matter, and spot fires leaped ahead, immediately consuming large areas while leaving other sections untouched.

Cattle fled, keying in on the rampage of a longhorned matriarch who enjoyed the reverence of all other animals—calf, heifer, steer, and bull alike. Indeed, once the boss lady decided to strike out for more congenial surroundings, it was only moments before nearly five hundred head of all denominations were in on the chase, following Number One for several miles, high up onto the timbered flanks of Red Mountain. Here the Maidus found their cattle happily grazing on bunch grass, aspen saplings, deer browse, and chokecherry leaves.

The fire in Childe's Meadows, however, driven by wind through a trench valley, roared northwest to Upper Mill

477

Creek Canyon and the edge of Circle-S land, dying there but moving in the direction of Black Butte, spotting up toward Mt. Lassen, and finally exhausting itself due to lack of burnable materials on steep canyon walls.

Blustery winds through the next several days continually fanned new blazes into life, however, and dead trees stood everywhere in irregular pattern, thousands of skeletons, many of them still trailing wisps of smoke.

DANIEL CLAYTON'S REMAINS were never found, and it was presumed the rancher must have perished in the inferno of his blazing ranch house. Several other men were missing as well, and Sheriff Jack Bannon from the county seat at Quincy, along with half a dozen deputies, made a thorough search of the area without finding the least evidence of foul play.

A number of Clayton's men, upon returning to the main ranch near Table Mountain, told stories of being set upon by a hundred or more Oidoing-koyo Indians just as fire was sweeping toward the Childe ranch house and barn, and this message, routed through official channels, was passed on to Jack Bannon.

The sheriff and his men rode across the low divide to Ben McCain's place, and learned of the deaths of both the owner and his wife as well as several of the Maidu Indians resident there.

A young man named Woodpecker claimed Ben and his squaw had been shot by Clayton and that Clayton's men had killed seven others and set the grass and scrub brush afire—so that the Oidoing-koyos had been obliged to spend an entire night cutting a firebreak and otherwise attempting to protect their own homes and the McCain buildings. Many of their cattle had run off in fear, Woodpecker said, and a number of the Indians were still scouring the hills in search of them.

Bannon checked brands on those cattle presently in the pastures, concluded everything was as it should be, and then demanded to know who was now actually in charge of the McCain holdings.

"Bill McCain," Big Woodpecker replied. "He's been down in Reno on business for the last week and a half. Poor bastard doesn't even know about the fire yet. Him and his lawyer— they're trying to get the inheritance thing straightened out

College kid, Sheriff—Bill's been back East for several years. Wasn't even here when Dan Clayton went nuts and shot his folks. He's not interested in cattle, but I don't think he's going to sell out. Word has it that Bitler'll be managing the place. Me, I'm just the straw boss. They tell me what to do, and I do it."

Bannon made a few notes and then nodded.

"I think there's more here than meets the eye," he said. In Reno, you say? Happen to know where Bill McCain's staying?"

Big Woodpecker shrugged again.

"Fanny Bitler's place—The Emporium, I think it's called."

"I'll be damned—he's staying in a whorehouse? You ain't telling me *The Queen of Reno* is related to this Bitler who's just bought Stump Ranch—or am I connecting things that ain't?"

"Yep. She's Hank Bitler's stepdaughter, though not many now it."

"Bitler's moved in, then?"

Big Woodpecker shook his head.

"Came up yesterday to pay his respects to Ben and Acorn Girl. Don't know how he'd heard about them getting killed. Guess Bill must have told him. Beats the hell out of me. Like I say, I just work here. Keep my nose out of Whiteman's affairs. Safer that way."

Bannon wrote down two or three more things, nodded to his deputies, mounted, and rode back toward Childe's Meadows.

"Try to get information out of a damned Injun," he mumbled. "Either it's like pulling teeth, or they fill a man's head with horsecrap. I'm sure of one thing, though. Those Maidus haven't been on any damned warpath. Hell, they're tamer than spaniels."

"So what happened to Clayton?" a deputy asked.

"Just a wild guess—but I figure the boys who rode off probably set the fire themselves, an' I'd be willing to bet they slugged old Dan and left his carcass in the house to cook. Well, that's a problem for Tehama, not Plumas. With half the county burnt up, we already got more troubles than we can handle."

*   *   *

NEAR THE END of September, light rain began to fall, continu
ing for three days. When skies eventually cleared, Wahgal
was transformed once more to a brilliant white, autumn wa
in the air, and frost appeared on window glass and alon
cedar rails of the McCain corral.

Hank Bitler finally got moved to his new operation a
Stump Ranch and talked to anyone who'd listen about th
advantages of raising thoroughbred horses. Even Tall Gras
Tillie at the cafe in Chester got her ear bent—though pei
haps she was actually interested, since she rode off with Han
and didn't return for three days.

Bitler was reunited with Auna-yi and was astonished to fin
"his" Fanny all grown up and, from the looks of things, nc
only a highly successful businesswoman but also soon to b
married to Young McCain, his neighbor a few miles up Nort
Branch. True Bear McCain seemed interested in horses, an
that was good. Furthermore, the man was willing to assist i
getting Bitler some reliable ranch hands from among the loc
Maidu Indian people.

A FORMAL MARRIAGE was celebrated at Upper Eden, wit
none other than Salty Dan Dolliver reading from the Goo
Book and Willow, his new partner, acting as bridesmaid
while Big Woodpecker stood next to True Bear as best man

But the festivities had a melancholy side to them as well—
for Ustu time had arrived, and on the ridge above the ranc
house, skinned pine poles had been erected and strung wit
woven baskets full of food and various trinkets, things dc
nated from among the Oidoing-koyos. Then fires were lit—i
memory not only of the Maidus who'd been slain by Clayton
men but of Bear-who-cannot-see-well and Acorn Girl alsc
Blue Loon presided, along with Short Ears and her husband
and as flames leaped up to consume the laden baskets, Tru
Bear, Auna-yi, Big Woodpecker, and Yellow Grass stood by
solemnly watching.

After a time the fire began to subside, and Yellow Gras
nodded.

"They're on their way to Upper Meadows now," she said
"They're stepping off the top of Wahgalu and out into th
stars that run across midsky. It's a beautiful story, and I hop
it's true."

True Bear and Auna-yi anticipated spending their wedding night in the newly-added-on bedroom they'd attached to the McCain ranch house, but with Dan outside, involved in a high-stakes hand-game with Goat's Head—and Willow, quite drunk, serenading them with obscene ballads—the newly married couple found it reasonable to slip unnoticed through a back door and make their way to the stables—where Renegade, the sorrel mare, and a pack mule had been prepared in advance against just such an eventuality.

MORNING FOUND THEM at Lake Helen, below the dome of Wahgalu. They were lying together, locked in one another's arms beneath a pile of blankets, and when they peered out at the new day, they saw heavy bands of dark, threatening clouds streaming overhead.

"Squaw gets up first to make the fire," True Bear murmured, biting at Auna-yi's earlobe.

"Like hell she does. Wake me when breakfast's ready."

"Modern times, modern times," he mumbled as he rose, pulled on his clothing, and began to pile twigs.

After a quick meal and several cups of coffee apiece, they rode on up the mountain until they reached a point where their horses were having difficulty with footing in the inch or two of snow that remained in the aftermath of the equinoctial storm.

Then they walked, setting their feet carefully, to the mountain's broad back.

Wind was bitter now, cutting through their clothing, and the sky looked ever more ominous.

"Are you certain we have to do this, True Bear McCain? It's quite true—I've never been to the summit before, but couldn't we choose a better day for the venture?"

"We're almost there," he replied.

They continued to trudge forward, beyond some last wind-deformed junipers now, moving ahead along a nearly featureless slope through half a foot of crusty snow.

True Bear stopped, pointed.

"Would you look at that!"

Several jets of steam hissed from between cracks in the back of the mountain, creating a roughly circular snow-free area.

A whistling noise, almost as though something alive were down underneath and trying to dig its way to the surface.

"The old Sacred Mountain's not finished yet, Auna-yi. At the moment her fires are banked, but they're still quite alive. One of these days. . . ."

"Will you be happy then—when hot rock pours down and covers our house? I think you will."

"Possibly," he replied. "Come on, the summit's just ahead."

Then they stood on the crest, stared out into grayness in all directions.

"I thought you said we'd be able to see Shasta and even Yaina from here. I can't see anything but clouds. You lie, True Bear."

"You're not looking hard enough," he replied. "There's a trick to it—you have to look *right through* the clouds. If you do that, you can see clear to God's Heavenly Mansion."

Auna-yi stared northward.

"I see snowflakes coming down. Now we'll be trapped on the mountain's top. Next year someone will climb up here and find us frozen to death."

True Bear laughed.

"If so, they'll find us stuck together like a pair of lovesick coyotes. Why do you think I brought you here?"

"Because you know I've got something to give you."

He looked into her eyes and tried to frown.

"And just what might that be, Fire Woman?"

"Oh . . . maybe a little one. You've noticed I haven't been feeling well some mornings. If it's a boy, I want to name him False Bear."

McCain grinned, and gazed off into the now swirling snowflakes.

"I like it," he said.

THEY DESCENDED the mountain, and when they drew close to where they'd left their horses, they heard the animals snorting and whinnying.

Downslope, a huge gold-red grizzly was sitting on its haunches, looking like Buddha in a fur coat.

Then the creature grunted, leaned forward so as to put weight upon its forepaws, and went waddling off toward a thick stand of hemlocks.

Author's Note

In the year 1911, on August 29th to be exact, a wild Indian was captured near Oroville, California. According to reports, he was half-dead of exposure and hunger. He was made welcome in the Whiteman's world by being clapped into jail "for his own protection," The man spoke no English, and first attempts to communicate with him proved futile. Soon, however, he came under the protection of anthropologists Alfred L. Kroeber and Thomas T. Waterman, who took him to the University of California Medical Center in San Francisco, worked with him, became his friends, and learned much from him.

To the world he's been known as Ishi, but that was not his name. At one point, being pressed for details concerning his identity, he delivered a long tale about the courting problems experienced by Wood Duck. With no more information than this, and a fiction writer's intuition, I chose to call the young Yahi boy in this novel Wood Duck.

With Ishi's death on March 25, 1916, the last of the Yahi people had vanished into darkness.

The mountain called Wahgalu is, of course, Mt. Lassen, elevation 10,457 ft., southernmost of the great Cascade volcanic peaks. The area surrounding the mountain is now a national park, perhaps our least visited.

As Mt. St. Helens demonstrated a few years ago, the Cascade volcanoes are far from extinct. Mt. Lassen erupted in May of 1914 and continued until 1917, during which time there were nearly three hundred significant explosions. Just south of the peak is the fragmented caldera of old Mt. Tehama, which geologists tell us was a far greater mountain that blew up at some indeterminate time in the not-too-distant past. Lassen itself is a "new" mountain, perhaps as little as five to eight thousand years old. Numerous vents, fumeroles, steam jets, and hot springs are active close by.

About the Author

BILL HOTCHKISS is a poet, critic, and novelist whose most recent books include *People of the Sacred Oak, Mountain Lamb, Spirit Mountain, Ammahabas, Soldier Wolf, Crow Warriors,* and *The Medicine Calf.* Born in New London, Connecticut, in 1936, Hotchkiss grew up in California's Mother Lode country and was educated at the University of California, San Francisco State University, and the University of Oregon. He's the holder of several graduate degrees, including a Ph.D. The author and his wife, Judith Shears, live in Woodpecker Ravine, near Grass Valley, California. He is currently at work on a new novel to be published by Bantam Books in the near future.

TERRY C. JOHNSTON

Winner of the prestigious Western Writer's award for best first novel, Terry C. Johnston brings you two volumes of his award-winning saga of mountain men Josiah Paddock and Titus Bass who strive together to meet the challenges of the western wilderness in the 1830's.

☐ 25572-X **CARRY THE WIND** $4.95

Having killed a wealthy young Frenchman in a duel, Josiah Paddock flees St. Louis in 1831. He heads west to the fierce and beautiful Rocky Mountains, to become a free trapper far from the entanglements of civilization. Hotheaded and impetuous, young Josiah finds his romantic image of life in the mountains giving way to a harsh struggle for survival—against wild animals, fierce Indians, and nature's own cruelty. Half-dead of cold and starvation, he encounters Titus Bass, a solitary old trapper who takes the youth under his wing and teaches him the ways of the mountains. So begins a magnificent historical novel, remarkable for its wealth of authentic mountain lore and wisdom.   Coming in October 1986.

☐ 26224-6 **BORDERLORDS** $4.50

Here is a swirling, powerful drama of the early American wilderness, filled with fascinating scenes of tribal Indian life depicted with passion and detail unequaled in American literature, and all of it leading up to a terrifying climax at the fabled 1833 Green River Rendezvous.

Look for these books wherever Bantam books are sold, or use this handy coupon for ordering: